Yes, Mama

HELEN FORRESTER

Yes, Mama

GUILD PUBLISHING LONDON

This edition published 1988 by
Guild Publishing
by arrangement with William Collins Sons & Co. Ltd

Copyright © Helen Forrester 1988

CN 3662

Printed in Great Britain by
Richard Clay Ltd, Bungay, Suffolk

To
Nora Walton (Sylvia Poole)
who was my friend when I most
needed one.

'*The prejudices remain within society,
within families and, above all, within the law.*'

Virginia Ironside and Jane Horwood,
*How can I explain to my daughter that
she isn't a little bastard?*
WOMAN magazine, November, 1986.

Chapter One

I

Much to her mother's annoyance, Alicia Beatrix Mary decided to be born on May 12th, 1886, during a visit to Liverpool of the dear Queen to open the International Exhibition of Navigation, Travelling, Commerce and Manufactures. On the day of Alicia's slightly premature birth, the Queen was to drive down the Boulevard from Princes Park, on her way to St George's Hall. As a result of Alicia's arrival, her mother, Elizabeth Woodman, missed the chance of seeing her Sovereign.

Mrs Dorothea Evans, the wife of a Liverpool shipping magnate, had graciously invited Elizabeth to view the procession from her bedroom window, which faced the Boulevard. 'If you wore a veil and a large shawl and came in a carriage, no one would realize your – er – condition. You could watch in absolute privacy from behind the lace curtains.'

Elizabeth had been thrilled by an invitation from such an eminent lady, who was herself to be presented to the Queen. She had looked forward to extending her acquaintance with Mrs Evans. She guessed that it would please Humphrey exceedingly if she were to make a friend of the wife of such an influential man – and Elizabeth knew that in the months to come, she would have to do a lot to mollify an outraged Humphrey Woodman, her husband of twenty-two years.

Between the painful contractions, as her forty-year-old body strove to deliver the child, she was consumed by anxiety, an anxiety which had commenced when first she knew she was pregnant.

Had Humphrey realized that the child was not his?

It was always so difficult to be sure of anything with her husband, she worried fretfully. He was so wrapped up in his multifarious business activities and the woman in the town whom he kept, that he rarely talked to his wife, never mind slept with her. But, of late, his usual bouts of temper had been so violent that she felt he must suspect her. And yet he had never commented on her condition.

Could it be, she wondered, that her huge skirts and swathing shawls had been a sufficient disguise, and that he had never realized her condition? She had found it difficult to believe, but she had still clung to the idea, hoping that she might miscarry. Now she prayed that, faced with a living child, he might use his common sense and accept it.

Peevishly, between gasps of pain, she commanded that the heavy, green velvet curtains be drawn over the ones of Nottingham lace. 'The sunlight's hurting my eyes,' she complained to the midwife. Mrs Macdonald, a stout, middle-aged woman in an impeccably white apron and long, black skirt, sighed at her difficult patient and hauled the heavy draperies over the offending light. The huge, brass curtain rings rattled in protest.

'I'll need some more candles, Ma'am.'

'Well, ring for them,' panted Elizabeth.

'Yes, Ma'am.' Mrs Macdonald went to the side of the fireplace and tugged at the green velvet bell-rope.

Though the bell rang in the basement kitchen, the distant tinkle was answered immediately by Fanny, a skinny twelve-year-old skivvy, who had been posted outside the door by Rosie, the housemaid, with orders to bring any messages from her mistress to her while she snatched a hasty lunch in the basement kitchen.

The child opened the bedroom door an inch, and hissed, 'Yes, Missus?'

'Fanny, tell Rosie to bring us some more candles immediately and make up the fire,' ordered Mrs Macdonald. 'And bring another kettle of water – and a trivet to rest it on.'

'I'll do fire afore I go downstairs.' A hand with dirt-engrimed nails gestured through the narrow opening of the door, towards the brimming coal scuttle by the fireplace.

Mrs Macdonald was shocked. 'Good gracious me, no! A young one like you can't come in here. Send Rosie up to do it.'

'Ah, go on with yez. I 'elped me Auntie last time.'

'Don't be so forward, young woman,' snapped the midwife. 'Get down them stairs and tell Rosie.'

'She int goin' to like doin' my job. Fires is *my* job.' Fanny shrugged, her thin lips curved in a grimace as she turned to do the errand. She was stopped by the sound of a querulous voice from the bed. 'Mrs Macdonald, ask Fanny if Miss Florence has arrived yet – or Miss Webb. Or Mr Woodman?' The voice sounded flustered, as Elizabeth named her husband.

'Nobody coom to the front door, Ma'am, not since doctor coom an hour ago,' piped Fanny.

'Where is everybody?' muttered Elizabeth exasperatedly. She moaned, as another bout of pain surged up her back and round her waist.

Mrs Macdonald answered her soothingly. 'It's early hours, yet, Ma'am. There's no hurry. Just rest yourself between the pains.'

Elizabeth grunted, and clutched the bedclothes. The thud of Fanny's big feet on the long staircase seemed to shake her and added to her fretfulness. Would the girl never learn to walk lightly?

Mrs Macdonald picked up a clean sheet and leisurely began to wind it into a rope. She looped this over the mahogany headrail and laid the twisted ends beside Elizabeth's pillow, so that her patient could pull on it when the need to bear down became intense. On the bedside table by the candlestick lay a new, wooden rolling-pin; Mrs Macdonald knew from experience that mothers giving birth needed something to clutch when their pains really began.

'Dr Willis should have stayed; he knows I need him,' Elizabeth complained, as the surging misery in her stiff body subsided.

'He promised to look in again in a couple of hours, Ma'am. Would you like a cup of tea, Ma'am?'

'I'd rather have a glass of port.'

'I wouldn't advise it, Ma'am. It might make the baby sleepy.'

Elizabeth sighed. 'Very well. I'll have tea.'

'That's better. I'll make a good, strong brew.'

Mrs Macdonald moved through the shadowy room to the fireplace to put a small, black kettle on to the fire. On a side table, lay a tray with a flowered teapot, a tea caddy and cups and saucers. The midwife liked to have tea handy and not be dependent upon a far-away kitchen. Tea always diverted a patient, made them feel that something was being done for them.

A soft knock at the bedroom door announced the arrival of Rosie, the housemaid, bearing a kettle of water and a brass trivet. Several long white candles stuck out of her apron pocket. She had not yet finished her lunch, and was cursing her employer under her breath, as she waited for Mrs Macdonald to bid her come in.

As she entered, Rosie composed her face. She handed the kettle, trivet and candles to the midwife and then made up the fire. She made a polite bob towards the bed and turned to leave.

'Rosie,' called Elizabeth from the depths of her supporting pillows.

'Ma'am?'

'Tell Maisie to show Miss Webb straight up when she arrives. You will all take your instructions from her. I also want to see my daughter, Mrs Browning, when she comes. Tell Cook that both ladies will probably be here for dinner.' Elizabeth paused to take a big breath as a stab shot through her abdomen. Then she went on, 'And, Rosie, none of the servants is to leave the house without Cook's permission.' She twisted suddenly in the bed and arched her back. 'Ah!' she cried.

Waiting to be dismissed, Rosie stood woodenly facing her,

while the spasm passed. 'Blow her,' she thought, 'just when I were thinkin' I could nip out a few minutes to see the Queen. And Miss Webb is a *single* lady – she won't want to come into a birthing room, any more'n she'd want to look into a midden full o' garbage.'

Mrs Macdonald wrung out a cloth in cool, scented water and began solicitously to wipe the patient's face. Elizabeth pushed her impatiently aside. 'Has Mrs Ford come?' she gasped to Rosie.

'Yes, Ma'am. She's bin waitin' in the kitchen this past three hours.'

'Send her up – I'll see her – while I still can,' Elizabeth ordered pessimistically.

II

Mrs Polly Ford was a widow, aged twenty-three. Six weeks before the Queen's visit, her husband, a docker, had fallen into the hold of a ship and had died, almost immediately, of his multiple injuries. Two nights later, in her parents' crowded cellar dwelling, his frantic widow had given birth to her first child.

Born on to a pile of rags in a windowless, waterless, heatless home, without even a clean sheet to be wrapped in, the baby boy had decided, three weeks later, that life was not worth living and had quit it. Polly wished passionately that she had been allowed to follow him. She was, however, a strong, healthy woman and, despite her despair, her milk surged in her.

Weeping helplessly, she had sat by a tiny fire lovingly built for her by her father, James Tyson. He had walked down to Seaforth sands to search for driftwood, in order to provide a little heat for her.

'We didn't know the babe was goin' to come so quick – or be born here – and we run out of coal and money,' he told her almost apologetically, his bearded face turned up towards her, as he knelt to feed the flames with chips from an old railway sleeper which he had found on the shore.

'I know, Dad,' she told him gently between her sobs. 'You shouldn't've took the wood from the sands – you could've been arrested for it.'

'Och, I know that. Devil take the bleeders!' He got up off his knees and stood leaning against the rough, brick chimney, the firelight catching the golden hairs of his beard and eyebrows. 'What you goin' to do now, duck?'

Her mother, Bridie Tyson, had been sitting beside Polly on the backless bench. Wrapped inside her shawl, to keep him warm in the foetid cellar of the court house, lay Billy, Polly's baby brother. His wide brown eyes glittered, as he peeked out of the enveloping shawl to watch the dancing flames of the fire. Now his mother sighed, and asked, 'Aye, what to do?'

'She can stay with us,' responded her husband immediately.

'Aye, Dad, you've got enough trouble without me,' Polly told him.

She looked helplessly round the tiny room, dimly lit from the open door leading to the steps up to the court itself. Down those steps, on wet days, trickled sewage from two overflowing earth lavatories which served the fourteen houses surrounding the court, to add to the overwhelming misery of the ten people living in her parents' windowless room below ground level. But her father was a casual labourer on the docks, and this, though he was as good a man as ever heard a Wesleyan sermon, was the best he could provide for his family from his irregular earnings. Also living with him was his widowed sister-in-law and her five children.

Polly's aunt had been sitting, almost unnoticed, on a three-legged stool tucked up by the fireplace. Under her black shawl, her stomach was swollen with pregnancy. She cackled suddenly, 'Youse wet with milk. You could mebbe wet-nurse.'

Polly's breasts ached with milk. She had let her little brother, Billy, suckle from her to ease the pain, but still the milk pressed within and damped her calico dress.

'Some fine lady'd pay good for that – and you'd be well fed to keep it up,' her aunt went on.

'Aye, you'd live the life o' Riley,' her mother agreed eagerly.

James Tyson looked down at his womenfolk and shrugged. This was woman talk, and, anyway, it was time to go down to the dock gate again, to stand in the rain and hope to be picked out for half a day's work. He patted Polly on the shoulder as he passed, and left them to it.

Through a grapevine of female cousins and aunts, inquiries went out to ask anyone in service whether their mistresses were expecting.

From Fanny, the little skivvy in the Woodmans' house, came the information via her aunt, that the Missus was expecting any day and was proper mad at it. In Fanny's considered opinion and judging from the gossip in the kitchen, she would be glad enough to be relieved of feeding the expected child and of looking after it; its nearest brother, Master Charles, was ten years old and had gone away to boarding school. *His* nurse had long since been let go.

On her Sunday afternoon off, Fanny visited her aunt in her tiny house in Shaw's Alley and confided to her that a real blow-up about the child was expected daily, between her Master and Mistress. 'It int his kid,' Fanny told her. 'And he's got a temper like you'd nevaire believe. Always pickin' on her, he is – and yet *he* can't talk – he took up with a woman as keeps a tobacco and sweets, back o' Water Street, downtown.'

Fanny bent to wring out a rag in a pail of cold water and reapplied it to one of her aunt's eyes, which her husband had blackened the previous night. Her aunt was hardly listening to her niece; she was wondering dully if, after last night, she would be in the family way again, and she sighed at the very thought of it. It would be the fifteenth and, out of the whole bloody issue, only three of them full grown.

Wearily, she tried to give her attention to what Fanny was saying, and replied, with pity, 'Well, you talk to Rosie and Mrs Tibbs about Polly Ford. The poor gel is broken-'earted and 'er Mam is near out of 'er wits over it.'

III

While Elizabeth Woodman's affairs were discussed in one of Liverpool's worst slums, Elizabeth herself had wandered round her handsome Upper Canning Street house through the last days of her pregnancy, and viewed with dread the birth of her child.

She had done her best to get rid of the child. She had drunk bottle after bottle of gin and had sat for hours in hot baths, while Fanny stoked up the kitchen fire to heat the water in the tank behind it, so that Elizabeth could keep renewing the water in her fine mahogany-encased bath in the bathroom. To no purpose.

She had even contemplated throwing herself down the main staircase in order to dislodge the foetus, but when she had looked at the steepness of the flight her courage had failed her.

She watched with horror her expanding figure and worried at her husband's complete lack of comment about it. As the months went remorselessly by, his silence began to terrify her. They had not slept together for months. He must *know* it's not his, she agonized. Is he going to ignore the fact or will he throw me out at some point? And where shall I go? What shall I do?

Perhaps it will be born dead, she thought hopefully. Then he won't *have* to say anything.

But Alicia Beatrix Mary had no intention of being born dead; Elizabeth, Polly and Fanny would all have their lives totally altered by her existence.

Chapter Two

I

Fanny consulted Rosie, the Woodmans' housemaid, about Polly. Rosie spoke to Mrs Martha Tibbs, the cook-housekeeper, an unmarried lady graced with the appellation of a wife because it was the custom.

In consideration of receiving Polly Ford's first month's wages, if she got the job, Mrs Tibbs graciously agreed to broach the subject of a wet-nurse with Elizabeth Woodman. Since nothing had been said to the domestic staff about the impending addition to the family, Mrs Tibbs went about the matter very delicately.

Bored to tears by three months' confinement during the more obvious period of her pregnancy, anxious to keep the child away from her husband as much as possible, assuming it were born alive, Elizabeth was almost grateful to Mrs Tibbs and agreed to look at Polly.

It took the efforts of all her extended family to make Polly look respectable for the interview. She had a black skirt in which she had been married. A black bodice was borrowed from a distant cousin down the street; she had had it given to her by the draper whose tiny shop she cleaned. It had been eaten by moths at the back, but with Polly's own black shawl over it, the holes would not show. A battered, black straw hat was acquired for a penny from a pedlar of secondhand clothes, after hard bargaining by Polly's married sister, Mary. Polly's mother washed and ironed her own apron to an unusual whiteness, so that Polly could wear it for the occasion. Polly had boots, though they were worn through at the bottom and were bursting round the little toes. 'I'll keep me feet under me skirt,' said Polly dully.

Through all these preparations, Polly wept steadily. At her mother's urging she suckled little Billy. 'It'll nourish 'im and it'll keep the milk comin', luv,' her mother consoled her.

It was comforting to hold the small boy to her. Though as grubby as a sweep, he was a merry child, who laughed and crowed and tried to talk to her.

Before Polly could aspire to a job as an indoor servant, she had, somehow, to acquire a reference from another lady. At first, Polly's mother had suggested that Mrs Tibbs' recommendation would be enough, but, through Fanny, Mrs Tibbs herself insisted that Polly must produce a written reference.

'Aye, she's right,' Polly agreed. Then, trying to make an effort for herself, she added, 'Now I've got a hat, I could go and see that ould Mrs Stanley, and ask 'er.'

Before her marriage, Polly had cleaned the doorsteps and the brass bells and letterboxes of a number of elegant houses in Mount Pleasant. For five years, she had donkey-stoned the front steps of a Mrs Stanley, an ancient crone who claimed that she had once danced with King George IV. Mrs Stanley lived with a white cat and an elderly married pair of servants.

With feelings akin to terror, Polly pulled the bell of the servants' entrance of Mrs Stanley's house. The same bent, bald manservant she remembered answered it. He did not recognize her, and asked, 'And what do you want?'

She told him.

'I'll ask the wife,' he told her, and shut the door in her face.

She was almost ready to give up and go home, when a little kitchen-maid opened it and said shyly, 'You're to coom in.'

She was led into a well-scrubbed kitchen where, on a bare, deal table, a meal was laid for four. Bending over to poke the roaring kitchen fire was an elderly woman-servant. A good smell of roasting meat permeated the room; it made Polly's mouth water.

The old woman straightened up. She wore a white, frilled cap tied under her chin and a grey uniform with a long, starched apron. Poker still in hand, she turned and said, "'Allo, Polly. What's to do? Didn't expect to see you again, after you was married.'

Polly explained her need for a reference. 'To say I'm honest, like.' She omitted to tell the woman that she had been widowed, because she thought she would start to cry again if she did so.

The older woman looked at her doubtfully. 'Well, I'll ask for yez,' she said slowly. 'I doubt she'll even know your face, though. Ye 'ardly ever saw 'er, did yer?'

'Not much,' agreed Polly humbly.

'I'll go up. Sit down there.' She pointed to a wooden chair set by the back entrance. Polly obediently sat on it.

A bell suddenly bounced on its spring in a corner of the ceiling and ting-a-linged impatiently. The manservant put on his jacket and went to answer it. The little kitchen-maid stirred the contents of an iron pot on the fire and carefully put the lid back on. A young woman in a pink-striped, housemaid's dress put her head round the door leading to the rest of the house, and shouted, 'Mary Jane, the Mistress wants her bath water. Hurry up.'

The kitchen-maid put her ladle down on to an old plate in the hearth. A somnolent kitchen cat slunk from the other end of the hearth and quietly licked it clean. The girl took a large ewer from a hook and swung it under the oven tap at the side of the huge kitchen fire. Boiling water belched into it. She grinned at Polly, as she waited for the water jug to fill.

Polly smiled faintly. Jaysus! Was she going to have to wait for the ould girl to bath and dress?

Two and a half hours later, by the clock hanging on the kitchen wall, Madam completed her toilet. The servants came at different times to eat their midday meal at the kitchen table. They ignored Polly as being so low that she was beneath their notice.

The morning-room bell tinkled. The manservant wiped his lips on the back of his hand, put on his black jacket and went upstairs. A few minutes later, he returned and said gruffly to Polly, 'Mistress'll see you.'

Her chest aching, her throat parched, her heart beating wildly from fright, Polly followed the old man along a dark passage and up two flights of stairs equally Stygian. 'You're lucky,' he piped. 'Mistress don't bother with the likes of you that often.'

Polly kept her head down and did not answer. Surreptitiously, under her shawl, she scratched a bug bite on her arm. She was so inured to vermin bites that they did not usually irritate. Her mother had, however, insisted that she wash herself all over in a bucket of cold water, scrubbing her yellowed skin with a rough piece of cloth. It had made her itch. After that, both of them had gone over the seams of her clothes to kill any lice or bugs that she might be carrying. 'You can't help your hair,' her mother had said. 'I haven't got no money to buy paraffin to kill the nits in it.'

The old servant pushed open a green baize door and suddenly she was in a blaze of sunlight coming through the stained glass of the hall window.

Blinking against the light, she tiptoed after the servant across the hall rug to a white-enamelled door.

The servant knocked gently, paused and then entered the room, while Polly, terrified, quivered on the red Turkey door-mat.

'Come on in,' the old man breathed irritably. 'She's waitin'.' He shoved Polly forward and closed the door behind her.

Before she lowered her eyes, Polly caught a glimpse of an incredibly thin woman, her heavy white hair done up elaborately on the top of her head. She was waiting bolt upright in an armless chair and was staring out of the window at the garden. Nestling in the folds of her grey silk skirt was a huge white cat. Heavily ringed fingers tickled the cat's ears.

Polly stood silently looking at the richly patterned carpet, and waited to be noticed.

'Well?' the old lady barked.

Polly swallowed and then curtsied. She wanted to run away

and cry, cry herself to death, if possible. 'I'm Polly, Ma'am,' she quavered, 'wot used to scrub your steps and do the brass . . .'

'I know who you are,' snapped the voice. 'What do you want?'

Polly glanced up at her erstwhile employer. The lady was still staring out of the window; the cat stared at Polly. 'Well, Ma'am, I – er . . .'

'For Heaven's sake, speak up, girl.'

'Yes, 'm, I'm wantin' to get a job as wet-nurse to a lady called Mrs Woodman in Upper Canning Street – and I was wonderin', Ma'am, if you would write a letter to her about me.'

'A reference?'

'Yes, Ma'am.'

'A wet-nurse, humph? Have you been in trouble? I don't believe in helping servants in trouble.'

'Oh, no, Ma'am.' Polly was shocked out of her fear. 'I were a married woman.' Her voice faltered, and for the first time, Mrs Stanley turned to look at her.

'Lost the child?'

'Yes, Ma'am. He was born a bit early – 'cos me 'oosband were killed – in the Albert Dock, Ma'am. It must've bin the shock.' She gulped back her tears, and then went on. ''E fell in an 'old, Ma'am.'

'How very careless of him.'

'Yes, 'm.' Tears coursed down the girl's cheeks.

Madam stared at her thoughtfully. Everybody lost children; she had lost all hers. Still, it was depressing. And doubtless Mrs Woodman, whom she had met once or twice at parties, would be glad of a wet-nurse. She understood that, nowadays, they were difficult to obtain.

'Have you been in service before?'

'Yes, Ma'am. I were a tweenie when I were ten, 'elping the 'ousemaid empty the slops, and like. The Missus died . . . and then I found I could earn more specializin' in doin' door-steps.'

'Humph.' Mrs Stanley's lips curled. The lower classes were remarkable in their ability to survive.

'And for how long did you – er – clean my doorsteps?'

'Five year, Ma'am.'

'Why don't you go back to it?'

Polly heaved a sigh. She was so tired that she thought her legs would give under her. 'Me Mam wants me to improve meself,' she burst out, with sudden inspiration.

'Very commendable. And do you go to Church, Polly?'

Polly had never been to Church in her life. And only once to an open air Wesleyan meeting with her father. She knew, however, what the answer must be. 'Oh, yes, Ma'am. I go to St Nick's – I mean, St Nicholas's.'

'Humph. Protestant, then?'

'Yes, Ma'am,' replied Polly promptly, wondering suddenly what she really was, since her mother was a Roman Catholic and her father a Wesleyan.

'Mrs Woodman is a Protestant, I believe.'

Polly did not care if Mrs Woodman worshipped golden idols, like the blackie seamen who walked the streets of Liverpool in silent, single files. All she wanted was three meals a day, to lessen the pain in her stomach, and a baby to suckle, to ease the pain in her chest; even the thought of suckling made her breasts fill and she could feel the milk trickling down to her waist.

Mrs Stanley smiled thinly. She did not care for Mrs Woodman, a fluttering widgeon of a woman with an upstart husband who dabbled in many commercial enterprises in Liverpool. Distinctly lower-class. She thought it might be amusing to send them a wet-nurse who was probably lice-ridden.

'Bring my desk from over there and put it on this table beside me.' Mrs Stanley gestured towards the far wall.

Polly did not know what a desk looked like and glanced, bewildered, towards the furniture indicated by the delicate white hand.

'*There*, you fool – that – er – sloping box.'

Polly carefully lifted a pair of crystal inkwells and a matching candlestick off the desk and laid the desk on the table indicated. She then replaced the inkwells and candlestick.

Irritated, Mrs Stanley moved inkwells and candlestick to the back of the desk, so that she could open the lid and extract a sheet of paper, a goose-quill pen and a piece of sealing wax. In exquisite copperplate, she wrote To Whom It May Concern that Polly Ford was honest, industrious and had worked for her as a charwoman for five years. She was desirous of improving herself, and Mrs Stanley felt that she would give satisfaction.

She sanded the paper to dry the ink. She then took a phosphorus match from the candlestick, struck it and lit the candle. She held the stick of sealing wax to the flame and allowed a small drop to fall upon the letter and seal it closed. Into the molten wax, she pressed a ring from her forefinger, to imprint her own seal.

'There.' She turned in her chair and handed the note to Polly. With a bit of luck, that would give the odious Woodmans a fair amount of trouble.

'Oh, thank you, Ma'am.' Polly's voice was full of genuine gratitude as she made a deep curtsey.

Mrs Stanley gave a stiff nod of acknowledgement, and then ordered, 'Put the desk back on to the far table.'

'Yes, 'm.' Polly did as she was bidden, being particularly careful not to spill the red and black inks from their crystal containers. She then backed to the door, bobbing little curtsies as she went.

'James will show you out. Pull the bell by the fireplace.'

The only thing by the fireplace which could be pulled was a long piece of embroidered canvas hanging from the ceiling. Polly hoped for the best and pulled it. Then she stood with hands neatly clasped in front of her and examined the pattern on the carpet. She was stupid, she told herself. She should have realized that she would have to be escorted out of the house in case she stole something. Not that I would, she told herself crossly.

The old manservant arrived with commendable promptness. 'Yes, Ma'am?'

'Show this woman out – by the servants' entrance.'

'Yes, Ma'am. Of course, Ma'am.' He twisted his toothless mouth into a tight knot. As if he would ever show a member of the lower classes out of the front door. After fifty years of service, Madam ought to know that, he thought irritably.

II

Sent upstairs by Rosie, Polly stood with head meekly bowed and examined the blue and white Chinese carpet in Elizabeth Woodman's room, while her new mistress looked her over for a second time.

The young woman seemed healthy enough; and with a reference from the high-and-mighty Mrs Stanley *and* a personal recommendation from her cook-housekeeper, Mrs Tibbs, she should be satisfactory. Yet, Elizabeth smelled a rat. Mrs Stanley was notorious for her perverted sense of humour. A leftover from the wilder days of King George IV and King William IV, the old devil was capable of all kinds of japes and capers.

As she peered in the candlelight at the humbly bent head, a much sharper pain shot through her and she cried out. Mrs Macdonald came to the bedside immediately. She picked up the rolling-pin from the bedside table and handed it to the sufferer. 'There, there, Ma'am. Hold on to this.'

Elizabeth clutched at the pin and gritted her teeth, as she waited for the next pang. She felt tired already, worn out from worrying over the coming child's existence. She was petrified at the thought of the outburst which might occur from Humphrey when he actually saw the baby.

But if she employed this Polly Ford, the child could stay in the old nurseries on the top floor for months, and as far as Humphrey was concerned, out of sight might be out of mind. And she herself would be freed from the boredom of feeding the baby. She could go out and fulfil her social obligations, be free to spend afternoons with darling Andrew, as before, though they would have to be much more careful.

She let another spasm go over, managing not to cry out. Then she said to the midwife, 'Mrs Macdonald, tell Mrs Tibbs to see that this woman is bathed, her head rubbed with paraffin, and her present clothing wrapped up tightly and sent to her home. Mrs Tibbs should have her uniform ready by now.'

'Yes, Ma'am. I'll ring for Rosie.'

Polly kept her head down. This was much better than she had expected. Both she and her mother had been worried about getting her a uniform, fearing that the pedlar might not give them credit. Now the clothes were to be given to her. If she had dared, she would have sighed with relief.

Elizabeth knew from sad experience that vermin could come into a house in a servant's trunk. She took no chances and always provided uniforms.

Polly endured without comment the humiliating complaints of her fellow servants, as a tin bath was lugged up to the windowless box room which would be her bedroom. Loquacious Fanny hauled two ewers of hot water and one of cold up the endless stairs from the basement kitchen, together with a bottle of paraffin, a bar of laundry soap, a piece of flannel and a worn bath towel. 'Mind you don't make no splashes,' she warned Polly.

Polly had never had a bath in her life; she had simply rubbed herself cursorily with a bit of cloth wrung out in cold water. Now, Fanny laid an old copy of *The Times* on the floor and said, 'Take off all yer clothes and put 'em on this. Mrs Tibbs'll get next door's gardener's boy to walk down with 'em to yer ma's.'

Polly looked at the girl appalled. Take off *everything*?

As if she could read her mind, Fanny said, with a grin, 'Everythin', 'cept yer stockin's and boots – you're to keep them.'

'Well, you go away, Miss, while I does it,' snapped Polly defiantly. Even Patrick had never seen her completely naked.

At the thought of Patrick, tears welled. Fanny saw them, and said sympathetically, 'Don't take on so. They did this to me when I coom. Fussy, the Mistress is – wash all of you every day, she allus says.' She glanced up again at Polly, still standing uncertainly by the bath. 'These days, I fancy a bath meself now and then – takes the aches out of yez. I'll bet she'll make you scrub your dairies every day.' She nodded her head like a disapproving old woman. 'Proper finick, she is.'

While she waited for Fanny to leave the room, Polly sat down and unlaced her boots. One of the bootlaces broke and she looked at it ruefully, wondering where she would get a halfpenny from to buy a new one. 'What's the Master like?' she inquired carefully – her mother had warned her long ago, when she had been a ten-year-old tweenie in a big house, to keep out of the way of the men of the house.

'Himself? Och, you don't have to worry about him. He's got a fancy woman downtown. Maisie – she's the parlour-maid – says the woman keeps 'im exhausted!' Fanny chortled and looked wickedly at Polly. Then she said more soberly, 'They do say as once he got a maid in trouble and the Mistress sent her packing. Nowadays, he don't even notice you're there, though. He's got a lousy temper, though. Just keep out of his way of an evening when he's drunk.'

Polly digested this advice, and then, as Fanny picked up her empty ewer and moved towards the door, she asked, 'What part of town do you come from?'

Fanny laughed. 'I dunno, for sure. I got an auntie wot lives in Shaw's Alley, but I coom 'ere from the Workie. I were born in there – and bloody glad I was to get out of it. At least the Mistress don't beat you. It were me auntie that got on to you.'

'Is your Mam still in the Workhouse?'

'Not her. She died when I was only an itty-bitty kid. The Workie Gaffer hit her one day for something she said – and she lay down and I remember she were cold.'

Polly did not bother to ask her where her father was. In her experience, fathers often remained unknown. She sighed and said, 'It must've bin proper hard for yez.'

26

Fanny's eyes twinkled. 'I wouldn't give a dead farthin' to go through it again,' she replied forcefully. Swinging her empty ewer, she turned and plodded down the stairs to the basement.

Polly quickly stripped off her blouse, skirt and stockings. She put a cautious toe into the steaming water and then stepped into it. It felt comfortable, so she carefully lowered herself into it and reached for the soap lying on the floor. She took the hairpins out of her plaits and loosened her hair. She found that holding the hot flannel to her breasts eased the ache in them and she was able to expel some of her milk. It would be a day or two, she realized, before the baby would be able to suck, and, in the meantime, she must keep the milk coming.

After she had dried herself, she kneeled down by the bath and uncorked the bottle of paraffin. Holding her breath because of its smell, she rubbed it liberally into her damp hair, until it dripped into the bath. Then, using a fine-toothed comb which her husband, Patrick, had given her as a present, she combed the long, damp locks until she reckoned she had all the lice out; the paraffin would kill the nits, so, if she were lucky, she would be free of them.

Two full-skirted, ankle-length, cotton dresses with petticoats to go under them had been provided. In Polly's eyes, the dresses were beautiful, far nicer than anything she had ever worn before; they had narrow, blue and white stripes. There were three large white aprons to wear over them and three white cotton bonnets to pin over her hair. To go out-of-doors, there was a navy-blue jacket, and a navy coif to go over the white caps.

She would have to find stockings and shoes for herself, and she wondered if her mother could prevail on the pedlar to let her have them on two months' credit. Her first month's wages would be appropriated by Mrs Tibbs, the cook-housekeeper, as her fee for getting her the job. As she thought about this, she replaited her hair and wound it into a neat bun at the back of her head.

When Fanny came back up the stairs, carrying a pair of slop pails in which to remove the bath water, she gaped at the newly created Nanny. 'Well, I never,' she exclaimed. 'You look proper pretty.'

Her spirits revived, Polly gave the girl a playful cuff about the head for her impudence. Then she asked, 'Wot time is servants' meals?'

'Breakfast at six-thirty, dinner 'alf-past eleven, tea at five. If Ma Tibbs is in a good mood, you get a bit o' somethin' afore bedtime – depends on wot's left from the Master's dinner. The Mistress isn't mean, but Ma Tibbs is. She takes food to her sister's house.'

'I'm awfully hungry,' admitted Polly, her voice trembling slightly.

'Oh, aye. *You* could get a mug o' milk or ale anytime you want – and I suppose I'll 'ave to bring it up.'

She plunged her slop pail into the scummy bath water.

'Bring me some milk and a piece of bread now,' wheedled Polly. 'There's a pet. I'm clemmed.'

Fanny glanced up at her. 'And the baby not even born yet?' she teased.

'Come on, Fanny. I'll share it with yez.'

'Well, seein' as I know yez, I'll ask for it.'

Chapter Three

I

At half-past eleven that warm May night, Alicia Beatrix Mary yelled her first impatient complaint in this world.

Dr Willis declared her a healthy child and Mrs Macdonald gave her her first bath. To ensure a flat, well-healed navel, a flannel binder was wound tightly round her stomach.

On a dresser lay a pile of baby clothes originally prepared for a brother, who, eight years before, had died within a month of his birth. Mrs Macdonald picked up a cotton napkin and one of terry towelling and enclosed Alicia in these. Then the child's tiny arms were pushed into a flannel vest. A long cotton petticoat followed and then a flannel one, each tied at the front. Over all this went a fine white baby gown, frilled and embroidered and hemstitched in an Islington sweat shop. The long petticoats and gown were folded up over the protesting little feet, and she was finally wrapped in a warm, white shawl crocheted for her by her mother's spinster friend and lifelong confidante, Miss Sarah Webb.

Almost smothered by the amount of clothing, Alicia carried her complaints to Humphrey Woodman.

Humphrey had been called from his booklined study by Dr Willis to inspect the new addition to his household and was uncertain, at first, whether he should go up. He had been startled when Maisie, the parlour-maid, had told him that his wife had commenced her labour. He had hoped to the last that his wife would miscarry, so that he would not have to face directly the fact of her infidelity.

Maisie was waiting, politely holding the door open for him, so he slowly pushed himself away from his desk and got up.

As he straightened his velvet smoking jacket and gravely marched upstairs, a slow anger burned in him. He did not care a damn what Elizabeth did as long as she was discreet; but having a child at the age of forty was, alone, enough to interest the gossips and raise speculation.

Since Dr Willis and Mrs Macdonald were present, he kissed his wife dutifully upon her white cheek, and, afterwards, went to inspect the minute bundle lying in the frilly, draped cot which had served all his children.

His breath began to come fast as he gazed at the crumpled red face, and he seethed inwardly; at that moment he would have liked to murder Elizabeth and her lawyer, Andrew Crossing, whom he was fairly sure was the child's father. Yet, in a sense, he also felt defeated. There was no question of his divorcing his wife; he must maintain his carefully built-up image of a well-respected city businessman with an impeccable home-life. To maintain society's rigid proprieties, he would have to accept the baby as his. He knew it and he guessed that his wife was counting upon it – the sanctimonious bitch!

At the back of his mind, too, was the need to protect the future of his daughter, Florence, who was standing by him, bending over the little cot and tenderly touching her newborn sister with a careful finger. Florence was herself seven months pregnant. She was the wife of the Reverend Clarence Browning, a gentleman with small private means bent on a career in the church. A divorce between her parents, or even a separation, might put an end to his hopes of obtaining a bishopric one day.

Humphrey loved Florence. She was the only person to whom he showed any real affection. Her marriage portion had been as handsome as he could make it. Though at this moment he itched to beat her mother to death, he knew he would never make a single move that might injure his little Flo. When Alicia's time came, however, he thought savagely, she would not get a penny out of him.

'Isn't she lovely, Papa?' cooed Florence.

Humphrey continued to gaze expressionlessly at the crabbed little face, as he said politely, 'Yes, my dear.'

While Dr Willis went to use the Woodmans' magnificent new water closet, Mrs Macdonald stood, hands folded over her apron, at the foot of the bed, waiting for the series of visitors to pass. She would stay to nurse Elizabeth for a couple of days, before handing her over to her friend, Sarah Webb, to be cared for during the rest of her ten days' lying-in.

As Humphrey turned to leave the room, he felt suddenly drained. His anger began to subside and he thought longingly of his Mrs Jakes. Most of his friends had a *little woman* tucked away somewhere in the town, and Mrs Jakes was his woman. Her well-patronized sweets and tobacco shop, on the corner of one of the crowded streets behind his office in Water Street, offered a fine excuse for visiting her. His need for tobacco for his pipe and the occasional gift of sweets for his children accounted easily for his going there. When the shop was empty of customers, he would slip behind the counter and through the door to her living-quarters. She would send her dull, thick-waisted daughter to tend the shop, lock the intervening door and draw the lace curtains over the window in it. They could be very cosy together behind the lace-draped door, sitting in front of her blazing coal fire; or they could go up the stairs which led to her bedroom above. It was a discreet, mutually agreeable arrangement. Why could not Elizabeth have been equally circumspect? he fumed.

Now, ignoring his wife, he said goodnight to Mrs Macdonald and told Florence to go to bed soon. Mrs Macdonald, much experienced in these matters, drew her own conclusions.

Downstairs, Humphrey waited in his study until the doctor should be shown in. Dr Willis, when he did come, accepted a glass of port and lifted it in a toast to the newborn. Humphrey bent his head slightly in acknowledgement, but he did not raise his glass. As Dr Willis drank from his glass, his eyebrows rose slightly – so his own wife's gossip about Elizabeth Woodman had a sound basis. Woodman was showing none of the jovial relief at a safe delivery that most men exhibited. He hastily finished his wine, put down his glass and said that he would call again the following morning, to check both mother and child.

II

Upstairs, Mrs Macdonald was deferentially solicitous and wondered privately who would pay her bill. She said, as she fussed round her patient, 'Miss Webb wondered if you would like a bite to eat, Ma'am?'

Sarah Webb, being a spinster, would not visit her friend until the morning; not having been married, she was supposed, officially, not to know how babies arrived. The following day seemed to her to be a polite time to come up. She had, meanwhile, taken over the housekeeping, and Mrs Tibbs had had a long, uncomfortable evening as Sarah began to cope with a kitchen unused to being visited by its mistress.

Florence reinforced the suggestion of food. She said, 'Yes, Mama, you should take something to eat. You have to keep up your strength.' Florence was deadly tired, her bundly body aching in every direction, but she spoke brightly to her mother.

'Very well, dear,' Elizabeth responded wearily. 'Tell Mrs Tibbs to make me a plain omelette and toast – and some Madeira to drink.'

Mrs Macdonald pulled at the bell rope.

Elizabeth continued to talk to her daughter. 'I have a wet-nurse for the child,' she told her with a wan smile. 'I don't propose to feed her myself. At my age . . .'

Florence nodded understandingly. She had not been informed of her mother's pregnancy until a week before the birth. Elizabeth had not felt able to tell a pregnant daughter that she was expecting an infant. At forty, it was indecent to be in such a situation; she herself had not expected it to happen.

As her mother's figure burgeoned under the flounces and

heavy drapery of her elaborate dresses, the situation had been clear to Florence for some time. She was, however, much too well brought up to mention the subject until her mother cared to bring the matter up and she expressed suitable surprise when Elizabeth suddenly blurted out that she would be brought to bed within the month. She had been much alarmed that her mother would not survive and had prayed earnestly each night that she be safely delivered. Now, she thought, she must pray for herself.

As if the midwife divined her thoughts, she turned towards her and smiled faintly, 'You look very well, if I may say so, Ma'am. You'll soon know the joy of your own wee babe in your arms.' There was oily comfort in every word.

'Thank you, Mrs Macdonald,' responded Florence graciously, 'With your help, I'm sure I will.'

In answer to the bell, Maisie, the elderly parlour-maid, arrived and was instructed regarding a meal.

'Tell Mrs Ford she may now come to remove the baby,' Elizabeth told the maid. 'I trust a fire has been made in the nursery – and in baby's bedroom?'

'Oh, yes, Ma'am. Fanny's bin watching both fires ever since afternoon.'

Up in the nursery, Polly, lulled by the heat, had gone to sleep in an old easy chair set by the fireplace. In the glow of the coals, she looked softly pretty, tidier, more clean than she had ever been in her life.

When Fanny clumped in with yet another hod of coal, she woke up with a start.

'Coom on, now,' Fanny commanded her. 'The Missus wants you to take the baby.' She dumped the heavy coal hod into the fireplace, picked up a pair of tongs and lifted a couple of lumps of coal on to the blaze. 'Maisie and Rosie'll bring the cot up.' She yawned enormously, her stunted little body stretching as she did so. 'Aye, I'm that tired. Seems to me as if none of us is goin' to get to bed tonight. And I got to be up at five, 'cos ould Tibbs raises Cain if she don't have a hot oven by six o'clock, ready to put the bread in.'

Polly got up and stretched. Then she peeked into the mirror over the dresser, to check that her hair was still neat and her cap on straight. 'Fancy having a mirror,' she thought to herself gleefully. She picked up the candle from the table.

'Aye, don't leave me in the dark,' protested Fanny. She hastily tipped the rest of the coal into a brass coal scuttle at the side of the hearth. 'It's proper ghosty up here, what with Mr Charles and Mr Edward gone away and not usin' the rooms on the other side o' the passage.'

Polly waited for the little skivvy and then, carrying the candle, led her down the dark staircase, the coal hod clanking like chains behind her.

On the floor below lay Elizabeth's bedroom and beside it the dressing-room in which Humphrey had slept for the last year or so. Also on this floor, lay Florence's old bedroom, a guest room and the main drawing-room; the latter was shrouded in dust sheets, because Elizabeth could not entertain in the last months of her pregnancy; it was not the thing. At the back of the house, on this same floor, was Elizabeth Woodman's latest status symbol, a brand new water closet and a handsome adjoining bathroom with hot and cold water which belched from shining brass taps.

'You're not allowed to use the water closet,' Fanny warned Polly, as they passed it. 'You got to come down to the closet outside the back kitchen door – or you can use a chamber-pot and empty it yourself down there. I 'aven't got no time to be running up and down with a slop pail to clear it for yez. There's an old slop pail in the nursery cupboard if you want to use it.'

Polly reached Elizabeth's door at the same time as Maisie was about to enter, so she followed her in. They both stood just inside the doorway, hands folded, eyes down, waiting for orders.

Elizabeth was sitting up in bed, wrapped in a pink shawl, her hair plaited neatly over each shoulder. She was feeling better and, though her eyes were black-ringed, some of her normal high colour had returned to her cheeks; the birth had, in fact, been quite an easy one. She fully expected that, thanks to Mrs Macdonald's modern ideas of well-scrubbed hands, boiled aprons and sheets, she would be spared that plague of new mothers, childbed fever.

Replete with omelette and half a bottle of Madeira, her breasts bound tightly by Mrs Macdonald to prevent the flow of milk, all she wanted now was that the child be taken away, so that, as much as possible, she could forget it. She hoped, also, when trouble with her husband had blown over, that she could be reunited with Andrew Crossing, only in a more private place than on her drawing-room settee.

'Polly,' she snapped at the trim, black-haired wet-nurse. 'Take the baby upstairs. See that it is fed every three or four hours and has its napkin changed frequently to keep it dry.' She turned to Maisie. 'Take the tray away. That will be all for tonight.'

'Thank you, ma'am,' Maisie replied, took the tray and fled thankfully to her bed. Polly approached the cradle cautiously and picked up the tiny bundle which was Alicia Beatrix Mary. The infant opened its eyes and whimpered.

'Polly.'

'Yes, 'm?'

'There is a good supply of clothing in the chest of drawers in the nursery. Fanny will remove any washing including your own. She will also bring up your meals. The washerwoman will come twice a week. See that the dirty clothes and sheets are down in the wash cellar by six o'clock every Monday and Thursday morning.'

Polly bobbed a small curtsey to indicate agreement.

'I have instructed Mrs Tibbs to feed you well and let you have as much milk as you can drink.'

Having met Mrs Tibbs, Polly did not have any great hope of these instructions being followed properly. She whispered, however, a faint 'Thank you, ma'am.' She allowed herself a small shivering sigh – it had been a long and eventful day for her – and then asked, 'What's baby's name, ma'am?'

'Alicia Beatrix Mary,' replied Elizabeth, having decided

that it was better to name the child herself, rather than ask Humphrey his opinion. Though she would not have liked to admit it, there was the thought in the back of her mind that, like its baby brother, it might die within the month, anyway; and that would solve a lot of her problems.

Andrew had assured her that since she and Humphrey lived together the child was legally his, unless he repudiated it. Nevertheless, she supposed she would have to go herself to register its birth, as soon as she felt well enough; Humphrey was hardly likely to do anything about putting *his* name on the birth certificate. She must also write a note to Andrew, she reminded herself, telling him of Alicia's birth; she could say that she wanted to alter her Will slightly to include a small legacy to the new baby. She sighed, and hoped he would come soon.

'You may go,' she told Polly, patiently standing in front of her with the baby in her arms.

III

Unaware of the inconvenience her arrival had caused, Alicia Beatrix Mary was carried up to the attic nurseries. To Polly, the child was sent by the Holy Mother herself to replace the little boy she had lost and to comfort her in her widowhood. For her part, Alicia learned to turn to Polly for mothering; it was Polly's voice she knew first and Polly's face that she first recognized.

Chapter Four

I

Alicia had barely learned how to suck, when Elizabeth, after ten days' of lying-in, descended one afternoon to the pleasant, sunny morning-room on the ground floor. She was escorted solicitously down the stairs by her friend, Sarah Webb, and was met by her elder daughter, Florence, in the little sitting-room.

As her own confinement drew near, Florence looked white-faced and drawn. She dreaded the birth of her baby, because she had no idea how it would make its way into the world. There did not seem to be an aperture big enough to give it access! She wondered if she would split down the middle, like a pea pod giving up its peas, and the idea terrified her. She was much too afraid of her stout, dogmatic husband, the Reverend Clarence Browning, to ask him. Having been taught nothing about sex and having been horrified when Clarence took her on her honeymoon, she felt that life was vulgar enough, without giving him further opportunity for lewd remarks and disgusting behaviour. She simply did not believe frustrated Clarence's assurance that their sex life was normal.

She was relieved to see her mother looking very elegant in a copper-coloured gown with the hint of a train at the back and a velvet collar edged with cream lace. It was comforting to realize that her mother had always survived childbirth, despite whatever ordeals it presented.

With the aid of her friend and her elder daughter, Elizabeth was gently eased into an armless easy chair near her work table in the window. Florence had brought a bunch of fat, pink roses from her own garden and had set them in a silver bowl on the table. She had also thoughtfully placed her mother's workbasket by her chair. Her mother still followed the old custom of making and embroidering her own petticoats and drawers, though Messrs George Henry Lee, a fashionable shop in the town which made her dresses, cloaks and hats, would have been happy to undertake the work for her.

Florence had already been up to the nursery to see Alicia, and now she asked her mother if she had seen the child that day.

Elizabeth was silent for a moment. Then she said heavily, 'No. Polly will bring her down at teatime.'

'She *is* thriving, isn't she?'

'I believe so.'

Though Florence had herself been cared for by a nanny, she was worried about the little mite so summarily handed over to a wet-nurse. The baby seemed contented enough, but her mother showed no interest in it; and the nursery, when Flo had visited, appeared neither clean nor tidy. She had spoken sharply to Mrs Tibbs and to Polly about the need for cleanliness. Mrs Tibbs, all indignation, had promised to order the housemaid to turn the room out immediately.

Now, with Sarah Webb nodding agreement, she strove to awaken her mother's interest in Alicia. 'Polly needs supervision,' she told her.

Her mother merely sighed absently, unable to tell her daughter of the sweating fear within her. She asked Florence to serve each of them with a glass of port from the decanter on the sideboard and to hand round biscuits from the biscuit barrel; when her glass was given to her she drank the contents with unmannerly speed.

'It's a pity Papa won't keep a carriage, isn't it, Mama? Such a lovely afternoon. We could have gone for a drive round the park.'

Elizabeth replied acidly, 'You know that your father has money for everything – railways, roads, ships, are all he's interested in. Never thinks of my needs.'

Sarah Webb, anxious to cheer up her friend, broke in, 'Dear Elizabeth, if you don't mind being driven in a governess cart,

I should be delighted to take you out. I stabled it in Crown Street during your confinement, so that I would have it close by. As you know, I can handle the reins quite well.'

The idea of being seen in her old friend's extremely shabby, humble vehicle, made Elizabeth shudder.

'No, no, Sarah, thank you. If I wished, I could, I suppose, hire a carriage from the stables. Thanks to my own dear Papa, I am not without funds for such things. And Andrew has managed my portion so well that it has increased.'

Elizabeth's dowry, legally tied up so that Humphrey could not touch it, provided her with a good wardrobe and sufficient pin money for small luxuries, like a hired carriage to take her shopping. But if Humphrey was so mean that he would not provide her with a fashionable vehicle, she preferred to put him in the wrong by being a martyr among her better-equipped friends. So, while Sarah and Florence sought to raise her spirits, she sighed and sulked, and looked forward with absolute dread to her husband's return from his office in the city.

She had not seen Humphrey since the night of Alicia's birth. As he had done for the past year, he had slept in the dressing-room next to their bedroom; in addition to the entrance to the bedroom, it had a door leading on to the landing, so he came and went without entering her room. Today, unless she feigned fatigue and returned to her bed, she would have to meet him at dinner. Later in the afternoon, Sarah and Florence would both go home and there would be no one present to make it necessary for him to control himself. The prospect made her feel sick, and she wondered what Andrew would do, if she ordered a carriage and fled to him.

As she drank her second glass of port and listened to Sarah and Florence talking about the joys of motherhood, she wanted to cry. Where was Andrew? He could have called or, at least, have sent some flowers from his wife and himself. He was her lawyer. He had every right to call on her. But in her heart she knew Andrew. He was in many ways weak; he would avoid a troublesome mistress as if she had the plague.

'Babies are such darlings,' gushed Sarah, none of whose nephews and nieces had ever been presented to her by their nannies, unless dry, fed and sleepy. She herself would not have known what to do with a sopping wet, hungry, howling infant, except to coo over it.

Florence was smart enough to realize this. She remembered her younger brother, Charles, with whom she had shared the nursery for a while; he had been anything but lovely. Clarence had told her flatly that they could not afford a nurse for their baby and that she must do the best she could with the aid of their cook-general and kitchen-maid. Because Charles was a boy, she had never seen him either bathed or changed. How did you change a small, wriggling creature like a baby? Or bathe it? Or put it to the breast? She hoped, rather frantically, that Mrs Macdonald, the midwife, would instruct her; she could not ask such vulgar questions of Mama. In some despair, she had made a point of arriving at her mother's house quite early, during the past ten days, having taken the horse-bus from home, so that she could go upstairs to watch Polly struggling with Alicia.

II

Polly was herself learning on the job, though she knew much more about birth and babies than poor Florence did. Before coming to the Woodman household, she had received some strict advice from her mother and from her Great-aunt Kitty, herself a midwife to the slum women around her. The result was that, much as she protested, Alicia was scoured twice daily from head to heel. To Fanny's irritation, the child was changed the moment she was damp; it was poor Fanny who had to carry the pails of dirty napkins, petticoats and gowns down to the cellar ready for the washerwoman.

'All for nought but a little bastard,' Fanny had muttered, as she heaved the heavy pails down the stairs.

To the Woodmans, Fanny was nothing but a quiet, little

shadow responsible for all the coal fires in the house. As she went from room to room, she had become well aware of Andrew Crossing's interest in her mistress; raucous jokes at his expense had been a real source of entertainment on quiet evenings in the kitchen, as the maids sipped their fender ale.

Fanny had also seen something of the bitter fights between Elizabeth and Humphrey. When she went through the house to make up all the fires and they heard her knock, they would stop their shouting and upbraiding and would stand rigidly staring at each other while she poked up the fire and added more coal; as soon as she was out of the door, coal hod in hand, she would hear them renew the battle.

It was Fanny who danced out into the street to find a cab to take Florence home. She took her time because it was so lovely to be out in the afternoon sun, and, when she found one, Florence gave her twopence for her trouble.

Florence was thankful that her mother had insisted on giving her the money to pay for the cab; otherwise, she would have had to take the horse-bus again. Though Elizabeth had great faith that the Reverend Clarence Browning would make his way upwards in the Church and would, in due course, be able to afford a carriage, Florence was acutely aware that he was far too outspoken, far too direct, ever to be recommended for high office. Florence herself was content to preside over the little vicarage they occupied, thankful that a man so intent on the saving of souls had managed, in spite of church politics, to rise to a vicarage. She asked no more – except for a nanny.

In order to conserve her strength for the coming confrontation with Humphrey, Elizabeth tried to take a nap in the afternoon, but she was so filled with anxiety that she returned to the morning-room in time to take tea and to receive Polly and Alicia.

Alicia was hungry and was screaming. Elizabeth inquired of Polly if she had everything she needed for the child and then sent her thankfully back upstairs.

III

When Humphrey bowled swiftly into the dining-room for dinner, his white-faced wife was already seated, and Maisie, the parlourmaid, was hovering over the laden sideboard.

Humphrey ignored both of them. He indicated that he was ready to be served by simply shaking out his table napkin and spreading it across his stomach. In complete silence, Maisie served them both.

Never a man to waste anything, Humphrey ate his way stolidly through soup, roast beef and steamed pudding. He knew, as his wife had already sensed, that this was the evening to make clear his attitude towards Alicia, who, like his wife, he had hoped would either miscarry or be born dead.

Impotent rage surged through him. Hemmed in by the constrictions of social propriety, he was certain there was not a great deal he could do about the situation without coming to grief himself, and this knowledge added to his boiling anger. He helped himself to hot mustard and cursed under his breath when the condiment stuck to its spoon. He banged the tiny spoon on the side of his plate and in the tensely quiet room it sounded like a pistol going off.

Elizabeth kept her eyes down and picked uneasily at her food. Her mind leaped wildly between fear of Humphrey and heartbreak that she had not heard from Andrew.

She jumped when Humphrey asked for a second helping of pudding and more wine. Really, the man ate like a hog. The only thing he seemed to notice in the house was when Mrs Tibbs' cooking was not up to its usual standard.

Humphrey had, indeed, not noticed for months that his wife was pregnant. When he did, he had hastily checked his office diary. It told him with certainty that the child could not be his. Plump, comfortable Mrs Jakes kept him so exhausted that he had rarely slept with his wife. Elizabeth had not seemed to care about his neglect.

Elizabeth had been more than thankful to be relieved of her wifely duties. Her lifelong friend, Andrew Crossing, had been only too willing to meet her needs, since his wife was a useless invalid. As Maisie took away her untouched roast beef, she thought agonizedly of how she had rebelled against marrying Humphrey, how passionately she had loved her childhood playmate, Andrew. At nineteen, Andrew had had no money and had failed his first year at University; her father had been adamant that he was not suitable for her. In contrast, at twenty-five, Humphrey was already well-established with his father, in a brokerage business and, as the elder son, he was to inherit the entire enterprise. What her father had not realized, Elizabeth fulminated, was that Humphrey was not only physically repellent to her, but also had the hoarding instincts of a jackdaw; his ambition was to accumulate capital to invest in shipping or railways. He lectured her regularly, from the days of their unhappy honeymoon onwards, on the fact that capital accumulated by personal savings was the only sure way to expand a business. Money made in a business should be ploughed back in. He had rationed her and, later, poor Flo, to two pairs of black woollen stockings and one pair of white silk every winter of her married life; any extra ones had had to be bought out of the money left her by her father. And he still went over Mrs Tibbs' account books with her each month and railed at her for waste.

It had taken twelve months of unmitigated pressure by her parents to make her marry him, twelve months during which no other young man had been allowed to get more than a single dance with her and she was never left alone.

It was Andrew himself who finally had broken her resolve.

At a banquet and ball given by the Mayor, Mr Gardner, to celebrate the marriage of the Prince of Wales to Princess Alexandra of Denmark, he had pushed his way through the throng, to find her sitting demurely beside her mother and her aunt, while her bearded father and his brother had gone to join their friends for a drink. He had formally asked for a waltz.

Her mother had answered frigidly for her. 'Elizabeth's programme is full, I am sorry.'

Elizabeth, faced with the handsome, blond, young man, had said desperately, as she handed him her tiny programme, 'I have one more dance to fill, Mama.' Two chaperones sitting near were watching the little exchange with interest, so, rather than cause a public fuss, her mother had said no more.

They had hardly taken a dozen steps, after Andrew came to claim her, when he blurted out, 'It's no good, Liz. I've tried to get the old man to persuade your father to allow an engagement, with no luck at all. He's furious with me for muffing my exams, and he's insisted that I begin all over again in law. Law's what I always wanted to do, anyway, but he was dead-set on my entering the church, so I had to do Divinity.'

'I can wait for you.' Elizabeth remembered her utter despair when she had realized that Andrew himself was backing out.

As they whirled amid the colourful throng of dancers, she had looked up at him and seen the tremulous uncertainty in his face; he had always been weak, she thought bitterly, as she contemplated her steamed pudding, and in her heart she knew without doubt that he had again deserted her. She wished that Mrs Macdonald had not been quite so skilful, and that she had died having Alicia.

Her reverie was broken by Humphrey's saying to Maisie, 'The Mistress will take her tea in the drawing-room.'

Elizabeth swallowed. Humphrey was choosing the field of combat, the upstairs room from which loud voices were least likely to be heard by the servants.

'Yes, Sir. I'll ask Fanny to make sure the fire is made up.'

While Humphrey ate his gorgonzola cheese and biscuits there was a flurry in the kitchen as a swearing Fanny fled upstairs with a shovel full of burning coals from the kitchen fire, to start a fire in the drawing-room. She had been so sure that the room would not be used that evening, there being no visitors, that she had not bothered to light the fire.

Elizabeth thought resignedly, 'So be it. What does it matter?' and went up to sit by the struggling blaze. Though it was May, the room was cold and clammy. Outside the tall, velvet-draped windows, a fine rain was falling. Elizabeth picked up a shawl and flung it around her shivering shoulders.

If Andrew had been anything but a family lawyer, she would have taken a chance and run to him now, told some suitable story to his fragile, rheumaticky Eleanor, and simply stayed with him, daring him to say a word. But in his profession, he dealt with the Estates of a number of widows, with Trusteeships like her own dowry. The slightest hint of scandal and he would lose a lot of business.

When she had told him of the coming child, he had immediately and fearfully repudiated any idea that he was the father. It had hurt her immeasurably.

'Humphrey will know it is not his,' she had replied dully.

'You're married to him, so the child will be born in wedlock.'

'Not if he denies it.'

They had been sitting, arms around each other on the big sofa facing her now, and he had drawn away from her. He had walked stiffly up and down the room, while she stared at him aghast. He had finally turned towards her and said through lips that quivered slightly, 'Come on, Liz. It can't be mine.'

'It can be and it is.'

'I simply don't believe it. I've never fathered a child before.' He came to sit down beside her, and added in a wheedling tone, 'Anyway, you can manage Humphrey, I'm sure.'

Tears sprang to her eyes. 'You don't know him. He's got a a murderous temper.'

She had wept and had implored him to take her away – to Italy, to anywhere they could live together. But the irresolute boy had grown into a vacillating man, and gradually she had realized that, if she pressed him, he would abandon her entirely.

She had bravely dried her tears and said that, somehow, she would brazen it out with Humphrey. In an almost motherly

45

fashion she had decided that he probably needed protection against a scandal more than she did.

'Don't worry, sweetheart,' she whispered, as he thankfully said his farewells. 'Just find a place where we can meet more safely than this. I love you, remember.'

He had replied, somewhat woodenly, that he loved her, too, and that he would find a trysting place.

His visits had grown rarer, however; he did not attempt to make love to her and she began to despair. Through the last months of her pregnancy, she had reassured herself again and again that he was merely being careful for the sake of the child, but, in more realistic moments, black hopelessness had almost overwhelmed her.

'Well, you slut. What have you to say?' Her husband had come into the room so quickly and so quietly that she had not heard him. Without warning, he clouted her across the back of her head.

Determined to feign innocence, she cried out indignantly, 'Humphrey, what did you do that for?'

'I suppose you think you're going to fob off Crossing's brat on me? Thought you'd get away with it?'

The blow had made her reel in her chair. Now she tried to rally herself. 'Humphrey, how could you say such a thing?' She angrily pushed some hairpins back into her bun. 'And to strike me, when I've only just got up from childbed. You must be drunk.'

He stood facing her, head thrust forward, his lips drawn back from tobacco-stained teeth. 'Don't try that on me. I know what's been going on – and now we've got a bastard in the house.' His hand shot forward and slapped her a stinging blow across the mouth, followed by another one with his left hand. 'And you, milady, are going to pay for it. This brat isn't mine and you know it.'

Shocked and terrified, she stared back at him, in too much pain to speak.

He pushed his face close to hers. 'You know, don't you?'

She edged to the side of her armless chair and slid out of it with what dignity she could muster. 'You must be mad!' she muttered, from between her swelling lips. 'You're my husband – it's normal to have babies.'

'I've not been with you for over a year – and you must know it. *And* I know about your happy afternoon hours with Crossing.'

Her eyes shot wider open, but she answered as steadily as she could, 'Andrew's my lawyer. He has to manage father's Trust for Clara and me, so, of course, he comes to consult me. Anyway, we've known him for years.' She held her hand to her mouth and closed her eyes with pain. Then she said, half-crying, 'If my brother were in England, you wouldn't dare to say such dreadful things – or hit me! And for no reason!'

'That jigger rabbit is three thousand miles away, in Ceylon. He'd be ashamed of you, anyway.' He advanced towards her and she hastily put the width of the chair between them and began to back towards the door. As she fumbled with the handle, he caught her by the shoulder and spun her back into the room, her full skirts splaying out round her. She stumbled and fell, face down.

He whipped his razor strop out of his pocket. Raising his arm, he brought it down across her shoulders with all the force he could muster. She screamed and covered her head with her arms as the wicked leather strap whistled down on her again. Four months of suppressed outrage were vented on her, as she sought to crawl away from him and reach the door.

'I've been waiting for this,' he yelled at her. 'I hope you enjoy it.' The strop came down again across the back of her head.

Her screams stopped. She lay immobile.

He paused, scarlet-faced, panting over her, the desire to rape her urgent in him. He heaved up her heavily gathered skirt, but she was tightly entangled in her three petticoats. He tore at his trousers and emptied himself over her.

'You damned Jezebel,' he snarled and kicked her in the stomach. She did not move.

'Go to hell,' he shrieked. 'Look at another man, and I'll make sure you do.'

He flung open the door, and ran down into the hall, buttoning up his trousers as he went. He seized his hat and stick from the rack and went out of the front door muttering like a madman. Five minutes later, he was sitting primly on the horse-bus on his way to visit Mrs Jakes.

Chapter Five

I

Fanny found her when she came to rake the cinders out of the fireplace before going to bed.

With a frightened squeak, she dropped her coal hod and knelt down to turn her mistress over. When she saw the swollen lips and tear-stained cheeks, she knew what had happened; she had seen the same thing so often in her aunt's home.

'Oh, Missus! Can you sit up, Missus? Look, I'll turn yez on your back and give you a heave up.'

Elizabeth moaned as she managed to turn and raise herself sufficiently to lean her head against the little skivvy's shoulder. Fanny swallowed, and looked desperately around. 'Is anythin' broke, d'yer think?' she asked.

Elizabeth shuddered, then whispered, 'I don't think so.' She began to cry.

'Well, let's try and get you on that low chair there, and then I'll run and get Maisie to help you up to your bed.'

'Not Maisie,' Elizabeth murmured. 'Or the others.' She paused, her breath coming slowly and heavily. 'Ask Polly – she'll mind her own business.'

She cried out in pain as Fanny slowly sat her upright while she brought the small chair closer, and moaned again as she was eased up on to it.

'There, Ma'am. Lean your head against the high back, and I'll be back with Polly in half a mo'.'

As she flew to the door, Elizabeth halted her by saying hoarsely, 'Not a word of this – from either Polly or you – to the other servants.'

Fanny had been thrilled at the idea of telling everyone about the drama on which she had stumbled. But, as Elizabeth spoke, she realized that to her mistress it was a terrible humiliation. She warmed with pity and said reassuringly, as she went out, 'Of course, Missus. Don't worry, Missus.'

Once Elizabeth had been laid gently on her bed, Polly sent Fanny back to the kitchen, where Mrs Tibbs promptly scolded her for being so long in doing her raking out, and sent her off to bed.

Elizabeth said stiffly, 'I shall be all right now, Polly.' She lay on her side, legs curled up, arms crossed over her injured face.

'I'll help you undress, Ma'am. Fanny said she thought your back was hurt. Let me have a look, Ma'am. If you've got any arnica, I could paint it on the bruises. First, will I get some brandy from the Master's study?'

'No!'

'Don't worry, Ma'am. He's out. He won't miss a small glass, Ma'am.'

With one hand, Elizabeth gestured to indicate reluctant agreement.

In the hope that it would ease her mistress's pain, Polly brought a generous glass of Humphrey's brandy, and, after Elizabeth had swallowed it, she allowed Polly to unbutton her dress.

'Jaysus!' Polly exclaimed, when she saw Elizabeth's back. Weals ran across it from the hairline to just below the waist. Where her corset had softened some of the blows, the marks were scarlet; above that, they were purple. 'It's a miracle if nothin's broken, Ma'am. We should get the doctor.'

'We can't, Polly.' She looked up at the other woman, tears beginning to course again down her ravaged face. She had given no explanation of her situation, because it was obvious that both Polly and Fanny had guessed what had happened; wife-beating was common enough amongst the lower classes, though it might have surprised them how often it occurred amongst their so-called betters.

'No, Ma'am. I do understand, Ma'am. I'll get the arnica from your medicine chest and maybe that'll do the trick.'

While she carefully sponged the bruised back with cold water and then applied the arnica, she was thinking fast. 'Would it be best, Ma'am, if you went to stay with someone? 'ave you got a sister or anybody? Till things blow over, like?'

Her mistress winced, as Polly dabbed on the tincture, and replied frankly, 'Last time he beat me, I went to my sister in West Kirby. She told me it was my fault and I shouldn't provoke him. She's unmarried and doesn't understand,' she finished brokenly.

Polly sighed. 'What about Miss Florence's?'

'She has a difficult life herself – and her baby is due any moment.' Elizabeth's voice strengthened. 'I don't want *anyone* to know, Polly. The disgrace would be more than I can bear. That's why I sent for you instead of Rosie or Maisie. You seem to keep to yourself.'

'Aye, you was right. I'll keep me mouth shut.' She eased her mistress's nightgown over her head, and then she blurted out, 'It were that Maisie wot is the root of the trouble. She told 'im every time, accordin' to Rosie.'

Elizabeth's eyes opened slowly. 'Told him what?'

'Told 'im when Mr Crossing called – and 'ow long 'e stayed.'

'Good Heavens!'

'He give 'er a shillin' every time.'

'Ach!' Elizabeth was sickened. 'Are you sure, Polly?'

'I wouldn't put it past her.'

Never in her life before had Elizabeth spoken so frankly to a servant. But never before had she needed an understanding friend more. Now she said grimly, 'I'll dismiss her. And I'll make sure she's gone before Humphrey finds out.'

'Yes, Ma'am.' Polly was putting her mistress's clothes away. Now she examined the back of the gown Elizabeth had been wearing. 'I think your dress is ruined, Ma'am.' She held it up for Elizabeth to see and lifted the candle closer to it.

Elizabeth heaved, and Polly hastily dropped the dress and picked up the bowl holding the water she had used to bathe the bruises. 'Take a big breath, Ma'am,' she ordered the sickened woman.

The nausea subsided, only to rise again each time she remembered what Humphrey had done. 'Oh, Polly,' she moaned, 'how could he?'

'Better outside than inside, Ma'am,' replied Polly with a quick quirk of humour. 'You can do without another baby.' Elizabeth heaved and brought up the brandy and what little dinner she had eaten. Afterwards, she said, 'Wrap up the dress and put it in the midden – bury it under some of the rubbish.'

'Oh, aye, Ma'am. Don't you worry about it.'

Polly put it about that Elizabeth had tripped over her gown and had fallen, hitting her face on the doorknob of her room. 'Made a couple o' rotten bruises on her cheeks and mouth,' she told Mrs Tibbs.

Mrs Tibbs had heard similar excuses several times before and simply shrugged slightly and went on with her cooking.

While Humphrey went on with his life as if nothing had happened, Elizabeth stayed in bed for three days. When she was ready to descend, she put on a black silk dress with a high neck edged with white frilling and dressed her hair low on her neck, to disguise the terrible bruise now yellowing there. A heavy dusting of rice flour helped the marks on her face. She sat silently in her favourite chair in the morning-room, her sewing untouched on her lap, and hoped Florence would not call for a few days more.

At dinner, she sat at her usual place at the foot of the table. She never raised her eyes, except to order Maisie to serve or to clear the table. Humphrey smiled at her – it was not a pleasant smile and it filled her with dread; in the months that followed she rarely spoke to him.

For several months, she cancelled her At Homes and invited no one to dinner, neither did she accept any invitations; she gave as the reason that Alicia's birth had been difficult. As time went by and Andrew Crossing did not communicate with her, she felt physically and mentally ill.

She waited patiently until Humphrey went to Manchester to stay with his brother, Harold, for a few days. Then she gave Maisie a week's pay in lieu of notice and told her to pack her bags. When Maisie protested, Elizabeth told her that they had decided to reduce staff.

'I want to speak to the Master,' retorted Maisie mutinously.

'Don't be insolent,' ordered Elizabeth coldly. 'I decide who works in this house. And it is I who will write references for you. Do you want to be turned off without a reference?'

At this deadly threat, Maisie caved in. Rosie was promoted to wait at table. When Humphrey noticed that Maisie was missing, he was forced to ask his wife where she was. She told him frigidly, between clenched teeth, that she was not going to be spied upon by a servant and that Rosie was quite satisfactory as parlourmaid. To get even with her, Humphrey told her that she would have to manage without a replacement girl.

Rosie came into the room, bringing another bottle of wine for which Humphrey had sent her, so Elizabeth sat stonily eating her dessert and did not reply.

Rosie and Fanny had to carry the work of a housemaid between them, and Rosie remarked thankfully that she would be married to the milkman by the end of the year. Fanny, who to her joy had had her wages quietly raised by a shilling a week, said nothing. She was learning to be a housemaid and that was real promotion for her.

II

'When is Alicia to be christened, Mama?' inquired Florence, when finally her mother ordered a carriage from the stable and went out to visit her.

'Well, I thought dear Clarence might do it in your church. It would be so nice to keep it in the family, wouldn't it? I'll get Mrs Tibbs to make a christening cake.' She paused and took a nervous sip of the Reverend Clarence's atrocious sherry from the glass in her hand. Then she babbled, 'Charles went straight from school this year to stay for a few days with one of his friends – I thought as soon as he came home – a nice little family party?' Her voice trailed off. She knew she could not face having the christening in her own church, St Margaret's in Princes Road. It was almost certain that Humphrey would not attend it – and that would cause enormous speculation, a fresh flurry of unwanted interest.

Florence felt that her mother was being unreasonable in getting her to have the party; it could be quite a large one, she thought wearily, if all her father's relations came and her mother's friends, not to speak of Aunt Clara from West Kirby, who was such a professional invalid that she would rearrange the whole Browning house to suit her convenience. 'I hope that I'm not taken to bed at the wrong moment, Mama,' she said anxiously.

'Well, then we'll make it a joyful double christening,' responded Elizabeth unfeelingly.

III

Elizabeth had been thankful that her younger son, Charles, had been away in boarding school during the more obvious period of her pregnancy and during her lying-in; she had certainly not wanted the cold, dark blue eyes of a ten-year-old examining her during this confinement.

When confiding to Sarah Webb, her oldest friend, the secret of her unwelcome breeding, she had wept on Sarah's shoulder, afraid of Humphrey, afraid of the hazard of giving birth at forty years of age. Speaking of Charles, she had added, 'Children always sense when something is wrong. And Charles always wants such precise answers to a question.'

Sarah sighed, and stroked her friend's dark hair. She had not only known Charles all his short life, but had been friends with Elizabeth and with Andrew Crossing since they first attended the same children's Christmas parties together. She had watched with pity, as her beautiful young friend had been bullied by her parents into marriage with Humphrey.

But Elizabeth had loved languid, charming Andrew, fair as some Icelandic god, a boy who appeared slow and lazy to her parents. His charm had, however, served him well in his subsequent career as a family lawyer, Sarah ruminated; even she herself, plain and studious, had worshipped from afar. She had been present at a ball, a few years back, at which Elizabeth had met and danced with him again; up till then, his old senior partner had always dealt with the affairs of Elizabeth's father's estate, so they had rarely seen each other. That winter, Andrew's senior partner died and the care of Elizabeth's affairs came into the hands of Andrew. Sarah had been greatly worried when Elizabeth promptly asked him to her next At Home.

'Is it wise, my dear?' she had asked, as she arranged her furs in front of Elizabeth's mirror before going home. She was the last guest to leave and Elizabeth herself was prinking before the mirror.

'I don't care,' Elizabeth had hissed savagely.

'Well, ask his wife as well,' suggested Sarah.

'I did – but you know and I know she can't stir out of the house – she's stiff as a board with rheumatism and she has to be carried everywhere. And, anyway,' she went on defiantly, '*anybody* may call on At Home days.'

Sarah sighed glumly. 'It's foolish, my dear – very foolish.'

Elizabeth bridled, and twirled in front of the mirror to show her fine, plump figure.

Over coffee in Elizabeth's morning-room the following day, Sarah had argued again.

'I can't help it, Sarah.' Elizabeth's wide dark blue eyes, so like those of her son, Charles, had a hint of tears in them. 'I must see him,' she said, 'I simply have to. Humphrey has his fancy woman – surely Andrew and I can be friends.'

Sarah bit her lips and said no more.

IV

When young Charles finally came home at the end of June, Elizabeth met him at Lime Street station.

Charles had spent his Easter holidays with his Uncle Harold

and his cousins in Manchester, so he had not seen his mother since the previous Christmas. She looked suddenly much older than he remembered, but when he inquired about her health as the hackney carriage traversed Lime Street, she told him brightly that she was quite well. She added that he now had a baby sister called Alicia – and, of course new babies were notorious for being rather tiring little people.

'Well, that's nice,' he responded politely, 'having a little sister, I mean.' He was not really very interested. Babies came in all the households that he visited; they often died. He vaguely remembered having a baby brother who had died very young, though, when he thought about it, it was the memory of his elder brother, Edward, being upset about it that had stayed with him. Death had always upset Edward; funny that he should have become a soldier.

Reminded that Edward was now a fixture in the 11th Foot, he also recalled a conversation he had once overheard between his father and Edward. His father had been furious when Edward had refused to join his brokerage firm and had asked permission to join the army instead. He recalled his father shouting that it cost money to maintain a son as an officer in the army, and Edward replying nervously that it might not cost as much as sending him to university to study Divinity, so that he could enter the Church.

Charles guessed that the main thing Edward wanted to do after finishing boarding school was to leave home. He had been awfully stubborn and finally his father had given way.

Their father had, later, talked to Charles about the advantages of joining the family firm. Though Charles thought that buying and selling stocks and shares would be a dreadfully dull way of earning a living, he had not dared to say any such thing to his father; he had merely smiled what he hoped was a nice little-boy smile, and said nothing. His maths teacher, old Fancy Moppit, wanted him to take more chemistry and maths and think about going to university. He wondered, now, if his father would pay for university.

'Have you heard from Edward lately?' he asked Elizabeth. 'I got a card from him at Easter, but I haven't heard since.'

'Not *got a card,* Charles – *received* a card.'

Charles grimaced, and said, 'Yes, Mama.'

'I heard from Edward quite recently. He is in Burma – and he's a full Lieutenant, now.'

'Oh, cheers!'

Charles was glad to be home for the remainder of the summer. Though nothing very interesting ever happened there, Mrs Tibbs produced all his favourite dishes and his mother didn't mind how much he read. Probably the family would go, as usual, for two weeks' seaside holiday in North Wales, and he would be able to add to his extensive collection of shells; he already had a glass case full of them, each neatly tagged with its Latin name.

After he had been down to the kitchen to see Mrs Tibbs, he climbed the five flights of stairs from the basement to the top floor, to see his new sister, Alicia. 'Her nurse's name is Polly. Be polite to her,' his mother had instructed.

Rosie and Fanny were left to toil up the stairs with his trunks.

'Holy God! Wot's he got in 'em?' puffed Fanny, as they paused for rest on the second landing.

'Books,' opined Rosie. 'Proper little bookworm, he is.'

Polly was glad to have a young boy sleeping in the back room across the landing. As Fanny had said, it could feel ghosty away at the top of the house; Rosie and Fanny shared a basement room and Mrs Tibbs had her own private bed-sitting room off the kitchen.

In case Charles came into the nursery while she was feeding Alicia, Polly took to wearing a shawl over her shoulders so that she could cover her breasts. She had been instructed by Elizabeth to keep Charles out of the day nursery at such moments, but, as Fanny said, 'If he don't learn now how a baby's fed, he may not know never.' So Charles learned a few interesting facts of life that summer. He also watched her being bathed, one day, and observed that she did not have a

57

penis; this confirmed what other boys had told him, that girls did not have such appendages. He found it very peculiar.

The day after his return, he went out to visit Florence in the company of his mother and Miss Sarah Webb, and attended Alicia's christening. He noted uneasily that Florence was uncommonly stout, but he dared not comment on it.

To Florence's mystification, Humphrey and Uncle Harold and his wife, Vera, did not attend the christening; they had urgent business to attend to in London that day. Elizabeth bought the customary silver christening mug and had it engraved, *To Alicia Beatrix Mary, from her loving parents, July 1886*.

Elizabeth had written to Andrew and his wife, inviting them to the christening. She received no reply and, after the christening tea, she had retired to Florence's privy and wept at the snub. She wondered if Mrs Crossing had even been shown the invitation.

As the long summer holiday progressed, Charles began to feel bored. He inquired of his mother when they would be taking their holiday in Wales. He was taken aback when Elizabeth snapped at him sharply that Papa was far too busy this year to think about holidays.

Feeling contrite about her peevishness, Elizabeth asked him if he would like to spend a few days with his Aunt Clara at West Kirby.

'Not really, Mama,' he replied. Though Aunt Clara lived by the sea, her many ailments did not make her appealing to him.

He began to accompany Polly when she wheeled Alicia in her pram through Princes Park. He liked Polly; she had never seen either shells or seaweed or even sand and had shown a most respectful interest when he had explained what they were.

In the park, she always paused for a little chat with a young gardener weeding the flower beds; he regularly managed to be working somewhere along the usual route of their walk, and Charles teased Polly about him.

In the course of one of their walks, Charles discovered that

Polly could not read. He stopped in the middle of the sandy carriageway, and stared up at the handsome young woman. 'Really?'

She smiled down at him mischievously. 'Aye. I don't know nothin', 'cept lookin' after Miss Alicia and a few things like that.'

He began walking again, kicking a stone along in front of him. 'I'd have thought you would be able to read easily. Servants always know so much.'

'I suppose they do – folks like Mrs Tibbs. But me? I only scrubbed doorsteps and cleaned brasses and helped me Mam sell fents in the market sometimes, afore I were married.'

'What are fents?'

'Bits of old or damaged cloth – for dusters, like.'

'I see. I didn't know you were married.'

'I'm not no more . . .' Her voice faltered. In the weeks since she had been with the Woodmans, she had wept fairly constantly, alone in her windowless garret. Her only comfort had been the delicious sensation of Alicia's contented sucking at her breast. 'Me oosband,' she picked up again, 'he were killed in the docks.'

'How dreadful!' Charles was genuinely shocked. He understood that to be a widow was very hard; even the Bible said that you had to look after the widowed and the fatherless.

'It were proper awful,' Polly confided to him. 'And me baby died – so I come to look after Miss Alicia.' She smiled sadly down at the sleeping child in the old basketware pram in which Charles himself had been wheeled as an infant.

'Well, I'm glad you did come. These hols are boring enough. Say, would you like to learn to read? It's easy, once you know how. I've still got my first books up in my bedroom – and I bet there are some girls' books in Flo's old bedroom. I could teach you in the evenings.'

So that summer Polly learned to read and discovered a wonderful dream world.

She also learned to sew better than she had previously done. Elizabeth sent up to the nursery loads of sheets and other household linens, demanding that they be neatly darned or patched; servants should be kept busy, according to Elizabeth.

At first, Polly had been appalled at the huge pile of mending, but Elizabeth had told Rosie to instruct her, particularly on how to patch and how to turn a sheet *sides to middle*, and they both spent long evening hours by Polly's single candle carefully weaving their needles in and out of the heavy linen cloth.

When Alicia had acquired a pattern of sleep and it was fairly certain that she would continue to sleep for an hour or two, Polly took a piece of sewing down to the big basement kitchen and sat for a little while with Rosie and Mrs Tibbs round the roaring fire in the kitchen range. 'I'll go crackers if I don't have a bit of a jangle with somebody,' she told Mrs Tibbs, and Mrs Tibbs had agreed that a little gossip was necessary to one's sanity. Except for minor squabbles, they got along together fairly well and they would talk about the neighbours and their servants, about the Woodman family and their own families, while Fanny toiled through the washing-up and the scouring of the big, soot-covered iron saucepans.

From these agreeable sessions, Polly began to learn how such a fine house was run, how you could acquire a few perks to take home, like a half-used tablet of soap, nearly finished bottles of wine or perfume, odds and ends like buttons, discarded in the wastepaper basket. In addition Mr Bittle, the gardener, according to Fanny, would sometimes provide a few windfall apples or pears or even a seedling geranium in a pot. 'Me auntie were made up when I bring 'er a little geranium,' she confided to Polly, as she sat down on a nursery chair to rest, after bringing up a hod of coal. 'Mrs Tibbs makes quite a bit on the side, Rosie says. She'll take a slice or two off a joint or a little bitty butter or cheese – not much, but it adds up to a meal or two by the time 'er day off come around. She takes it to 'er sister.'

Another time, she remarked, 'Ould Woodie is a mingy master, a proper pinchpenny, so he's askin' for theft. I suppose the Missus is used to 'im being mean and pokin' his nose into the housekeepin' book. And him payin' out for his fancy woman; the poor Missus must lose out because of her,' she giggled knowingly.

Polly laughed. Then she said more soberly, 'It's hard when you've no man interested in yez.'

As Polly's grief over Patrick diminished, she had begun to look for someone to replace him; she was young and strong and could not imagine life without a man in it. But she lived in a world of women domestics, and the valet of the Colonel who lived next door was, she soon found, not interested in females. 'And he a fine lookin' man,' she tut-tutted to Fanny. Fanny's reply was ribald in the extreme.

Every time Polly went home to see her parents, however, she was reminded how lucky she was. The stench of sewage and the lack of even a decent cup of tea had not bothered her in earlier days – she had taken hardship for granted; but not any longer.

The overcrowding had been lessened by the removal of her paternal aunt and her five children to another cellar, but she was grieved to see her struggling mother grow progressively wearier and her unemployed father more despairing. She gave them most of the two shillings a week she earned, and, after her few hours of freedom, she would return thankfully to the nursery, to have only the smell of the baby round her and to know that tea might not be a very large meal but it would certainly arrive.

Though not given to pondering on what the future held, she began to consider how she could continue working for the Woodmans after Alicia was weaned. As a possible alternative, she dreamed occasionally of the gardener in Princes Park. He had never asked her out but he always seemed glad to see her. If he were promoted, he might be given a tied cottage in the park; they were sometimes provided for more senior gardeners. There he might be able to keep a pig and grow some vegetables – and keep a wife.

Unlike Rosie, she did not meet the tradesmen who came to

the house and lingered round the back door until they were sent packing by Mrs Tibbs or, in the case of the grocer, invited into her private bed-sitting room to discuss the week's groceries.

In the darkness of the early morning, Rosie, the house-parlourmaid, used to scurry down the path in the back garden, to get a kiss and a quick fondle from the milkman, who was courting her. Then, trembling with desire, she would rush back into the house and tear upstairs to wash out the great bath with its mahogany surround, before Humphrey Woodman got up. She would lay out his cut-throat razor, his moustache scissors and his shaving cup on the bathroom dressing-table and wipe down his leather razor strop which hung on the wall beside the sink.

'He used to tan 'is sons' hides with his razor strop,' Rosie told Polly. 'I remember Master Edward gettin' it so hard once, he fainted. And even then he never lifted a finger against 'is Pa. Loovely young man, Master Edward is; always says "thank you".'

Rocking the baby in her arms as she paused at the doorway of the bathroom she was not allowed to use, Polly remembered the dreadful state of Elizabeth's back after she had been beaten and she wondered if he had used the strop on her. No one, she thought passionately, should use a strop on such a pretty lady, no matter what she had done. Since that day, she had more than once found her Mistress with tears on her face. She wondered what else he had done to her, and she shivered.

Chapter Six

I

Elizabeth had no idea whether her husband had expressed any
feelings in public about the new arrival in the family, but she
suspected that Maisie had done so and that the news of Alicia's
doubtful origins had reached some of her acquaintances. Certainly, the number of invitations she usually received had
dropped off, and one or two ladies appeared not to have seen
her when she met them while out walking.

Her conscience told her that, as Andrew and she moved
through their usual group before the birth, mutual friends
must have sensed the attachment between them – and her
pregnancy, at so late an age, must have caused speculation
behind delicately waving ball fans.

She decided that she did not care; she would brazen it out.
And Humphrey could take himself to hell, as long as he kept
her. Once she had recovered from the beating, she had done
some urgent arithmetic, and had decided that she could not
possibly live on her marriage settlement from her father; it
provided pin money, but that was all.

In her despair, she had considered writing to her brother
in Ceylon and asking if she could make a home with him; but
he had always been a poor correspondent and lived up country
on his tea plantation, sharing a house with his partner. Two
bachelors together, she thought wryly, would not want to be
saddled with a woman. And it was said that men sometimes,
well, sometimes did intimate things together – and she could
not face the possibility of that.

So she decided to use Humphrey to her own advantage. If
he threatened to beat her again, she would say sharply that

she would show the bruises to the wives of his business associates. Stiff-necked Presbyterians, most of them, they might feel she deserved it, but faced with it, they would freeze out Humphrey. They'd be a pack of Pontius Pilates, she thought maliciously.

The armed truce prevailed, with occasional tiresome arguments which never resolved anything.

II

Though Elizabeth's friends might snub her, Humphrey found, to his embarrassment, that when he met business acquaintances accompanied by their wives, several of the ladies inquired after Elizabeth's health and whether the baby had been a boy or a girl.

The same thing happened when he attended social events alone. Where was dear Elizabeth and how was the new baby?

He knew he must, to save unwanted conjecture, persuade Elizabeth to accompany him occasionally, and he must learn to reply civilly to polite inquiries. He could not ignore both mother and daughter indefinitely. His Manchester brother, Harold, and his wife, Vera, had been offended at not being asked to the christening, and he had told them that it had been very quiet because Elizabeth was still weak and Florence was in the family way herself. Though his brother accepted this, Vera felt that it confirmed her own suspicions.

At St Margaret's Church, Humphrey and Elizabeth stood side by side each Sunday morning in frigid silence. He hoped that she had been privately Churched, attended a traditional service of thanksgiving; otherwise, the minister would ask awkward questions.

Elizabeth had, indeed, been Churched. One morning, she had kneeled alone before the priest, while he intoned over her Psalm 127, with its uncomfortable references to men with quivers full of arrows, and she wept quietly for Andrew Crossing, the darling of her youth, who had deserted her. In a worldly way, she knew he had been wise to slip quietly out of her life, by the simple process of handing over her legal work to one of his partners. She knew he should have done it long before. But it hurt.

It was common enough for women to cry after giving birth, so the priest ignored the tears stealing down Elizabeth's cheeks. He was, however, kind enough to invite her into the vicarage, where he handed her over to his sister, who kept house for him. She was a fussy, plain woman who produced a strong cup of tea and ten minutes' bracing conversation on the joys of having children. It gave Elizabeth time to blow her nose, before walking home.

III

Alicia's first Boxing Day was a Sunday. Harold and Vera Woodman, accompanied by their three sons, came to spend the day with Elizabeth and Humphrey. At tea time, Alicia was brought down by Polly and laid in her mother's arms; she behaved admirably and gurgled and smiled at the company.

Aunt Vera stroked the fine down of ash-blonde hair on the child's head. 'She's as fair as a lily – and with such light grey eyes,' she remarked, watching Elizabeth's face.

Elizabeth bent her own dark head over the baby and kissed it. 'My brother is quite fair,' she lied; at least *he* was not likely to come home for years; with luck, his black hair would have turned white before he returned to England.

Humphrey chewed his moustache and turned to look out of the lace-draped window. His brother and nephews joined him – babies were not very interesting, particularly when they were girls.

Vera pursed her lips and made no further comment. She brought out from her reticule an ivory ring with two silver bells attached to it. 'Here, Alicia,' she said. 'Here is a pretty present from Father Christmas for you.'

Alicia clutched at the ring, and Elizabeth sighed with relief.

When, the following year, the Queen's Jubilee was being celebrated in Liverpool, Elizabeth's sister, Clara, came to stay and to join in the festivities. She was older than Elizabeth and lived in a small house left her by their father, in the village of West Kirby on the Wirral Peninsula. She had been ill with bronchitis at the time of Alicia's birth and this had left her with a painful cough, making travelling too arduous for her. Thanks to the patient ministrations of her companion-help, she was now feeling better, and had come to see her new niece.

She was a spinster and sometimes quite lonely. When she saw the little girl in Polly's arms, she said impulsively to Elizabeth, 'You must bring her to stay with me. The sea air will put some colour into those pale, little cheeks.'

When Elizabeth demurred that the presence of a young child might put too much strain on her delicate health, the older woman replied, 'Let Polly come as well.'

So Alicia's early childhood was enlivened by visits to the seaside, occasionally accompanied by Elizabeth, more often by Polly. Though frail and slow-moving, Aunt Clara taught her niece how to build sandcastles and took her to collect shells and to paddle in the shallow pools left by the tide.

Polly had never seen the sea before and was, at first, terrified of its bouncing waves. She soon discovered with Alicia the joys of paddling and she, too, looked forward to these little holidays.

Humphrey had invested money in a railway line to link West Kirby with Liverpool. Because it failed to draw enough passengers and part of it had to run in a tunnel under the Mersey, which was more expensive than expected, he suffered a resounding financial loss. When, finally, it did go through, it was a joyous occasion for Alicia, because dear delicate Aunt Clara could then so easily visit the house in Upper Canning Street. Humphrey was consoled by the fact that a piece of land that he had, years before, bought in West Kirby suddenly became immensely valuable because it lay close to the new station. He sold it for housing development, at a handsome profit.

IV

'Wot you goin' to do when our Allie goes to school?' Fanny asked Polly, as, one night, she snatched a moment in the nursery to rest her aching feet. She had asked a similar question when, at eighteen months of age, Alicia had finally been weaned.

At that time, Polly had been very troubled. The under-gardener in the park, of whom she had had hopes, had failed to appear during two successive walks. According to a surly park-keeper, he had been dismissed for impudence. Polly's dream of presiding over a tied cottage with a small pigsty vanished with him. A brief encounter with a regular soldier, also met in the park, had come to an abrupt end when his regiment was sent to India. Statistics were against Polly's ever marrying again; the district had far more women than it had men.

The longer Polly continued to live in the comfort of the nursery attic, the less she wanted to return to the teeming slum in which she had been raised. A high standard of living, she found, was very easy to get used to. She had been thankful when Elizabeth had used her, in part, to replace Maisie.

Fanny was now a small, pinched seventeen-year-old and had replaced Rosie as a housemaid. Rosie had married the milkman as soon as he was satisfied that she was pregnant; a working man had to be certain that his wife could have children to maintain him in his old age.

A tweenie was no longer employed to care for fires, empty slops and carry water. Instead, Humphrey ordered Elizabeth to employ a charwoman, who came early in the morning to clean out the fireplaces and remake the fires. She also filled all the coal scuttles. To cut down on the carrying of water, more use was made of the bathroom taps, though the servants were still not allowed to wash themselves or use the lavatory in the bathroom. Elizabeth ended a custom of centuries, abandoned the chamber-pot under her bed and trailed along to the bathroom; she felt it was a real hardship.

Safe in the nursery with Polly, for many years Alicia understood little of the bitterness which lay between her mother and Humphrey Woodman. She learned early, however, from Polly that Papa was to be feared and that she should keep out of his way. As soon as the child could talk Polly taught her that the pretty lady who lived downstairs was to be obeyed without question, no matter how unhappy her decisions made little girls and nannies. Nannies said, 'Yes, Ma'am, of course, Ma'am.' Little girls said, 'Yes, Mama,' she instructed.

Alicia's first day at Miss Schreiber's Preparatory School approached and Polly was again worried.

'I suppose I'll have to look for another place,' she sighed to Fanny. 'It'll fairly kill me to leave little Allie – she's my baby more'n anybody else's.' She glanced across to where Alicia was kneeling on a chair at the table. She was quarrelling with Florence's elder son, Frank. They were playing Snakes and Ladders and she was protesting to the boy that he must slide down every snake on which his counter landed. He retorted that if he wanted to he could slide down only every other one. A fight threatened, and Polly got up to settle the squabble.

'Now, you play nicely, Master Frank, or I'll send you home.'

Frank looked at her mutinously, picked up the board and tipped the counters off it, then slid down from his chair to go to the rocking-horse. Still watching Polly, he climbed on to it and began to rock as hard as he could. 'Cheat!' shouted Alicia, and, aggrieved, went to sit on Polly's lap.

'You could wait at table.' Fanny grinned wryly at Polly. 'The Missus says I'm even worse'n Rosie was.'

'I don't know how neither.'

'Ask the Missus to train you. You and her is as thick as thieves – she'll jump at the idea. Now the Master is wantin' to have more dinner parties, she'll need a proper parlourmaid.'

''Ow d'you know he wants more people in?'

Fanny looked wise, 'I 'ear it all.'

When Master Charles came home for the summer holidays, soon after Alicia's fifth birthday, he found his old friend, Polly, waiting at table. For the first time, Alicia was allowed to have lunch with him and with his mother in the dining-room. He noticed, uneasily, that Elizabeth was most impatient with the little girl, as the child floundered over the various knives and forks. He teased her gently that she would soon be a grown-up young lady and the threatening tears turned to a shy giggle.

'I'm going to school soon,' she confided proudly, and wondered if she dare ask for another spoonful of strawberry jelly. She looked up at Polly, hovering over her mother, water-jug in hand, and decided not to. She had long since joined the silent conspiracy of servants in the kitchen; she knew that after the meal she could go down to the basement to ask Mrs Tibbs for a bit more and would be given it gladly.

After this first venture at lunch in the dining-room, she asked Polly, 'Why are you dressed up differently in the dining-room?'

''Cos as well as lookin' after you, you cheeky little bugger, I got to be the parlourmaid in a parlourmaid's uniform.'

Miss Schreiber, at the preparatory school, was horrified when, one morning in September, Alicia called a teasing boy a cheeky little bugger. For the first time in her life, the child received a sound slap. She learned quickly that there was more than one English language.

Alicia tended to be secretive and very quiet when in her mother's company. Miss Schreiber's complaint forced Elizabeth to pay more attention to her daughter's language, and this made Alicia more than usually tongue-tied. Only in the kitchen, where she was treated with easy affection, was she able to express herself freely.

She also tended to be struck dumb in her sister's home, where she was taken by her mother to play with her nephew, Frank. Frank now had a small brother and a baby sister.

'They're no good to play with yet,' he told her, in reference to his siblings. 'He wets his trousers and she only sleeps – do you know, she hasn't got any teeth?'

The latter interesting fact stirred Alicia out of her usual wordlessness. 'Perhaps she's lost them,' she suggested. 'Aunt Clara lost hers once – we found them in her dressing-table drawer.'

For months after that, Frank checked his teeth from time to time, to make sure that they were still firmly fixed in his mouth.

Alicia was always thankful, after these visits, to be returned to the safety of the kitchen in Upper Canning Street; Frank tended to push her about and she did not enjoy it.

Chapter Seven

I

Several times in her life Alicia was visited in her nursery by a man so tall that it seemed to her that his head would touch the ceiling. He was very thin and stood awkwardly in the open doorway of the nursery, until he was invited in by Polly, who curtsied to him.

He was dressed in tweeds which smelled of tobacco smoke and his black hair was cropped close to his head. He always went to stand with his back to the fire and then he would survey the room and say, in a deep friendly voice, 'This is the only place in the world which never changes – and old Toby is still there!' He would move over to pat the head of the rocking-horse, which Alicia loved to ride.

At first, Alicia tended to shrink behind Polly's skirts; her knowledge of men was limited to Humphrey, who had never been known to enter the nursery, and the Reverend Clarence, who never spoke to her. Polly hauled her out, however, and said, 'Come on, now. You know your big brother, Master Edward. He's come all the way from India to see yez. Come and say how-do-you-do.'

With the offer of an ivory elephant, just the right size to hold in her hand, she was beguiled on to his knee while he talked to Polly. Polly made up a story about her *furrie* elephant; it was some time before Alicia realized that she meant a fairy elephant and not a fur-clad mammoth such as she had seen in a picture in one of Charles's old books.

Perhaps because the room was Edward's childhood nursery and Polly was not unlike the nanny he had known long ago, his military stiffness left him. While Alicia dozed in the warmth of the fire, her head on his shoulder, he talked easily to buxom, blue-eyed Polly.

Polly watched the yellowed, strained face and fell helplessly in love with every line of it. On other nights, while Alicia slept in the next room, she listened avidly, with her sewing needle poised above her mending, to his stories of the jungles of Burma filled with small, brown men who wore only loincloths. Glad to have a genuinely interested audience, he described the wild beauty of the Himalayas and a particularly dangerous spot called the Khyber Pass, where wicked men in turbans hid amongst the rocks and fired at British soldiers. Normally, he was a quiet, dull man, who, as a boy, had tried to live up to his father's expectations and had failed. To escape, he had joined the army – a nondescript foot regiment – and he knew he would never be a particularly outstanding soldier either. To Polly he seemed a wonderful person, and she treated him as such.

'Aye, he's a lovely man,' she said wistfully one day to Fanny, who, quick of eye, had noticed the blush which rose to Polly's cheeks when Master Edward's name was mentioned in the kitchen and had later teased her about it.

'Does 'e coom to your room?' inquired Fanny with great interest, as she quickly dusted the hallway of the top storey.

Polly was changing into her afternoon uniform, ready to open the front door to Elizabeth's callers, and she paused in tying her apron.

'Aye,' she whispered, 'but don't tell no one, Fan. He's a really good man and I wouldn't want 'is Mam to find out.'

'Watch out you don't get in the family way,' Fanny warned, as she commenced to dust down the bare wooden stairs that led up to the nurseries. After a moment, she looked up again. 'Be careful. *He* could tell someone. Some of 'em is real organ-grinders. When did it start?'

Polly adjusted her frilly cap and prepared to come down the stairs. 'He'll never tell nobody,' she replied firmly. Then, in answer to Fanny's question, she went on, 'It all coom about, the year 'e coom down with malaria. Remember, 'e coom home and the mistress and me 'ad to nurse 'im? He were home a long time, till 'e got over it.' She sighed. 'It were then – when he were better and not yet called back to 'is Regiment.' As she sidled past Fanny on the stairs, she giggled suddenly. 'He couldn't do it, first time – he were too weak!'

'Do 'e give you anythin' for it?'

'No. I don't want nothin'. I love 'im.' The dark head with its frilled cap was raised proudly, as she paused, hand on banister, to look back at her fellow servant.

Fanny opened the staircase window and leaned out to shake her duster. She laughed. 'Aye, you've got it bad, you 'ave.'

Polly sighed again. 'Aye. I wish he didn't 'ave to go to them furrin parts. The Missis told the Master as he's goin' back to India soon – he's bin in Aldershot so long, I begun to think he'd be there always. It makes me sick to me stomach to think about them blackies in their turbans, with their guns.'

When Edward did return to India, this time to the Punjab, Alicia began to get regular letters from her brother. He would invariably end them by sending his love to her and asking her to remember him kindly to Polly, who, he trusted, was well. In neat script, seven-year-old Alicia would equally invariably reply that Polly was well and sent her best respects.

II

In an effort to re-establish herself, Elizabeth had, about a year after Alicia's birth, plunged into the fashionable world of charitable undertakings. The ladies of St Margaret's Church found her so useful, when planning church bazaars, that they began to ignore the occasional innuendo which reached their ears about their fellow parishioner.

With one or two other ladies from the church, she became a fund-raiser for the new Royal Infirmary and for the Sheltering Home for Destitute Children in Myrtle Street. She was occasionally snubbed, but a number of the ladies appreciated her hard work and, with them, she was sometimes asked to receptions given for the many important visitors who passed through Liverpool. Humphrey soon discovered that she was acquainted with the wives of men he would like to know, and he suppressed his smouldering anger with her sufficiently to be able to address her and encourage her to ask these people to dinner.

A handsome, well-dressed woman in her forties, forced to deny her natural sensuality, she became, as the years went on, extremely peevish with those who served her.

'Forever pickin' on yez,' Fanny complained to Polly, while they prepared the dining-room for a formal dinner in September, 1896. She pushed a mahogany chair more exactly in position at the glittering table. Quick and impatient, she could be nearly as irritable as Elizabeth was.

'Aye,' agreed Polly, 'and I'll get it if I don't hurry. Got to collect Allie from Miss Schreiber's.'

'She's risin' eleven now. She's old enough to take 'erself to school and back.'

'The ould fella says as she's to be escorted. I heard 'im. Gettin' at her, he was, pickin' on her for nothin'. Tryin' to make things awkward for her. *She* said as Allie were old enough.'

'Don't want 'er to stray like her Mam,' opined Fanny, positioning finger bowls round the table with mathematical precision. 'It's herself what needs escorting. She's still fine lookin'.'

'Fanny!'

'Well, she's forever trailin' her petticoats afore one man or another. You watch her tonight.'

'Nothin' comes of it,' Polly responded forcefully. 'It's just her way – and she must be all of fifty by now – an old woman. You shouldn't say such things – and about a good Mistress an' all.'

'Aye, she's quite good,' agreed Fanny reluctantly. She turned to poke up the fire. 'How do we know what comes of it? Anyway, who's comin' tonight?'

'A professor and his missus and two other couples. They're

all at that big meeting in St George's Hall. A real famous doctor come to talk to 'em. Read it in the paper. Name of Lister.' Polly surveyed the table, set with Elizabeth's best china and Bohemian cut glass. 'Well, that's done, anyways.'

'Better snatch a cup o' tea while we can,' suggested Fanny, putting down the poker on its rest in the hearth.

'Not me. I must run to get Allie.'

III

After school, Alicia sat by the kitchen fire, watching a harassed Mrs Tibbs baste a huge joint of beef, while Fanny stirred a cauldron of soup. Polly thrust a glass of milk into the child's hand and told her that after she had drunk it she should go into the garden and do some skipping in the fresh air.

'Do I have to?'

'Aye, coom on, luv. I'll come with yez and count your peppers for a mo'. Then I got to help Cook.'

She put her arm round Alicia and together they went out of the back door, which led into a brick-lined area, and then up well-washed stone steps to the long, narrow walled garden. A straight, paved path ran from the area to a wooden door in the high, back wall. The wind was whirling the first autumn leaves along the path and over the lawn, and the single aspen tree at the far end shivered, as if it already felt the cold of winter. Opposite the tree, on the other lawn, stood an octagonal summerhouse, where Alicia occasionally played house with a little girl called Ethel, who also attended Miss Schreiber's school. Nearer the house, an apple tree bore a crop of cooking apples almost ready for picking.

At Polly's urging, Alicia did a fast pepper, her skipping rope thwacking the path quicker and quicker. Polly counted, and they both laughed when Alicia finally tripped over the rope.

'Seventy-two,' shouted Polly.

The latch on the back gate rattled suddenly, as it was lifted. A grubby face, topped by wildly tousled hair, peered cautiously round the door. A very thin boy, about eleven years old, entered like a cat on alien ground. His breeches were in the last stages of disintegration and were topped by a ragged jacket too large for him. He wore a red kerchief round his neck and was bare-legged and barefooted. Alicia smiled at him; he was Polly's brother who came sometimes, when he was unemployed, to beg a piece of bread from her. Though he smelled like a wet dog, Alicia accepted him as part of her small world, as she did the coalman, the milkman and the postman.

This visit was obviously different. The boy was blubbering like a brook in spate, and when he saw Polly he ran into her arms.

'Why, Billy! What's to do?' She hugged him to her white, starched apron.

'It's Mam,' he told her. 'She's took bad – real bad. Mary's with her and Ma Fox from upstairs. Dad says to come quick.'

Unaware that his sister had suckled both of them and was equally loved by Alicia, he ignored the girl and clutched at Polly.

'Jaysus! What happened?'

'She's bin sick of the fever for nearly a week and she don't know none of us any more.'

Fever was a scary threat, and Alicia interjected impulsively, 'Polly, you must go. I'll do my homework while you're away.'

'I'll have to ask your Mam. We got a dinner party.' She looked down at the mop of hair on her shoulder and gently pushed the boy away from her. 'Don't grieve, luv. I'll come, somehow.'

Billy stepped back and wiped his eyes with the backs of his hands. This left a dirty smear on either cheek.

For the first time, he seemed to realize that Alicia was there watching him, her skipping rope dangling from one hand. He stared at her for a second and then, obviously trying to re-establish his manliness after such a bout of tears, he carefully winked at her. While she giggled, he turned on his heel and trotted back down the path. The garden door banged behind him, and, as he ran, they could hear his bare feet thudding along the back alley.

With Alicia hurrying behind her, Polly fled back to the kitchen. She was met by an anxious Fanny.

'The Missus is in, and in a proper temper, askin' why you wasn't there to open the door for her. I told her as you was in the garden with Allie, but she's real put out and sez you've not put the claret glasses on the table.'

'Bugger her.' Polly stripped off her kitchen apron, snatched up her frilly parlour one and whipped it round herself. The ribbons of her cap streamed behind her, as she shot upstairs, leaving a surprised Fanny facing Alicia and asking, 'And what's to do with her?'

IV

The dining-room door was ajar. Elizabeth, still in her osprey-trimmed hat, was standing in the doorway, tapping her foot fretfully.

The moment the green baize door to the back stairs opened to reveal a breathless Polly, Elizabeth turned on her. 'Polly, claret glasses, girl, claret glasses – and couldn't you find a more interesting way to fold the table napkins?'

Polly's panic over her mother immediately gave way to her mistress's wrath, and she responded humbly, 'I thought it was your favourite way of havin' the napkins, Ma'am.'

'It is not. And the claret glasses?'

Polly bobbed a little curtsey. 'I'll get 'em immediately, Ma'am. I wasn't sure which wine you was having.'

Aware that she was not being quite fair to a woman she respected, Elizabeth tried to control her irritability, and turned to pass through the hall and climb the red-carpeted staircase to her bedroom. Polly followed her anxiously to the foot of the stairs. 'Ma'am, may I speak to you, Ma'am?'

Her plump white hand on the carved newel post, Elizabeth turned to look down at her. 'Yes?'

'Ma'am, I just had word that me Mam is very ill and is callin'' for me. Can I go to her?'

'Really, Polly!' Elizabeth burst out. 'What has come over you? First the dinner table, and then this! How can you go anywhere when Professor Morrison is coming to dinner? Who is going to wait at table?'

'I thought, perhaps, Fanny could do it, for once. Mam's real ill – she wouldn't send otherwise.'

'Fanny is too clumsy – and I am sure other members of your family can care for your mother for a few hours.' Elizabeth was shaking with anger. 'If you *must* go home, you may go immediately after you have brought in the tea and coffee trays. Fanny can clear up afterwards. But make sure you are back in time to take Miss Alicia to school in the morning.'

Polly kept her eyes down, so that Elizabeth should not see the bitter anger seething in her. I'll get another job, I will, she raged inwardly. Friend? She's no friend. Aloud, she said, 'Yes,'m. Thank you, Ma'am.'

As she got the claret glasses out of the glass cupboard, she cried unrestrainedly for fear of what might have happened to her mother.

When she went down to the basement kitchen, it was in turmoil. Mrs Tibbs missed not having a kitchen-maid and she still tended to lean on Fanny for help. Fanny worked hard. During the day, she still had to carry hods of coal to all the fireplaces in the house, in addition to her cleaning duties as housemaid. Though she resented the totality of her work, she was, like Polly, thankful to be reasonably fed and warm under a mistress who did not usually penetrate to the kitchen. Polly, also, found herself hard-pressed to keep up with the work of parlourmaid and take care of Alicia, as well as do the extensive mending required and the careful pressing of Elizabeth's elaborate dresses, while Humphrey strove to keep the costs of his household down.

Today, his housekeeper-cook, Mrs Tibbs, usually fairly calm, was in full spate in the steaming kitchen. She shouted to a reluctant Fanny to fill up the hot water tank by the blazing fire and then to peel the potatoes. The light of the fire danced on her sweating face, as she tasted the mock turtle soup and added a quick shake of pepper to it.

Polly was weeping as she came through the door, and Mrs Tibbs, Fanny and Alicia all looked up. They listened in shocked silence as Polly told them what Elizabeth had said about her going to her mother. Polly turned to Fanny. 'Could you manage the clearing up, Fan?'

''Course I can, duck. Mrs Tibbs and me – we'll manage, won't we, Mrs Tibbs?'

'I'm sure I don't know how – but we will,' sighed Mrs Tibbs. She picked up a ladle and opened the big, iron oven at the side of the fireplace to baste the joint of beef in it. Then she carefully closed the door on it again. She turned to Polly, who was wiping her eyes with a corner of her apron. 'Now, Polly, make yourself tidy again, and then you could beat the cream for the trifle – and give Miss Alicia her tea.'

Alicia had come forward to watch Mrs Tibbs deal with the meat. The cook asked her, 'Would you like a bit of our Shepherd's Pie, luv?'

'Yes, please, Mrs Tibbs. Can't I help you – or do some of the dishes for Fanny?'

Mrs Tibbs smiled at her. 'No, luv. It wouldn't be proper. Your Mam wouldn't like it.'

So Polly carried a tray containing Shepherd's Pie and trifle up to the nursery – Mrs Tibbs had made the dessert in a little glass dish specially for Alicia.

As Polly put the tray down in front of her, Alicia asked, 'Why doesn't Mama let me come down to dinner, now? All the girls at school have dinner with their parents. I'm nearly grown up – and it would save you such a lot of running up and down, Polly.' She shook out her table napkin and put it on her lap. 'I could even eat my meals in the kitchen with you and the others. And, you know, I could have helped Mrs Tibbs today, so as to free Fanny to wait at table.'

'Bless your lovin' heart.' Polly bent and gave her a quick kiss on the top of her flaxen head. Then she hastily rewound the plaits of her own hair more tightly and settled a clean cap on top of them, while she considered how to answer the girl.

'It's not proper for you to eat with the servants, luv. And your Papa gets cross very quickly, as you well know. So your Mam probably wants him to have his dinner quiet, like.'

'I don't think it's because of that, because I can be as quiet as a mouse. I think they don't like me, not even Mama. There must be something wrong with me.'

'Och, no! Parents always like their kids,' Polly lied.

'Well, I don't understand why I can't be with them.'

No you don't, thanks be, thought Polly. I'd hate you to find out. She was anxious to get back to her work, but Alicia was following her own line of thought, so she lingered for a moment, as the child asked her, 'Do you think Mama would be grumpy, if I asked Mrs Tibbs to teach me to cook? Some of the girls at school are learning from their Mamas. You see, I could then help Mrs Tibbs.' She looked earnestly up from her dinner.

'Well, you could ask your Mam. But don't say nothin' about helpin' – she might not like that.'

'Surely I can help a *friend*?'

Polly did not respond. She merely said she must get back to the kitchen and fled before she had to explain the limit of friends allowed to little girls.

Alicia licked both sides of her trifle spoon and sadly scraped the empty dish. She put the dish back on to the tray. As she slowly folded up her napkin and pushed it into the ivory ring which Edward had sent her from India, she thought there was no explaining the idiosyncrasies of parents. She leaned back in her chair and her lips began to tremble – she wanted to cry. It was so strange that the other girls at school had parties at Christmas and birthdays and went on holidays with their mothers and fathers, and no such things ever happened to her – she was not even taken shopping by her mother – Polly took her to Miss Bloom, the dressmaker, to have her dresses and coats fitted, or to Granby Street to buy the few Christmas gifts she did not make herself. Polly even took her to All Saints Church most Sunday mornings.

She got out her spelling book to do her homework for the following day. But the letters seemed to jump erratically, as she realized suddenly that not only had she never given a party; she had never been invited to any other girls' parties, either.

Chapter Eight

I

James Tyson did not take much notice of his wife, Bridie's, complaints of fatigue and of pain in her legs; women always complained of their feet and that they were tired. He himself suffered chronic pain in his back, a relic of his work as a docker; it made it impossible, now, for him to find work, except occasionally as a nightwatchman. It was Bridie selling her rags and old buttons in the market who kept them from starvation. When one morning she failed to get up in time for the opening of the market, it was suddenly brought home to him that her complaints were not the usual ones.

'Me head,' she nearly screamed to him. 'It's me head!'

She was hot with fever, so a worried James suggested that she should go to the public Dispensary to ask for medicine.

'I couldn't walk it,' she gasped. 'I'll be better later on.'

James woke Billy and sent him off to work; he had a job cleaning up after the horses in a stable belonging to a warehouse. On the way, James said, he was to call in on his sister, Mary, and ask her to come to her mother. Mary arrived at Bridie's bedside half an hour later, her newest baby tucked inside her shawl. She was followed by her daughter, Theresa, a fourteen-year-old who plied the streets at night. They both stared down at Bridie tossing on her truckle bed; neither knew what to do.

Finally, Mary sent James upstairs to the tap in the court, to get some water to bathe Bridie's face with. 'Looks as if she's got the flu,' she suggested, as she handed her baby to Theresa to hold.

Nobody else attempted to put a name to the fever; there

were all kinds of fevers, and people either got better from them or they died. And pain such as Bridie's was something you put up with.

The news went round the court that Billy Tyson's Mam had the flu. Nobody wanted to catch it, so they stayed away. James went to peddle Bridie's fents in the market.

Word that Bridie had the flu very badly reached her Great-aunt Kitty, who lived in the next court. She hobbled down the stairs from the attic in which she lived and, slowly and painfully, dragged her arthritic limbs into the Tysons' cellar room. She was panting with the effort as James, returned from the market, made her welcome; few people knew as much about sickness as Great-aunt Kitty did. She pushed her black shawl back from her bald head and bent over to talk to the patient.

'Ow you feelin', Bridie?' she croaked.

Her eyes wide and unblinking, Bridie tossed and muttered unceasingly.

'Lemme closer,' the old lady commanded Mary. 'And give me the candle so I can see proper.'

As was the custom, Bridie still had her clothes on; clothes kept you warm at night as well as in the daytime. Only her boots had been removed, to show black woollen stockings with holes in the heels and toes.

As she shuffled closer to the bed, the old lady muttered, 'Well, it int cholera, praise be, or she'd be dead by now. Is 'er stummick running?'

'No. She ain't even pissed.'

Aunt Kitty paused and looked up at Mary. 'She truly 'asn't?'

'No. Not a drop. I bin 'ere all day.'

'That's bad.' Aunt Kitty bent still lower, the candle dripping wax on Bridie's blouse, while she lifted the sufferer's chin and held it firmly in order to take a good look at her face. 'Lord presairve us!' she exclaimed. She touched a dark encrustation at the corners of Bridie's mouth, and then drew back thoughtfully.

She turned to Billy and James and ordered, 'You turn your backs. I'm goin' to take a real look at 'er all over.'

Filled with apprehension, Billy followed his father's example.

Great-aunt Kitty gestured towards Mary with the candle. 'Lift up her skirts. I want to see her stummick.'

Mary hesitated, her brown eyes wide with fear of what her great-aunt might deduce.

'Come on, girl.'

Kitty was said to be a witch, so rather than be cursed, Mary did as she was bidden, though she felt it wicked to expose her mother so.

Underneath the black woollen skirt were the ragged remains of a black and white striped petticoat. Mary lifted this and her mother's stomach was exposed; she wore nothing else, other than her stockings.

Holding the candle so that it did not drip on Bridie's bare flesh, Kitty ran her fingers over the sick woman's stomach. She bent down to peer very carefully at it. Beneath the grime, she was able to see dark red blotches. Her lips tightened over her toothless mouth.

She felt down the rigid legs and her sly old face, for once, showed only a terrible sadness. Very gently she took the petticoat and skirt hems from Mary's fingers and laid them back over Bridie. 'You can look now,' she told the male members of the family.

While she made her examination, James had retreated to the back of the tiny room. Now she turned to him.

''Ad any rats 'ere lately?'

'There's always rats, you know that,' growled James.

'Hm.'

Billy interjected, 'Mam found a near-dead one in the court a while back. Proper huge it were – like a cat. She threw it in the midden with the rubbish.'

'I knew it,' muttered Great-aunt Kitty. 'I seen it before. She's got gaol fever, God help us all.'

A hissing sigh of fear went through the other members of the family.

'Typhus?' James whispered.

'Aye. Haven't seen it for a while. But I seen lots of it in me time.'

'What'll we do?'

'Doctor from Dispensary might come.'

'They'll be shut by now.'

'Well, first light tomorrer, you go after 'em. Aye, this'll cause a pile of trouble.'

'What?'

'They'll burn everythin' you got, to stop it spreadin'.' She pointed to Bridie, still staring at the blackened rafters above her head and chattering incoherently. 'They'll take 'er to the Infirmary no doubt – keep 'er away by herself.'

'To die by herself?' James was aghast.

'That's wot 'ospitals is for, int it? To die in.' She gave a dry, sardonic laugh. 'They daren't leave 'er here, 'cos everybody in the court could get it from her.'

'Christ!' He rubbed his face with his hands. 'Are you certain sure?'

'Aye, I'm sure.' She hesitated, and then said, 'Well – almost.' She looked round the little room, lit only by the candle in her hand, at its dirty brick walls, its earthen floor, its empty firegrate. 'And you take care o' yourself and our Bill,' she warned. 'Take all your clothes off and wash 'em, and kill every bloody louse and flea you can find. The cleaner you are, the better you'll be.' She turned to Mary, and asked, 'Anybody else bin in here?'

'Our Theresa and the baby was here. I sent 'em home just now.' Mary began to cry.

'Well, you got a copper in your house. You go home and put all your clothes in it – and Theresa's and the baby's and our Billy's and your Dad's stuff. And boil the lot real hard.' She looked disparagingly at the fat, rather stupid girl in front of her. 'And if it's wool and it can't be boiled, borrow an iron and iron it well. Go over all the seams – with a good, hot iron, mind you.'

She turned back to Bridie, who periodically was letting out short shrieks. She put her hand on her niece's forehead again, and then turned to James. 'See if you can get a bit of milk from somewhere and feed it to her.' She swung back to Mary and snarled at her, 'Stop wingeing.'

Mary sniffed and wiped her face with the end of her shawl. She cast a glance of pure hatred at the humped back bent once more over Bridie; witches ought to be burned, in her opinion. Aloud she said, 'I'll go and get the fire lit under the copper. Tell our Billy to come straight over to our 'ouse – I'll do 'im first. While the water's gettin' hot, I'll run back with a bit of conny-onny for Mam.'

Kitty straightened up and sighed. She felt around in her skirt pocket and brought out a penny. 'Get a pennorth o' fresh milk, as you go by Mike's dairy. Conny-onny int goin' to do her much good.'

With a pout, Mary took the proffered coin, said goodbye to her father and clumped up the steps to the court.

'I'll stay for a while,' the old woman told James, who had moved closer to look anxiously at his tossing wife. 'Gi' me a chair, Jamie boy.'

James hastily moved a small stool closer to the bed and she slowly lowered herself on to it. ''Ave you got any firing? I could use a cup o' tea.'

'Aye, I got some driftwood.' He took the water bucket up to the court to draw water for tea from the common tap.

Crouched against a wall, Billy had listened dumbly to Great-aunt Kitty's diagnosis. His mother was his world. Sharp-tongued and quick to slap, nevertheless, she kept the family together. Without her, there was only darkness. Now he crept forward, to ask, 'Is she goin' to die, Aunty?'

His great-aunt looked up at him from her stool, her blood-shot eyes glittering in their black hollows. 'Coom 'ere, duck.'

The lad moved closer to her, and she put a long bony arm round him. 'She might,' she said. 'She 'asn't got no strength.'

Billy began to blubber like a small boy, while his mother raved on her bed. 'Na, then, luv.' Great-aunt Kitty's arm tightened round him. 'There's a time when all of us has to go.

You must pray nobody else gets it.' She sighed. 'Your Pa should've asked the Dispensary for 'elp before.'

'Mam didn't want 'im to. She's afraid of us all endin' up in the Workie.'

The very word 'Workhouse' was enough to make anybody panic, thought Great-aunt Kitty, so she nodded understandingly.

'Well she *is* real ill now, lad, and the Dispensary is the only one what might save her.'

II

Wrapped in a black woollen shawl, her straw hat skewered by two huge hatpins to the top of her plaited hair, Polly ran through the ill-lit city. Though she was by no means young she was nervous in the Woodmans' neighbourhood of being cornered by half-drunk, smartly dressed men out for an evening's entertainment; further into the city itself, prostitutes paraded followed closely by their pimps, all of them anxious to defend their own particular territory. As she cut through side streets to reach her home near the junction of Scotland Road and Cazneau Street, homeless men dozing in doorways called to her, and an occasional group of seamen on shore leave shouted after her. She gave them all wide berth.

The narrow street off which the court led was almost dead dark, and she feared she might not find the entrance. As she passed, she let her fingertips brush along the rough brick wall, watching that she did not trip over front steps which occasionally protruded on to the pavement.

A slight difference in the light and nothing under her fingertips told her that she had found the narrow archway.

As she entered, the smell hit her, the appalling reek of the midden full of a month's rubbish and the overflowing earth lavatories. Very faintly, from the steps leading down to the cellar, came the glow of a candle. She walked lightly towards it, afraid of slipping on the cobblestones, greasy from half a century of filth. Then she ran down the narrow outside staircase and into the room.

Though there were only three of them, the cellar seemed full of women, wrapped in their black, crocheted shawls, all watching tearfully, as her mother on her straw mattress muttered softly. The light of the solitary candle barely reached her father, who was pacing up and down a narrow space by the fireplace. He was beating his breast with one clenched fist, in time to the movement of his feet. Crouched on another palliasse laid on the floor, his head against the wall, Billy dozed, his tousled hair shadowing his face.

Polly's quick footsteps on the stairs woke the boy, and all heads turned towards her.

Polly had eyes only for her mother, and the women edged back as she ran to the narrow bed and flung herself on her knees by it. 'Holy Mary!' she breathed, as she saw the black-encrusted mouth and the frightening staring eyes. She laid her arm round her mother's head and whispered, 'Mam.'

Bridie ignored her, and continued to toss and mutter with an occasional near shout.

Polly looked round wildly. 'Aunty! Aunty Kitty, what's to do with her? Can't you do somethin'?'

Perched on her stool like a roosting crow, her great-aunt said heavily, 'I think it's gaol fever.'

Polly drew back from the bed in horror. 'Has anybody bin to the Dispensary to ask the doctor?'

'Billy'll go as soon as it's light – mebbe somebody'll be there.' She looked down at the terrified girl. 'You come away from 'er, duck. You can't do nothin', and you might catch it.'

Mary let out a sudden wail, 'Aye, we'll all die unless we're lucky – and our Billy wouldn't come over and 'ave hisself washed and 'is clothes boiled.'

'Now, Mary, don't take on so. Time enough for that later.' This from Mrs Fox, Bridie's distant kinswoman and the family's landlady, who, to her credit, had come down from her ground floor room to see if she could help.

But Bridie was beyond help. She died before midnight in the arms of her old aunt, her half-nourished body unable to withstand the ravages of the terrible disease.

In the first light of morning, as they listened to the unearthly sound of keening coming from the Tysons' cellar, her Catholic neighbours formed an uneasy knot on the far side of the court; occasionally, one or the other of them would cross themselves.

They whispered questions to each other, and, finally, a woman ran across to the iron railing guarding the cellar steps. She leaned over. Great-aunt Kitty was sitting exhausted on the bottom step, and she asked her, 'What's to do?'

The old woman looked up and replied, without hesitation, 'Typhus, I reckon. It's our Bridie, dead from typhus.'

The woman flung her hands across her chest, as if to protect herself, her face a picture of horror. 'Jaysus, save us!' she screamed.

At her shriek, panic went from face to face. People not yet up leapt from their palliasses to the windows and flung them up, as the woman turned and spread the news. Nobody came near the cellar, tending instead to bunch themselves in the far corners of the foetid yard and draw comfort from excited talk with each other.

James wept unrestrainedly, not only because he had lost his wife, but also because she would have to be given a pauper's funeral, the last great humiliation.

''Aven't even got a sheet to wind her in,' he sobbed bitterly. 'Will they 'ave to strip 'er?'

'Aye, for their own safety, they'll have to take everything of ours off 'er and burn it,' Great-aunt Kitty told him. 'They'll bring a shroud, though.'

III

Though his neighbours did not come near him, it seemed to James that that day, the rest of the population of the city tramped through his miserable dwelling.

Money being a terrible necessity, Billy was sent, weeping,

off to work. On his way, he ran to the Dispensary to put a note, written by Great-aunt Kitty, through the letter-box. An anxious doctor arrived within the hour. He confirmed Great-aunt Kitty's diagnosis.

He said he would inform the Medical Officer of Health immediately, so that the court could be fumigated and cleansed in an effort to contain the disease.

As he was going out of the court, he was stopped by a middle-aged man who wanted to know if the disease was typhus. The doctor said it was and that the authorities would assuredly do their best to stop others getting it. He explained about fumigation to get rid of fleas and other vermin.

When this information was passed to the other inhabitants of the court, they were very upset, and they blamed Mrs Fox, James's landlady, for harbouring Catholic Bridie's Protestant husband, a man who was known to have attended Methodist revival meetings.

'It's the wrath of God, it is, strikin' at us for havin' a heretic here,' one old biddy raged.

Fear of catching the disease by touching anyone who had been near the corpse, however, forestalled the donnybrook which might otherwise have ensued. They contented themselves by shouting obscenities at James and Billy whenever they emerged. Father and son, wrapped in their own grief, hardly heard them.

Billy longed for Polly to comfort him, but after her mother died, Great-aunt Kitty persuaded Polly that, for her own sake, she should return to the Woodmans' house. 'Good jobs is hard to find,' she told her practically, as she held the younger woman to her. 'Your Dad and Mary and me, we'll manage. Away you go, now. And change your clothes and wash them.'

Weeping all the way, Polly obeyed.

IV

Knowing that the undertaker would not touch the corpse unless it was washed, Great-aunt Kitty, assisted by a frightened, sobbing Mary, took off the dead woman's clothes and gently sponged her down; her jaw was bound with strips torn from her petticoat and two pennies, provided by Great-aunt Kitty, were placed on her eyelids after Kitty had closed them. They had nothing better to cover her with, so they spread her thick black skirt over her. With her arms crossed over her breast, Bridie looked, in her nakedness, a dreadful travesty of the woman she might have been.

The undertaker and his assistant were by no means as inhumane as James had feared. They wrapped his wife's remains in a coarse shroud and laid her carefully in a rough coffin. Mary had shamed her husband, Mike, into coming to help to carry her coffin, and he did help James and Billy to lift it out of the court and to lay it in the undertaker's horse-drawn van.

Alerted by Mrs Fox, the landlady, a local Roman Catholic priest arrived, just as the van was about to move off. He scolded James for not calling him earlier, so that Bridie could have received Extreme Unction before her death. James simply stared at him unseeingly. He made no objection, however, when the priest undertook to read the service for the committal of the dead; and the four men trudged through the uncaring streets, following the slow clip-clop of the horse's hooves.

V

Early the following morning, an extremely perturbed sanitary inspector arrived at the court; he knew only too well how major diseases could sweep through parts of Liverpool. He had not yet gone through all the houses, when he was followed by the midden men to empty the rubbish from the midden and a rat catcher to check for rodents; it all caused no little stir amongst the fuming, fearful inhabitants.

The house in which James lived would have to be fumigated, the inspector announced, which meant all the twenty-one inhabitants would be homeless for a day while the smelly job was done. The same people would all have to be examined by a physician. Mrs Fox felt free to have a strong attack of hysterics and allow herself to be comforted with sips of rum provided by her sympathetic neighbours.

Though in one way the neighbours were angry with James for his heresy and the upset which they believed it had caused, they also enjoyed the excitement of being the centre of so much attention; it gave them something new to talk about and they felt suddenly important. They were sorely disappointed, however, to hear that there there would be no Wake.

The rent collector representing the absentee landlord, having heard from the sanitary inspector in extremely strong language about the state of the property, felt the need to look as if he were doing something about it, and sent Mrs Fox once more into hysterics. He not only demanded that James be kicked out of his cellar, which, several years back, had been condemned by the sanitary authorities and boarded up, but gave Mrs Fox and her numerous tenants notice to quit.

Stout and ferocious, the landlady took her fight with the rent collector outside, where she screamed, 'I never miss me rent, you stinking bugger – and do you think I'm goin' to let me own flesh and blood sleep in the streets when I got a cellar wot only needed the boards takin' down?'

The rent collector backed, only to find himself hemmed in by a delighted crowd. Arms outflung, Mrs Fox appealed to them, stressing her own kindness and humanity. She threw herself down at the rent collector's feet, as he tried to protest that the house was overcrowded. Enjoying herself thoroughly, Mrs Fox turned on her back, to kick her heels like a child in a tantrum and reveal legs like the pillars of St George's Hall.

The subtenants began to gather closer round the beleaguered man. 'Want to swallow a fist full o' knuckles?' inquired a bony youth, thrusting a leathery clenched hand into his face. Another man laughed. 'Throw 'im in the midden,' he suggested, while Mrs Fox screamed louder and a dazed James watched from the top of his cellar steps.

The rent collector turned, pushed his way through the jubilant crowd and fled.

Mrs Fox turned off her screams immediately. Triumphant, she rose from the cobbles and shook out her skirt. She simpered at the younger men, and said sorrowfully, 'Charity it was, to let the cellar to our Bridie, seeing as how 'er 'ubby int what he might be.' She sniffed slowly and dramatically, 'Out of love of God and love of 'er, I did it, pore dear.'

'Well, put him out,' snarled a wizened hunchback.

Mrs Fox looked down at him. 'I'll think about it,' she responded loftily, and went back into her house.'

VI

The Roman Catholic priest mentioned to the minister of the Wesleyan chapel in Scotland Road that there had been a case of typhus in the parish; they were well-acquainted with each other and often cooperated in schemes to improve the lives of the teeming parish. James was not a member of his chapel but the minister had met him at a Revivalist meeting once and had visited him a few times over the years. Now, without hesitation, he struggled into his shabby jacket and walked down to the court dwelling.

It always took him all his courage to enter closed courts; if the attitude of the Roman Catholic inhabitants should turn ugly, there was only the single narrow exit. When he arrived, however, the only people in the court appeared to be two housewives, buckets in hand, gossiping by the water tap, their children playing in the dirt at their feet, and two labourers shovelling out the midden.

To avoid others getting the disease, Bridie's burial had been necessarily fast and Billy had gone straight from her funeral to work, because the need for money was desperate. When the minister knocked on the cellar door, Mary with her suckling baby at her breast, answered it. James, nearly out of his mind with pain in his back, was seated, teeth clenched, on a bench. In the light of a guttering candle, the room looked even barer than usual, because both the straw palliasses had been taken away to be burned.

Pushing her straggling black hair back from a tearstained face, Mary invited the minister to enter, and James rose slowly from his bench. 'Come in, Sir. Sit down, Sir.' He pointed to a stool opposite him.

James was sober, observed the minister with relief; temperance vows sometimes got forgotten, and the homes he visited would be packed with drunken, wailing relations, not to speak of the corpse propped up in a corner so that it could view the proceedings.

He found that talking to James was rather like addressing a corpse. The man sat as if deaf, hearing nothing of the minister's homily on accepting the Will of God or the subsequent prayers delivered by him. Only when he was leaving did James bestir himself.

As he dumbly followed the minister to the foot of the steps, he suddenly broached his worries about Billy. He said, 'Our Billy is only a young 'un yet; me daughters is all right – one married and one in service.' He cleared his throat, and the minister paused to listen. 'He's a good lad. If aught should 'appen to me, would you look out for 'im? Mary here 'as her own to care for – and more to come, no doubt. There's nobody to look for our Billy.' He laid his hand on the minister's arm, and implored, 'Don't let 'em put 'im in the Workhouse, ever.'

The minister nodded, 'I'll do my best. You know, Billy should come to chapel and then we can keep an eye on him.'

'We don't have no money to give – and no half-decent clothes to wear – and Billy's Mam raised 'im more of a Catholic, like.'

'Well, you'll probably live a long time yet,' replied the minister briskly, 'and you'll see the boy safely started yourself.'

'Oh, aye. Maybe.' He let his hand drop from the minister's arm, and half turned away.

The minister felt a stirring of guilt; James was the type of person John Wesley had first tried to succour. He hesitated, and then said, 'I'll ask one of our lay preachers to make a point of visiting you.'

'That's proper kind of you.'

Mary had said nothing during the visit, but when the visitor had left, she buttoned up her black blouse, hitched the shawl more tightly round the sleeping baby, and said, 'I'll go 'ome to make a bit to eat. You and Billy come over and share with us. I'm goin' to wash Billy's clothes, anyways, tonight, and you stay over with us, till you find somewhere else to live.'

'Ta, luv,' James responded dully, as she ran up the steps.

He closed the door and then stood in the middle of the room and looked round him. Without Bridie and her piles of fents, the place was desolate. Beside the stool, the stripped truckle bed gave not even a remembrance of her. A few dishes and two saucepans, with the gutted candle in a bottle, cluttered the deal table, the water bucket underneath it. From nails in the walls hung James's docker's hook, unused for a year, the rope he used to tie wood from the river into bundles, and his ragged jacket. A mouse ran across the floor.

He was shaking with hunger and pain, but there was no food. He continued to stand uncertainly for a minute. Then he moved the stool to a more central position.

He took down the rope from its nail, made a noose in it and tied it firmly to a meathook in the rafters. He climbed on to the stool, put the noose round his neck, kicked the stool from under him and, not very quietly, hanged himself.

The fumigators found him the following day.

Chapter Nine

I

Sick at heart, Billy went straight from work to his sister's house, so he was spared the shock of finding his father dead.

For fear of bringing more trouble to the court, no one there was prepared to talk to Health Officials. Faced with a wall of silent dislike, the medical officer did not manage to trace any of the Tyson family and, in consequence, was unable to quarantine them. Looking like an offended empress, Mrs Fox swore that she had never been near Bridie. 'I got more sense,' she told the harassed, overworked doctor.

Defeated, the authorities sent in an additional rat catcher and had the court itself thoroughly sluiced down with water and carbolic, after Mrs Fox's house had, over her protestations, been fumigated.

By the time Mary's husband, Mike, returned home from his job as stableman in a dairy, Billy, sniffing miserably, had had the first bath of his life, in Mary's wooden washtub. While he rubbed himself dry in front of the kitchen fire, Mary heated a borrowed iron on the fire and pressed his jacket and breeches, to kill the lice and fleas. He wore nothing else, except a red handkerchief round his neck, so she did not have to heat up her clay and brick wash boiler.

Mike greeted the boy surlily; he was mortally afraid of contracting typhus himself. He and Mary had had a tremendous row, when she had insisted that they must give a temporary roof to her father and her brother. Though he had struck her several times in the course of the quarrel, she had persisted stubbornly that it was the least they could do. To save face, he had shouted that Billy must pay his wages to him, and if her father did not like it he could get out. She sullenly agreed.

When she had to tell Billy of their father's death and that he would be buried in a suicide's grave, the boy clung to her, unable to cope with the destruction of his small world. Her children played in the street, unaware of the tragedy; only her eldest daughter, Theresa, watched with sly, knowing eyes. Mrs Fox, who had brought the news, sat in Mike's chair by the fire and wiped her eyes, said it was proper awful and had a most enjoyable cry.

II

Since officially there were no Tysons available to deal with poor James's funeral, Mrs Fox undertook to cope with the city authorities. This did not stop Polly asking Elizabeth Woodman for a half-day off, so that she could follow her father's coffin to the cemetery. Permission was reluctantly given, and she, Mary and Billy waited a few yards away from the undertaker's van until the coffin was brought out of the court. They then quietly followed it, and only their prayers consigned his remains to the earth.

Because of Polly's absence, Alicia was allowed for the first time to go to school by herself. Elizabeth Woodman had put on weight and climbing stairs or hills made her pant, so she did not consider taking the child herself.

'I simply cannot spare Fanny to go with you,' she fretted to Alicia. 'It's At Home Day, and I cannot think how we're going to manage without Polly. Go straight to school and come straight home again. And don't speak to any strangers.'

'Lots of girls go to school alone,' Alicia assured her. 'I'll walk part of the way back with Ethel – she lives in Falkner Square.'

'Is that the child who came to play with you once or twice?'

'Yes. I've asked her several times since, but she's so busy.' Alicia sighed. 'She swots a lot.'

'Swot is slang, Alicia,' Elizabeth responded mechanically. Blast them, she thought. The girl's parents must have found out that Alicia was illegitimate; Ethel would certainly not be allowed to associate with Alicia in future. Aloud, she said, 'Never mind, dear.'

Alicia confirmed her mother's suspicions by saying pensively, 'Ethel says that her mother chooses her friends for her – and she doesn't like it much.'

'Some mothers are unreasonably fussy.'

Alicia was sitting on a small stool facing her mother, her hands neatly folded in her lap. 'When will Polly come home?'

'She had better be home tonight or I shall be very cross with her. I can't endure these constant absences.'

Alicia gazed doubtfully at Elizabeth. 'She cries a lot,' she said. 'I suppose parents' funerals are important?' She was genuinely curious. With a father and a mother whom she rarely saw and with few friends, she wondered about the relationship between parents and children.

Elizabeth was shocked by the question. She thought, for a moment, that Alicia was being sarcastic. The child's face with its light grey eyes was so innocent, however, that she stifled her sharp reply and sat staring at her daughter. She carefully put down her after-lunch cup of coffee on the table beside her, before she replied, and then she said, 'Parents care a great deal about their children; children should therefore grieve very much if their parents die. As the Bible says, parents are to be honoured.'

A little bewildered, Alicia said, 'Poor Polly! I don't know what to say to comfort her.'

'Oh, servants don't feel as we do. Polly will soon get over it. She shouldn't cry in front of you. I'll speak to her about it.'

Alicia opened her mouth to disagree with Elizabeth, and then thought better of it. If you wanted to avoid being spanked, you agreed with everything Mama said. Polly always said that Mama knew best. So she muttered, 'Yes, Mama,' and wished that she had not mentioned Polly's grief. She stood up, preparatory to going back to school for the afternoon and waited for her mother to dismiss her. She rubbed her black-stockinged leg with the toe of her house shoe.

Rather put out by the whole conversation, Elizabeth told her irritably to stop fidgeting.

Alicia immediately stood straight, like a small soldier. She said, 'I'm sorry, Mama.' Then, since her mother still did not dismiss her, she said politely, 'Of course, Mama, I would be sad if I had to go to *your* funeral.'

Jolted, Elizabeth looked up from contemplation of her wedding and engagement rings. Her daughter was smiling gently. 'Would you?' Elizabeth asked her.

'Of course, Mama.'

'Ah, well, I hope you won't have to for a long time. Run along now.'

III

In a new black alpaca dress, Elizabeth sat calmly and charmingly through her At Home. She dispensed China tea from her best silver teapot, while Fanny proffered small iced cakes from a silver cake-basket. She wished Florence was with her, to help to keep the conversation spritely. But Florence had six children now and had little time for social occasions.

All the usual ladies called, to sip tea and exchange gossip. Some brought daughters who had just Come Out. One had brought her newly married daughter, shyly pretty in a fine tweed costume and one of the new big hats.

Viewing them from behind her teapot, Elizabeth felt sadly that none of them were ladies of substance, except for her lifelong spinster friend, Sarah Webb, who was the daughter of a baronet; she was sitting quietly in a corner as a single gentlewoman should. All the women present, though prosperous, were of a lower social class than herself; the wives of Liverpool's truly important men had dropped her, now that she felt too tired and depressed to continue her charitable efforts.

As she watched the painted rose at the bottom of each teacup slowly drown in the tea she poured, she fretted about Alicia. What was she going to do when the girl grew older? She could not live forever in the attic nurseries with Polly. Even now, if she had been an ordinary daughter, like Florence, it would have been expected that, after school, she would join her mother in the drawing-room, to be made a fuss of by her friends and be encouraged, perhaps, to recite a piece of poetry.

Fortunately, some of the ladies present were barely aware that she had a younger daughter and those that knew would not wish to face the fact, because they would feel that they had to drop Elizabeth if they did so – and Elizabeth was their social superior and worth cultivating from that point of view. It was certain, however, that if Elizabeth began to introduce the girl, the old rumours would come up again and both mother and daughter would be snubbed. Elizabeth, passing the sugar bowl with a smile as sweet as its contents, thought bitterly that, with this mob, out of sight was out of mind.

Behind her bright chatter, her anguish grew. Alicia was becoming more like Andrew every day, a constant reminder of her lover's defection. The more apparent the likeness became, the less she wanted mutual friends to observe it; Andrew was, after all, a well-known family solicitor who moved in good circles in the city; some people would have actually met him in the Woodmans' house when, before Humphrey realized what was happening, she had asked him to parties. If in a few years' time she Brought Out Alicia, even amongst her despised guests the connection would be made, and, without a very large dowry, Alicia would not stand a chance of marriage.

But Alicia was growing up and was beginning to ask questions – childish ones, but nevertheless very disconcerting to her Mama.

After her second *petit four*, Sarah Webb delicately dabbed her three chins with a lace-edged napkin, and inquired, 'How is dear Florence these days? And little Alicia? I don't think I've seen Alicia since last Christmas. She seems to have been at school whenever I called.'

Sarah was assured that dear Florence was well, though still a little delicate after her last baby. And, according to Miss Schreiber, Alicia was doing very well at school. Elizabeth wished crossly that Sarah had enough sense to keep her mouth shut. But Sarah loved her godchild and did not agree with Elizabeth's keeping her in such seclusion.

Bent on suggesting a different future for Alicia, Sarah said cheerfully, 'Perhaps Alicia will follow Charles into university – I hear he's doing well at Cambridge.' She looked coyly at the other ladies, and studiously evaded Elizabeth's warning eye. 'Perhaps she'll become a New Woman!' she speculated, and accepted yet another *petit four* from the silver basket.

The suggestion of university for a girl set off a heated argument; even if she were accepted, what use would such an education be? They all agreed that men did not like to marry educated women.

'I wish I could have gone to university,' responded Sarah wistfully. 'I would love to have studied botany.'

The ladies felt that botany might be a suitable study for a woman – it was quite *nice*. 'But what would you have done with your learning, Miss Webb?' inquired one of the younger ladies quite earnestly.

Sarah looked bewildered. Then her chins wobbled, as she laughed and confessed, 'I really don't know. But it would have been so good to understand the theories behind it all. And, you know, some young women *are* continuing their education, nowadays.'

An elderly widow, her black veil flung back from a wizened face, retorted, 'It is not nice for women to be exposed to vulgarity, when sitting at lectures with a host of young men to whom they have not been introduced!'

Two or three other guests nodded their heads in agreement. Sarah Webb was a fool who had not succeeded in getting married.

A very blonde lady in a fashionable hat loaded with white

veiling, giggled and suggested, 'University won't teach you how to manage men!'

The guests laughed, and agreed.

The conversation and Sarah Webb's remarks about university remained with Elizabeth long after the guests had departed. She dined with her husband, and the meal was as usual practically silent.

After dinner, Humphrey normally retired to his library to drink brandy and coffee while he read the evening newspaper; Elizabeth took tea in the morning-room, where she continued her endless embroidery of underwear or made beautiful hand-stitched clothes for Florence's children. This night, however, after the cheese and fruit had been brought in, she took her courage in both hands, dismissed Fanny to the kitchen, and said to an unsuspecting Humphrey, 'I have to speak to you about Alicia.'

IV

Humphrey always did his best to ignore the plain, shy child he met from time to time on the stairs or in the hall. On the rare occasions when the family was gathered together, such as at Christmas, he tolerated her presence rather than face awkward questions from Florence or her children, but he avoided speaking to her. Florence's husband, the Reverend Clarence Browning, appeared to understand the situation because he also ignored the child. It was Humphrey's brother, Harold, who, when visiting from Manchester, pitied Alicia and brought her little tins of chocolate drops; he persisted in this, even when his wife, Vera, protested that the little girl was 'not quite the thing'. 'What nonsense,' he would reply. 'She's only a child.'

Alicia had once said wistfully to Polly that she wished she could have a birthday party where her father would be present. 'Ethel's father actually played Blind Man's Buff with them last time,' she said.

'Your Papa is a very busy man, luv,' Polly had told her. 'And you had a nice birthday last time, remember? Miss Webb took you on the ferry boat to New Brighton, and Mrs Tibbs made you a birthday cake for when you come 'ome.'

Alicia's eyelids had drooped and she had bitten her lower lip, and agreed. Polly had cut the cake in the nursery, and Alicia had taken a piece down to the morning-room for her mother.

Elizabeth had thanked her and looked as if she were going to cry. She had fumbled amid the muddle of her sewing and brought out a tissue-paper parcel which she handed to Alicia.

It contained a coral necklace which she said she used to wear when she was a little girl, and Alicia had been so delighted that she had kissed her mother on her cheek. Her mother did not respond.

Now a very nervous but determined Elizabeth surveyed her husband's red face at the other end of the dining-table, his scarlet neck oozing over his stiff white collar, his stubby fingers wielding the cheese knife. As he transferred a piece of gorganzola to his plate, he said icily, 'Alicia is your business. I don't want anything to do with her.'

Elizabeth's hand trembled so much that she was unable to peel the grape on her plate. Under the table, her feet were tensed against the floor, so that if Humphrey threatened her, she could jump from her chair and make for the door.

'I'm fully aware of that,' she managed to reply. 'However, since she lives here, she's officially your child.' She abandoned the grape and clenched her hands in her lap. 'That means that you have to go through the motions expected of a parent. She's ten years old now and a clever little girl.'

Humphrey took out his ivory toothpick and asked, 'And what particular paternal duty did you have in mind?'

Elizabeth ignored his sarcasm. 'I want to send her to Blackburne House School. Miss Schreiber says she's clever and recommends that we do so.'

'Why don't you send her to boarding school? That would get her out of the way until she's eighteen.'

'Would you pay the fees?'

'No, I would not!' Humphrey shook his toothpick at her. His face was rapidly turning purple.

Though she was deadly afraid, Elizabeth's temper began to rise. 'Precisely. Blackburne House would be much cheaper.'

'If you think I'm going to pay for your bastard to go anywhere, you're mistaken.' He pushed back his chair and slapped his linen table napkin down on the table. 'She doesn't need an education – she can marry.'

'It's doubtful if she can ever marry – unless you dower her – she might stand a chance then.'

'Me? Dower her? Don't be absurd. And don't expect me to provide for her after my death.'

'Really, Humphrey, you've carried on this vendetta too long. It's not the child's fault.'

'No, it isn't her fault, is it? Ask yourself whose fault it is – and don't expect me to bear the burden of it.'

Elizabeth swallowed her rage; anger only ended in her being struck, and the older she became the less she was able to endure it.

Her husband glided from the room, his house shoes making no noise on the Turkey carpet. The door clicked shut.

Alone, she bowed her head and thought bitterly that, apart from the running sore which was Alicia, her husband blamed her that their eldest son, Edward, was stupid, incapable of adding two and two when it came to arithmetic, and was still dependent upon an allowance from his father to augment his army pay. He also despised Charles, a thin, bent bookworm taking Chemistry as a major in university. 'Who is going to carry on the business?' he would shout at Elizabeth in his frustration.

Sitting defeated at the table, she longed to rest her head on the shoulder of a gentle, sympathetic man; she did not go so far as to admit that she would like to slip into bed with one; she fought her sexual desires as if they were an importuning dragon to be slain.

She leaned forward and rang the bell for Polly.

She had her elbows on the table and was resting her head in her hands, when Polly arrived carrying her big clearing tray.

"'Ave you got an 'eadache, Ma'am?' Polly inquired solicitously.

'Yes, I have, Polly. I think I'll lie down for a little while. You may clear the table.' In a slow dignified fashion, she rose from the table and made her way out of the room.

'She's bin cryin' again,' Polly reported to Fanny, in the great cavern of a kitchen. 'His Nibs must've bin at her.'

'Take her up some tea to her bed,' advised Fanny. 'She always likes that.' She looked compassionately at Polly, whose face was pinched, her mouth tight with unexpressed grief. 'And 'ave a good strong cup yerself, luv. Funerals is 'ard to bear.'

Chapter Ten

I

After taking a tray of tea and ratafia biscuits up to a tear-sodden Elizabeth, Polly fled up the remainder of the stairs to the day nursery. She flung herself into the old easy chair and wept unrestrainedly.

She ignored Alicia sitting at the centre table, struggling with her Saturday task of history homework. Shocked at her nanny's distress, Alicia slipped from her chair and ran to her. She put her arms round Polly's shaking shoulders. 'Please don't cry, Polly,' she pleaded. She fumbled for her handkerchief neatly tucked into her waistband, and handed it to the distraught woman.

Polly took the embroidered scrap of cambric and held it to her mouth, while she tried to control herself.

'Is it about your Papa, Polly? Has anything else happened?'

Polly leaned her head on her little charge's shoulder, and sobbed. 'It's me poor Dad. He 'ung himself – so this afternoon they put 'im in a suicide's grave – and there wasn't no priest. It were awful.'

Alicia stiffened. Outside the covers of novels, she had not heard of a suicide. Did people *really* take their own lives? The idea was awesome, and she whispered in horror, 'Oh, Polly!'

Polly lifted her head and blew her nose on Alicia's handkerchief. She looked at the white, anxious little face before her, and said hoarsely, 'He couldn't make do, without me Mam.' She began to cry again.

'I assumed he'd died of fever like your Mama,' Alicia said, her voice puzzled. She had never seen Polly's home or her parents, and she asked with wonder, 'Did he love her so much?' She felt as if she had stumbled on a true romance.

'Aye, I think he did. His back were so bad, he could 'ardly work, and she took care of him.'

In Alicia's mind, the humble labourer joined other star-crossed lovers, like Romeo and Juliet. She began to cry, too.

Polly lifted her on to her lap and held her close. They wept together as if they were mother and daughter joined by a common sorrow.

Polly knew then that no matter how irritating Elizabeth Woodman became, she could never leave Alicia.

II

The next morning, dressed in her morning uniform of pink-striped dress and well-starched apron, she carried Elizabeth's breakfast up to her bedroom. Elizabeth was awake and was sitting up in bed; she looked as weary and hollow-eyed as Polly did.

As Polly laid the tray on her bedside table, she inquired, 'The funeral? Is everything settled in your family, now?'

Polly fought back her tears. 'Yes,'m.' She went to the window to draw back the velvet curtains.

'Good.' Elizabeth began to pour herself a cup of tea. 'Next term, Polly, I shall enrol Miss Alicia at Blackburne House. I think she will be able to walk there quite safely by herself, except in winter when it will be dark and you'll have to take her.'

Elizabeth had as yet only a glimmer of an idea of how she was going to pay Alicia's school fees, but she felt that by telling Polly it might be more certain to come about; it would strengthen her resolve to have Alicia educated sufficiently for her to be a governess.

'Yes,'m. Of course, I'll take her.' Polly was not sure what Blackburne House was exactly nor did she know where it lay. 'Is that everything, Ma'am?'

'No, Polly. In future, I want you to see that Miss Alicia is dressed for dinner. Unless there are visitors, she will take her meal with us.'

'Yes, Ma'am. Shall I tell her, Ma'am?'

'No. I will tell her.' Elizabeth's mouth trembled. Humphrey was going to be furious at having to eat his dinner with Alicia and even crosser if she managed the fees for Blackburne House.

As Polly prepared to leave the bedroom, Elizabeth asked casually, 'What did your mother die of, Polly? I trust she was not in pain?'

Polly paused, her hand on the doorknob. After a second's thought, she said carefully, 'She had a fever, Ma'am. She weren't that strong – she couldn't stand up to it.' She closed her eyes and saw, for a second, her tortured mother tossing on her palliasse. She dared not say that it had been typhus; she might lose her job, as a frightened mistress tried to distance herself from such a virulent infection. 'Doctor didn't put a name to it.'

'I see.' She already knew from Polly that James Tyson had committed suicide. She disapproved strongly of this – suicide was a sin. She picked up her silver spoon and began to crack her boiled egg.

Outside the door, Polly began to cry silently.

Later on, she mentioned to Mrs Tibbs that Alicia would be coming down to dinner in future.

'Oh, my! Maybe the Master's got used to her bein' around and got to like her,' Mrs Tibbs suggested.

This opened up a new point of view to Polly, and she replied quite enthusiastically, 'Oh, aye, I hope you're right, poor lamb.'

While Elizabeth ate her breakfast egg, she also considered Alicia. Sarah Webb's idle remarks at the At Home had reminded her sharply that Alicia was past the usual age for confinement to the nursery. If the girl did not soon join the rest of the family for the main meal of the day, acquaintances would hear from the servant grapevine that Alicia was not being treated as the daughters of others were. It would confirm the rumour of her illegitimacy, and no doubt the story of

Andrew Crossing and herself would be dug up again. She felt, with a sense of panic, that Andrew's name must never suffer more besmirchment than had already been the case.

Then she asked herself why she should care about him – he had hurt her dreadfully. The answer came readily, 'Simply because I love him – and always will.' She leaned her head back against her pillows and closed her eyes in an agony of remembrance.

School fees were a different problem. She herself had managed to pay Miss Schreiber's fees out of the allowance sent her each month by Andrew's partner, who now administered her father's Estate. She had not been consulted about the transfer and, when she inquired, young Mr Simpkins had explained that the firm was the Trustee, so any partner could attend to the administration. No doubt, Mr Crossing would explain to her the internal reorganization of the office on the death of their most senior partner. Mr Crossing never had explained, thought Elizabeth fretfully; the stupid idiot had never been near her since Alicia's birth.

During the night, it had occurred to her that Sarah Webb might help with the Blackburne House fees, since she was Alicia's godmother. Or Elizabeth's elder sister, Clara, in West Kirby, might do it simply to spite Humphrey whom she detested. But Sarah at least knew the true story of Alicia, and she loved the child.

As Elizabeth nibbled her last piece of toast, she felt a guilty pang that she did not love Alicia. She was honest enough to admit that she resented her very existence. And to look at her was to see a small mirror of Andrew, which was of no use to a woman who longed passionately to feel his hands upon her, hear him whisper to her as he assuaged the mad sexual urge within her. If Alicia had not been conceived, they might have continued lovers indefinitely; she might have been expecting him that very afternoon. She put down her toast and began to cry.

Later on, she pulled herself together and, when Alicia came home for lunch, she sent for her in the morning-room and told her that Polly would dress her that evening and she should come down to dinner.

Alicia was thrilled. She said, 'Oh, thank you, Mama,' dipped a little curtsey and, without waiting to be dismissed ran out of the room and down the back stairs to tell Polly.

III

Humphrey Woodman sometimes thought that, to a large degree, he lost effective control of Elizabeth on the day that Alicia first came down for dinner.

Before banging the dinner gong in the hall, Polly carefully seated her little charge in the mahogany dining-chair which had been occupied by Edward whenever he was home. Alicia's hair had been combed rigidly back from her face and plaited down her back. She wore a white cotton dress trimmed with lace and had a narrow blue ribbon tied round her waist. On her feet were her best white slippers; they pinched slightly because she was growing fast and they were becoming too small for her. Her hands were clasped tightly in her lap and her eager expression bespoke her excitement.

'Now, you mind your manners,' Polly instructed her, as she plaited her hair. 'You don't open your mouth till you're spoke to, remember. Hold your knife and fork proper, like your Mama does.'

Bubbling with excitement, Alicia promised to be perfect.

Now, as Polly spoke down the blower to Mrs Tibbs in the basement and ordered the soup to be sent up in the dumb-waiter, Elizabeth entered. She cast a quick glance over Alicia and the table settings, and then sat down.

'Remember, Alicia, to be quiet,' she told the girl. 'Mr Woodman dislikes chatterboxes.' She wondered nervously what exactly Humphrey's reaction would be to the girl's presence.

Alicia smiled up at her mother and responded, 'Yes, Mama.' Then she added shyly, 'You do look pretty in your dinner dress, Mama.'

While Polly leaned over to pick up the serviette by Alicia's plate and spread it over the girl's knees, Elizabeth acknowledged the compliment with a slight smile.

Despite a feeling of fatigue which nowadays sometimes bothered him in the evening, Humphrey bowled into the room with the same small, purposeful step that at other times propelled him rapidly along Castle Street to the Exchange Flags, where, amid eddying groups of top-hatted businessmen, he searched for the right contacts, the right pieces of inside information, to promote his considerable investments.

On meeting the nervous, pale eyes of Alicia, he paused, disconcerted, and glanced at his wife. She clenched her teeth and stared coldly back at him. Through her teeth, she said firmly, 'Alicia will have her evening meal with us, in future. She's a big girl now; she has to learn how to behave as a grown-up should.'

At the sideboard, her back to the room, Polly stood, for a second, soup ladle poised over a dish, waiting for the outburst.

Faced with the anxious stare of a little girl he hardly knew and with a servant in the room, probably dying with curiosity and ready to run into the kitchen to relay anything he said, he was for once nonplussed. He sniffed, and with great dignity pulled out his chair and sat down. He shook out his huge linen table napkin as if it were a flag and placed it neatly across his knee. While he considered the situation, he bowed his head and muttered, 'For what we are about to receive may the Lord make us truly thankful, Amen. Where's the soup?'

'Amen,' responded Elizabeth and Alicia in quiet chorus, while Polly hastily slipped a bowl of soup in front of Elizabeth and another in front of Humphrey. She then brought a small helping for Alicia.

Painfully aware of the tension between her parents which she did not understand, Alicia carefully drank her tomato soup with a huge tablespoon. 'God, don't let me spill anything on the tablecloth or on my white frock,' she prayed earnestly.

If Humphrey did not initiate a conversation, Elizabeth rarely did, except when visitors were present. Their verbal exchanges were usually limited to complaints by Humphrey or reports of household needs by Elizabeth. On that day, Humphrey never said a word, while, out of the corner of his eye, he watched the quiet child negotiate her way through the meal.

Dead spit of Crossing, he brooded, and was surprised to find that, though on the surface of his mind, he was irritated at Elizabeth's temerity in bringing Alicia to the dining-room and the fact that she cost him money to maintain, his fury of earlier times had gone; he realized that he simply did not care; his life, his real life, had been transferred out of this house. He was content amid the swarm of businessmen on Exchange Flags, behind the Town Hall, or in the clubs and restaurants of the city.

He found physical comfort curled up in Mrs Jakes' feather bed; he never felt a twinge of desire for Elizabeth – let her and her damned daughter rot, he thought savagely.

Occasionally, he glanced up from his plate to look at Alicia, and he noted that the girl would sometimes lift her eyes towards Polly, as if to inquire if she were doing everything properly, and the parlourmaid would give her the faintest smile of approbation.

He did not normally notice who was waiting on him, because he was so used to a pair of hands putting food in front of him; they were simply a necessary part of the furniture. Now, he idly examined Polly, as she deftly went about her work. She was quite old, at least thirty, he surmised, a trim-looking woman with a good waist, though beginning to show the heaviness of middle age. He recollected that he paid her three pounds a year plus uniform and keep, and she obviously got along well with Elizabeth. For a moment, he toyed ma-liciously with the idea of dismissing her, simply to annoy Elizabeth, and then decided it was not worth the rumpus which would probably ensue.

Although Alicia was used to being alone a lot, resigned to being quiet, she was not without pluck. The silence of the dining-room, however, was almost unbearable and her disappointment very great. Promotion to the world of grown-ups had suggested something exciting. Instead, she had become acutely conscious of the animosity between Humphrey and Elizabeth. By the time Polly served the caramel pudding, she was so unnerved that she could hardly eat it and was grateful when Polly whipped her dish away.

At bedtime, soon afterwards, as Polly unbuttoned her dress for her and slipped it over her head, she asked tremulously, 'Do I have to go down every day, Polly? I'd much rather be as before – or I could have my dinner in the kitchen with Mrs Tibbs, if it would save you trouble?'

Kneeling in front of her, the dress in her arms, Polly smiled at her, 'Your Mam wants you to learn nice manners – to be a young lady, luv. That's why she wants you down. Perhaps she'll begin to take you out with her a bit, now you're a big girl. That would be a bit of all right, wouldn't it, now? You might get to know some other girls.'

'I suppose it would be nice.' She sounded so forlorn that Polly put her arms round the skinny child and hugged her to her.

But the remorseless dinner hour came round every day; Alicia found herself unable to eat much and Polly began to worry that she was losing weight. The maid wondered if she should point this out to Elizabeth. She talked it over with Mrs Tibbs and Fanny. They decided unanimously that they should not intrude on the delicate balance between husband and wife. Instead, Mrs Tibbs made a little bedtime supper for the girl and invited her to come down to the kitchen and sit by the fire to eat it. This hour in the warmth of the kitchen became the highlight of Alicia's day and she gained weight and joined gaily in the spirited repartee between the three servants.

Very lonely herself, Elizabeth began to call the child to the morning-room for half an hour or so after dinner. Though still handsome, Elizabeth had lost her vivacity and Alicia found these sessions boring. Her mother did not take her out with her, because she rarely went out herself; to entertain or to be entertained seemed increasingly tiring, and tradesmen were only too happy to send their errand boys with an assortment of goods on approval, from which she could choose; there was no need to go shopping.

The presence of Alicia in the morning-room provided a little undemanding company. She was also useful. She helped to wind knitting wool and sorted out Elizabeth's cottons and embroidery silks. And, increasingly, when the Reverend Clarence Browning and Florence called, she minded any off-spring which Florence might have decided to bring with her.

Her hair hanging in untidy wisps round her face, her hands reddened in a most unladylike way, Florence had for years been much too harassed by her unruly family and the calls made on her as a Vicar's wife, to pay much attention to her half-sister, about whose birth Clarence had told her a most shocking story.

When Alicia had been small, she had been sometimes sent to stay with Florence for a few days; but Alicia had dreaded the visits. Her eldest nephew, Frank, was a big, heavily-built boy who, as he grew older, bullied his siblings ruthlessly. He had once pinned a terrified Alicia in a corner of the garden wall and demanded that she lift up her petticoats and dress, so that he could see what she was like underneath. She had instinctively fought him off, and the encounter had been mercifully interrupted by one of his younger brothers in pursuit of a ball. After that, though he stalked her from time to time, she had made sure she always stayed close to his sisters. Fortunately for Alicia, as time went on, it became increasingly expensive for Elizabeth to hire a carriage to take her to the Vicarage, so she had not been to her sister's house for at least a year before Edward came on a leave long delayed by tribal uprisings near the Khyber Pass.

IV

On the day after her first essay into the dining-room, Polly told her on the way to school, 'Your Mama says Mr Edward's comin' home on leave tomorrer. Let's ask him to take you down town, to see the Punch and Judy show on the Quadrant.'

Alicia looked up, and asked in sudden hope, 'Do you think he would?'

'Oh, aye, he will. Don't ask 'im the first day, 'cos he'll be tired after the voyage.' I'll make sure he does take you, me darlin', she promised herself.

Edward did not dock in time to have dinner with his family the following evening. He did, however, come up to the nursery before Alicia went to bed, to see his little sister and Polly.

Despite his tanned face, he looked ill. Periodic bouts of malaria had taken their toll, and his sideburns were flecked with grey. His face lit up, however, when he entered the nursery. He swung Alicia up into his arms and told her that, in the three years since he had seen her, she had become a young lady. While Polly watched gravely, she put her arms round his neck and giggled delightedly. He looked over Alicia's head at her nanny, and Polly knew, with joy, that her time would come. She was so lucky, she thought, that Fanny and Mrs Tibbs slept in the basement. Only when young Master Charles was sleeping in his room on the nursery floor, did she and Edward have to be really careful.

Edward produced an ivory goddess from his pocket for Alicia and it was carefully installed on the mantelpiece, next to a paperweight which Charles had given her the previous Christmas.

Polly looked down at her little charge, as the child chatted animatedly with Edward, and was glad of the affection between the two. Alicia was not nearly so close to Charles – Master Charles had always struck Polly as someone who tolerated his family, but did not really *belong* to it, perhaps because he had been sent to boarding school so young. But Edward was grateful for love.

In response to a request whispered to him by Polly in the small hours of the morning, Edward declared his intention of going downtown to see the Punch and Judy Show and invited

Alicia to accompany him, and to have ice cream and lemonade in Fuller's Tea Rooms, afterwards. A thrilled Alicia acceptd the invitation.

The ladies taking afternoon tea in Fuller's glanced surreptitiously at the straight-backed, rather distinguished-looking dark man in civilian clothes that were too loose-fitting to be smart, and at the ash-blonde little girl in a plain white linen dress and untrimmed straw hat. 'A singular combination of colouring for a father and daughter,' murmured one elegant woman to her friend.

Edward and Alicia were blithely unaware of the watching eyes; they were both enjoying themselves, two shy, diffident people who could relate to each other.

As he watched Alicia mop up her strawberry ice, Edward thought about Polly. He could barely understand why he had felt so happy to slide, once more, into Polly's narrow bed. She was, after all, only a maid and no longer very good-looking. But she was totally unlike the girls of the Herring Fleet, as they were called, who came out to India each winter in the hope of finding a husband. Each year he looked at these young, hopeful products of ladies' seminaries, and swore that he could not afford to marry. But he knew that the real reason was Polly. Polly gave everything and asked nothing and, had she been of the same class, he knew that he would have married her long ago, and somehow juggled successfully with his finances. But even in a modest Foot Regiment, she would be ostracized by the other officers' wives because she was not a gentlewoman; marriage was out of the question.

Troubled about what might happen to her, he had, the previous night, fished around in his net purse and had given her a sovereign.

She had flushed, and had handed the gold coin back to him. 'You don't need to pay me,' she told him as she quivered against him and nuzzled into his neck, before kissing him goodbye behind her bedroom door.

He embraced her tightly and refused to take the money back. 'It's not a payment, my dear. It's a keepsake for a rainy day, because I dare not bring you a present; if Mother spotted anything unusual in your room, she'd dismiss you – and then what would we do?' He smiled down at her, the candlelight catching the harsh outlines of his face. 'You can put this away safely somewhere, because it's small. Servants – I mean, people – normally have savings for their old age.' He stroked her black hair tumbling down her back. 'I'm going to add to it – and you never know, you might be glad of it.'

So she accepted the gift and hid it in an old black and white cardboard pill-box at the back of the ancient chest of drawers in her bedroom.

Edward remained in England for a year, teaching modern tactics at Aldershot Military Camp. He had frequent leave, and Alicia became actively aware of a close relationship between her brother and her nanny, which she did not understand. She had taken their friendship for granted; after all, they both loved her – it was, to her, natural that they should be friends. It seemed to her, however, to be one of those many things which nobody ever mentioned, so she never brought the matter up. Throughout her life, there had been a close conspiracy between her and Polly against 'Them, downstairs'; she added the sound of soft footfalls, voices and a creaking bed next door, to her list of secrets, though, as she grew older, she wondered sometimes why Edward visited Polly only at night.

To Polly, it was a wonderful year. She lived in a mixed state of joy at having her lover so often with her and fear of having a child. As a defence against pregnancy, she used a wad of cottonwool, soaked in vinegar, tucked inside her, something she had learned from Great-aunt Kitty.

The single sovereign grew into a small pile, as Edward sought to give her a nest egg.

Chapter Eleven

I

On the evening on which Edward had returned from India, Alicia had taken her skipping rope into the garden. She was surprised to find Billy, Polly's brother, kneeling by Mr Bittle, the gardener, helping to weed a flowerbed. She had always regarded herself as Mr Bittle's assistant, and she approached the two bent figures with a sudden feeling of jealousy.

Billy scrambled to his feet and touched his forelock respectfully. Mr Bittle half turned to look up at her.

'Evenin', Miss Alicia,' he greeted her, his toothless mouth spread in a grin.

'Good evening, Mr Bittle. Good evening, Billy,' Alicia replied, a little frostily. 'What are you doing here, Billy?'

Billy swallowed. How to tell this pretty little girl that he was keeping out of the way of his drunken brother-in-law? Billy cleared his throat and responded uneasily to Alicia's question, 'I coom to see our Polly, only she's busy, like. So I asked Mr Bittle if I could help 'im – to fill in the time, like. I hope your Dad won't mind?'

'I see.' Alicia swung her skipping rope and continued down the path.

Though Billy dutifully handed his week's earnings over to his brother-in-law, Mike, his life with Mary and her husband was, within a week of his father's suicide, almost intolerable. Mike's iron fists and vindictive temper became a menace to him, so he had found temporary refuge in the Woodmans' garden.

On the second evening, Alicia paused to talk to him, as she passed him sitting on the steps. He was munching a large slice of bread which Polly had given him. He stood up immediately and took his cap off. She asked if he were going to help Mr Bittle weed that evening; Mr Bittle liked to get every scrap of weed out of the garden before the winter set in.

'Yes, Miss. He said 'e'd be glad of help.' He grinned shyly.

'Well, I might as well get my sackcloth apron and help, too.'

Amused at having two volunteers, old Mr Bittle thankfully left them to kneel and weed, while he pruned.

II

Eight days after James's suicide, his granddaughter, Theresa, Mary and Mike's eldest daughter, gave birth to an illegitimate daughter, father unknown. As she lay on a straw mattress and shrieked with the pain of childbirth, her cries were, most of the day, almost drowned by the sounds of singing and raucous laughter in the court. A seaman had returned home with three months' pay and his friends, including Mike, were busy drinking it away for him. A barrel of beer had been purchased and had been set up in a corner, and the stone flags of the court resounded to dancing boots.

As Mary worked with her daughter to speed the coming of the afterbirth, and the new baby squawked on its child-mother's breast, the beer barrel became empty and the party began to break up. Mike's unsteady tread could be heard in the downstairs room.

'What the hell's to do?' he shouted up the stairs, as he heard the baby's thin cry.

'Our Theresa's baby coom,' his wife shouted back, as she eased a fresh wad of newspaper under her daughter's buttocks.

'Christ!' Mike swung unsteadily into the tiny windowless bedroom. The smell of blood made him want to heave, as the afterbirth came clear. Behind him, Billy tried to peer round Mike's back to see what was happening. He had never seen a human birth, though he had watched the horses foal in the warehouse stables.

'Another bloody mouth to feed,' Mike growled, anger against his daughter rising in him. 'Haven't you taught her enough to make her keep clear o' the boys?'

'Now, Mike, you know how she got the kid,' Mary said in as soothing a voice as she could manage. 'She can't help it, with what she's havin' to do – and Father Gallagher frightened her so much, she wouldn't swaller wot Auntie Kitty offered her to get rid of it.'

Bubbling with frustrated rage, unable to accept that his daughter walked the streets, he turned about and bumped into Billy.

'Hm! Maybe she got it from nearer home,' he snarled down at the boy. He seized Billy by the shoulder and shook him. 'Eh?'

Billy cringed. 'Me? I never touched 'er. I never bin with a woman yet.' He tried to back down the narrow staircase. Mike gave him a push, and he turned and half tumbled, half stumbled, down the stairs. Mike came down after him.

'If this one isn't yours, the next one likely will be,' he shouted suddenly, and clouted the staggering boy across the face.

Billy squealed.

Mary deserted Theresa and rushed down the stairs.

'You leave our Billy alone, Mike. The lad's only just past eleven! Don't be daft.'

Billy tried to move towards the door. Mike lurched forward and caught him a stinging blow across the head. 'You keep out o' this,' he yelled at his wife. 'Months ago I seen him making eyes at her. He'll get her again, for sure.' Billy was caught in a corner of the room and whimpered helplessly, as he was struck again.

'Mike!' Mary caught his upraised arm and clung on to it. 'You know how she got this kid. It weren't Billy. I don't know how we'd go on without her money.'

'You sayin' I don't provide?' The question was full of drunken outrage.

'No, Mike!' Mary dropped his arm and backed away from

him. 'But without wot she brings in, we'd not eat, many a time.'

In his furious frustration at their need for his daughter's earnings, Mike forgot about Billy, and the boy slid noiselessly out of the open door into the court, where he stood panting against the blackened wall.

He heard Mary shriek, 'No, Mike! No!' and the thwack, as Mike hit her.

'She's no bloody good to anyone,' Mike yelled back. 'I'll larn her to bring a brat to disgrace us – and I'll larn you, too, you lazy bitch.'

As Mary began to scream steadily under Mike's beating, Billy burst into tears. He felt his way through the now deserted court to the street and began to run.

III

He ran down into Great Homer Street and trotted aimlessly along it. Where could he go? What could he do? It was almost certain that Mary would not dare to take him in again. He had given his last week's wages to Mike. He would have to work for nearly a week before he got any further wages, and he was already hungry. Tears made grubby lines down his face, as his feet thudded along the empty pavement and a fine rain began to soak through his clothes. His face throbbed and his teeth ached from the blows he had received. He was used to being trounced by the men with whom he worked, but nobody struck as hard as Mike did.

As darkness closed in, the public houses shut their doors and drunken groups began to roll slowly and unsteadily along the pavement. Billy became nervous for his immediate safety – drunks were not fussy if they found a boy, instead of a woman.

He hid himself in the dark doorway of a warehouse, huddled down and snivelled miserably. He longed despairingly for his mother.

Dare he go to Polly? What would her mistress say, if she heard him knocking on the back door in the middle of the night, even supposing the garden door leading to the alley were unlocked?

He wiped his nose on his sleeve. He decided that it did not matter how caustic Polly's mistress turned out to be, Polly was the only person he could ask for help with any hope of getting it. He heaved himself to his feet and set out through the drizzling rain on the long hike to Upper Canning Street.

He was much too afraid to go to the front door of the house; nobody of his low origins ever set foot on a front doorstep. He tried the gate, which was the tradesmen's entrance and opened on to a set of steps leading down to the front basement kitchen door. The cast-iron gate was locked and the spiked railings guarding the twelve-fo 't drop from the street did not encourage him to climb over.

He walked again down the street to the entrance to the back alleyway. Beyond the flickering gaslight at the entry, the darkness was so intense that, at first, his courage failed him. How was he going to find, in the dark, the correct, unnumbered, wooden back door?

Frustrated, he leaned his forehead against the unfriendly brick wall and cried again. He would have to wait until morning.

Behind him, on the pavement, he suddenly heard the measured tramp of heavy boots. The scuffer on the beat, he guessed. Fears of being arrested as a vagrant or for loitering with intent shot through his mind. As lightly as he could, he fled straight across the road and dived round a corner.

He found himself in a street of small shops and he crouched down in the darkest doorway he could find. The rain did not reach him there, and he dozed uncomfortably.

He was roused by the clip-clop of horses' hooves and the rattle of drays, as milkmen and coalmen began their rounds. The rain had passed and the street shone in the early morning sun. He had little idea of time, except that it was early, so he remained where he was, cramped and aching, until he heard a window being flung open and a woman's voice from the shopkeeper's flat above him.

Unsure of exactly where he was, he got up and stretched and then joined a growing number of people hurrying to work. Caught up in the crowd, he was soon lost.

In a desperate need to relieve himself, he turned into a back alley and thankfully paid a call against the wall. Then he went slowly back to the street he had left, to glance rather hopelessly up and down it. Finally, he stopped another youth, dressed as poorly as he was, to ask where Upper Canning Street was.

'Oh, aye. You're best off to come along o' me. I work in Falkner Square garden.'

In their clumsy boots, they walked along together, and the gardener's boy pointed out the side entry which led to the house's back alley.

'Ta, ever so,' Billy said gratefully.

When he tried the door, it was bolted on the inside. He looked up at the ten-foot high brick wall guarding the garden; to deter thieves and vandals, it had great shards of glass embedded in the top.

'Oh, Jaysus!' he wailed.

He stared at the door's unyielding woodwork and was just about to turn away, to see if the tradesmen's entrance at the front was yet unlocked, when there was the sound of a woman's quick step on the other side and the bolt was drawn back.

The door was opened, as if the woman were about to glance into the alley. Instead, she was faced with a small, but strong-looking youth.

'Oh!' she shrieked, and slammed the door in his face. He heard the bolt grating shut again.

He shouted, 'Don't be afraid, Missus. You know me. I'm Polly's brother – Polly Tyson.'

'Whoja say?'

'Billy Tyson. I'm looking for me sister, Polly.'

The bolt once more squeaked open. Fanny put her head cautiously round the door, to take a good look at him. Then she opened the door wide. 'Give me a proper fright, you did, standin' there. I were lookin' for the midden men.' She surveyed his dusty rags of clothing, which looked even worse than usual after being soaked and then slept in in a doorway. 'Coom in. You can sit on back step, like always. She's up and layin' breakfast for the Master. I'll get 'er for you, though.'

Billy followed her up the garden path, past the pretty summer house and well-laid out flower beds, one or two roses still in bloom. To him, the garden always looked fit for the old Queen herself to sit in.

As they descended the steps into the brick-lined area surrounding the back door, Fanny said, 'I'll tell Mrs Tibbs you're here and I'll get Polly; but you'll have to wait.'

Billy nodded and sat down on the steps still wet from rain. He shivered with the damp.

When Fanny opened the kitchen door, a delicious smell of frying pigs' ears was emitted, and Billy could have cried again, this time with hunger.

Polly came hurrying out of the kitchen door, her face wrinkled with anxiety. 'What's to do?' she asked.

He told her, and then went on, 'I can't go back, Pol. Mary'll get it again, if I do – I'm sure of it.' He looked at her imploringly.

Polly sighed. 'I don't know what to do for yez, luv. I really don't. Nor for poor Mary neither.' She clasped her arms across her breast, and looked round her in perplexity. Then she said, 'See here. I got to serve the Master and take up the Mistress's breakfast, and give Miss Alicia hers and get her ready for church – and I got to take her to church.' She looked round, seeking somewhere dry for him to sit. 'You sit on the loo here and wait for me.' She opened the door of the servants' lavatory, as she looked at her brother's bruised face and bloodshot eyes. 'You bin out *all* night?'

'Aye.'

''Ve you got any money at all?'

'No.' He snuffled miserably.

'Well, you stick here, and I'll ask old Tibbs if she can spare a bit o' porridge for yez.'

Used to Polly's begging a little food for Mr Bittle's helper, Mrs Tibbs splashed a ladle of thick porridge into an old soup bowl and pushed a tin spoon into it. She shoved it across the kitchen table to Polly. 'I don't know what the Master's goin' to say, if he ever finds out what I give that kid,' she grumbled.

'Ah, he won't find out if you don't tell 'im,' Polly assured her. 'Ta, Mrs Tibbs.' She took the bowl out to her brother and then flitted silently back upstairs to the dining-room in time to hear Humphrey Woodman's quick steps coming downstairs. 'Send up porridge, quick,' she panted down the blower to Mrs Tibbs. ''Is Nibs is comin'.'

While Mrs Tibbs prepared Elizabeth Woodman's boiled egg and thin bread and butter and tea, Polly came out to the area carrying her own bowl of porridge. Billy opened the lavatory door as she put the dish on the step. She ran back into the kitchen, to return with two big mugs of tea drawn from the enamelled teapot on the back of the kitchen range. 'There's lots of sugar and milk in it,' she told her brother with a smile, as she handed him one. A small grin relaxed his pinched face, before he eagerly gulped down the hot drink.

Polly leaned against the door jamb of the lavatory, as she began to shovel porridge hastily into her mouth. She said, 'I bin thinkin' what to do, and what I think is that you should go to Great-aunt Kitty. She's only got one little room, but she'd never deny you a corner to sleep – and she might be glad to have a strong lad with her at her age. You can give her your wages for your keep. It'll keep you out of the workhouse or an 'ome.'

It was an idea that had not occurred to Billy, but he looked uneasily at Polly, as he replied, 'She's a witch.'

Polly laughed. 'Not her. She's an old, old woman wot knows a lot, that's all. She's not even off 'er chump, like some old biddies. Remember how gentle she was with Mam?'

Billy reluctantly nodded agreement; she'd been gentle with him, too.

'She might be able to think up somethin' better for you. I don't know what – but she might. She knows everybody.'

The tea and porridge restored Billy's spirits a little. And Polly's suggestion at least gave him hope of avoiding the workhouse – God and his Angels preserve him from *that*. Nevertheless, Great-aunt Kitty was uncanny – she seemed to know what you were going to do, even before you thought of it yourself!

'Think she'll do it?'

'Sure she will. What else, anyway? And mind you go to work come Monday.'

He laughed suddenly, and gave her a playful nudge. 'You sound just like Mam.'

Then, at the memory of his tart, capable mother, his face fell and he looked down at his boots. There was a silence between them.

Polly gave a tremulous sigh. 'Poor Mam,' she said.

She rummaged in her skirt pocket and brought out a six-pence, which she handed to Billy. 'Here's a tanner to help you out, duck,' she added more briskly. 'I got to get back to me work – there's Mrs Tibbs callin' me.' She picked up the mugs and porridge plates from the steps. 'Away, now. Give me love to Auntie, and tell 'er as I told you to come to 'er.'

IV

Though Great-aunt Kitty was surprised she was not displeased to see Billy at her door. He told her that Polly had sent him. She grasped his elbow with long, bony fingers and drew him into her tiny, foetid room.

'Coom in, and tell me what's to do,' she invited, in her high-pitched, cracked voice. 'Like a cuppa tea?'

Without waiting for a reply, she pushed him towards a wooden settle and then picked up a pair of bellows from the hearth and inserted them at the base of a few embers in her fireplace. She blew the embers into tiny flame, then added a few small pieces of coal to them and plunked a sooty kettle on top. She pushed an indolent black cat off a rocking chair and sat down herself. The cat stalked over to Billy and sniffed at him.

Billy shuddered and recoiled slightly from it, movements noted with amusement by his great-aunt. 'Tea won't be long,' she assured him. 'It's not that old.'

The cat sat down opposite Billy and yawned. It seemed to Billy that it was looking through him with its great green eyes; a real witch's cat.

He jumped when Kitty got up suddenly and went to a wall cupboard. She opened it, to reveal a surprisingly large store of food for one so poor and elderly. She took down a loaf and a piece of cheese and put them on the table, together with a bottle of whisky. With a knife which looked like a dagger to a nervous Billy, she cut a big slice of bread and then a slice of cheese to put on top of it. ''Ere you are, duck,' she said, as she handed it to him.

With his mouth full, Billy began to relax and he told her about Theresa's child and her father's rage.

'Aye, I saw Theresa when I were with your Mam; I know'd the kid were about due. And I know Theresa's on the game. She should've done wot I told her; then she wouldn't have had to 'ave it.' She paused to reflect, while Billy watched her over his slice of bread and cheese. Then she said, 'Anyways, Mary should've called me to help with the lyin'-in. Mike wouldn't 've touched either of 'em, if I'd bin there.'

Billy swallowed his current mouthful of bread with a gulp, as he again shivered. He had no doubt that Great-aunt Kitty, with her unearthly powers, could stop Mike dead, if she wanted to.

The old lady took the kettle off the fire and poured the reboiled tea into two tin mugs, one of which she handed to Billy; the other she laid on the hob to keep warm for herself. She slopped some milk from a milkcan into both mugs and followed it with generous spoonfuls of sugar from a tin. Then she offered the boy another slice of bread which, despite his timorousness, he accepted eagerly.

He wondered how she managed to have such a handsomely

full food cupboard, though the rest of her room looked as skint as that of a family the day before payday, when everything pawnable would have been pawned.

Great-aunt Kitty was, in fact, a busy woman. Like many elderly women, she was in demand to help to deliver infants or nurse the sick or lay out the dead, for which she was paid a little either in cash or in food. Her main income came, however, from moneylending, illegal lending to hard-pressed housewives in nearby streets. She would lend them sixpence on a Monday, provided they paid her back eightpence on the following Saturday, when most of them got their housekeeping money from their husbands. The women were enormously grateful to her. She enjoyed their goodwill until they fell behind with their payments and she arrived like an angry raven on their doorsteps to collect. Knowing the borrowers' ignorance of the law she frightened them with threats of Court proceedings, or, more practically, with the wrath of their husbands if she told tales of the wives' borrowing. If they failed to pay her, even after being solemnly cursed with gruesome maledictions, she still made a tremendous profit from those who did meet their obligations.

When she had heard Billy through to the end, she leaned forward and shovelled a small pile of damp, slack coal over the little fire, to keep it burning slowly without having to use larger lumps. Then she sat back in her wooden rocking-chair and thoughtfully stroked her chin, which was as thickly covered with white hairs as that of an old man.

After a minute or two, during which Billy watched her nervously, she suddenly asked, 'You a Methody or a Catholic? I were never sure.'

Billy was nonplussed. He had never been to any kind of church. Caught between a harried Roman Catholic mother and a father who was an oddity who went to open air Wesleyan meetings, and living in a court not very often visited by clerics of any persuasion, he had no idea what he was. His mother had once taught him how to say a rosary; his father had been firm that one must pray directly to God, though, mostly, he

128

had assured Billy, prayers were not answered. For himself, as a toddler in the court, Billy had learned that it was essential for survival to join the solidly Roman Catholic male population in ambushing and beating up Protestants on Orange Day – and to duck participation in Roman Catholic Processions on Saints' Days if he did not want a pummelling from Protestant lads.

Nonplussed by Kitty's query regarding his religious affiliations, he muttered, 'I dunno.' He did not dare to take a chance on settling upon one or the other religion, in case it turned out to be the wrong answer to give a witch.

'Well, if you was a Methody, now, that Holy Joe wot come to see your Dad, he might help you.' Her toothless mouth spread in a wry grin. She considered herself a Roman Catholic, but she knew that if she asked a local priest to help Billy, the boy would probably end up in the Kirkdale Industrial Home or some similar institution, which in her opinion would be like condemning him to hell everlasting. She said aloud, 'And I don't want you to end up in the Workie either.'

The mention of the Workhouse was enough to make Billy begin to blench. 'Oh, no, Auntie! Can't I stay with you?'

She looked at him not unkindly. 'It's whether I can stay with *you*, duck. I 'aven't got that long.' She was silent while she considered the increasing swelling of her stomach, the fierce ache in her back, her sticklike thinness, and the opium she bought from Vietnamese sailors to ease her pain. No, she had not long. But she, too, was determined to stay out of the Workhouse by never going near the Dispensary, never mind a Workhouse doctor. She would die in this very room, she was determined of that, and in her mattress lay enough silver coins to pay for a decent funeral.

Billy stared at her. His heart raced with a fear of the ruthless discipline of charitable Homes and the semi-starvation in the Workhouse, of the beatings, the confinement, the bullying and misuse of him by other inmates, the toil of grinding bones or breaking stones. Holy God, preserve him from such places! He had heard that in the Workie you were kept so hungry that it was a relief to eat the rotting marrow out of the bones before you crushed them for fertilizer.

Like everyone else, he was terrified of crossing the path of a Workhouse Master. Better to go to gaol, any day – at least there, you eventually came to the end of your sentence and were let out.

'Let me stay, Auntie,' he pleaded. 'If you want to move to another room, I could help you. I'm strong.'

'You can't help me where I'm goin',' she replied drily. She sucked her toothless gums and poured herself another cup of black, stewed tea. Then, with shaking fingers, she managed to pull the cork out of the whisky bottle and splashed some of the contents into her cup.

She rammed the cork back into the bottle, and said to Billy, ''Ere, put this back into cupboard for me, before a neighbour comes in and spots it.' A decent display of abject poverty was, she had always felt, necessary to her personal safety.

As Billy obeyed, she continued the line of conversation. 'If I were to send you to live with anybody we knows, the same thing would happen as 'as happened at Mary's – the man wouldn't want you around – particularly as you grows bigger. You could work your heart out and give 'em everything you earned, without keeping a meg for yourself – but soon they'd get fed up with yez – and out you'd go. And you'd have no place – and that could mean the Workie.' She sipped her laced tea thoughtfully, as Billy's heart sank ever lower.

She noted his expression, and grinned at him. 'It int that bad, duck. The more I think about it the more I think you'd better be a Methody – after all, your Dad was – and I think we'll do it. Tomorrer we'll go down to the chapel and see the Holy Joe wot came after your Mam died. He might have some new idea – and we can always say No, if we don't like it.'

Chapter Twelve

On the last day of September 1896, as the rays of the evening sun gleamed softly over the smoking chimney pots, Billy Tyson eased open the Woodmans' alley door and crept quietly down the path towards the kitchen.

'What do you want?' inquired a disembodied female voice.

Billy whirled round. He could see no one. He glanced nervously up at the house windows above him; they were empty of people.

There was a chuckle from high in the apple tree to his left. He turned and looked up. A pair of long, black-stockinged legs topped by divided drawers swung suddenly down to a lower branch. Then Alicia jumped in a flurry of spreading calico pinafore and pleated serge skirt. He caught an embarrassing glimpse of the prettiest little white bottom, as she landed on all fours, bringing with her a shower of small green apples and loose leaves. She picked herself up and rubbed her hands free of bits of damp grass.

Though Alicia had accepted him with almost the same ease that she did Mr Bittle, Billy was aware of the big social gap between them. He whipped off his cap and waited cautiously for her to speak.

'How are you, Billy?' she asked cordially.

'I'm all right, thank you, Miss.' Then, unable to contain his excitement, he burst out, 'I got some good news for our Polly.'

'She's clearing up dinner, but I can get her for you, if you like.'

He blushed and glanced uneasily away from her, and then answered, 'If you would, Miss – for a minute, like.'

She noticed his change of colour under the heavy grime, and she smiled. She flitted across the grass and down the steps to the kitchen door, her silver-fair hair, for once unplaited, flowing softly behind her. He watched her, fascinated, as she lifted the latch and went indoors; she was so white, unlike the young girls in the courts.

When Alicia entered the kitchen she found Polly unloading the dirty dishes from the dumb-waiter. On hearing that Billy wanted to speak to her, she left her work and hurried anxiously into the brick area and up the stone steps towards him.

When Billy saw her worried face, he laughed and shouted to her, 'I'm going to Canada, Pol. Day after tomorrow – to work on a farm.' He ignored Alicia, who had followed behind her.

Polly paused at the top of the steps. Her mouth fell open. Then she gasped, 'To Canada? Holy Mother save us! How come, luv?'

He persuaded her to sit down on one of the steps, while he explained to her about Great-aunt Kitty's and his visit to the Methodist minister.

'I'm going proper quick 'cos I'm taking the place of a boy what died last week; the Methody is fixin' it. Ordinary, like, they don't send kids out at this time – they send 'em at the beginning of summer. But they got so many that they're sending this lot special through the Kirkdale Home.'

Polly was appalled. For her brother to be delivered to the untender mercies of the Kirkdale Industrial School, even for a few days, was shocking enough to her; to be sent to Canada was like being tipped over the edge of the earth.

Billy was babbling on about the Methodist minister. 'He says I'll get a farm of me own one day, if I work. A farm, Pol!'

'You'll never come back, our kid,' Polly wailed. 'People go there – and that's the last you ever hear of them.'

'I'll come back,' he promised earnestly. 'I'll come and fetch you when I got a farm.'

Polly's eyes glistened with tears and she twisted the ends of her apron with agitated hands. Alicia had crouched at her nanny's feet while she listened. Now she put her hand on Polly's knee, and said, 'Don't cry, Polly, dear. Billy'll write to you, won't you, Billy?'

''Course, I will, Miss. I'm not that good at me letters, but I know enough to write – don't you fret, our Polly,' he reassured his sister. 'Anyways, when I work on a farm, the farmer has to send me to school. The Methody promised.'

Alicia looked up at Polly. 'There, you see. You don't have to worry.'

Polly nodded her head hopelessly. 'But it snows all the time there – and there's the Red Indians and the Frogs – I mean the French – it int safe.' All the novels that Polly had read about the American West came to the fore of her mind.

'I'm goin' to get warm clothes given me,' Billy assured her. 'And I'm not going where the French are.'

'Where are you going, Billy?' Alicia asked.

'I don't know exactly, Miss. It depends where the farmer is who wants me. I have to write home and say where I am, soon as I get settled.' He turned to Polly. 'Cheer up, Pol. There's lots of us going – all orphans, like me.'

'It's dangerous, chook. It's too dangerous.' She wiped her damp face with her apron.

'It's not – they wouldn't send us if it was. I'll save me wages and I'll buy a farm.' He sighed blissfully. 'What a chance, Polly! Dad would've jumped at it.' He leaped up and spread out his arms to encompass the pretty garden. 'When I got a farm, you can come and make a garden like this for yourself.'

Polly threw her apron over her head and began to keen. 'It'll take ages. How will I go on without you? There'll only be Mary and me.'

'And me,' interjected Alicia softly, suddenly shaken by the idea that Polly could leave her.

Though Billy was still young, he had all the common sense of his mother. But for the moment he was far away, dreaming wildly of a little house on land as big as Sefton Park, a house with apple trees around it. Flitting in his mind's eye was a little creature living there with him, a creature with long fair hair and a wicked chuckle who liked climbing apple trees. After the destruction of his way of life that sad September, he had suddenly been handed a little hope and it was almost too much for him to cope with.

Chapter Thirteen

I

The winter came to Liverpool with gales howling in from the Atlantic. Rain pelted on the burgeoning city, swirled in the filthy courts, flooding the latrines and spreading stomach ailments amongst the sodden inhabitants. Hardly strong enough to creep across the yard to the privy, Great-aunt Kitty took to her bed, swallowed a large dose of a drug bought some time back from a Thai stoker, and died alone.

It was two days before the tenant of the house noticed her absence, and it was only when Polly went to visit her three weeks later, on one of her afternoons off, that the family learned of her death. By then, the room was occupied by someone else, and the landlord said that all the old lady's possessions had been thrown in the midden in case she had died of something catching.

Through her tears, Polly upbraided the man for not sending for Mary or Mrs Fox. 'You knew where to find them, you lousy bugger,' she shouted at him. But in her heart she knew that the room had been picked clean by him and he had then reported the death to the Medical Officer as being that of a destitute old woman. Like her niece, Bridie Tyson, Great-aunt Kitty had had a pauper's funeral.

Polly had seen it happen before. Boiling with anger but unable to prove any misdoing, she went away to see Mary and to grieve with her for the death of a wise old woman. She did not mention her loss to Alicia.

II

One day in January, as Alicia sat at the nursery table carefully sketching into her botany exercise book the root system of a piece of Shepherd's Purse, Polly looked up from her mending, and said, 'You know, I'm that raddled with worry about our Billy. Three months and no word from him.'

'You could go to see the Reverend Whoever-he-is at the Methodist Chapel, and ask if he's any news.'

'I already done it on me Sunday off. He were proper nice and he said the children reached the Home in Toronto safely. He says, though, that each kid is supposed to write home to say his exact address, 'cos they get sent all over.'

'I suppose he can write, Polly?'

'Aye, he can a bit. Me Mam sent 'im to dame school, same as me. 'Course, I never learned me letters proper – it were Master Charles wot really taught me.' She bit her cotton off with her teeth, and then said, 'But he's smart enough to get someone to help 'im, if he needed to.'

Alicia leaned back from her drawing and put her pencil down on the table. 'Perhaps Canadian stamps are too expensive for him,' she suggested.

'Well, I dunno. Surely wherever he's workin', they'd give 'im one stamp, so as he could write home?'

III

Alicia was right. Everything is too expensive to those who have nothing. Even if Billy had been free to go to the Metis village some twenty miles from the tiny sod hut in which he found himself, he had no money to buy a piece of paper, a pencil or a stamp.

To a street arab like Billy, though used to the discipline of work, the Canadian Children's Home which was his first destination felt like a prison. With the sixty other children who had travelled with him, he endured it for a week, while he was supplied with warm clothing, new boots and a Bible to put in the almost empty tin trunk given to him by the Kirkie. He then said a cheerful goodbye to the other children and was put on an immigrant train travelling westward, in the care of the conductor.

For twenty-four hours, the train chugged its way through what appeared to be endless forest and gradually his spirits fell. The immigrant families in the train spoke other languages and ignored him. He ate the two slices of bread given to him by the Home.

In the chilly, early morning hours, the train stopped at a wayside halt, and the conductor let him down on to the tiny wooden platform. There was no sign of any building or people and he could not see anything which indicated the name of the place.

As the conductor helped the boy lift his small trunk down from the train, he said cheerfully, 'I've no doubt somebody'll be along to collect you as soon as it's light.'

As he blew his whistle for the train to proceed, he looked down at the thin, small figure in its shabby secondhand over-coat and cloth cap standing forlornly by the tin trunk, and he thought with compassion, 'Another poor little bastard, God help him.'

As the train vanished into the forest, Billy looked around him and absolute terror began to grip him. Beyond the end of the tiny platform huge pine trees, black in the dawn light, pressed in upon him. The eery silence was broken only by the soughing of the wind through the wall of ever-greens.

Where was he?

He wanted to scream in terror, and run – run anywhere. He looked along the shiny track of the railway lines over which he had travelled. It had been like this – just trees – all day yesterday, with only tiny settlements in clearings by halts like this or a solitary Indian watching the train pass.

He sat down on his trunk and clasped his arms round his knees and tucked his head down. His breath came in quick gasps, making a small cloud in the cool air.

'Holy Jaysus, send somebody,' he prayed. 'Anybody!'

There was a rustle in the undergrowth and stories of bears rushed into his head. He screamed, and clutched himself tighter.

'You William?' a voice inquired.

At first the question did not penetrate his paralysed mind, but when it was repeated, he slowly looked up.

What he saw was not reassuring. A strangely garmented man with a dark face framed by black plaits down either side loomed in the half light.

The boy took a moment to find his voice. Then he quavered, 'Yes. I'm Billy Tyson.' He got slowly to his feet.

'Come.'

Billy looked uncertainly down at his trunk. The man bent down to take hold of the handle at one end and gestured to Billy to take the other end. Watching the stranger all the time, Billy did as he was bidden. The man smelled strongly of wood smoke, and his coarse, woollen coat was heavily stained at the front. His trousers, tucked into knee-high laced boots, seemed to be made of skin and were equally dirty.

Without a further word, the man led him down a narrow, slatted slope at one end of the wooden platform and along an almost invisible track through the trees.

The path led into a cleared circle in the centre of which were huddled several log cabins. Smoke curled from stone chimneys. A dog barked at their approach and was joined by a chorus of yapping from numerous other tethered canines, all with big fluffy tails and heavy coats.

As they came towards the cabins, the wind brought another odour besides that of burning wood, an odour all too familiar to Billy from his work in dockside warehouses, the sickening smell of untanned or partially tanned hides.

They put down the trunk at the threshold of one of

the cabins. The man opened the door and preceded him inside.

As Billy hesitated on the doorstep, it seemed to him, in the poor light of an oil lamp and an open fire, that he saw nothing but eyes. They peered out at him from rough bunks against the walls; they stared up at him from the floor and from round a wooden table.

Gradually the eyes had faces added to them and then untidy bodies. A woman was squatting by the fire, cooking something on a heated stone. She wore a long, brightly printed cotton skirt with what looked like a black, woollen bodice. As the man sat himself down at the table, she glanced up at Billy and said to him in a strong Scottish accent, 'Come to the fire. You must be cold.'

As Billy nervously advanced towards the blaze, she rose and gingerly picked up some of the hot bannock she had been cooking and put it in front of the man at the table. She spoke to him in a strange language, as she took down a mug from a shelf and poured out coffee for him from a pot which had been standing in the hearth.

The dark brown children – for most of the eyes belonged to children – slowly began to gather round Billy. They touched his long overcoat and giggled, black eyes reflecting the dancing flames of the fire. He felt suddenly safer and grinned back at them.

Their mother was going to a tumbled bed at the further end of the big, stone fireplace. She carried a mug of coffee with her, and a thin, wrinkled hand took it from her. A white head was turned. For a second, Billy was the recipient of a glance so piercing that it seemed to the boy that in that moment a total inventory of him had been taken. Then the eyes were politely averted.

Billy timidly extended his hands to the fire and rubbed them. If the weather was as cold as this in October, he wondered what it would be like in January; he wished he had some gloves.

He looked surreptitiously round the hut. The interior was

not unlike the cellar dwelling in which he had grown up, except that the smell was different and the fire seemed enormous.

The woman put a warm piece of bannock into his hand and then distributed pieces to the children. He stood near the fire with the other youngsters and wolfed down the food gratefully, while the woman explained to him in good English that he was to wait with them until full daylight and then a man would come for him.

She turned to her husband and spoke to him in their own language. He nodded, and grunted agreement. 'Macdonald,' he said directly to Billy.

The woman poured coffee for herself, and Billy watched her shyly. Then he ventured a question. 'Are you farmers?'

She took a sip from her coffee, and then answered, 'No. We trap.'

The blank look on Billy's face made an older girl begin to giggle, and her mother, realizing that he did not understand, explained, 'We trap animals – beaver and foxes mostly – for their fur. Soon it'll be time for my husband to set his trapline.'

At this interesting reply, a whole mass of questions tumbled into Billy's head, but the parents were obviously taciturn, so he ventured one more only; he felt he had to know the answer. 'Are you Red Indians?' he inquired, with breathless interest.

The woman smiled, and glanced at her silent husband placidly stirring his coffee. Billy realized suddenly that, unlike the rest of the family, her eyes were blue like his mother's. 'No,' she responded slowly. 'We're Metis people.'

Billy was very disappointed; he had looked forward to meeting a Red Indian, complete with feathered headdress and tomahawk, as described to him by Polly. He wondered what a Metis was.

The mother turned to the children and said something in the second language. A small boy opened the door. The morning sun was flooding the clearing with light, and the children wandered out into the warming sunshine, except for two babies crawling about on the floor. The biggest youngster, a girl with a long black plait, pulled at Billy's sleeve and indicated that he should go out with her. He glanced back at the woman and the quiet brown man drinking his coffee. She nodded agreement, so he followed the girl outside, at the same time struggling out of his coat. He laid coat and cap on top of his trunk. Without them, he hoped that other people would not stare at him; his jacket, breeches, long socks and black boots would, perhaps, look similar to the garments of his Metis host.

The girl indicated to him to wait, while she went to pick up a couple of buckets from beside the corner of the cabin. The tiny settlement was gradually coming to life. A man in a tall, widebrimmed hat brought out a horse, mounted it and rode away into the forest. An old woman crouched over a smoky fire with fish drying over it. Innumerable children ran about and then came to stare at him. The girl turned to shout at them in the strange tongue, which everybody except himself seemed to understand.

As the girl returned with a clanking pail in each hand, he asked, 'Can you speak English?'

The girl was the same height as he was. Her almond eyes twinkled at the question. 'Yes. Why?'

'Well, nobody else seems to, except your Mam.'

'A lot of us can speak it – if we feel like it! Even Dad knows it, though he speaks Algonquin mostly. Mother's father was from Scotland. He came out here to buy furs and then he married Grandma and stayed, to trap himself.'

While Billy digested this information, she led him along a path from behind the cabin to a little river, where two women were filling buckets with water.

Steadying herself by holding on to an overhanging tree branch, she reached down and filled the buckets from the swiftly flowing water.

Billy insisted on carrying one of the filled buckets back for her and in tipping its contents into a barrel by the cabin door. It took three trips to the river to fill the barrel, and Billy's aid to the girl brought forth some good-humoured jeering from a couple of youths lounging in the doorway of one of the homes.

Billy did not understand the words, but realized they were disparaging, and he asked, 'What did they say?'

She hesitated, and then said, with a grin, 'They said you were doing women's work and you must be like a woman.'

Billy scowled. 'Dirty bastards,' he snarled, but decided that it was not worth a fight, particularly when the opponents were taller.

They had just put away the buckets, when a heavily-built white man clumped past them and, without knocking, entered the cabin.

He came out again almost immediately. Billy stared apprehensively at him. 'Come on, you,' he ordered the boy testily. He bent and pushed Billy's overcoat and cap into the dust, to pick up the trunk and swing it on to his back.

Billy picked up his coat and cap and then glanced back at the girl. Her face was expressionless. His earlier fears returned to him, but he said to her, 'Thank your Mam for me.' Then he ran after Macdonald.

His new master crossed the railway line. On the other side was a lane where a horse and cart stood waiting. The man slung the trunk into the back of the cart and indicated that Billy should climb in after it.

He scrambled up beside a heavy sack of flour and stood uncertainly for a moment, not sure what to do.

'Sit down, you stupid bugger,' Macdonald snarled.

Billy hastily squatted down, his back against the side of the cart. Some of the children from the settlement had followed them and were standing on the higher ground of the railway embankment. He waved to them and they waved back. He felt better.

Macdonald mounted the driver's seat, cracked his whip and the horse started forward. The sudden upward jerk of the two-wheeled cart sent both Billy and his trunk skidding backwards to the tail. Macdonald laughed.

Ruefully rubbing a banged elbow, Billy crawled to the front

of the cart and sat with his back to the driver. His fears returned.

The lady at the Toronto Home had explained to him that he would be bound to this white man until he was eighteen – and that would be nearly seven years. He was to work for him and, in return, he would be fed and clothed and sent to church and to school. At sixteen, he would be entitled to wages – two or three dollars a month. But in the streets and warehouses of Liverpool, Billy had seen types like Macdonald before and he was filled with dread.

Peeping over the side of the cart, he watched with despair the everlasting ranks of trees on either side of the track. Where was he? The train conductor must have known the name of the halt, but Billy had been expecting a proper station with a name on it, so it had not occurred to him to ask the man. He peered once more at the crumpled label tied to the buttonhole at the neck of his coat; it had a confusing series of numbers and Macdonald's name; how could he have known that the numbers were a surveyor's description of a particular quarter-section of land in an area of forest just opened up to settlers?

Chapter Fourteen

I

The cart bumped its way slowly along a narrow lane thickly carpeted with pine needles. Once or twice, between breaks in the trees, Billy caught a glimpse of a twist of smoke against the intensely blue sky, a suggestion of human habitation. There seemed, however, to be no sound left in the world, except for the squeak of the cart's wheels and the muffled clop of the horse's hooves. To Billy, used to the hurly-burly of the docks and the city, to a boy who had never even seen the English countryside, it was extremely frightening. But most of all, he feared the man who was driving. At one point, he got up enough courage to kneel up behind him and ask him, 'Where are we? What's the name of the place we're goin' to?'

The response was curt. 'Sit down, and mind your own business.'

Billy sat down. He longed for something to eat and for a horse blanket like the one Macdonald had across his knees, to wrap round himself to keep out the chill invading him.

They turned off the track they had been following on to an even bumpier one, and then several more turns, each time on to a narrower path. The pine trees closed in more tightly than ever, brushing their fronds against the cart and shutting out the sunlight. Billy felt as if a gaoler had closed the door on him.

In the afternoon, when it seemed as if they would never get out of the forest, the track debouched into an area where raw tree stumps indicated a fresh clearing. There was a large vegetable patch partially harvested; and newly washed clothes had been laid out to dry over a few bushes which had already lost their leaves to autumn. From a rise in the ground, came an unexpected plume of smoke. A baby wailed in steady, demanding notes, and from a nearby tree, a tethered goat complained loudly. Billy looked at the goat in bewilderment and decided it must be some kind of sheep.

The driver shouted at the horse and the cart stopped at the rise in the ground. Billy kneeled up to see over the side of the cart. To his astonishment, he was in front of a cabin half-buried in the ground. The roof was covered with turf.

Nearby, a rough enclosure had been made of logs and looked as if it were in process of being roofed with timber.

A woman holding a tiny baby wrapped in fur came up out of the cabin. She had on a black skirt and shawl, such as Billy's mother had worn; her long, narrow face was red, as if she had been in the sun too long; her hair was scraped back from it and tied in a knot on top of her head. As Macdonald climbed down from the cart, she said in a strong Scottish accent and without preamble, 'I want some water.'

Billy climbed carefully over the back of the cart and dropped to the ground. He was stiff with cold and the long hours of sitting in an awkward position. 'Give 'im the bucket,' Macdonald growled.

To Billy he said, 'Put that fancy overcoat down and get 'er some water.' He pointed to a narrow path leading into the trees on the other side of the clearing.

Bewildered and scared, Billy was slow in finding a place to lay his coat down. The man came to where he stood glancing anxiously about him, and shouted into his face, 'Get a move on. When I tell you something, you *run* and do it. Understand?' Bloodshot eyes glared at him from a bristled face.

Billy hastily bundled up the coat and laid it near the logs which formed the visible part of the cabin. Mrs Macdonald picked up a galvanized bucket and handed it to him. He snatched it from her and ran towards the path which had been indicated. The pines' long fingers seemed to lock over his head, but after a couple of hundred yards the pencil-thin path sloped down to a narrow swift-flowing river with more close-packed forest louring at him from the further bank.

For a moment, he could not think how to dip the bucket into sufficiently deep water to fill it without getting his boots soaked. In a semi-panic, he scouted up the river a few yards, following another little path. At the end of it he found a point where the river swirled in and out of a slight curve in the bank. He lay on his stomach and dipped the bucket in.

When he first tried to lift the vessel out, it was so heavy that he splashed half the contents over its sides. He tried filling it again and, when hauling it out, he rested it, half way, on a jutting stone. He scrambled to his feet and managed to get it up on to the bank. He carried it slowly and carefully back to the cabin.

'You took your time,' the woman snarled at him, and snatched the pail from him so clumsily that she splashed herself. 'Careful!' she shrieked at him, as he looked helplessly at her, his throat constricted with dread of the whole place and its inhabitants.

He spent until nightfall helping Macdonald roof the unfinished building he had noticed on his arrival. He was sick with hunger.

For the most part, the time was spent in silence, but he did learn that Macdonald was clearing his first quarter-section. This alerted Billy to the fact that an immigrant could, indeed, own land, and he ventured a cautious question or two as to how the quarter-section had been acquired.

Macdonald told him that when he first came out from Dundee, he had worked on the farm of an established settler. Later on, when he had obtained the land, he had commenced to clear it during quiet months on his employer's farm. The family had lived in a lean-to tent while he built the cabin. He had hoped to get a crop in that summer, but had managed only a large vegetable patch.

'If we get through this winter,' he told Billy gloomily, 'it'll be a bleedin' miracle. The other boy they sent me was no help.'

More fear clutched at Billy's throat; he knew how, even in Liverpool, a bad winter could pick people off.

As the sun went down, Billy was ordered to put away the saws and axes, while Macdonald milked the goat.

Macdonald had actually driven down to the Metis village the day before and had continued on to a farmer who owned a small mill. There, he had bought a sack of flour for the winter and had picked up Billy at the railway halt on his return journey. Together, they now heaved the sack into the cabin.

Mrs Macdonald complained that she did not know where to store it. Macdonald told her sharply to shut up; she was lucky to have it.

The interior of the cabin seemed to Billy's weary eyes infinitely cosy. A good wood fire blazed in a stone hearth. The floor was earthen, but that was no different from the floor of the cellar in which he had lived with his parents. The walls were made of logs chinked with clay. Near the top of one wall a pair of shutters opened to the fresh air. At one side a sacking curtain was drawn across the little room and on another side was a closed door, which Billy later discovered led to a storeroom. A couple of benches and a table, obviously homemade, and a bunk against a wall, appeared to be the only furnishings. On the walls were hung tools, basins, a tin bath and some articles which Billy did not know the use of.

A pannikin of water lay on the table and Macdonald rinsed his hands and face in it and dried himself on a piece of rag. He indicated to Billy that he could do likewise and should then take the pannikin outside and empty it on the vegetable garden. Billy did as he was told. When he seized the handle of the shallow pan, he slopped the water on the floor, and Mrs Macdonald's tight lips exploded with an angry 'Tush! Look what you're doing.'

He came back into the cabin to find a modest dish of rabbit stew and potatoes waiting for him. He thankfully ate this whilst standing at the table. The Macdonalds sat down on a bench side by side, the baby sleeping in its mother's lap, and ate much larger helpings.

As soon as Billy put down his empty plate on to the table,

Macdonald told him, 'Go out and split some logs from the woodpile and bring them in for the Missus.'

'Lay them at the side of the chimney here, to dry,' Mrs Macdonald chimed in, as she rose from the table, holding her baby against her shoulder.

Billy looked longingly at the remains of the stew in an iron saucepan on the table, but the hint was not taken. He turned, and trailed slowly up the wooden steps to the door.

Billy had expected that outside it would be dead dark, but once his eyes got used to it, he found he could see fairly well in the starlight. He went, first, down to the privy, a hole in the ground inside a shack as yet unroofed.

As he split the logs, he remembered when he had helped his father do the same thing. They would go at night to the shore to steal driftwood, bits of wrecks, wooden boxes, even trees, swept on to the river shore by the tide, and the next day they would reduce them to firing easy for his mother to handle. Swaying with fatigue and lack of sufficient food, he let the tears fall. 'Aye, Mam,' he cried to the uncaring pines.

He stumbled back and forth to the stove with the firewood, until Mrs Macdonald said it was enough and that he could go to bed in the bunk by the storeroom door. He took off his boots and, after opening them out to dry, he fell into the coffinlike bed and spread over himself the coarse blanket he found there. Without even a straw mattress or pillow, the bed was hard, but he was so exhausted that he slept immediately. He awoke, feeling very cold, when Macdonald shouted to him from behind the sacking curtain to make up the fire.

Except for a few embers on the hearth, the cabin was dark, and Billy could not at first think where he was. Then memory reasserted itself, and he stumbled out of the bunk to do as he was bidden.

It was still dark outside, when Mrs Macdonald shook him and told him it was time to get up. The baby was sobbing heartily and, from behind the sackcloth curtain, Macdonald shouted to her, 'Can't you shut the brat up?'

She did not answer him. Working by the light of the fire,

she was stirring something in a saucepan; the baby, to Billy's complete astonishment, was hanging in what appeared to be a bag hung on the wall beside the fireplace. He dared not remark on it. Agonizedly stiff and cold, he staggered towards the warmth of the fire, and was immediately handed a plate of porridge. 'Eat up,' Mrs Macdonald commanded, 'there's coffee in the pot on the hearth there. Then get your boots on and get the goat out of the barn. See if you can find a tree to tether it to where the grass is clear of snow.'

So that was what the animal was. A goat!

'Will it let me?' asked Billy, as he knelt by the hearth to fill a mug of coffee. He sipped the bitter brew cautiously; he had never tasted coffee before. 'I've never seen no goat before.'

The woman laughed, as she put porridge out for her husband. 'Where've you kids been all your lives? You're the second boy we've had and neither of you've seen a goat!'

Macdonald pulled back the sackcloth curtain and emerged, tightening his belt buckle as he came to eat his breakfast. He laughed with his wife. 'Take the little pail off the nail there – try milking her when you've tied her up.'

Billy learned to hate that goat. He hated it even more than he had hated the subnormal boy who had bullied him as a child in the court.

Shivering in the cold of the October morning, he forcibly dragged the reluctant goat out of the relative comfort of the barn, found a tree with less snow under it than most, and tethered the animal to it. Then he put the pail under the suspicious animal, squatted down by it and attempted to milk it as he had seen the cows milked in the dairy where Mike worked. The goat edged away, turned and butted him crossly. Billy unbalanced and toppled sideways. The goat backed away from him to the furthest extent of its rope, put its hard little head down and prepared to charge. Billy scrambled out of reach, his hands freezing in the snow.

From the doorway, Macdonald guffawed with laughter. He came forward, picked up the pail and motioned Billy to watch him. He went up to the angry animal, spoke surprisingly softly to her, squatted on his heels and put his head against her side and she let him milk her, while she took occasional bored nips at tufts of grass poking through the snow. Occasionally, she raised a resentful, malevolent eye towards Billy.

The goat did not produce much milk, and Macdonald said she was nearly ready for mating again, but the nearest billygoat was almost fifteen miles away; it was a long way to take her.

'Is that the nearest farm?' asked Billy, thoughts of escape to the forefront of his mind.

'Yes. And there's only a narrow trail to it; I can't get the cart through from this side.'

He handed the pail to Billy and told him to take it to Mrs Macdonald.

'Anybody else live round here?' asked Billy, trying to sound casual, as they walked towards the cabin.

'There's the Metis village that you saw, but that's nearly twenty miles from here. They trap, and there's one or two more as come from further away; they've got traplines along the river.' He pointed to the water barrel. 'Fill it up for her. Then we'll finish roofing the barn. The horse's got to have cover for winter.'

The following day, Macdonald took the horse to the field he was clearing for ploughing in the spring; there were, apparently, numerous tree roots that he had either pulled loose or dynamited out and he needed to clear them away, if they had not already frozen to the ground.

Billy was left to help Mrs Macdonald. He hauled more buckets of water from the river than he cared to remember, to fill the water-barrel and a tin bath for doing the washing. By the time he was finished, he was sopping wet down one side of his breeches and his boots squished as he moved around. The water was bitterly cold, and he was thankful when Mrs Macdonald called him indoors to build up the fire for her, while she kneaded bread dough, using a piece of old dough as a raising agent. His boots were hardly steaming in the hearth, when she took him outside again to show him, quickly, how to fire a clay oven which her husband had built for her near the door. She said she would bake the bread and a rabbit pie in it.

The baby yelled, and he was told to stay out of the cabin while she gave the child her breast. Later, while the baby, swaddled in its rabbit skins, slept in its parents' wooden bed behind the sackcloth curtain and the bread was left to rise on the hearth, she and Billy pulled out the last of the carrots from the vegetable patch; not having time to harvest them earlier, she had hastily heaped earth and leaves over them in the hope they would not freeze. In these temporary clamps, they appeared to have survived, so they buried them in wooden boxes of river sand which Mrs Macdonald had dried at the side of the fireplace.

Finding that Billy was interested in what she was doing, she began to talk a little. She told him that the barrel in the corner of the cabin was filled with sauerkraut. He did not know what that was, so she explained that it was shredded, salted cabbage being allowed to ferment in its own juice. 'A German showed me how to do it,' she volunteered.

She asked if he could fish, because she had learned from the Indians how to dry fish, though there was not much time before the really intense cold set in. 'We've done well this year to have such a mild autumn,' she told him.

'I never learned to fish,' Billy said, in response to her question. 'There isn't many fishes in the Mersey now. Me Dad told me that when he were a boy he went fishin' with his Dad, and they always ate fish of a Friday. Now you got to go out to sea to get it – into the Bay, like.'

'There's a lake near here full of them,' Mrs Macdonald informed him. 'But Angus hasn't got the time; he must get the land cleared.' She sighed. 'If I'd got some money, I could buy any amount of fish from the Metis. Somehow, I'll get Angus to teach you how to ice fish – that would help feed us in the winter.'

In the late afternoon, Macdonald returned. The horse was dragging a spruce which had been roughly cleared of most of its branches.

151

Billy's immature muscles already ached as if he had been beaten, but after a piece of bread and a cup of coffee, Macdonald ordered him to take the other end of the saw and help him reduce the spruce to logs. When Billy did not pull or push hard enough, Macdonald cursed his ineptitude.

From the general tenor of the tirade, Billy learned that the same threat that beset Mrs Macdonald with her store of carrots, onions and sauerkraut, also bedevilled her husband. The winter.

The wood pile must be built up and up. Every scrap of food they could raise or barter for must be stored before the winter fell on them. Hay and oats and anything that could be culled from the forest or begged from the settlers he used to work for – the neighbour with the goat – must be collected to keep the horse and the goat alive.

When Macdonald paused to wipe the sweat off his face, Billy said, 'The Missus says as you'll teach me to fish.'

'Aye, I will. And to trap rabbits.'

The pain in Billy's back when he was roused the next morning made him cry out. Mrs Macdonald laughed at him and said he'd get used to it and to go and get her some more wood.

Outside, it was freezing and a powder of fresh snow lay on the ground. His damp boots were soon icy, as he hefted the split logs into the cabin.

At the end of a month he was still as hungry as he had ever been in Liverpool, and he was struck or kicked far more by both husband and wife than he had ever been in the great port.

No matter how he phrased the question, neither husband nor wife would tell him where he was. That information, they reckoned with a sly grin to each other, would give Billy a basis on which to work out how to run away, like the previous orphan had.

Remembering that the Macdonalds were supposed to supply him with clothes, he asked Mrs Macdonald if she could give him a pair of gloves. 'Me hands is so cold they froze to the bucket handle this morning,' he told her, fear of what the cold might do to his hands making him desperate.

She looked at him as if he had asked something absurd. Then she went to a wooden trunk in the storeroom and rummaged through odds and ends of clothing. She fretfully flung him a pair of her husband's old socks with large holes in their heels.

As he caught the socks, hatred of her seethed in him. Young and terribly disappointed, he gave no thought to her despair. He was, however, thankful to slip his hands into the heavy, smelly socks.

The water-barrel had been moved inside the cabin. Now she told him to refill it, as usual. 'Remember to keep breaking the river ice, to keep it open round where you get the water. Soon you'll have to cut steps through it to get at the water.'

Billy nodded. He had already been breaking the ice for some time, with the aid of a dead branch. When he contemplated Mrs Macdonald's forecast, he began to shake with fear. Would he freeze, too?

Could he follow the railway lines back to Toronto? he wondered frantically. How far did a train travel in a day and a night?

A few days back, he had tried to retrace his way to the Metis village, because he could not even follow the railway track until he found its shining lines. He had hoped that the Metis family he had met on his arrival might listen to him and help him. But within twenty minutes, mistaking an animal track for one of the turnings he had originally taken, he became lost. Fortunately, in his subsequent panic, he walked in a circle, and in the forest's uncanny silence he had heard Mrs Macdonald's voice shouting angrily for him. He had stumbled back to her through the bush and got a sound cuffing for his pains. She also told him that, earlier in the year, her husband had shot a cougar trying to get at the goat, and that it was capable of eating a boy.

'What's a cougar?' he had asked, as he thankfully swept the floor of the cabin for her and got warm again.

'It's like a lion.'

After hearing that, Billy never left the clearing alone, except to go for water, and sometimes in the evening, if he had to walk the trail to the river, a rustling in the undergrowth would cause him to break out in a cold sweat.

One night, in the cabin, when he was whittling dowels for his master, he thought about the Metis children at the railway halt. He wondered if they went to school. This reminded him that he was supposed to be sent both to church and to school.

School seemed suddenly like a rest cure, five or six hours of perfect peace after the intolerable load of work he was doing. He did not care about church, but attendance would ensure a comfortable sitdown, a happy change from working seven days a week from long before dawn to after dark. He paused in his whittling, penknife idle, while it struck him that he did not even know what day it was.

Sunday had been a day when both his father and mother had been at home; frequently it had been a day on which they went down to the shore to pick amongst the rubbish thrown up by the tide for anything that might be useful, a day when Polly sometimes came, bringing her wages and interesting gossip. An agony of loneliness went through him.

Macdonald looked up from the horse-collar he was repairing, and Billy hastily resumed his careful whittling.

The prim lady at the Home in Toronto had promised that someone would visit him at the farm where he settled, to check that he was happy and behaving well. Not realizing the complexity of arranging such a visit, or that it might cost money, he had waited as patiently as he could for the visitor to arrive, so that he could ask to be moved. But, like many other such children, he was in a place so isolated that no local worthy could be recruited to visit – not that it would necessarily have done much good; children were usually interviewed in the presence of their employers and were too afraid to complain.

Since his arrival at the cabin, Billy had seen no other person than his employers, and he wondered, suddenly, if other settlers disliked the Macdonalds as much as he did.

With a small burst of bravery, he broke the silence of the cabin, by asking Macdonald, 'When will I be able to go to school? And church? Like the lady at the 'Ome promised?'

Startled out of his usual moroseness, Macdonald stared at the boy, his needle poised over the collar's leather. Mrs Macdonald laughed almost hysterically.

'Where'd you go? The nearest school is thirty miles off. And church the same. Have to wait for months, sometimes, for a priest to come through to marry you – or christen you.' He gestured with his needle towards the child sleeping on its mother's lap. 'He'll be on his feet before he's christened.' He resumed his stitching, and then went on, 'Anyway, you're too big to be wasting your time in school; I can't spare you.'

Having got the man to talk, Billy asked once more, 'Well, what's the name of this place and the name of the place where the school is.' He tried to sound casual and went gravely on with his whittling, as he waited for a reply.

Macdonald growled, 'None of them's got names yet.'

Billy picked up another piece of wood and began carefully to pare it into rough shape. He wondered if the boy Mrs Macdonald had mentioned before had run away. 'What happened to the boy you had before me?'

'Drowned. He tried to cross the river on the ice and it gave under him. That's what comes of running away.'

Billy was shocked at Macdonald's laconic response.

'That was proper awful!'

'Bloody fool. Should've known better.'

II

Was it always going to be like this? Billy wondered. His ears hurt as they warmed up again, after going for the day's water. He stood inside the cabin at the foot of the steps, brushing the last of the snow still on his boots with a besom Mrs

Macdonald had made. One boot had a small hole in the bottom and he had stuffed some straw from the barn into it to stop his foot freezing; he feared having to ask Macdonald for leather and tools to mend it.

Before he could take his overcoat off, Mrs Macdonald turned from feeding the baby cuddled under her shawl, to say, 'Go and open up the oven and get the bread out for me; it'll be more than done.' The baby lost her breast and whimpered. 'Take the basket off the shelf to carry it in.'

With a sigh, he swung the basket down, while she grumbled, 'After this lot we'll be down to bannock. It'll be too snowy out there to use the oven.'

'Oh, aye,' he agreed indifferently. If you had any sense you said as little as possible to the Macdonalds. Then you could not be clouted for impudence.

'Have you got the peel?'

He hastily unhooked, from a wooden peg by the door, a long-handled wooden shovel with which to get the bread out of the hot oven.

He had never been given this job before, but he had noticed that Mrs Macdonald was slowly pushing many of her household chores on to him – he had done a bath full of washing for her only a few days earlier, spreading the garments out on the bushes to dry. At first they had frozen; yet, to his astonishment, they had eventually proved to be almost dry.

He approached the oven with respect. He reckoned it must be very hot, but when he put his hand on the outside it was merely comfortably warm. Very cautiously, he opened the wooden door which was lined with metal. As the interior heat hit the cold air outside, a burst of steam blew into his face. The odour of the bread made his saliva run.

With great care, he first took out a covered stewpot and stood it in the shallow basket. Then, one by one, he shovelled out the round loaves and laid them in the basket, round the pot. When he had finished, he stood in the warmth still emitted by the oven and looked down at the bread. Hunger was a constant pain with him, and he suddenly pulled the sock off his hand, bent down and snatched up a loaf. Despite the bitter air, it was still extremely hot, but he broke it open and shoved a cob into his mouth. Though it burned the top of his mouth, it was good beyond words, and he tore another piece off and crammed it into his mouth.

Absorbed in the rapture of eating, he did not hear the quiet plod of the horse's hooves or the squeaking wheels. The whistle of Macdonald's buggy whip, as he bent from the seat of the cart and swung it across the boy's back, was the first indication Billy had of Macdonald's return from his field with a load of stones he intended to use to hold down the edges of the barn roof.

Billy nearly choked on the bread, as he cried out and swung round to face his attacker.

Red with fury, Macdonald leaped from the cart and caught him by the shoulder, forcing him to turn his back. 'I'll teach you to steal,' he roared. He raised his whip again and hit the boy across the back with the handle. The end of the lash snaked viciously round Billy and cut his lower lip.

Billy struggled to escape the remorseless grip as the blows rained down on him. 'I were that hungry,' he appealed frantically. He put his hand to his bleeding lip.

Macdonald hurled him face down on the oven's curved side and, holding him by the back of the neck, beat him unmercifully.

Twelve-year-old Billy was strong, but he was no hero. He howled so loudly that Mrs Macdonald came flying out, the baby crying in her arms. 'What's he done?' she cried. She stopped, to look bewilderedly at her loaves scattered in the snow and the stewpot, half-tipped over. Then she saw that Billy was bleeding at the mouth, and she yelled, 'That's enough, Angus! You'll kill him!'

Macdonald let go and threw Billy to the ground. Weeping and bleeding, he crawled through the snow to seek sanctuary behind Mrs Macdonald.

Ignoring him, Mrs Macdonald bent down to rescue the loaves and straighten the stewpot before it lost all its contents.

The baby objected to being jostled about and cried all the harder. The half-eaten loaf told its own story.

'You greedy bugger,' she fulminated at Billy struggling to his feet, and sped back indoors out of the cold.

Macdonald strode back to the horse, to lead it to the barn. He turned and barked at Billy, 'You get over to the barn and get the ladder out, and you lay these stones along the edge of the roof till I tell you to stop, you damned thief.'

Unable to straighten his back properly, Billy dragged himself towards the barn. Sobbing, he looked down at his long, clumsy overcoat. Added to its dirtiness, it now had bloodstains from his swelling lip.

The stones would be frozen, he thought hopelessly; Macdonald must have had to use a pickaxe to loosen them from the pile by the field. Fear of further beating, however, drove him painfully towards the barn, to wait sullenly by the ladder while Macdonald unharnessed the horse and tipped the cart to let the stones roll off it.

As Macdonald led the horse into the barn to join the goat bleating in a corner, Billy stood staring at the stones; a skiff of snow was already powdering them over. Rage took over from pain.

'I'll kill him,' he promised himself savagely. 'One day I'll kill him. And then I'll run away. I'll die in the forest before I stay here.' He slowly lifted the home-made ladder and set it against the barn wall; the stones were heavy and awkward to carry up a ladder which rapidly became slippery and every journey hurt his battered back.

It was Mrs Macdonald who came through the early darkness, a lantern in her hand, to tell him to come in. He had not put many stones in place but in the dark his poor efforts went unremarked.

'Come on,' was all she said.

They passed a silent Macdonald going to the barn to check the horse and put a blanket over it before he went to bed.

In the candlelit cabin, Mrs Macdonald told him to wash his face, while she put some stew out for him. Afterwards, he went to the fire and stood warming his frozen hands and feet. 'Get to bed before he comes back,' she urged, so he took his plate and spoon into his bunk with him. He was beyond talking, but his hunger was such that he managed to eat his supper despite his hurt lip.

'Holy Mother, hear my prayer,' he whispered to himself, rage gone from him leaving him cowed and exhausted. 'Holy Mary, Mother of God, send the lady from Toronto – send her soon.'

III

November and December slipped away in unremitted work. He fed the animals, cleaned tools, went for water, shovelled snow away from the door and kept a path open to the frozen privy, cut kindling and did the washing. He also helped Mrs Macdonald make a pair of knee-high mocassins for each of them out of roughly tanned skins. As the sun curved through the sky closer and closer to the horizon, he waited and hoped.

In their despair, the Macdonalds did not keep Christmas, and Billy spent Christmas Day chipping steps into the ice in order to reach water in the river. Macdonald taught him how to snare small animals, skin them, scrape their skins clean and prepare them for eating. Together, they walked through the bush to a small lake, frozen like everything else. There they built a rough shelter with spruce boughs, bored a hole through the ice and Billy learned to fish. If Macdonald had been a more kindly man, Billy would have enjoyed learning these new skills, but his employer was, at best, irascible, at worst a bully to be feared.

In January, the cold became a dreadful nightmare and carrying water from the river, in clothing suitable for an English winter, became a battle which Billy began to feel he would lose. He begged another pair of socks and an old woollen shawl from Mrs Macdonald. The shawl he wrapped round his head and neck over his cap, to save his ears and cheeks from frostbite.

One night, the cabin became lined with ice and the baby froze to death. For once, Billy was sorry for Mrs Macdonald. She did not cry, but sat silently by the fire, her hands in her aproned lap, her domestic tasks undone. Macdonald tried to rouse her, without success. It was Billy who took whatever game he and Macdonald had been able to find and made stews out of it and tried to persuade the woman to eat. It was Macdonald himself who had to take the tiny bundle which had been his son outside and cover it with some of the stones from his field so that it could not be eaten by predators, until Spring should come and he could bury it. Both of them began to fear that Mrs Macdonald had lost her reason.

In the latter part of the winter, when rabbits became hard to find, they lived on oatmeal and on the odd fish, caught on days when the weather eased a little. Macdonald tried to cheer up his wife by saying that with the first money they got from next year's crop he would buy a rifle, so that he could hunt moose to fill their winter larder. To Billy, he worried that the horse and goat might not survive; it was a simpler matter to replace a baby than it was to replace a draught animal.

Billy crept on from day to day, numbed by the gruelling cold and, alternatively, the confinement to the tiny cabin.

One March day, when it seemed that the weather was indeed a little warmer, despite its being overcast, they took the horse out and felled another tree. By the time it had been dragged home, however, snow was beginning to fall and Macdonald said uneasily that he thought they were in for a storm. They stabled the horse and put its blankets over it and fed it. Macdonald had built an inner enclosure for the goat and laid spruce branches thickly on the floor of it and the animal was surviving, though it had chewed all the bark off the logs forming its pen.

The snow came down heavily and a wind whipped it into

160

deep drifts, so that Billy was glad that Macdonald had earlier connected the cabin entrance to the privy by a rope; he knew that as long as he held on to the rope, he could find his way back to the cabin after relieving himself, no matter how thickly it was snowing.

It was this rope which led a trapper, caught in the white wilderness of the storm, from the edge of the clearing to their door. In his thankfulness at finding a warm refuge, he did not know that Billy was convinced that he had been sent by the Holy Mother herself.

IV

To Polly and Alicia in crowded England, it seemed impossible that Billy could have been in a place so isolated that it did not even have a proper name, only numbers from a survey map, a place where there were no shops or even another person, except his employers, until in a storm, a half-French, half-Red Indian man had sought shelter with them. Yet, there it was, all set out vividly in stumbling print over both sides of three pages torn from an account book.

Polly looked at the letter dumbfounded and then handed it to Alicia. 'It shouldn't happen to a dog!' she exclaimed. 'He were lucky that man told him the route down to the railway line; a simple way, even if it were longer – so he didn't get lost. Eight hours' walkin'. It's terrible!'

Alicia, too, was horrified by Billy's story. 'Poor boy! Thank goodness, he had enough sense to wait until the Spring came before he set out.'

'Aye.' Polly heaved a sigh. 'He never should've gone to Canada. I knew something awful would happen.'

'Well, it sounds as if he's all right now,' Alicia comforted her. 'The old pedlar who picked him up near the Metis village seems a decent sort. I'm sure he'll find it much easier helping him to sell buttons and cotton and things than working on a farm.'

Polly agreed, and then asked, 'But where's Winnipeg? That's where I got to write back.'

'It's in Manitoba on the Red River. I'll get the atlas and show you.'

Polly and Alicia had been tidying the linen closet opposite her mother's bedroom when the postman had brought the afternoon mail. Now she ran up the stairs from the second floor landing to the nursery and, more slowly, brought down her school atlas. While she looked for the page containing Canada, Polly said, 'He says that next Spring, they'll leave Winnipeg and go west.'

'Hm.' Alicia found Winnipeg and, leaning the atlas against the wall, so that Polly could see better where she was pointing, she said slowly, 'You know, Pol, there's an awful lot of Canada west of Winnipeg. I wonder where his pedlar's taking him?'

'Maybe when Master Edward comes home on leave – he's due soon – we could ask him if he knows the likely places.'

Alicia smiled. 'Of course we could.'

'I'd like to write back to Billy tonight. Would you help me, Allie? I'm not that good at writin' letters.'

'I'd love to.'

After dinner, Alicia sat for a short while with her mother and told her about Billy's adventures. Elizabeth did not appear very interested and Alicia was finally reduced to silence. Then her mother said, 'I want to talk to you about school.'

Sarah Webb had willingly agreed to share the cost of sending Alicia to Blackburne House School, so Elizabeth spent a few minutes explaining the advantages of the new school to Alicia. 'You will start in September,' she said.

'Yes, Mama.' She knew that the school was considered a good one, but she felt nervous about leaving Miss Schreiber and the girls with whom she was familiar. September was, however, a long way off, and in the meantime she had promised to help Polly with her letter, so she said no more and sat waiting for her mother to say she could go.

A little nonplussed at the absence of enthusiasm from Alicia at being sent to such an excellent school, Elizabeth dismissed her.

To help Polly, Alicia took her mother's tea tray down to the kitchen. Rosie, who had married her milkman at Christmastime, had not been replaced and Fanny and Polly were having to carry her work between them. They grumbled a great deal about the extra load and, recently, in bed at night, Alicia had felt sick with dread that they might hand in their notice and leave her faced with strange, new servants to take care of her.

Chapter Fifteen

I

In November 1899, Alicia lost an old friend.

After getting wet through on her day off, Mrs Tibbs caught pneumonia; she took to her bed with a temperature and a hacking cough, and Fanny and Polly grumbled at the extra work they had to undertake. It was assumed, however, that she would be up again in a couple of days.

Elizabeth endured several days of complaint from Humphrey about Polly's cooking before she descended to her cook-housekeeper's basement bedroom to inquire when she expected to be better.

Mrs Tibbs was obviously in pain and she did not recognize her mistress.

A frightened Elizabeth sent for the doctor, who on seeing the patient had her immediately transferred to the Infirmary. There, overnight, she died.

Elizabeth told Humphrey that she would try to find a good, new cook.

He glanced up from his desk in the library and replied, 'Teach Polly how to cook – we can't afford a full-time cook, anyway,' a remark which was far from true.

Elizabeth protested. Out of pure malice, Humphrey refused to budge. 'It wouldn't hurt you to do some of the cooking yourself,' he bellowed at her. 'Get off your fat bottom and do something, for a change.'

Shocked that he should mention any part of her anatomy, Elizabeth flounced out of the room.

In the hall, she bumped into Alicia on her way back to school after lunch. Her face flushed with rage, she paused and said angrily, 'I really don't know why Mrs Tibbs had to die so inconveniently. Polly will have to learn to cook from her cookery books!'

'Why, Mama?' Alicia had moved towards the front door and had her hand on the big, iron key, ready to turn it.

'Mr Woodman won't let me replace Mrs Tibbs.'

'He didn't let you get anyone instead of Rose when she got married.'

Fuming, Elizabeth ignored her daughter's remark, and said crossly, 'Fanny and Polly will simply have to split the work between them. Perhaps I can get a charwoman from the Workhouse to help in the mornings.'

'Yes, Mama.' As she opened the front door, her heart beat faster with apprehension. 'I hope Polly and Fanny don't feel the work is too much – and leave us, Mama?'

'I'll raise their wages,' promised Elizabeth, 'no matter what Mr Woodman says. I can't do it from my own money – with Charles to help – and then there are the Blackburne House fees . . . ,' she trailed off. Then she said impatiently to Alicia, 'Run along now – you'll be late.'

'Yes, Mama.'

Her mother swept across the hall to the dining-room where Polly was brushing up the crumbs from the linen tablecloth with a tiny crumb-tray and brush.

Alicia turned the key in the lock, swung open the heavy, oak front door and went slowly down the steps. She was deeply puzzled about Elizabeth's remark regarding school fees. She had always imagined that fathers paid for their children's education – and she knew from an overheard complaint of Humphrey's that he paid Charles's university fees – and, yet, if she had understood correctly, her *mother* was paying for her to attend Blackburne House. It seemed very strange and again suggested to her that there was something that made her different from other daughters.

II

Both Polly and Fanny were, at first, very resentful of the imposition of yet more work. Polly ventured to protest to Elizabeth that they already ran the house with two less staff than when she had first come to serve her. 'There's Maisie *and* Rosie gone,' she pointed out aggrievedly.

At the threatened loss of his remaining domestics, Humphrey grumpily gave in, and Elizabeth raised Polly's wages by thirty shillings a year and Fanny's by a pound – it was still much cheaper than replacing Mrs Tibbs. The two servants promised to think her offer over, and retired to the kitchen to boil up an extremely strong pot of tea and drink it with double helpings of sugar, while they angrily discussed their position.

Alicia came home from school while they were still talking. She ran to Polly and flung her arms round her. 'Guess what, Polly? I got full marks for my essay on Canada. Isn't it great? I'm sure it's because of writing to Billy and finding the places he goes to, on the map.' She turned excitedly to Fanny, 'I didn't even have a spelling error – first time it's happened.'

Fanny looked at Polly and began to laugh. Alicia looked at the two maids. She dropped her arms, and said crossly, 'Well, I don't think it's anything to laugh at.'

They hastened to comfort her and assure her that they were not laughing at her, but at themselves; they were both delighted at her success.

'I couldn't leave 'er, not if I tried,' Polly said to Fanny, when Alicia insisted on carrying her mother's tea tray up to her, to save Polly's legs.

'I knowed it – that's wot made me laugh,' replied Fanny, with one of her wide grins. 'And I don't know no other place. We'll manage somehow, we will.'

Polly made a list of the work to be done and submitted it to Elizabeth for approval. Elizabeth reluctantly agreed to it.

It entailed doing house-cleaning at times other than the weekday mornings, ''Cos Fanny'll never get through it, now she's got to wait at table while I cook – and most times she'll have to answer the bell,' Polly said.

It particularly irritated Elizabeth that the morning-room, which she regarded as her own private sitting-room, was not cleaned before she rose in the morning. Sometimes, the work was done on a Saturday morning, and Alicia never forgot the problem of routing her mother out, once she was settled in her chair.

She would put her arms under her mother's armpits and say, 'Let me help you up, Mama.' Then she would heave her forward from the depths of the chair. It seemed as if, every month, her mother grew heavier, and that she did not smell quite as nicely as she used to. Her favourite, grey morning dress always seemed to be a little spotted with tea and in need of sponging and pressing. Her magnificent hair was bundled carelessly into a snood at the back of her neck. As Alicia eased her carefully up the stairs to the big formal drawing-room to sit and have her coffee while the morning-room was cleaned, she would complain steadily, and Alicia would do her utmost to quell her own girlish impatience and respond non-committally by simply saying, 'Yes, Mama. I do understand how difficult it is for you.'

III

One by one, Elizabeth had given up her charitable endeavours; they had always been tedious to her and she found them increasingly tiring. Because they failed to attract the type of woman she would have liked to mix with, she ceased, also, to hold her weekly At Homes.

Added to the innuendo that followed Alicia's birth, ladies said behind their fans that she flirted too much at the dinners and dances which her husband insisted she attend with him. Her dresses were just a little too loud, her wit a little too sharp, and Elizabeth knew she was asked because she was Humphrey's wife, not from friendship towards her.

The ultimate humiliation had occurred at a private New Year Reception. She had heard a budding young medical specialist from the School of Tropical Medicine make a vulgar joke at her expense, and it had punctured her self-respect beyond repair – because it was so close to the truth. Afterwards, she began to lose her hold on life and to give way to her inward despair.

When she heard that Andrew Crossing's wife had died, she had enjoyed a few months of wild hope that he would seek her out, demand that she should divorce Humphrey and marry him. But after six months, he married his secretary.

Moving towards womanhood with all the dreams of a young girl, Alicia found it more and more difficult to endure her mother's moods; yet Polly assured her that it was her duty to do so. 'She's your Mam,' she reminded the girl sharply. 'You be patient with her; daughters have to bear with their Mams.'

On the rare occasions when Alicia went to church, the preachers would point up the need for young people to honour their parents. She also knew of older single women in the district who cared for ageing parents. She decided that Polly must be right. It irritated her, however, when Florence on one of her brief visits would take it for granted that it was Alicia, and not herself, who was going to do the honouring. 'Does marriage let you off?' Alicia wondered crossly.

IV

If it had not been for Polly and Fanny, Alicia would never have seen anything of the excitement of the special New Year which ushered the world into the twentieth century.

While her parents drove in a hired carriage to the home of one of Humphrey's friends for a New Year dinner, Alicia had eaten her own dinner at the kitchen table, rather than have Polly bring a tray up to the loneliness of the day nursery.

On her way down to the basement, she had been unnerved by the sound of quarrelling coming from her parents' bedroom. She knew that Humphrey sometimes hit her mother and the idea of anyone being struck sickened her, though Polly had often slapped her when she had done something wrong.

Elizabeth had failed to get up on the last day of the century. Humphrey had insisted that they *must* attend the dinner to which they had been invited. Finally, he had rung the bell furiously, and Polly had shot upstairs to answer it.

'Help your mistress get washed and dressed,' Humphrey had ordered her. His face purple, his white moustache quivering with rage, he had gone back into the dressing-room to change into his dinner clothes. 'The carriage will be here in an hour,' he had shouted to the women, as he slammed the door after himself.

Elizabeth was not ill. She simply did not want to make the effort, yet again, to be civil to women who obviously did not really want to know her. Since Polly was there, politely waiting, she did reluctantly rise from her bed, and within the hour Polly managed to have her washed, dressed and her hair well brushed and neatly braided round her head, though the style was most unfashionable. As she handed her mistress her long, white satin gloves and an ivory brisé fan, she felt some pity for her. 'You look very fine, Ma'am, in that plum colour,' she whispered encouragingly.

'Thank you, Polly. I had better put on my heavy cloak, though it doesn't match this gown.'

Polly got out the black velvet cloak and wrapped it round Elizabeth. Then she helped her down the stairs.

Humphrey was already waiting in the hall, his cloak over his shoulders. He carried a top hat and was impatiently drumming his fingers on its hard top. 'Hurry,' he called to his wife. 'We mustn't keep the horse waiting.'

He'd keep me waiting for hours, Elizabeth thought savagely, whenever he felt like it, but not a horse – not a horse.

The minute the front door had been shut after the Master

and Mistress, the atmosphere of the house changed. Alicia had gone to wash her hands after her meal, and when she returned to the kitchen, she found the two maids sitting before the fire with their feet on the steel fender, a fender which badly needed polishing. On the floor between them was a jug of porter. They each held a mug in their hands.

'Coom on, luv,' invited Fanny, shifting her kitchen chair to make room for the girl. 'It's a proper shame they never thought of you havin' a bit of fun tonight.'

Alicia was so used to having to fill her evenings and holidays herself that this point had not occurred to her. Left to herself, she would have done her piano practice and then read until bedtime.

'Pull up a chair, duck,' Polly encouraged her, her plump face and blue eyes gentle to this child who was almost a woman.

As Alicia turned to get herself a chair, Fanny said, 'Polly and I was thinkin' we'd go up to the crossroads – you know, at Smithdown Road and Lodge Lane – afore midnight. Do you want to come?'

Alicia smiled. 'Why would you want to go up there?'

'Don't you know? Thousands a people goes every New Year. We have a great time. Everybody joins hands and the circle goes in and out of all the streets that meet there. And we sing and we have a good laugh. Then the men go first-footing, 'specially the dark ones 'cos they bring good luck.'

'What's first-footing?' Alicia asked, as she plunked herself down on the edge of her chair.

Fanny looked at her in amazement. 'Hasn't Polly never told you about it? You *have* bin missin' out. That's where they goes knockin' on all the doors, to come into the house – to be the first visitor, like. They has a bit o' bread in one hand and a bit o' coal in the other. And they get a drink for it.'

'It brings good luck to the house,' Polly interjected. She took a sip of porter and wiped her mouth with the back of her hand.

'Does anybody first-foot our house?'

'Well, when you was a little girl, when your Mam used to give a party, the Reverend, Miss Florence's husband, used to come, 'cos he's as dark as can be.' Polly took another sip, and sighed. 'But not no more. Do you remember, luv, at all?'

'Not really. They were grown-ups' parties. I used to hear them, sometimes, when I was lying in bed.' She paused, and reverted to Fanny's suggestion that they should go up to the crossroads. 'I don't think Mama would like me to go out in the dark.'

'Och, you'd be safe enough with the two of us, wouldn't she, Pol?'

'For sure you would. And if you don't tell your Mam, she won't know nothin'.'

Alicia did not reply. She felt that she could not forbid the maids to go; she guessed that, for years, those girls not likely to be missed by her mother had gone cheerfully off to this gathering. Tucked up in the attic nursery bedroom, she could often have been left alone in the house, if her parents were out, and she would not have realized it.

Now she was nearly grown up, Polly did not fuss so much about bedtime; and here she was, sitting with her two best friends, and, outside, the magic of this special New Year beckoned. What would the twentieth century be like, she wondered, lurking out there in the darkness, a mysterious unknown. And passionately she wished that it would be fun, that she might have a bicycle and go spinning out to the countryside on it – or even learn to play tennis, like Charles.

She looked up and smiled at Polly. 'What should I put on?' she asked.

'Wrap up warm,' Polly told her, as she got up from her chair and took her empty beer mug to the sink. 'And put your grey shawl up round your head and shoulders – then you'll look like everyone else up there and nobody'll know you.' She was suddenly uneasy that someone might recognize the girl; but then not many people knew her that well, she reassured herself.

They set out about half-past eleven, skipping along together. They passed out of the quiet streets and squares which formed their own salubrious neighbourhood, into a district of older small houses and shops. They soon joined a stream of humanity, the majority young working men. The whole concourse was extremely merry, and, with two mugs of porter inside each of them, both Polly and Fanny were very talkative. The excitement of the crowd was infectious and Alicia tripped along gaily between the two maids.

They joined a huge ring of people holding hands. Alicia's shawl fell back from her white-gold hair and her plait swung behind her, as she laughed up at Fanny.

A burly man in blackened labourer's clothing pushed between the young girl and Fanny. 'Allo, la, Fan. The ole girl let you out tonight, aye?' He grasped Alicia's hand, without looking at her, so as to keep the continuity of the ring.

Fanny laughed at him, and shouted back, 'I coom, anyways.'

'Must've known I'd be here.'

'Don't flatter yourself.'

Alicia clung on to Polly, on the other side of her. The crowd lifted their clasped hands and danced forward, converging on the point where all the streets met. Then they retreated backwards down each individual street as far as they could, without loosing hands, until, in the narrowness of the roadway they were face to face with part of the human chain on the other side of the street. Alicia found herself almost nose to nose with three well-dressed young men about seventeen years of age. They were all staggering and were largely held on their uncertain feet by the force of the people on either side of them.

'Alicia Woodman!' hiccuped one of them, as he recognized the daughter of a neighbour much talked-about by his parents. Loose-mouthed, he grinned at her before he was nearly thrown off his feet by the movement of the crowd as it reversed. He was hauled up by his friends and a moment later they staggered forward again towards a frightened Alicia.

One of the other youngsters shouted, 'Who is she?' and the

original speaker replied, 'She's a neighbour. The Woodmans' kid.'

'What's she doing here? A lady?'

They were so close to her now that Alicia could smell the alcohol on their breath, and she was sickened.

They stared at her with an unpleasant intentness. She gave no hint that she knew who they were and dropped her eyes behind her gold-rimmed glasses.

As the dancers parted again, there came one of those tiny silences that occasionally occur in the biggest crowds, and she clearly heard the first speaker snigger and say, 'Like mother, like daughter; they say she's a bastard.'

The words were filled with scorn and Alicia's heart leaped with apprehension. A bastard? What did that mean? Clearly something not very nice. She glanced up at Polly; she urgently wanted to go home to the safety of the nursery. But Polly was singing at the top of her voice, as they swayed back down a narrow street with the rest of the dancers; she did not look down at her charge.

Bent on flight, Alicia became aware of the huge hand clasping her on the other side. She knew the face of the man, though it was not as black as usual; it was the coalman. When she looked up at him, he grinned down at her in a friendly way, and she felt a little comforted. But what was a bastard?

'Enjoyin' yerself, me duck?' he asked.

'Oh, yes,' she replied politely.

As if ordered, the crowd stopped moving and stood very quietly.

Through the cold, mist-laden air, hooters blared from the ships in the river and then church bells began to ring.

There was a great united shout. 'Happy New Year! Happy New Century!' It was followed immediately by hundreds and hundreds of voices singing 'Auld Lang Syne'.

At the end of the song, arms were raised in a kind of last farewell to the old year, and the ring broke up. The coalman caught Fanny round the waist and gave her a smacking kiss.

Still holding her, he turned to Alicia. 'A happy New Year to yez, Miss,' he said.

Struggling to stay near to the couple in the surging crowd, she replied, 'Thank you, and a very happy one to you, too.' Then she jumped in fright, as from behind her two arms encircled her waist. She half turned in the unexpected embrace and one of the hands was shifted to fondle her small young breasts beneath her shawl. 'Happy New Year,' her youthful neighbour breathed.

Alicia was aware of Fanny's shocked face half behind the coalman. The coalman took one look at the youth, and said to Alicia, 'You'd better go home, luv.' Then to the boy he growled, 'You, mister, you leave go of her.'

Alicia panicked and began to struggle. 'Let go,' she whispered.

The grip tightened and the fondling began to make her feel very odd indeed.

A large dirty fist was interposed between the back of her neck and the nuzzling nose of the youth. 'See this,' roared the coalman. 'You bugger off or I'll smash your bleedin' face in.'

For a second, the hold on her loosened and Alicia broke free. She ran into Fanny's arms. She was trembling all over and cried, 'Take me home, Fanny. Where's Polly?'

'In a minute, luv. We'll have to let the crowd go a bit.' She eased the girl and herself behind the comforting bulk of the coalman.

The young man had raised his fists and squared off, ready to fight. His friends, seizing the opportunity of a small break in the press around them, tried to haul him backwards. This unsteadied him and he sat down suddenly on the cobbled street, to the amusement of a circle which had begun to form around the adversaries.

Alerted to trouble, Polly struggled back to Fanny and Alicia. She heard the stream of abuse hurled at the coalman by the fallen youngster and instead of stepping over his straddled legs, she deliberately trod on his ankle, as she passed. The abuse ceased in a shriek of pain.

A couple of women wrapped in black shawls nodded approval, and one cackled at the youth, 'Serves yer right, yer cheeky bastard.'

Alicia, held tightly by Fanny, heard her and decided that if it were a term of abuse, a bastard must be a dreadful thing. Her trembling was renewed.

'Get outta here, quick,' the coalman ordered the maids and Alicia. Still facing the seated boy, who was now being tended by his anxious friends, he backed away a little. Then he hitched up his trousers, bent slightly and with a horrible grimace, he snarled, 'Get back to your Mam afore I marmalize you.' He turned and with deliberate slowness lounged after the scared maids.

The deflated little group was swept down Upper Parliament Street by the homeward-bound revellers, Polly muttering bracingly to Alicia, 'Soon be home, luv. Time for bed.'

In the comparative quiet of Grove Street, they paused to say goodnight to the coalman. 'You shouldn't've took her,' he scolded Polly and Fanny. 'It's not fit.'

Both women were very sober now and Polly was crestfallen as she answered him, 'We wasn't to know we'd bump into a little runt like that. He should've bin in bed – in his cradle.'

The quick walk had calmed Alicia, and now she said earnestly to the coalman, 'It's very kind of you to bring us home. I'm all right now, and I'm most grateful to you.'

The coalman looked down at the white, worried face glimmering in the gaslight from the street lamps. 'Aye, it were nothin', Miss.' With the grey shawl over her head, she looked oddly like his little sister. He smiled, teeth flashing red and yellow against the coaldust ingrained in his skin. 'You'll be safe with our Fanny and Polly now.' He turned away with a muttered, 'Tara, well,' to the maids and strode up the almost deserted street.

While they drank their bedtime cocoa, seated round the dying embers of the kitchen fire, Alicia did not contribute much to the conversation, except to say that the coalman was a very nice person. Within her lay a cold snake of fear. What was a bastard? Before she got into bed, she took down her school dictionary from the nursery shelf to look up the offending word. It was not in it.

V

Charles was spending his Christmas and New Year's holidays with friends in London. Even if he had been at home, thought Alicia wistfully, he would have been out most of the time; she suspected that he avoided his family as much as possible because Papa shouted at him so much. Papa thought that university was wasted time. She sighed, as, on the last January day of her school holidays, she strolled alone through Princes Park under trees dripping with sea mist, the grass seared, the silence absolute. If Charles had been at home, she could have asked him, perhaps, what 'bastard' meant. 'Could it be a slang word?' she wondered. 'Even if it were, what did it mean?' She wished Edward would come home from the war; he knew so much.

After her walk, she took her mother's four o'clock tea tray up to the morning-room.

'Where's Polly?' asked her mother, looking up from the rose she was embroidering on a party dress for Florence's eldest daughter.

Alicia explained that Polly was very busy preparing dinner.

Elizabeth nodded, and accepted a cup of tea from her daughter. Really, there was no reason why Alicia should not make herself useful in the house, she thought suddenly.

Alicia was often at a loss for conversational gambits when with Elizabeth. Today, however, she remembered that Elizabeth had been to a New Year Party, so she inquired if she had enjoyed it.

Elizabeth roused herself sufficiently to describe the menu and the guests. Alicia listened politely. She found sitting with her mother much more tedious than sitting with dear old Sarah Webb, her godmother, who was always delighted to discuss the news or ideas about education or religion or anything else that Alicia might be interested in.

She wondered if she dare ask Elizabeth what 'bastard' meant. She did not want to ask Polly, because if the word had a bad meaning, Polly would be sure to ask where she had heard it and she would have to own up that it had been thrown at her when they were out together; it might make Polly feel badly.

On consideration, she concluded that her mother might be the best person to ask. On another matter, Polly had said quite forcibly that it was a mother's duty to explain things. A thoroughly scared Alicia had gone to Polly to say that she was bleeding – underneath. Had she caught consumption or something?

Polly had hugged her and told her calmly that all women bled every month and this simply meant that Alicia was now a young woman.

Alicia had gaped at her.

'It's true, duck. I'll boil some rags and show you how to keep it off your petties. Don't be frightened, now. It don't mean nothin' more. I'll tell your Ma.' She stroked the girl's hair and kissed her. 'If you get a pain, you tell me.'

Alicia did not get a pain. She learned, however, that mothers had at least one duty – to tell their children things – what things, she was not quite sure. She poured her mother another cup of tea, and asked, as she handed it to her, 'Mama, what's a bastard?'

Elizabeth blenched. At first she thought she must have misheard. Then, as she realized that Alicia had indeed asked such a diabolical question, she exclaimed in horror, 'Alicia! Where did you hear such a dreadful word? It is most vulgar – never used by a lady under any circumstance.' Her breath began to come in short gasps, as she tried to control her sense of panic.

'I'm so sorry, Mama. I didn't know that. I – I – er just thought it was another word I should learn how to spell. Are you all right, Mama?'

'I feel faint. Get my smelling salts – they're on the table here – somewhere.' She leaned back in her chair and closed her eyes, unable to grapple with the inference of Alicia's question.

Alicia jumped from the straight chair on which she had been sitting and scrabbled anxiously amid bits of satin and hanks of embroidery silk until she found the tiny blue glass bottle. She whipped off its top and her eyes blinked as the ammonia fumes hit them.

'Here you are, Mama.' She held the open bottle under her mother's nose.

'Thank you,' Elizabeth gasped as she inhaled. She took the bottle from Alicia and held it under each nostril in turn. Alicia watched her apprehensively; she had not expected such an extreme reaction to her query.

After a few moments, with eyes still closed, Elizabeth asked, 'Where did you hear such a dreadful word? You are not to mix with people who use such language.'

Nonplussed that one word could make a person feel faint, Alicia did not know how to reply. Finally she said, 'An old woman in a crowd called a boy it, and I heard her.'

'I see,' Elizabeth swallowed. 'You really must be careful about words you pick up from the lower classes. Fortunately, Polly speaks fairly well now – but even with her you should be careful about new words.'

Alicia agreed in a very subdued voice, 'Yes, Mama.' What could a bastard be? She glanced up at Elizabeth whose complexion was slowly returning to a reasonable pink. 'Do you feel better now, Mama? Would you like me to get you some fresh tea?' she asked, anxious to make amends.

'No, thank you. I'll rest in my chair for a little while.'

'Then I'll take the tray back to Polly.' She looked contritely at her mother. 'I'm truly sorry, Mama, to distress you.'

Her mother did not answer; her mind was in a tumult. She had never before faced honestly the fact that, despite the restricted life Alicia led, sooner or later, she was likely to learn of the scandal her birth had caused. The neglected child was now a young woman, and Elizabeth prayed that she never asked Humphrey what a bastard was.

VI

A very puzzled Alicia took the teacups off the tray and put them into the kitchen sink. Then she turned to Polly making pastry at the big square table in the middle of the kitchen.

'Polly, what's a bastard?'

The rolling-pin stopped dead. Polly raised startled eyes to Alicia's solemn little face. She had not heard the young man's remark on New Year's Eve, so she did not know what had sparked the question. She looked down at the pastry and carefully gave it a long slow roll. Then she said honestly, 'It's a kid wot don't have no real papa.'

Alicia's eyes widened in surprise. She approached the table and gazed up at Polly's averted face. 'But, Polly, when we were out on New Year's Eve, that drunk young man called *me* a bastard – and I've got a papa.' Her lips trembled, as Polly continued to roll the pastry. 'And he made it sound wicked – and he was rude about Mama. He frightened me, Pol.' The last words were entreating as she begged for reassurance.

Polly turned to the girl, forcing herself to smile, as she inwardly cursed Elizabeth for not, in some way, preparing Alicia to face her illegitimacy. She said cheerfully, 'Anybody as called you that is only tenpence to a shillin'. You poor kid – don't you worry your head about it. The Master 'as you in this house, so he's your papa all right – all proper and legal.'

Alicia clicked her tongue fretfully, and then fumed, 'Well, I don't understand why he should be so rude about Mama and me. Is it really wicked to be one? And how can anybody *not* have a proper papa?'

'It's not wicked to be one,' replied Polly firmly. 'Kids can't help being born. What happens is sometimes people fall in love and maybe they can't get married – no money or somethin' – but a baby comes. And that baby is called a bastard. It's proper sad and it's real hard on the kid's Mam. But the baby isn't wicked – the nice name for him is a love child – somebody special, like.'

Poor Polly hoped she had laid the matter to rest and she lifted her pastry carefully into a piedish. But worse was to come.

'I didn't know you could have a baby without being married!' exclaimed Alicia, her high, white forehead wrinkled by her complete confusion. 'I don't even know how babies come, except I'm sure they don't come in the doctor's bag – they'd smother in it.'

'You don't have to be married,' Polly floundered. 'Hasn't your Mam ever spoken to you about it?'

'No.' Alicia heaved a sigh. 'Should she? She nearly fainted when I asked her what a bastard was. She didn't tell me.'

I bet she didn't, thought Polly sourly. Aloud, she said, 'Well, it int a word that ladies use.'

'How do babies come, Polly? Ethel at school says she saw a cat have kittens once – and she really believes that babies come the same way. She said it was awfully messy. She said that Fluffy opened up between her legs and the kittens squeezed out – and there was blood and things.' Her voice faltered, and she looked appealingly at Polly as if she hoped Polly would deny it.

Better she knows, thought Polly. She had heard Elizabeth talking to Humphrey about the necessity of Alicia going to Blackburne House School, so that she was educated enough to be a governess, if she did not marry. And in Polly's opinion, governesses needed to know as much as housemaids did, since they were just as vulnerable to unwanted advances. Why hasn't the bloody woman said something to her about men? Polly cursed. Now she had the job. That Ethel should've kept her mouth shut.

'She's right,' she blurted out. 'Oh, aye, she's right.'

Alicia was so startled by this revelation that she knocked the recipe book off the table.

'You mean women – we open like that?'

Polly piled apple slices into the tart she was making. She

180

looked up with a small grin. 'Yes, chook. Don't be scared. It's as natural as anything.'

'But doesn't it hurt? Babies are quite big.'

Polly rested her floured knuckles on the deal table. 'It does a bit – not much,' she admitted. 'And you forget about it when the kid's in your arms.'

Alicia recovered herself slightly and bent to rescue the cookery book from the floor. She laughed nervously, as she straightened up. 'You're teasing me, Polly, and in a vulgar way. How could a baby get inside its mother, in the first place?' she asked, as she sat down on a stool.

Holy Mother, save me! I'm lost, thought Polly anxiously. Aloud, she insisted, 'I'm not teasing, luv. It's God's truth.'

Alicia still doubted her and was angry; Polly should not tell such stories when she had asked a serious question. 'Well, how do we get there?' she demanded.

Polly sighed and lifted more pastry on to the wooden pastry board, ready for rolling. At least they had got away from the direct subject of bastards. 'I think you should ask your Mam,' she advised.

'Oh, Polly!' Alicia exclaimed crossly. 'You know she never talks to me about anything much.'

Polly swallowed and then nodded. Here I go, she fretted. 'And I hope I don't lose me job if the Missus finds out.' She paused in her rolling and was quiet for a moment, ad then she began, 'Well, you know as I was married once and had a little baby? And he died?'

'Yes.' Alicia was tremblingly alert now. 'I'm sorry he died.'

'Well, I loved our Pat, me hubbie, somethin' terrible.' She heaved a sigh at the memory of him, though, with no photograph to help her, she could not always remember his face clearly. She leaned on her rolling-pin and cleared her throat. 'When you love a person like that you don't mind what they do to you – you don't mind 'em touching you anywhere.'

Demonstrating with her floured hands, she explained very simply, and Alicia listened, wide-eyed and nervous, yet not frightened. This was what all the mystery was about, this simple action. And when she thought about the world around her, it was a logical explanation.

'It feels lovely,' Polly finished up, 'and you and your hubby are happy afterwards.'

Alicia sat shyly examining her fingernails, and then she asked, 'Do you and Edward feel happy like that?'

Polly had picked up a piece of pastry to cover her apple tart. Paralysed by the question, she stood staring at Alicia, while the pastry drooped and stretched. A slow red flush went up over her forehead and down her neck.

'Now, our Allie!' she protested, giving Alicia her baby name.

Alicia grinned mischievously. 'I'm sorry. I shouldn't ask personal questions. But I thought you must be feeling awful with his being in the war in South Africa – if you do love him.'

Polly gulped and closed her eyes, so that Alicia should not see her agony of mind. Then it burst from her. 'Oh, I do, luv. I worry all the time.'

Alicia slipped from her stool and impulsively wound her arms round the back of her nanny, leaning her head on the maid's bent back. 'Oh, Polly, I'm so sad for you. I love him, too. It makes me feel sick to think of Africa.' She sighed. 'Being a soldier is a dreadful life, isn't it? When you think about it – having to kill other men before they kill you. It must be terrible for Mama.'

Polly turned round and, despite her floury hands, she clung to Alicia.

So rarely did Elizabeth say much to either of them that neither realized that she did not know that her son was in South Africa. Edward wrote to her about once a quarter and never to his father; no mention was made in his letters of where he was, in case the missives fell into enemy hands. He also sent little notes to Polly, care of her sister, Mary, who now had a decent house provided by the City Council, where the postman delivered daily. He signed his notes only with his first initial. Polly treasured them, and it was she who had told Alicia that she was fairly certain Edward had been moved to South Africa – last time he was home they had agreed on a code word by which he could tell her approximately where he was.

The apple pie which Polly had been making was not a great success, because Polly forgot to put in the cloves and cinnamon. Alicia forgot that Polly had not exactly explained how she came to be called a bastard, though a small, nagging apprehension remained with her.

Was she really Alicia Beatrix Mary Woodman? If she was not, who was she? She surreptitiously combed the dictionary in the library; it told her no more than Polly had. And Polly had been quite firm that she was legally Papa's child.

Reading novels with a new alertness, she found there were many in which the heroine was 'betrayed' and often seemed to die in the Workhouse while having a baby with no husband to love and take care of it. Was that how a bastard was born? It was all very vague, except that the baby's life was invariably very difficult.

She never thought of asking Fanny, who could have enlightened her in a few seconds, having been born one herself and having watched the progress of Elizabeth's love affair. Though Fanny was a dear friend, she was not, in Alicia's opinion, very knowledgeable and Alicia had a tendency to lecture her, which sometimes made Fanny laugh.

Chapter Sixteen

I

As Elizabeth grew older and her mind dulled, she rarely read more than the headlines in the newspaper. Polly and Alicia, however, read them quite thoroughly after Humphrey had put them into his wastepaper basket, both anxiously watching the news from South Africa.

At dinnertime, when such news might reasonably have been discussed, Alicia never spoke for fear of having Humphrey snarl at her to hold her tongue. She listened to her parents' conversation, and hearing their quarrelsome arguments made her question Fanny's and Polly's assertions that marriage was a highly desirable state. She herself was always thankful to escape from them to the nursery or the kitchen. She did, occasionally, share afternoon tea with her mother, and, one day, she remarked, without thinking, that it was worrisome to have dear Edward involved in South Africa.

'He's in *India*,' responded Elizabeth lazily. 'Mr Woodman remarked that the Bank was still sending his allowance there – he said that since he was a soldier, he *ought* to be in South Africa.' Elizabeth had, for years, not given much thought to her stodgy elder son, of whom she had few real memories and occasionally forgot completely.

Alicia swallowed, realizing her slip, and hastily agreed that he was probably still in Amritsar. Poor Polly! She had inadvertently nearly betrayed her. She would not have known what to say, if her mother had asked why she imagined Edward was in Africa. How could she tell her that Edward wrote letters to her maidservant? Polly would be dismissed without notice simply for receiving such a missive.

II

One morning late in March, when Mr Bittle's daffodils were blowing cheerfully in the back garden, Humphrey was handed his letters by Fanny, who was waiting on him at the breakfast table. He looked through the envelopes and then quickly extracted one from the War Office. Apprehensively, he slit it open.

Good God! Edward! Dead of the typhoid? He was as shocked as if Edward had been his most beloved son, instead of a constant irritation to him. And he'd died at Ladysmith?

A searing pain went up his chest and neck; he could not breathe properly. And the boy had not even managed to be killed in action, dying for King and Country! That hurt. The pain leapt through him, and he had a flash of memory of a little boy bowling an iron hoop and bumping into him and his being very sharp with him for such careless behaviour. As he fought for breath, a muddled sense of guilt went through him.

Fanny was tidying the sideboard and had her back to him. Now she heard him gasp, 'Brandy!'

She whirled round.

Her master was clutching his chest, obviously in great pain.

She whipped open the sideboard cupboard, snatched up a glass and the crystal decanter and ran to him. She slopped a little brandy into the glass, putting her arm round his shoulders to steady him. He managed to swallow a sip as he leaned against her starched apron. The pain receded slightly, and he muttered, 'Help me – library couch. Call the Mistress.' His speech was slurred.

She was a tiny woman and thought he would collapse on to the hall floor, but she did manage to ease him into the book-lined room and he tumbled on to the couch. He struggled to breathe, as she shook out a crocheted shawl lying at the end of the couch and put it over him. 'I won't be a mo', sir.'

She ran out of the room, hitching up her calico skirts as she took the stairs two at a time.

She hardly stopped to knock, as she flew into Elizabeth's bedroom. 'Oh, Ma'am, please come quick. The Master's took sick.'

Elizabeth put down her teacup carefully on to her breakfast tray. 'Really? Where is he?'

'On the couch in the library. Please hurry, Ma'am.'

Elizabeth slowly reached for her dressing-gown hanging on the bedknob, pushed back the bedcovers and extended one fat leg. Fanny took her hand and helped her out. As Elizabeth carefully tied the cord, Fanny wanted to yell at her, 'Hurry up, for Christ's sake!'

Her mistress stood unsteadily by the bed. Her head ached abominably. 'What happened?'

'He can't breathe, Ma'am, not proper, that is. He were holding 'is chest.'

Herded by a distraught Fanny, Elizabeth staggered to the door and stumped downstairs. When she entered the library, she found Humphrey lying slumped against the raised curve of the end of the couch. His eyes were closed; his breath was coming in irregular gasps.

His wife stood over him, trying to gather her wits together despite her throbbing head. 'What's the matter, Humphrey?'

'Get Willis – heart attack.'

'Are you sure?'

'Yes. Quickly.' His voice faded and he moaned.

Fanny was fluttering nervously in the background. She turned to the mahogany desk, picked out a piece of notepaper from the stand and laid it on the blotting pad. 'Here you are, Ma'am,' she said to Elizabeth.

Like a sleepwalker, Elizabeth went to the desk. Fanny dipped a pen into the silver inkwell and handed it to her. Obediently, Elizabeth wrote. She recollected that she had not had to call Dr Willis since Mrs Tibbs had been taken ill. Mrs Tibbs had died, she thought dully.

'I'll run with it, Ma'am.' She hesitated, and then inquired, 'Shall I ask Polly to come up – to be with you, like?'

Elizabeth looked indifferently at the suffering man. She felt far away from the proceedings, as if she were watching a boring play. In answer to Fanny's question, she said mechanically, 'Yes. Ask her to bring up a glass of brandy – two glasses.'

Polly arrived very speedily with the brandy and suggested that she should watch her Master, who seemed more comfortable after the restorative, while Elizabeth got dressed for the doctor's visit.

Elizabeth tossed down her glass of brandy at a gulp. Then, feeling a little stronger herself, she agreed to go and dress.

Polly did not dare to sit down in front of the Master of the house, so she stood at the foot of the couch, hands clasped tightly in front of her, alternately glancing at the sick man and then through the lace curtains, to see if the doctor's carriage was coming.

She was surprised when, in a whisper, Humphrey addressed her, his eyes still closed. 'Polly.'

'Sir? Are you feelin' better, sir?'

'A little. Polly, I have to break it to your Mistress that Master Edward died at Ladysmith. I want you to be here, in case she faints – that is, if Dr Willis hasn't arrived by the time she comes down again.'

Polly swayed on her feet, as if he had struck her. Strength seemed to run out of her and she thought *she* would faint. Edward, dearest Edward. She clutched at the edge of the desk behind her.

Unaware of the distress he had caused, Humphrey lay perfectly still and tried to breathe normally, as the pain threatened again. The only sound in the room was that of a fly buzzing on the windowpane.

Polly did not answer Humphrey. She could not. She simply stood, trembling from head to foot, trying not to scream or sob, for fear the stricken man before her noticed.

Fanny knocked on the door. When she received no reply,

she opened it cautiously. She was still panting from her fast run to Dr Willis's. 'Aye, Polly, I thought the Mistress would be here. Doctor's comin' now.' Then as she saw Polly's evident anguish, she asked in alarm, 'What's up?'

Polly fought to keep her senses. 'Fanny, watch the Master till the Missus comes back. I got to go upstairs.' She pushed past the little maid to the hall. Holding hard to the banister, she went quickly up the two flights of stairs to her narrow bedroom next to the day nursery. She flung herself on to the bed and let blackness roll over her.

Humphrey was vaguely aware of the verbal exchange between the maids, but his need to rest was paramount. As long as someone was there to deal with the hysterics he expected from his wife, he did not care.

III

Dr Willis consigned Humphrey to bed indefinitely. He promised a bottle of medicine and ordered a light diet. 'And no cigars.'

At the latter instruction, Humphrey's eyes shot open. 'Surely, Willis, I can smoke?'

'I have found that my patients' bouts of pain are much reduced, if they don't smoke,' the doctor declared firmly. 'You may have whisky and an occasional glass of wine. I shall, of course, come in each morning.'

Elizabeth had left the room, while the doctor conducted a physical examination of his patient. Now Dr Willis rose from his chair by the couch and announced that he would go to explain to her what Humphrey could eat. From under heavy grey eyebrows, he looked down at the exhausted man on the couch. 'Have you a manservant to help you to bed?' he inquired.

'No. I'll send for my son-in-law.' It was an effort to speak. 'Probably my brother – Harold – come from Manchester.' He paused to get his breath. 'I can stay here for a couple of days, if necessary.' The pain threatened again and he winced.

Dr Willis took some cushions from an easy chair and gently propped the patient into a more upright position. 'Carefully, Sir,' he warned. He turned to drop his stethoscope into his Gladstone bag.

'Willis, I need your help.' The request was barely a whisper.

'Of coure, sir. What can I do for you?'

'Tell Mrs Woodman that our son, Edward, died at Ladysmith. Letter – under the shawl here.'

'My dear fellow! I'm dreadfully sorry! Of course, I'll tell her. And we were all so thankful last month to hear that the town had been relieved. How very sad for you.' He again looked keenly at Humphrey. 'Was that the cause of the chest pain?'

'I believe so.'

'My deepest condolences. Would you like *me* to send for the Reverend Browning and your daughter? I have an errand boy who could go on his bicycle.'

'Please, do.'

'May I see the letter – so that I can be more precise when talking to your poor lady?'

Humphrey nodded, too exhausted to find the letter for him.

Dr Willis felt round under the shawl and found the crumpled missive. As he read it, he moved slowly towards the bell-pull to call Fanny. 'Rest quietly, sir. I'll deal with this. Indeed, the Lord giveth and the Lord taketh away,' he added piously.

When Fanny showed him into the morning-room, Elizabeth was seated in her favourite chair by the window. Fanny brought him a straight chair and set it close to Elizabeth. He was a tall, elderly man, a product of Edinburgh Medical School, and when Elizabeth turned inquiringly towards him, he surveyed her puffy, overly red cheeks and bloodshot eyes with professional assessment. She smelled of port wine.

Fanny turned to leave the room but the doctor indicated, with a discreet gesture, that she should stay. If Mrs Woodman fainted or went into hysterics, he felt he might need help. He put down his bag and sat down.

Elizabeth's beringed hand was resting on the padded arm of her chair, and the doctor took it in his. 'I'm pleased to tell you, dear Mrs Woodman,' he began, 'that Mr Woodman will recover quite well, if he takes care now. He must stay in bed. And when he is well enough to go outside again, he must never go in cold or blustery weather.' He smiled. 'I'll send in a bottle of medicine later. See that he takes it whenever the pain threatens.'

Elizabeth inclined her head and thanked him. A glass of brandy followed by two of port had created a comfortable euphoria. The doctor sighed. 'I have, however, some very sad news to impart.'

Since she had just been assured that Humphrey would recover, Elizabeth could not think what news the doctor might consider sad, so she smiled slightly. Fanny, however, standing quietly behind her chair, stiffened. With insight and compassion, she again saw Polly's stricken face. Master Edward! It had to be.

Dr Willis told Elizabeth as gently as he could about her son.

Elizabeth did not faint. She sat suddenly very upright. 'Why did not Mr Woodman tell me himself?'

'The news was the cause of his heart pain, I believe.'

'I see.' She was breathing rather heavily and took a moment to let it subside. Then she said, 'To die of typhoid in a foreign land is dying for one's country, is it not, Doctor?'

'Indeed it is, Mrs Woodman, and you may be proud of your son. Disease causes more deaths in the army than actual fighting does – and our men know, when they go forth, that they have to face both enemies, both deadly.'

The doctor continued to sit and pat her hand, expecting tears to burst forth any minute. But they did not. Finally, he told her of the arrangement with her husband that his delivery boy would take a message to Florence and her husband. Then he added, 'My daughter attends Blackburne House and I seem to remember her telling me that your daughter's there. Would you like me to send for her, as well? I'm sure that you'll wish your maids to remain with you, and not go on messages.'

She looked around her rather helplessly. 'Yes – um – yes, I would, if your boy would take a note to her Head Mistress. Fanny, where are you, Fanny?'

'Here, Ma'am.' Fanny came swiftly from behind her.

'Bring my writing case.'

The doctor rose. 'I'll just look in on Mr Woodman again. Someone should sit with him for the next few hours.'

Elizabeth nodded agreement, and she scribbled a note to Alicia's Head Mistress and then folded it up. 'Where's Polly?' she asked Fanny.

'She were took poorly, Ma'am. I think it were her stummick.'

'Dear me!' exclaimed Dr Willis, as he picked up his bag. 'Would you like me to see her?'

'No, thank you,' responded Elizabeth stiffly. 'See Dr Willis out, Fanny, after he has looked at the Master again.' She held out her hand to the doctor and he shook it.

'I'll send in a draught which you yourself might be glad to take at bedtime,' he promised her. She was much too quiet, he thought; she should be shrieking like a steam locomotive. But, then, perhaps she was too drunk to realize completely what had happened. 'I will come again tomorrow morning,' he assured her. 'In the meantime, if there is a recurrence of the pain, please do not hesitate to send for me.'

When Fanny had closed the front door after the kindly doctor, she hesitated as to whether she should go back to her mistress or go to Polly.

She sprinted silently up the stairs to the top floor.

Polly was curled up on her narrow, iron bed, a bundle of sobbing misery. Fanny flew to the bedside and knelt down by her. 'Aye, I'm sorry, luv,' she said as she gathered the weeping woman into her arms. 'There, Pol. There, there,' she crooned.

After rocking her backwards and forwards for a minute, as if she were a child, Fanny urged her to get up and wash her face. 'The Mistress'll want us both, and she mustn't know, luv.

She mustn't never know what was up between you and Master Edward.'

'I don't care if she does.'

'You got to care, Pol. Or you'll be out on the street without a reference.'

'I don't care. I want to die.'

'Come on with yez. Think of our little Allie. What's she goin' to do without you? You're her Mam, really; it's you who loves her. And she'll be home in twenty minutes or so – Doctor's sendin' a note for her – maybe he thinks the Master won't live.'

At this, Polly slowly sat up and wiped her eyes with the back of her hands. 'She loved Eddy,' she said brokenly. 'He was forever sendin' her little presents. Aye, he were a lovely man.' The tears burst forth again.

Fanny got up off the floor and went to the washstand. She poured some water from the flowered pitcher into the bowl, took up a flannel and wetted it. 'Wipe your face, luv. You got to go down.'

Still crying, Polly obediently took the flannel and washed her face. Fanny handed her the towel.

After drying herself, she staggered up off the bed and went to a small mirror on the wall. She hastily pulled out her hairpins and redid her hair.

'Where's your cap?' Fanny asked, hunting round the pillow for it.

'Get me a clean one out of the cupboard.' Polly was struggling, now, to quell the storm of grief within her.

When Fanny returned to the morning-room, Elizabeth asked irritably where she had been. 'I've been ringing the bell for ages,' she complained.

Lying glibly, Fanny told her that she had had to attend to the butcher's delivery boy at the back door and that Polly was now making a sponge cake and dare not leave it in the middle. 'Would you like to lie down a bit, Ma'am? Polly or me'll watch the Master. I'm proper sorry about the young Master, Ma'am.'

'Thank you, Fanny. Ask Polly to make some coffee and bring it to the library. And make up the library fire.'

'Yes,'m.' Fanny helped to heave her out of her chair and, teetering slightly, she went into the hall and through to the library. There, she peered down at her husband. He appeared to be sleeping, but his cheeks, drained of their usual ruddiness, were wet and a tear had got caught in his moustache.

'I should be crying, too,' thought Elizabeth vaguely. 'But I can't. I've seen so little of him – and he was always so dull, not a bit like Charles.' She sat down by the embers of the fire, and thought of the three miscarriages which had followed Edward's birth; they had left her weak and depressed. She decided fretfully that probably Edward had been happier with his nanny than with her.

Down in the untidy kitchen, Polly mechanically set a tray, including a cup for Humphrey.

'Make a good strong cup for yourself as well,' Fanny instructed her. She had been to the coal cellar and had a full coal scuttle in one hand. Her sackcloth apron and her hands were black with coal dust. 'Put a drop of the cooking rum in it,' she advised Polly, as she crossed the kitchen. 'Keep yer goin', it will.'

Still sobbing, Polly nodded agreement.

Chapter Seventeen

I

'Polly! Polly!' Alicia sped down the area steps and pushed open the heavy back door. 'Polly! What's happened? Why am I sent for?' She slammed the door behind her to keep out the chill March wind, and slung her satchel on to the floor. She pulled off her hat. Her face was more than usually pale and was wet from the rain through which she had run.

Polly put down the kettle which she was filling at the sink and quickly skirted the big deal table. She took Alicia by the elbow and ushered her towards the kitchen range. 'Come by the fire, duck, and get warm, and I'll tell you.'

In the heat of the fire, Alicia struggled out of her damp coat and looked at Polly.

'Polly, you've been crying. Something awful's happened. 'what is it?'

Polly sank down on to a wooden chair, her starched apron poofing out in front of her. She put an arm round Alicia's waist. 'It's Master Edward, luv. He died at Ladysmith – caught the typhoid during the siege.'

'Oh, Polly!' Alicia gasped in consternation. 'Oh, Polly, Polly!' She put her arms round her nanny's neck and buried her face in her shoulder. 'And we'll never see him again?'

'No, duck. Try not to grieve, luvvie. He were a soldier, and he were brave; so we have to be brave like him.' Her voice quavered and broke; she wept unrestrainedly.

Alicia cried with her. 'He wasn't just my brother, he was my very best friend,' she moaned. 'And he's gone.'

Ever since their conversation over the apple pie on the subject of bastards, Alicia had understood the relationship between Polly and her brother, and, after her first burst of tears, she tried to comfort her nanny. She patted Polly's bent back, and whispered, 'Dearest Polly, I'm so sorry for you. It must be terrible.'

The young girl's understanding made Polly jump. She pushed Alicia gently a little back from her and looked into the concerned light grey eyes. 'God bless the poor little lamb,' she thought, and hugged her close again, as she sniffed back her tears. 'Aye, Allie, dear, I could wish myself dead.'

'Oh, no, Polly. What would I do without you? And we have to help Mama – just think what she must be feeling! I'd better go up to her.' She took her handkerchief out of her blouse pocket and wiped the tears from Polly's lined face. Polly looks so old, she thought with a pang, and she feared suddenly that she might lose her, too.

As Polly slowly got up from her wooden chair, Alicia turned away and blew her nose. 'Has anybody told Papa? And Florence and Charles?' she inquired.

Polly sniffed and swallowed. 'Aye, and that's another thing,' she said, and told Alicia about Humphrey's heart attack and that Dr Willis was sending a message to Florence.

Alicia looked at her as if she had seen a ghost. 'And Mama?' she stammered.

'She's all right. She's sittin' with your Papa. I don't think she's cryin' or anythin'.'

'She's probably tipsy,' Alicia thought unhesitatingly, and she glanced despairingly around her; she felt hemmed in.

She heaved a great sigh and said courageously, 'Look, Polly, dear. Everybody's going to need to eat, so you make lunch – you'll feel better if you're busy, I think. Make enough for Florence and Clarence. And I'll go to see Mama and Papa.' She wiped her nose again and it shone red in the firelight.

Polly nodded. 'You're right, me little duck; you're a good little girl. You go to your Mam.'

'What's Fanny doing?'

'She's bin makin' up all the fires, because the wind's cold today, and now she's changin' the sheets on the Mistress's bed and puttin' in hot water bottles to warm it. When the Reverend and Miss Florence come, we'll get the Master up to bed – he's in the library at present. And Fanny'll make up the bed in the dressing-room for your Mam so she'll be close by.'

As she picked up her damp hat and coat, Alicia felt reluctant to leave the safety of the warm kitchen, but she said quite firmly to Polly, 'I'll go up and see them.' She could not imagine her bad-tempered, taciturn father lying sick. He never spoke to her, except to reprimand, and she wondered what to say to him, what to do.

As she hesitated before climbing the stairs, Polly turned from poking up the fire, and called, 'Off you go now. They need you.'

The idea that her parents might need her was a new one to Alicia, and again she had the uncanny feeling of events closing in on her.

Mechanically she hung her coat and hat in the big hall cloakroom and changed into house slippers. Inside her was a hard lump of misery and she whimpered to herself, 'Edward, Edward, I always thought – hoped – you would come home for good one day and be with Polly and me.'

At the door of the library, she stifled her sobs and rubbed the tears from her eyes. She knocked and entered.

Humphrey looked pitifully small under the eiderdown Fanny had brought to cover him, an object of fear, now deflated like a burst balloon. Her mother looked slovenly, with untidy wisps of hair hanging round her flushed face. Alicia went cautiously towards her and gave her a light kiss on her cheek. 'I'm so sad for you, Mama,' she said. 'Polly told me.'

Elizabeth nodded, and said thickly, 'What a waste – to die of typhoid.'

'Yes, indeed, Mama.'

Her mother relapsed into silence, and Alicia turned timidly towards the man on the couch. 'How are you feeling now, Papa?'

He had been watching her since she entered the room. He

did not answer, but contented himself with a slight movement of his head, which seemed to Alicia to indicate that he was not feeling very good.

'I'm so sad about Edward,' she faltered, the tears threatening to brim over again.

With eyes closed, he nodded again.

She stood uncertainly between the couple, the silence clawing at her. What should she do? She stole a glance at her mother whose head had fallen forward as if she had suddenly fallen asleep. The reek of alcohol from her was sufficient for Alicia to realize that she would get no help from her. She yearned for Florence to come, though Florence never seemed to know what to do in any circumstances; she was a flurry of muddle and uncertainties, but at least she spoke to one, and she, too, might care about Edward.

'He's my brother,' she thought desperately, 'and Mama doesn't seem to realize that it hurts – it hurts most dreadfully – that he's dead.' In a flash of anger, she wanted to strike both parents. Her teeth began to chatter, and through it she stammered to Elizabeth, 'I'll see if Fanny's done the bedroom properly for Papa.' And she fled from the room.

She met Fanny coming out of the master bedroom, a pile of tumbled sheets in her arms. 'Oh, Fanny,' she wailed in relief.

Fanny dropped the bedclothes and put skinny arms around the frightened girl. 'It's all right, Allie, dear. Everything'll be all right in a wee bittie.'

Alicia hugged Fanny's small frame and kissed her on the cheek. Then she let her go. 'Mama doesn't seem to be very well, Fanny, so you make sure that everything is clean and neat up here, ready for Father – water in the carafe – and soap and towels – before the Reverend Browning gets here. He's so picky.'

Fanny knew perfectly well that Alicia meant that her mother was drunk again, so she said, 'Don't worry, pet. Polly and us'll manage together, won't we? We'll get your Dad better.'

Alicia nodded. She watched the tiny maid collect up the

sheets from the floor, and she asked, 'Fanny, will they bury Edward in Africa – in Ladysmith?'

Fanny looked up, a little confused, 'They must've done it already,' she replied slowly, as she straightened up.

'But he'll be so lonely.' Alicia looked up beseechingly at Fanny. 'Can't he be brought home?'

Fanny hesitated, anxious to comfort, but not sure how to do it. Then she said, 'He might like to lie with his friends, luv. A lot of men died at Ladysmith.'

'Perhaps he would.' Alicia managed a tremulous smile. Then her expression changed as she remembered Charles. 'I don't think anyone has thought about telling Charles,' she said. 'I must ask the Reverend Browning to send him a telegram.'

II

Alicia never went back to Blackburne House. Forced by circumstances, as her mother became daily more incompetent, she grew up very fast. She took over the management of the house and, under the guidance of Dr Willis, the care of Humphrey. When she wailed to Polly that everything was too much for her and that she did not know how to cope, Polly would say, 'It's your duty, duck, to look after your Ma and Pa. It's a daughter's job. Me and Fanny'll help you.'

Yes, thought Alicia, but you don't really have to face Papa.

Humphrey had no intention of remaining an invalid for the rest of his life. Because he refused to have a nurse in the house, for several weeks he had to accept the help of Alicia. It was either Polly or Alicia who emptied his bedpans, and Alicia, who had never in her life seen a naked male, who washed him. A curious, close relationship grew up between them, like that between prisoner and gaoler. There was no love between the thin wisp of a girl and the stout, frustrated man, but there began to be a reciprocal respect. In the end, Humphrey found it satisfyingly ironical that it should be Crossing's bastard who served him so faithfully.

Numbed by hatred of him, there was no sympathy from Elizabeth. Yet she feared that if he died, there would be only absent-minded, self-centred Charles to protect her. She rarely went into her husband's bedroom and spent most of her time slumped in her easy chair or, as the summer drew on, in a chair in the garden. Polly and Fanny bore as best they could her continuous complaints about slowness in answering her bell and lateness of meals; it was as if the reality of caring for an invalid, or the fact that she should be helping, had not impinged on her brain at all.

Following Humphrey's heart attack, Florence came to stay for a couple of days. When told about Edward, she sat and wept copiously and the next day went into black. After that, she returned to her impatient, fussy husband, who had brought her to the house and who had stayed long enough to help Humphrey to his bed, before he went back home to supervise those members of his rowdy family not yet in boarding school.

Alicia hid the key to the wine cellar long enough to get Elizabeth into one of her good, black dresses and keep her sober while she attended a Memorial Service for Edward arranged by her son-in-law. After the service, Elizabeth, clutching a black-edged handkerchief, received a stream of visitors who called formally to present their condolences; one or two went up to visit Humphrey as well, but he was very weak and could not stand long visits.

Humphrey's brother, Harold, and his wife, Vera, came from Manchester for the service, and Alicia soberly sat with them through lunch in the dining-room. 'Mama is lying down— naturally, she is rather indisposed,' Alicia explained. She did not say that her mother had a racking headache and was raging in her room, because she could not find the key to the wine cellar, nor could she find a single bottle of anything to drink in the rest of the house.

When, later, the couple went upstairs for a short visit to her, she was propped up in bed drinking tea and was barely civil to them.

In the next room, they conveyed their condolences to a

recumbent Humphrey, and Harold promised to come to visit him again the following week.

Charles came down from University and wandered round the house, looking helpless. He had grown a beard and had trimmed it in imitation of the dashing Prince of Wales, so that Alicia barely recognized him.

Charles had few memories of Edward and could not grieve at his death any more than if he had been a casual friend who had died. He did, however, sit with his father and refrained from any hot answer when Humphrey grumbled that he needed him at home now, to help him in the office.

Despite the gloom in the house, Charles joked with Alicia and told her she was managing everything wonderfully. A few days later he went thankfully back to Cambridge and his research.

At the end of two weeks, Elizabeth's cash box being empty, Alicia gathered up her courage and asked Humphrey for some housekeeping money.

'Mama doesn't seem to have any; and I must pay Fanny and Polly and the grocer and the butcher.'

He turned his head on his pillow and looked at her in astonishment, a thin slip of a fourteen-year-old – Andrew Crossing's bastard. Then he laughed. It was not a pleasant laugh and it frightened Alicia. But she stood her ground and waited.

'What's your mother doing? *She* should have come to me for her housekeeping.'

Alicia gulped. She did not want to say that her mother was often dazedly drunk or lay in her bed with racking headaches. Finally, she told him, 'Well, Mama is so upset about Edward – and about you – that she is not well herself; so I've been doing things.'

'I see. Get the housekeeping book from your mother and bring it to me – I check it each month. If she is well enough, ask her to come in to see me. Last time I saw it, the entries did not match the tradesmen's bills.' He looked suddenly exhausted, and Alicia felt a quick jolt of apprehension. Supposing he died, what would happen to her and to Mama – and Polly and Fanny?

'And may I have some money, Papa?'

'I must first speak to your mother.'

'Of course, it would be impolite for me to look after the housekeeping without first asking her,' responded Alicia soberly, as if she had not been battling with it for the previous two weeks.

Politeness was not what Humphrey had in mind. Now a little recovered, he wanted to know what his wife had actually been doing while he was ill. Was she so drunk that she could not run the house?

He rested for a moment while Alicia stood apprehensively by his bed. Then he took a large breath and made a further effort. 'You remember Mr Bowring, my clerk, who came to see me after the Memorial Service?' he asked.

'Yes, Papa.'

'Write him a letter to ask him to call on me tomorrow afternoon – at three o'clock. And get the maids to bring up the side table from the library – and a chair – and put them in the window, here, so that he has a place to work.'

'Yes, Papa.'

Outside the room, she stood in the upper hall and cried quietly to herself. How long was it going to be like this, she wondered. When would she be able to go back to school?

Chapter Eighteen

I

On January 22nd, 1901, the old Queen died after a very brief illness. Few of her subjects had ever known another monarch, and they felt bereft when they discovered that she was not immortal. Theatres closed and church bells tolled mournfully; they went on and on, until even the most devoted mourners had to grit their teeth to endure even one more slow dong-dong.

All the dressmakers in the city, including George Henry Lee's who usually provided Elizabeth's better dresses, were inundated by orders for funeral mourning.

On February 2nd, Humphrey and Elizabeth were bidden to the Cathedral Church of St Peter to attend a memorial service for the Queen.

When Humphrey found the invitation in his morning mail at the breakfast table, he felt that they should attend. Though not as strong as he had been, he was fairly recovered from his heart attack and had taken up again most of his usual pursuits.

He met his wife emerging from the master bedroom, after having had her breakfast in bed – he had long since returned to his single bed in the dressing-room; once his heart pains had retreated, he had announced that he preferred its more masculine atmosphere. This morning, Elizabeth was still wrapped in her grubby, blue woollen dressing-gown, her grey hair tumbling round her shoulders. She had assumed that Humphrey was already on his way to his office and she was now in search of a drop of brandy.

He informed her of the cathedral service, and she responded sulkily that she had no decent black dress to wear.

'Nonsense,' he replied shortly, 'you must have an enormous wardrobe.'

'Nothing fits.' Elizabeth sounded as if she did not care very much.

'Well, for God's sake, get a new dress or costume.'

'I still owe Lee's for the last one – and I know that Mrs Blossom has so much work that she can't promise a dress in less than a month.'

'Can't you even manage to pay your bills?'

'If you'd give more to Charles for his university expenses, he wouldn't be such a drain on *my* resources.'

'Charles should be in the office with me; I wonder if he'll ever learn that he must earn a living.'

Elizabeth ignored this old complaint, but went on unwisely, 'Alicia should have a black costume, also.'

Humphrey's little eyes nearly vanished in the folds of flesh around them, as he turned towards the bathroom door. 'Alicia's personal needs are your concern, not mine. She's lucky that I feed her and give her a bed.' He pushed the door open and then looked back over his shoulder. 'And don't forget, Madam, that I give *you* a roof – many men wouldn't. I shall order the carriage for 10.30 on Friday morning. See that you are ready. And make sure the servants have black arm bands sewn on their outdoor clothes.'

He stalked into the bathroom and closed the door.

Elizabeth shivered and wondered, for the hundredth time, whether her brother in Ceylon would give her a home on his tea estate, if she suddenly arrived there. Then she envisioned again dealing with the partner with whom he lived and with a totally strange country, and she discarded the idea; she rarely considered what would happen to Alicia if she left her husband; she did not enjoy thinking about the girl at all.

She went downstairs into the dining-room; the brandy bottle in the sideboard was empty. She pulled a chair away from the table and sat down on it. When Polly came up to clear Humphrey's breakfast dishes, she found her mistress weeping quietly, her hands screwing up her wet handkerchief in her lap. Tray in hand, Polly asked kindly if she could help her.

Elizabeth made no attempt to hide her tears. She mumbled, 'Yes, Polly. Find me a glass of port and my smelling salts.'

II

The fine black broadcloth costume, lined with silk and trimmed discreetly with black silk velvet binding was a miracle produced by two elderly ladies from George Henry Lee's who sewed nearly all night for several nights, first the calico fitting and then the dress material cut from the calico pattern. Though a seamstress was sent up to the house for the first two fittings, Lee's was so busy that Elizabeth had to go down to the shop for the final one.

When Elizabeth had said she would hire a closed carriage for this journey, Humphrey said she could hire anything as long as *she* paid for it. Otherwise, she could use the electric tram, as he did. This led to one of their tremendous quarrels, from which the whole household reverberated for the next twenty-four hours.

When Sarah Webb called and was told by Elizabeth about Humphrey's meanness, she promptly offered to take her angry friend down to Lee's in her governess cart; she herself always wore black as being the most economical colour. Elizabeth reluctantly accepted this modest form of door-to-door transport, and had the dress billed to Humphrey.

A new hat being too much expense, an old one was taken out and retrimmed with swirls of black velvet, taken from an evening gown with a twenty-two inch waist which Elizabeth could no longer get into. There was enough material in the skirt to furnish a dress for Alicia; this was made up for her by a new dressmaker who had recently set up in Crown Street; it neither fitted nor suited Alicia, who complained bitterly to Polly about it.

'It's the best your Mam could do; be thankful for it,' replied Polly unsympathetically.

Alicia thought uneasily about this apparent need for economy and then put on the hated garment.

Alicia herself bound four white handkerchiefs with black edging, two for Humphrey and one each for her mother and herself, not that Alicia wept much for the old Queen; she had a feeling that Edward VII might be more fun.

While her parents were at the service and the subsequent luncheon, Alicia thankfully took off her ugly mourning dress and put on an old summer frock, in order to help Fanny give the morning-room and the library a much needed cleaning.

The house was far too big for two maids to cope with, and Alicia had realized that parts of it were gradually becoming very neglected. Elizabeth took little interest in it. No parties had been given in it for some time. Few ladies called on a woman who did not have an At Home any more. Only Sarah Webb panted her way up the front steps at least once a week to sit with her old friend and visit her godchild.

Shabby curtains and rugs which might normally have been renewed went unnoticed by their depressed owners. When Alicia pointed out that moths had got into the dining-room curtains and suggested new ones, her mother retorted impatiently that it was too much trouble and, anyway, Humphrey would never agree to the expense. In this latter remark, she was probably right; Humphrey was finding his old friend, Mrs Jakes and her tobacco shop, quite expensive, at a time when he had suffered a number of financial losses, including money invested in a mad scheme to build a railway tunnel under the Mersey; the railway had been built, but had been a consistent money loser.

'Shall we take up the carpet, Allie?' This from Fanny in the morning-room. 'It needs beating badly.'

'There isn't time, Fan. They'll be back from Church before we're finished, if we take it up. Scatter tea leaves over it and give it a thorough brush with a stiff broom. We'll take the curtains down, though, and give them a good brush and shake in the garden; I don't think the velvet ones have been down for years.'

'You should leave me to do it, Allie. You should go out for a bit. Haven't you got a school friend you could visit? That Miss Ethel you used to walk home with sometimes?'

At the top of the stepladder, Alicia carefully lowered one end of the heavy brass curtain rail into Fanny's hands. Dust flew from the curtains as they slid to the end of the rail and Fanny pulled them off. Alicia sneezed, and this gave her time to consider her reply. She had learned to accept the fact that when she offered friendship to a girl, there always seemed to be an obstacle to its flourishing. She did not really understand why, and usually blamed herself for being uninteresting or not well-dressed enough to please the parents concerned.

Now, she wondered sometimes if there were another, darker reason. She had come to understand, after sly questioning of Polly, that illegitimacy was a dreadful burden for a child to bear; but, again and again, she came back to the fact that Papa was very much a presence in the house. He was terrifyingly bad-tempered and he rarely spoke to her, except to scold or swear at her. Nevertheless, he existed, so that when she had been called a bastard, it had seemed untrue. That her mother's long-held reputation for flirtatiousness, on top of the rumours of Alicia being the daughter of Andrew Crossing, made anxious mothers feel that their daughters should not be exposed to such an influence, did not occur to bewildered Alicia.

Fanny's suggestion that she should go to see Ethel disturbed her and she did not know how to answer. Finally, as she slipped another curtain off its rod, she replied, 'You know, Fan, I often feel a long way away from other girls, as if I were much older than them.' She climbed slowly down the stepladder. 'I met Ethel in the chemist's one day. She said she was swotting to go to university, which is something I would have liked to do; but which university is going to accept a lady?'

'I dunno anything about that. But it int natural for a young girl to have no friends,' responded Fanny firmly. 'Your Mam ought to do something about it. Who's going to come to your Coming Out Dance, if you don't know nobody?'

Alicia bent over to bundle up the curtains, to take them into the garden to shake. 'Mama hasn't said anything about my Coming Out yet – I'm really not quite old enough, am I?'

'Suppose you talk to Miss Florence about it?' Fanny suggested, as together they staggered out under their loads of drapery.

'Perhaps I will – one day,' Alicia replied doubtfully.

III

Except for a necklace of seed pearls from her godmother, Sarah Webb, and a book of children's poetry which arrived by post from Florence, Alicia's sixteenth birthday on May 12th , 1902, went unremarked outside the kitchen.

Polly baked a birthday cake and presented her with a pair of hand-knitted gloves; Fanny gave her two bars of highly scented soap. In addition to the cake, they had strawberry jelly for tea.

When Sarah called, Elizabeth was so deeply asleep that Alicia was unable to waken her to greet her old friend. Sarah kept her concern at this to herself and had a cup of tea and a piece of birthday cake with Alicia in the morning-room.

Alicia was enchanted at having a real pearl necklace and flung her arms round Sarah gleefully.

She did not tell her godmother that, as usual, her mother had forgotten her birthday and that Papa and Charles never seemed to remember anybody's birthday. She wondered sadly if there were other girls whose birthdays went unremarked; most of the girls at school, she remembered, had had not only presents but parties to celebrate the day, parties to which she was never invited. This persistent overlooking of her meant, she was by now convinced, that there was something seriously wrong with her own character, so that she failed to please – or that she was, indeed, by some odd quirk, illegitimate and, therefore, outside the social pale. These fears about herself tended to make her withdrawn, though not when with her quiet, charming, old godmother.

While she plied Sarah with tea, down in the basement kitchen Fanny voiced her usual complaints about the neglect of Alicia's birthday.

'Lady Mucks of Muck Hall round here, they are. Anywhere else, they'd've forgotten years ago wot 'er Mam did – and you'd think the Master would've guv up on it by now. But, no! The poor little bugger has to go on being put in 'er place, like she were born in the Workhouse, like me.'

'Her Mam's not well enough to see to her,' Polly defended her mistress.

Fanny replied tartly, 'There's nothin' wrong with her Mam, 'cept she drinks and totters round like a hen with the staggers. She's just gone to bits, she has.' Fanny wrung out the dishcloth, as if she were wringing Elizabeth's neck. 'If she'd a scrap of sense, she could've helped the kid get some friends, so they could've come to a do on her birthday.' And she added, as she emptied the washing-up water down the sink, 'There's no excuse for not givin' her a present.'

Polly had heard it all before and agreed with her friend, but she warned, 'Hush, Fan. It int our business.'

IV

On a warm, late September day, Florence and three of her children dropped in for afternoon tea. After enduring the children while Alicia served tea, Elizabeth suggested wearily that they should take the youngsters for a run in the garden, so Alicia and Florence took them outside.

Alicia pointed out with jubilation that, today, she had her hair up for the first time, and she turned her head so that Florence could admire the neat bun at the back of her neck.

Florence said absently that it was very nice, and turned to chide three of her children who were romping through a bed of delphiniums, the pride of Mr Bittle, the gardener. Her scolding was ineffectual and she felt wearily that she had not the strength to heave them bodily out of the flowerbed, so she turned a fretful face back to Alicia.

Alicia was saying, 'Flo, do you think I'm old enough to have a Coming Out Party?'

Away in her parsonage ever since Alicia was born, Florence had little idea of the day-to-day isolation of her half-sister, and she replied casually, 'I imagine you could have your friends in. The drawing-room is big enough for a little dance.'

'It needs a good clean,' replied Alicia ruefully. 'You had a dance, didn't you? And that's how you met Clarence?'

'Yes. Mama asked the sons of friends of hers, and he was one of them. The idea is to meet possible husbands.'

'Are you happy with him, Flo?'

The sudden question disconcerted the older woman. Under the brim of her straw hat, her eyes were troubled. 'Well, of course. Clarence is very good and the children are a great consolation. What else can one expect?'

'Were you in love with Clarence, I mean truly, romantically in love?'

'Really, Alicia, I think that is a rather impertinent question. Naturally one loves one's husband – it's the duty of a wife.' They sat down together on the garden seat and Alicia stretched her arms above her and then clasped her hands behind her head. 'I'd like to be in love,' she declared, 'really and truly in love.'

'Alicia! Don't stretch yourself in public; it's most unladylike. In love? Well, I hope it happens.' She thought how nice it would be to be sixteen and not know anything about the nastiness of love and the pain and exhaustion of child-bearing – and how totally unreasonable husbands could be. She pushed back errant wisps of hair from her face; she looked terribly tired and old, and Alicia pitied her.

'You know, Flo, if I get married, I'm not going to have a lot of children.'

Florence smiled sadly. 'You don't have any choice. They simply come.'

'Even if you don't get married?'

Florence hesitated. 'Well, you know that old maids don't have them. But you don't want to be an old maid, do you?'

'Aunt Sarah seems to be quite happy in her little house and with her pony and trap.'

'Ah, yes, but Miss Webster was left quite a competence by her father.'

'Well, won't Papa leave you and me something? I thought all fathers did.'

Florence did not know how to answer the question. Though Humphrey tolerated Alicia in his house, Clarence had not hesitated to state that Alicia was illegitimate and that her mother's morals had been a source of gossip for years. He had, at the same time, pointed out that a Vicar's wife must always be above suspicion.

Under Alicia's steady gaze, Florence squirmed uneasily. Though her father sent her generous monetary gifts for her birthday and at Christmas, she knew that he never gave anything to Alicia; he seemed to ignore the girl as far as possible. And Clarence was in part correct; her mother had been in times past rather a flirt and her clothes had tended to be extremely fashionable and too bright in colour for a place like Liverpool. Alicia was, however, waiting for an answer, so she said hesitantly, 'Well, I'm not sure. I suspect that he is not quite as well off as he used to be, so I can't say.'

The cheerfulness engendered by her mother's permission to put her hair up went out of Alicia, as she looked at her obviously embarrassed, prevaricating sister. Papa was certainly being quite careful about money; yet she felt that Florence was trying to evade replying to her question. As it had done many times lately, a sense of dread invaded her and made her stomach muscles clench. Without Papa, what would happen to Mama and to herself? If they could not pay Polly, she, too, would have difficulties and would have to find another job. Alicia wondered how she could live without Polly. She licked her lips, and tried to be practical, as she suggested, 'Perhaps I should forget about Coming Out; the girls at school used to say that it wasn't the party you gave yourself that was so much fun, but the parties of the other families to which you were invited. And who is going to ask me? I never see another girl these days – I mean, nice girls – when I go shopping; they are all in school.' She stopped, her expression pensive. Then she added heavily, 'I must be the most boring person on earth.'

Florence did not deny her last remark; Alicia was rarely spritely. She did feel, however, a sense of guilt. If her mother was not well enough to bring Alicia out, she should herself help the girl a little – though what Clarence would say if she suggested giving parties for Alicia would probably be unprintable.

Yet, Coming Out launched you on the marriage market, gave you a chance to meet eligible young men. Even plain girls like Alicia had to marry – what else were they to do? The few girls who earned their living in offices or stores were lower class. There was, of course, nursing, thanks to the efforts of Florence Nightingale; but if Alicia became a nurse she would have to live in the hospital amongst a lot of ignorant, Roman Catholic Irish girls, and Florence shuddered at the thought of the amount of floor-scrubbing and cleaning of bedpans she would have to do before she received her nurse's cap.

The very thought of giving even a Tea for Alicia made Florence feel tired to death, but she said reluctantly, 'I'll mention it to Mama, if you like.'

'Would you, Flo?' She looked wistfully at her sister. 'I would so love a party with a special dress – not made by old Miss Blossom!' She smiled at her own reference to the elderly dressmaker whose clothes always seemed behind the times.

'I'm sure you would.' Inwardly, Florence sighed. The hint that the girl was a bastard, added to that almost white, wispy hair, the light grey eyes with their pale lashes behind glasses, the quietness of the girl. There was nothing to recommend her to a well-placed youth unless she had a good dowry. She's pleasant and she's capable and that's all, thought Florence.

The recollection of Alicia's ability to organize her mother's house reminded Florence of her own need for additional help at home.

'You know, Alicia,' she said slowly, 'if Papa was not able to leave either of us any money, the Reverend Browning would give you a home; Clarence is a little stern, but he would never let you starve.'

Alicia's lips looked almost grim because at this remark she clamped them together so tightly. No, she screamed inwardly. Heaven preserve me from becoming an unpaid help in a brother-in-law's house, penniless, and without a moment's privacy or peace. Better to be a paid governess in the house of a stranger. She said aloud, 'That would be very kind of you both, Flo. Thank you.'

V

Florence broached the subject to her mother on one of Elizabeth's rare visits to the Vicarage.

Because Humphrey had had a new lock put on the wine cellar, Elizabeth was unusually sober. Seated in Florence's pokey little sitting-room, a glass of the Reverend Browning's poor quality Madeira in her hand, she was doing her best to sip the wine genteelly while she longed to gulp it down and ask for another glass. Her hands trembled and her mind had a tendency to wander.

Sarah Webb who had driven her out to the Vicarage noted her friend's predicament and thought that, later, she would warn Florence not to offer her mother alcohol. Poor Elizabeth would kill herself with drink, if she were not watched.

Elizabeth was caught off balance by Florence's request for a Coming Out for Alicia. She blurted in reply, 'Your father would never allow it.'

'But, Mama, I had one.'

'It – er – would be so expensive, nowadays.'

Florence tried again. 'It would not need a great deal, Mama. I'm sure we could cater it ourselves – and get flowers from the garden. I could play the piano for dancing. And that leaves only wine – which Papa probably already has in his cellar.'

Cornered, Elizabeth cast a frantic glance at Sarah.

Sarah knew all too well that a Coming Out Party would cause another round of malicious gossip and would probably not result in Alicia getting a husband. Elizabeth had already told her of Humphrey's angry remark that he would leave nothing to Alicia, and, of course, Elizabeth's capital left her by her father could not be touched; she could use only the interest, so, presumably, Alicia had no dowry.

Watching Alicia slowly take over the housekeeping, Sarah sensed that, in any case, Elizabeth simply did not want to alter the current situation; for once, Elizabeth and Humphrey were in silent agreement; it was convenient to have a trustworthy, unpaid housekeeper.

Anxious not to hurt Alicia, Sarah took a careful sip from her teacup, and said to Florence, 'Your Mama and Papa are far from well, dear – and the passing of Edward . . . the wear and tear of a party could be too much for them.' She turned to Elizabeth, and asked, 'Would Clara in West Kirby give a little party for her and invite the local young people?' That, she argued, might introduce the girl to a new group, give her a little chance.

'Clara is totally bed-ridden now; her companion-help has to do everything for her. She could not even come to Edward's Memorial Service. She's been very kind in asking Alicia to visit her to get the sea air . . . but I haven't been able to spare her lately . . .' Elizabeth could hardly hold her teacup steady and leaned forward to put it down on the side table, before she dropped it.

All this time, Alicia had been kneeling in front of the windowseat on which she and Florence's youngest daughter had spread a jigsaw puzzle. As she half-listened to the debate on her Coming Out, she felt a painful sadness; her mother's remark about her aunt's invitations, however, was comforting; dear Aunt Clara had not forgotten her, as she had often assumed. Now it struck her that arthritic hands and sheer age had probably made it difficult for her to write many letters and, naturally, she would write, when she could, to Elizabeth. Mama, being often drunk, had probably forgotten to pass on the gentle, kindly messages.

As her little niece triumphantly placed a corner piece in the puzzle, Alicia felt again that walls were closing round her – and the walls had no doors or windows. Though she had never had a social life, she had always hoped that as she grew up she would get a chance of making a circle of cheerful, intelligent friends.

Elizabeth was woodenly declaring that dear Alicia did not need to Come Out; her place was with her mother.

Alicia wanted to cry; the walls loomed even bigger and more menacing.

She had wept and raged one night recently, while helping Polly plough through the household mending. 'Why can't I be like other girls and go back to school? At least I was learning something there.'

Pitying her and anxious not to add to the girl's burdens, Polly had tried to rationalize the situation for her. She had said, 'Well, luvvy, your Ma and Pa need your help very badly at home; any girl would do the same as you and look after them. It's a single daughter's duty – you see it all the time.' She had put down her sewing on the table and had leaned over to touch Alicia's hand. 'You've got enough book-learnin', already, to last you a lifetime, duck.'

Alicia had hung her head, so that Polly should not see the rebellion in her expression, and had continued to cross-stitch round a patch in a flannel sheet.

Polly changed the subject to divert her, and asked, 'When I done this hem, will you help me write to Billy? Come on. Here's a hankie to dry your eyes.'

Resignedly, Alicia wiped her face, blew her nose and agreed to help. Billy did not write that often, but at least three or four times a year, a long, printed epistle would arrive, and his adventures in Canada were sometimes very funny, as he described them to the sister for whom he hoped to make a home.

Now, in Florence's dowdy sitting-room, young Beatrice carefully put the last piece into the puzzle and smiled up at Alicia in triumph. She scrambled down from the windowseat and went to ask Florence for a piece of cake.

Alicia got up off her knees and quietly took a seat by the completed puzzle.

As the debate on a party for her petered out, she felt defeated. She knew she had duties towards her parents, duties defined by the Church which she no longer had the time to attend and by a society which did not hesitate to keep a daughter at home and single, if it were convenient to her parents.

Doesn't anyone have duties towards me? she wondered forlornly.

VI

In an effort to alleviate the disappointment her godchild must be feeling, Sarah Webb changed the subject of conversation, by asking Alicia, 'Did you see the Indian troops pass through on the electric tram, dear? They're here for the Coronation.'

'Yes, I did,' replied Alicia a trifle defiantly, as she glanced at her surprised mother. 'Polly and I walked down to Sefton Park to see them.'

Her mother blinked. She was quite shocked. 'Alicia! You should ask before you leave the house. To go out with the common herd to gape at foreign troops!'

'You were asleep, Mama. I did not wish to wake you.' She did not add that her mother had been sleeping off a bottle of port which Elizabeth had ordered Fanny to go out and buy for her. 'I wanted to see the kind of men that Edward commanded.' Her nose went into the air in a movement like that of her mother in earlier days, and she added, 'They looked very fine – very handsome. I was safe there with Polly – and really a lot of most respectable-looking people had turned out for them.'

Elizabeth responded sharply, 'Well, it's not to happen again. You are not to leave the house without my permission.'

An outraged Alicia opened her mouth to protest, but Sarah took one of the girl's hands and pressed it urgently. Alicia swallowed her anger, and answered sullenly, 'Yes, Mama.'

Chapter Nineteen

I

Though Alicia never knew it, the idea of her being Brought Out was finally killed by the Reverend Clarence Browning. With his eyes on promotion in the Church, he forbade Florence to have anything to do with it. 'I cannot forbid you to see your *half*-sister,' he had fulminated, 'but the less attention drawn to her – and to her mother – the better it will be for us.'

Florence protested at the slur cast upon Elizabeth, but the biting sarcasms thrown at her sent her weeping to her bedroom. Alicia would have to fight for herself, Florence decided in desperation. And as for her mother, Florence had an uneasy feeling that she was losing her wits; she seemed so stupid at times.

Alicia would not have seen anything of the festivities for the Coronation of King Edward VII on August 9th, 1902, had not Sarah, pitying her confinement, persuaded Elizabeth that an old woman needed someone with her if she were to mingle with the crowds in the city.

'I know you don't want to go,' she said, 'so I want to borrow dear Alicia just for a couple of hours.'

'I can't imagine why *you* want to go – the city will be packed – full of vulgar curiosity seekers,' responded Elizabeth fretfully.

'I always did love crowds,' Sarah replied sweetly, so Elizabeth reluctantly gave her consent.

There was so much traffic on the roads to the city centre that the two ladies decided to go by electric tram; and it was a pleasure to Sarah to see Alicia's face light up when she saw the gay buntings and streamers strung from the lamp-posts and the delightfully decorated trams, one of which had been specially illuminated in honour of Alexandra, the pretty new Queen.

When Sarah's legs began to fail, they went into a small café much frequented by lady shoppers. Sarah ordered an assortment of iced cakes, lemonade, ice cream and tea and watched with pleasure as Alicia enjoyed them. The child can be quite vivacious, she ruminated, given a chance – but she does look dreadfully frumpy amongst the other young women in here.

On the way home, Alicia thanked her godmother profusely for the outing. 'I must be very frivolous,' she confessed, 'but I do love going out.'

'Nonsense, child. I wish I could take you more often.'

At sixty, Sarah was feeling her age and, though she hated to admit it, she could no longer afford such expeditions; like many others, her income inherited from her father now bought considerably less than it had twenty years before. She was preparing to give up her governess cart because she could no longer afford the stabling fees and she had already dispensed with her live-in maid; she now managed with the aid of a grey, silent charlady from the Workhouse, who came in every morning.

Despite her growing infirmities, however, she arranged another little outing for Alicia, one that did not cost anything. She insisted that she and Alicia should go to see the opening of the new Toxteth Branch Library. Elizabeth complained capriciously that she could not spare Alicia, to which Sarah had roundly replied, 'Rubbish, my dear. You should come along yourself; it is an important local event which we should be a part of. The library will make a lot of difference to this district.'

'I couldn't possibly come,' Elizabeth replied. 'Standing amid the rabble would be too tiring.'

'Well, then I promise not to keep Alicia more than two hours. Where is the child?' And she insisted that, there and then, Alicia be sent for, so that she could be invited personally.

She wanted to make sure that her godchild actually received the invitation; Elizabeth was most forgetful.

Polly was surprised when, the next morning, Elizabeth asked where Alicia was.

'Miss Webb came for her about an hour ago, Ma'am, to go and see the new lilbrary.'

Elizabeth looked a little bewildered and then answered, 'Yes, of course she did.'

As Sarah Webb and Alicia walked down to the new little brick building, Sarah's double chins wobbled excitedly as she told Alicia, 'Mr Andrew Carnegie himself has condescended to come to open it – you know, he has provided the money for it. It's a real chance to see a great man.'

Thankful to be out in the fresh air on a brisk October morning with leaves whirling in the gutters, Alicia cheerfully agreed.

'Once you join the library, you'll be able to borrow books ad lib – anybody can.'

'Could Polly? She loves to read.'

'Indeed, yes. She will be made welcome. It is meant to bring books within the purview of the poorest.'

'Mama says it's vulgar to belong to a free library, that one might catch diseases from the books.'

'Well, I'm not vulgar,' puffed the older woman firmly. 'I shall be happy to borrow books from this library; it'll save me having to go to town to get them from Lee's private library.'

They found a good position across the road from the new building and watched a constable keeping people back from the entrance. The wind was quite cold, and barefoot children ran in and out amongst the adults, to keep themselves warm.

One little tike with sores on his head thrust his hand out in front of Alicia, and asked hopefully, 'Gi' us a penny, Miss.'

Alicia looked down at the wizened, worldly-wise face and replied truthfully, 'I don't have any money with me.' She flushed slightly, feeling humiliated in front of Sarah, who produced a coin from her old-fashioned, black velvet bag.

It was some time since she had had any spending money of her own. From childhood, her mother had each Saturday given her a silver threepenny piece. Lately, she had not done so, and Alicia was worried that, from the current month's housekeeping, she had had to spend twopence on hairpins and then enter it in the account book; she feared greatly what Humphrey would say about it. As he had done with Mrs Tibbs, he queried almost every item.

'Naughty little thing,' Sarah said, with a chuckle, as the child slipped away.

After the ceremony, they strolled back to Sarah's house, where they were to have a cup of tea before Alicia went home. Sarah said gaily, 'You'll be able to tell your friends that you saw Andrew Carnegie, and even tell your grandchildren.'

Remembering that she had friends in Polly and Fanny, she was able to agree with Sarah, though some of her pleasure in the pleasant morning went at the thought that it would be a miracle if she ever had children, never mind grandchildren. There did not seem to be much future, beyond dancing attendance on her parents.

Once the library was running, she and Polly often sat up late in the nursery, sharing a candle – Humphrey was fussy about the number of candles consumed in the house – in order to read a stream of novels Polly borrowed.

Both of them dreamed of a great aristocrat who would ride into their lives and whisk them off to a gorgeous manor house. It was a delicious indulgence, but both of them knew that dreams were ephemeral.

The hard work which had been Polly's lot had taken her earlier prettiness. She was quite heavily lined and, when she was tired, her pale lips drooped and her eyes had a look of sad disillusionment.

Despite her love of Edward, she had in earlier years sometimes picked up a likely young man lounging round the waterfront, hoping to make a marriage which would release her from the bonds of domestic service. There was, however, in Liverpool South, a great shortage of men of her own age group, and, as she often said to Fanny, 'With no work, a wife's a luxury to a man – they can't afford to marry.'

She was thankful for the small store of golden sovereigns given to her by Edward and for the silver shillings from her wages which she had added to them; they would cushion her old age.

During the same month that Alexander Carnegie visited Liverpool, Sir Wilfred Laurier, the Premier of Canada, came to open the new Produce Exchange. When Polly read about it in the newspaper, her face lit up, and she ran up to the nursery, where Alicia was sponging and pressing her mother's winter dresses. 'Would he have news of our Billy?' she asked breathlessly.

Alicia laid her iron on a trivet and pushed it over the fire to heat again. Though she wanted to smile, she replied gravely, 'I don't think so, Polly. He comes from Ottawa in Ontario – and Billy's in a provincial district – Alberta – and it's a long way off – thousands of miles.'

Polly's face fell. 'Aye, I suppose you're right.' She sighed, and turned to go downstairs again. 'I wish he were 'ere,' she said wistfully. 'Our Mary and me, we miss 'im. He were such a good lad.'

II

Used to being part of a tight family unit, Billy did not forget his sisters and often wished they were with him as he scratched for a living in an alien world.

When a ragged tomtit of a boy had crept out of the bush at the side of the trail leading down to the railway halt by the Metis village and had begged Ben Reilly, an elderly pedlar, to show him the way to Toronto, Ben had picked him up and put the exhausted boy on the back of one of his horses. As they proceeded along the trail, the boy had wept and told him what had happened to him on the Macdonalds' farm.

Ben Reilly had seen such children many times in his travels, and as he plodded through melting snow, chewing on a plug of tobacco and listening to the tale of woe, he felt that Billy might help to solve his own problems. He, therefore, set up camp for the night at a distance from the Metis village, and he and Billy shared a sparse dinner of bannock and bacon, while they got to know each other. The boy was eager to help him and obviously knew how to handle horses.

Though Reilly came from southern Ontario, he was to Billy a bit like any Irishman on the Liverpool docks, and the man's language was similar; he certainly had the same flow of swear words, as he built a smoky fire with damp, dead wood. 'In a month or two, it'll be so dry, we'll have to watch we don't start a forest fire,' he asssured Billy, and Billy didn't miss the inference that they would still be together. He wondered suddenly if the man would expect to sleep with him and he watched him warily, as Reilly took a bottle from a saddlebag and settled down by the fire to drink. He motioned to Billy to sit near him. Billy carefully left a foot between them. The bent hobgoblin of a man laughed and spat his tobacco into the fire. 'I'm not goin' to touch you, lad.'

Billy smiled sheepishly, but kept his distance. 'Do you know *where* Toronto is?' he asked after a small silence.

'Aye, I do. But there's no way you can get there 'cept by ridin' the train. It's hundreds a miles away.' He chewed the end of his heavy, white moustache thoughtfully. 'Best I can do for you is to miss calling at the next village, 'cos they may remember you there, if Macdonald comes lookin'. We can go to the farms I usually do after that – they won't know your face. You could get work on the farms, but I tell you it wouldn't be any better than what you gone through already.'

Expert salesman, Ben Reilly had a merry, elfin quality about him, and Billy gradually relaxed.

According to Ben, the pickings for a travelling packman like himself were getting thinner in Ontario, as settlements grew, roads were built and shops were established. What he wanted to do, before he got too old, was to go further west. Had Billy ever heard of Calgary – or Edmonton?

Billy had not.

'You can get land for nuthin' out there – or next to it.'

Billy looked at him pop-eyed, his fatigue forgotten. Land for nothing? As the night wore on and the old pedlar, glad of company, began to talk out his ideas, Billy's almost forgotten dream of a farm of his own began to revive.

It was dead dark and the forest was full of night noises by the time Ben Reilly had worked his way round to asking Billy if he would like to go west with him and work as his assistant. 'All I can do is feed you, till we get started. You look an honest boy. You play fair with me and I'll play fair with you.'

Billy agreed, and for two months they travelled Ben's usual round. Under his tutelage, Billy extended his knowledge of how to bargain with both buyers and sellers, how to wheedle small animal skins out of isolated settlers in return for sewing cotton, needles, nails, nuts and bolts, screws and good knives. Fur traders in the cities were always interested in decent pelts, he told Billy.

When the warm weather came, they stowed away on a train bound for Calgary. They were kicked off it at Winnipeg.

Unperturbed, Ben took the opportunity to buy a number of small tins of simple remedies, like zinc ointment, which he assured Billy would sell very well in isolated places at twice the price. They then caught another train.

Though they did their best to lose themselves in a large group of Ukrainian immigrants, an angry conductor picked them out and threatened them with delivery to the North-west Mounted Police, if they did not pay up. While Billy tried to make himself invisible behind Ben Reilly, the pedlar resignedly slit the lining of his coat and produced the fare for both of them, swearing that they had joined the train at Regina.

The conductor had heard the same story a hundred times before; nevertheless, he decided to accept their protestations, rather than waste more time arguing that they had got on earlier.

With a contented grin at Billy, old Ben put his head down

on his pack and slept. Billy sat squashed on a wooden seat beside two restive children in fur waistcoats.

In Calgary, they found shelter in the straw-filled loft of a rooming house, which they shared with three young men, also new immigrants. Ben and the other men all smoked, and Billy spent a week of most uneasy nights, fearing that one or the other of them would set the straw on fire. He survived, however, and set out for the countryside with Ben, refurbished packs, and a horse of most uncertain temperament.

Ben Reilly never spent a penny, if he could help it, and Billy learned from him to do likewise, to cadge and beguile meals and a place to sleep. Sometimes, they ate off the land, snaring rabbits, catching fish, and adding wild plants to the subsequent stew.

After a while, they moved their base to Edmonton where the competition was less. Reilly began to feel his age as the years went by, so when Billy was seventeen he sent him north to St Albert and Lac Ste. Anne, to branch off wherever he found a settlement. Billy met housewives using many different languages and he took the trouble to learn the names of the objects in his pack in Russian, Norwegian, Dutch and Icelandic. His efforts brought friendly smiles to the faces of many lonely women.

Though he was strictly honest with Ben Reilly, he found ways of earning a few extra dollars on the side. A housewife whose husband had a closely guarded flock of sheep – the coyotes picked them off, if they were not careful, the woman said – used to spin and knit garments for her family. He offered to sell for her on commission any extra ones she had time to make. She persuaded an Icelandic neighbour to knit as well, and Billy had no difficulty in getting rid of the warm woollens in lumber and mining camps, where he sold tobacco. Well-established settlers sometimes had feathers to spare; Billy suggested to one lady that she put hers into bags made of a gay print which he provided, and he sold them as cushions, again on commission. Ben Reilly began to pay him a better commission himself. Cents became dollars, and Billy stitched them into his jacket. He grew into a short, amiable man, who kept out of the taverns and out of trouble, as best he could in a rough frontier world.

He did not drink or smoke, because in his opinion the cost was too great, and he had his eyes set on applying for a quarter-section of land. Though the land cost little, he knew he would need a horse and plough, seed and axes, if he was to get a good start; his wife, if he ever got one, was not going to pull the plough, as he had seen Ukrainian women do when their husbands were breaking land.

Because he was sometimes lonely, his letters to Polly became longer and more interesting as he ruefully described his adventures on the road. In the spring, when everybody was bogged down by mud, he helped the man who owned the stable where he had first lodged in Edmonton and made a lifelong friend of him. He told of going during the winter into logging camps where no women were, to sell tobacco, cigarette papers, boots, socks and pipes. He mentioned Chinese, some of them his competitors, who had worked on the railway and had never gone home because they did not have enough money. Some of them had opened tiny cafés and he found he liked the food they served. He was used to oriental faces on the docks where he had worked as a boy, and, unlike many of their customers, he would talk with them if they knew enough English; so now he had one or two Chinese friends.

'Chinese food!' exclaimed Polly incredulously. 'He must be starvin' to eat that.'

Alicia laughed – she had a pretty, tinkling laugh like her mother's. 'I read somewhere that the Chinese are the world's best cooks.'

'It's a good thing Mrs Tibbs int here to hear you,' replied Polly. 'Pack o' heathens. Seen 'em walkin' round down town – come off the boats, they had. Aye, poor Billy. What he must be goin' through!'

But Billy was happy. He felt he was on his way to better things. Very slowly, but steadily, the dollars sewn into his jacket increased.

Chapter Twenty

I

'Aye, 'e's dead,' Fanny assured Alicia lugubriously, her voice muffled. She was cleaning the flues of the kitchen range and puffs of soot flew round her, as she pulled out the long wire brush from the oven flue. 'Colonel Milfort's valet, next door, told me.' She turned away to sneeze, and then glanced at Alicia sitting by the white-scrubbed table. The young woman was wrapped in a dressing-gown long since discarded by her mother; her nose and eyes were red from a heavy cold and she was shivering in the unheated kitchen.

Alicia had come downstairs early, in hope of a cup of tea to ease her aching head, but the kitchen range had, the previous day, not been drawing properly, so the fire was not yet lit because of Fanny's cleaning efforts. Until she had finished, there would be no means of boiling a kettle and no hot water flowing from the bathroom taps – which would make Papa furious.

She leaned one elbow on the table and rested her head on her hand. It was nearly six o'clock, and outside the high, barred window overlooking the stone area, the February wind was howling, as it had done for the last twenty-four hours. In the kitchen, a single gaslight hanging from the high ceiling cast cold rays on grubby walls and grey stone floor.

Dear old Mr Bittle dead? He'd been the gardener since before she was born – and next May she would be twenty. A lump rose in her throat and she wanted to cry. She took out a much-used handkerchief and blew her stuffed-up nose. In her mind's eye, she saw the gardener's heavy, work-hardened fingers delicately splitting a seed so that she could observe its interior under her magnifying glass. She remembered how, as a little girl, he had recruited her to help him clear cluttered corners of the garden which might harbour wicked slugs and snails, how he had scattered lime round his precious seedlings and had encouraged starlings and toads, to reduce voracious pests. 'Natural things'll help you in a garden, if you let them,' he would say.

Fanny put away her long flue brush and picked up the poker to rake out the previous day's ashes. She said, of Mr Bittle, 'Colonel Milfort's man said he were found lyin' in the street in the middle of the storm yesterday. Proper awful, poor man. The wind must've bin too much for him, after he left here.'

Alicia winced. Dear humble man, out there in the cold. And nobody left in his little cottage off Crown Street to know or care that he had not returned.

She had felt depressed throughout the winter and this news added to it. A woman who did her duty was supposed to be content, knowing that she had done it; but, increasingly, Alicia felt she wanted to run out of the front door and dance and laugh and be free, swept along by the wild wind outside, into some madcap new world. Yet, she knew, from Polly and Fanny's stories, how cruel that outside world could be and the thought of facing it alone and penniless kept her rooted in Humphrey's house; at least Papa was a known devil.

After putting a new lock on his wine cellar door to protect his stock, Humphrey had told Alicia and the servants that, on no account, were they to provide Elizabeth with alcohol. Elizabeth vented her misery on Alicia.

Fanny, however, had had in some ways a very close affinity with Elizabeth, ever since she had found her badly beaten so many years ago. Armed with money from Elizabeth's allowance, she would sneak out to buy the occasional bottle of port or brandy for her desperate mistress. Such occasions were the only times when Alicia had a peaceful day, as Elizabeth slept it off. With her head spinning, Alicia dreaded today; since the weather was so bad, she would not even be able to persuade her mother to take a little walk in the fresh air.

Not that walking out with Elizabeth was exactly exciting. Accompanied occasionally by Sarah Webb, the most adventurous walk would be as far as Princes Park at the pace of elderly ladies. Alicia would dawdle along, watching enviously as working-class couples strolled past them, arm-in-arm, or cuddled close to each other on the park benches. She watched families picnicking or playing impromptu games of cricket on fine Sunday afternoons; and girls, not much younger than herself, enjoying equally impromptu games of rounders or shuttlecock and battledore. She had herself almost forgotten what it was like to play anything. In any case, her mother referred to the happy players as very vulgar. Was everything that was fun vulgar? Was she always to be an onlooker of life, never a participant? she wondered bitterly.

Yesterday had been a rotten day, she thought mournfully, as Fanny swept up the hearth after her cleaning. Papa had, when doing the household accounts with her, seized upon the butcher's bill and complained that it was far too high. She should, he said, scold Polly for extravagance.

'The price of beef went up recently,' Alicia had told him sullenly.

'Don't be pert, girl. Do as I say.' He had slapped the next month's housekeeping down in front of her, and she had picked up the precious gold coins, and whispered frightenedly, 'Yes, Papa.'

She ran from the room, forgetting to shut the door and had fled upstairs to the almost unused day nursery, not heeding Humphrey's angry bellow, as he got up to shut the door. She had sat down on Polly's chair and wept passionately, for the empty ache inside her and for her isolation.

Now, on this miserable February morning, Polly came whirling down the servants' stair, tying her morning apron as she came.

When she saw the empty fireplace and Fanny all covered with soot, she stopped. 'Aye, Fan!' she cried. 'Hurry up, luv. The Master will be wantin' his shavin' water and his brekkie.'

Fanny turned her smudged face towards Polly and shrugged helplessly. Alicia said savagely, 'Let him wait. It won't hurt him.'

Polly picked up a wooden tray and put it on the table. 'Now, Allie, luv, none o' that. Your Dad's a busy man.' She took a traycloth out of a drawer and laid it on the tray. Then she turned to the dresser to get the breakfast crockery.

'He should buy us a gas stove, Polly. I've asked him several times. But, no. Coal was good enough for Mrs Tibbs, so it's good enough for us.'

'Well, it would save us a lot of work,' agreed Polly, with a sigh. 'But mostly we can manage. Couldn't you do the flues at night, Fan?'

'Often the range is too hot, still,' Fanny replied, as she put a match to screwed-up newspaper she had laid in the grate. The wood on top of it began to crackle and she carefully added small pieces of coal.

'Ah, well, I'll give 'im scrambled eggs – they're quick. Tell 'im the pork butcher didn't 'ave no pigs' ears. Butcher says they're gettin' harder to get, anyways.' She picked up a tiny saucepan and went to the sink to fill it, and then gave it to Fanny. ''Ere you are, Fan. Put this on for 'is Nibs' shavin' water.'

'I can't do much until the fire gets going, so I'll go up and dress,' Alicia said wearily to Polly.

As the green baize door at the top of the stairs flipped closed behind her, Polly remarked worriedly, 'Our Allie is proper low these days.'

Fanny shrugged, and took off her sackcloth apron and hung it on a hook. 'Who wouldn't be? She don't have no fun, no friends, no nothin'. That old bastard keeps her kennelled like a dog, and her Mam's never lifts a finger to help her.' Fanny ran her tongue round her mouth and spat soot into the fire. Then she put the little saucepan over the flames. 'What that girl needs is a young man to walk out with, strong enough not to be afraid of her ould man. Pack of bloody nuns we are, in this 'ouse.'

Polly looked worried. 'God forbid she gets mixed up with a man,' she exclaimed. 'I don't want her in trouble.'

Fanny took a soot-blackened kettle, filled it at the tap and then hung it over the fire by a hook in the chimney. 'Never did *us* any 'arm,' she replied drily. 'A bit of playin' put and take would do us all good.'

Polly had to smile. 'You not doin' so well with the new coalie, as you did with ould Jack?' she inquired.

Fanny made a vulgar gesture, and then sighed, 'Jack were a good fella. I always fancied 'im. Kept 'is Missus goin' and me, sometimes.'

'No one better this side of Wigan,' agreed Polly, though she herself had not succumbed to Jack's charms. 'It were the dust from the coal that put 'im in the Infirmary – definite.'

Fanny nodded agreement. 'It'll be a bloody miracle if he ever gets out, with a cough like he's got.' She glanced round the kitchen, as she whipped the little saucepan off the fire. 'Where's old fishface's shaving mug?'

'Blast! I forgot to bring it down. It's in the bathroom. Run up and fill it for me, duck, while I finish the brekkie trays. Then you could light the fire under the copper. There's the tablecloths still to wash; I didn't have time Monday.'

'Oh, Jaysus!' moaned Fanny, and trotted upstairs, hot saucepan in hand.

She met Alicia coming out of the bathroom. The girl was shivering, having washed herself in cold water, as she usually did.

'Aye, duck, you should wait till the kitchen fire heats the hot water. Fire's blazin'. It won't be long.'

'You know Papa always lectured Charles and me on the benefits of washing in cold water,' Alicia replied morosely. 'Washing in warm water is waste of fuel, he says.'

'He uses hot himself; he'll raise Cain this mornin' 'cos the tap won't run that hot yet.' She took the lid off the little saucepan and poured the steaming water into a rose-wreathed shaving-mug on the bathroom table. She was about to say something more when Humphrey suddenly emerged from his

230

bedroom. He was wrapped in a heavy, camel hair dressing-gown and his fur-lined slippers could be heard brushing along the hall carpet.

'Beat it,' urged Fanny in a whisper to Alicia, and Alicia fled upstairs. The instinct to keep out of Humphrey's way was still very strong.

Later, Alicia ate a bowl of porridge with the maids and then again went upstairs to make her bed and clean her room.

'The kid's gettin' desperate,' declared Fanny, as she cleared the dishes and put them into the sandstone sink. 'Do you think you could talk to Miss Webb about her? Proper nice, the old girl is. Get her to talk to the Missus, now she's a bit more sober.'

Polly looked tired and troubled. The baker had just delivered the day's bread and she was putting it into the bread bin. She closed the heavy, metal lid slowly. 'I'll try again. She don't get any pocket money these days – and the Missus always gave her some.'

'It's Allie who pays us, so she's got money.'

'That's housekeepin' only. And it's time you and me got a raise. We haven't had one for years.'

Fanny made a wry mouth. 'Wages isn't goin' up much anywhere.'

II

Polly was still wondering how to broach the subject of Alicia's loneliness to Miss Webb when, the next day help came from an unexpected quarter. She answered a prolonged ring at the doorbell to find Charles, looking very cheerful, standing impatiently on the top step and stamping his feet to keep them warm in the bitter wind. His loose, tweed overcoat flapped around his legs and the ends of his long woollen scarf danced in the wind. On his head, he wore a greasy-looking deerstalker hat. One gloved hand clutched a Gladstone bag and the other a meerschaum pipe.

'Lost my key,' he explained, as Polly hastily shut the door before the house was totally chilled. 'How are you, Polly, my old love?'

She smiled and replied, 'I'm very well, thank you, sir.' She took his bag and put it on the floor, while he pulled off his scarf and overcoat. He handed the garments to Polly and took off his hat and put it on her head. 'Where's mother?' he asked.

Seated in the morning-room with Sarah Webb, Elizabeth had already heard her son's voice, and she got up from her chair unusually quickly and went into the hall. 'Why, Charles, this is splendid,' she cried, as he bent to kiss her. 'How long are you here for?'

'For a week this time.'

'You should have written.' She turned to Polly and ordered in her old, firm voice, 'Ask Fanny to open up the blue bedroom – put a fire in it and get it aired. And bring me another teacup.'

Charles shook Sarah's hand, and it was she who ushered him closer to the fireplace, so that he could thankfully rub his hands before its warmth.

As he exchanged pleasantries with both women, he felt that the room looked more depressing every time he returned home. The curtains were grey with dust and carelessly half drawn back, the chintz covers on the chairs were so worn that the pattern on them was barely visible. On every surface there was a clutter of books, sewing and old newspapers, something that he had not observed before. In her day, his mother had been such a methodical woman and he felt a sad pang when she sat down near him. She still had a fine, white skin, but a double chin and layers of fat had taken their toll. Her hair was bunched into an untidy bun covered with a snood at the back of her head.

After he had inquired politely about his father and Alicia, who was at the grocer's, and a cup of tea and some biscuits had been pressed into his hand, his mother asked him if he had just come to see her or whether something special had occurred.

With a mouthful of biscuit, he murmured, 'Of course, I've come to see you. But I've also got an interview at the University College. They're establishing a Chair of Bio-Chemistry.'

His mother's face brightened. At last the backing she had given her son in his studies was going to have some result of which Humphrey might approve, which would be a pleasant change.

Charles saw the change in her expression, and he laughed. 'No, Mama, I'm not yet qualified enough to hold a Chair. Where there is a Chair, however, there is usually a need for Readers and Lecturers – and laboratory staff – so I wrote a general, exploratory letter, and I received a very kind letter back from the man who will hold the Chair. He's asked me to come to see him.'

'That sounds very nice.' She was a little disappointed.

'It would mean, dear Mama, that I would not have to take any further financial help from you. You have been so good to me.'

At these personal disclosures, Miss Webb rose and said that she should go home.

'Oh, dear Aunt Sarah, don't stand on ceremony. She mustn't, must she, Mama? She knows all about us.'

But Sarah Webb, who did know all about them, nevertheless felt that it was only ladylike to leave, so Polly was rung for to show her out, and Charles accompanied her to the front door, to save his mother getting up again.

At the door, Sarah Webb took his hand in her tiny gloved one, and he bent to kiss her. She smiled and looked up at him. Then she said very earnestly, 'It would do your family a world of good, Charles, if you do come home. Your mother – and little Alicia, particularly – need you.'

While Polly stood in the background, politely deaf, blind and dumb, and inwardly rejoiced, Charles was suddenly very sober, not being clear in his mind as to her meaning. 'They do,' Miss Webb assured him. 'Goodbye, dear boy.'

Polly helped Sarah on with her cloak and handed her her umbrella. After Sarah's departure, Polly locked the door and

Charles said to her uneasily, 'Polly, what's up? Really up, I mean?'

Polly licked her lips and lowered her eyelids. She clasped her hands primly over her apron, while she sought for words. 'I – er – I couldn't tell you all in one go, sir,' she whispered, with a pointed glance at the open morning-room door.

'Is mother ill?' Charles whispered back.

'In a manner of speaking, she is, sir. Could I talk to you later, sir?'

'Is she going to die, Polly?'

'Oh, no, sir. It's not consumption or anythin'. It's her and Miss Alicia's spirits mostly.'

'I see. Mother may herself confide in me.'

Polly looked relieved. 'Yes, mebbe she will, sir.'

'When will the Master be in?'

'He usually comes about seven o'clock – for dinner.'

'Thank you, Polly.'

She was dismissed. Feeling dispirited, she went slowly down to the basement kitchen.

Very thoughtfully, hands in trouser pockets, Charles spun slowly round on his heels, gazing at the hall's fine ceiling, now hanging with spiders' webs. Alerted by Sarah, he was considering the state of his home with the same care that he would have used when looking at the results of one of his experiments. His eyes followed the worn carpet up the stairs. In the old days his mother would not have tolerated such a tattered stair rug, and he wondered if his father had lost money. The place reeked of neglect.

III

'Charles,' yelled Alicia in a most unladylike way, as she ran into the morning-room to greet him. He caught her in his arms and swung her round.

'My goodness!' he exclaimed. 'You've grown up.'

She tossed her head when he put her down. 'I'm nineteen.

I've been grown up for a long time – only you've never noticed it, you wretch.'

He grimaced sheepishly. It was true. When he came north, he would pay a short duty visit to his family and then go to visit the livelier homes of his old friends, now married and scattered round Merseyside.

As they sat around the fire, they discussed the reason for his visit.

'You'll live here, of course?' Alicia asked hopefully.

'Well, at first I would,' he hedged. He was determined not to be subject to his father any longer than he had to. If he got a post at the College, he would build a small house for himself and get a housekeeper.

Humphrey received Charles's news with more equanimity than his son had expected and promised to talk to him about it after dinner. He then went up stairs to wash.

As the brass tap in the bathroom trickled hot water into the huge porcelain basin, he peered at himself in the mirror which was slowly steaming up. He felt immensely tired, drained of his usual vigour. 'Damn her,' he muttered, to himself, 'damn her!'

IV

Humphrey had spent the previous two hours with Mrs Jakes. They had proved unexpectedly stormy. Instead of cosying up with him in her feather bed, she had first suggested a drink and had sat him down by her living-room fire. A little surprised, he had accepted a tankard of porter, while she took a glass of port.

After a few moments of silence, she had said, 'It's me daughter, our Stella May. You know she's not really the marrying kind – and she were twenty-five come last Christmas – and that puts her on the shelf, if you know what I mean.'

She took a sip of wine and then went on to suggest that Stella May would stand a better chance if she had a dowry, and Mrs Jakes hoped that dearest Humphrey would provide it.

Dearest Humphrey had huffily refused; this was not the first request that his mistress had made for additional money. 'She's not *my* daughter,' he said frostily. 'In any case, she'll inherit your shop. Wouldn't that be enough to tempt a promising young man?'

'Well, you know her,' replied Mrs Jakes, sipping daintly at her port, while she controlled her anger. 'She's all right behind the counter, but she don't know nothin' about tobacco or how to blend it – nor about accounts – and she don't seem able to learn.' She bridled, and went on, 'And in any case, I expect to live for many years myself, so I need the shop – it really don't keep more'n one comfortable.'

Humphrey considered the cloddish, amiable face of the young woman in question, and saw no reason why he should provide for her. 'Whatever Stella May needs is your business,' he told his paramour bleakly.

Mrs Jakes pressed and argued until Humphrey's irritation gave way to anger. He was sick of the whining bitch, he decided suddenly. He put down his tankard, rose from his chair and gathered up his top hat and gloves.

Suppressing her fury, Mrs Jakes smiled up at him sweetly. 'Don't go yet,' she urged. 'If you don't have the money, you could ask Mrs Woodman – make some excuse. I hear as she's a well-off lady.'

'My wife is no concern of yours.' Humphrey rammed his hat on to his head. He was outraged at the calm suggestion.

'Oh, but I always felt concerned for the pore dear. Bein' an invalid, like.'

Humphrey was perfectly aware of the implied threat behind the sweetness of the voice. It was the oldest of warnings from women like her: 'I'll tell your wife what you've been up to.'

Mrs Jakes looked reflectively at her empty glass, as she continued, 'If it isn't convenient, like, to get it from her, I did hear as you're likely to do very well out of the underground railway, when you've finished makin' it electric. You don't have to help our Stella May now, but, say, in six months' time. What about then?' she wheedled.

He was still standing stiffly on the hearth rug, as if ready to leave, and she hastily put down her glass in the hearth and began to fiddle with the buttons of her high lace collar. 'You think about it, dearie, and, meantime, let's have a bit of a roll.'

Slyly, she undid the buttons until the cleft between her heavy breasts was visible, and she smiled up at him knowingly.

Despite his fatigue, he felt a jump of desire; she would do anything for him in bed. But he was for the first time afraid of her, afraid of blackmail. It was one thing that most people, including your wife, knew that you kept a mistress – most well-to-do men did. But it was unpardonable if the mistress surfaced with loud complaints. He knew he must frighten her.

He snatched up his overcoat and moved quickly to the lace-draped door of the shop. With his hand on the knob, he said firmly, 'It seems that our friendship has come to an end. Good afternoon, Ma'am.'

Followed by an outraged cry of 'Humphrey!' he closed the glass-panelled door and marched through the tiny shop, with its rich odour of molasses. He ignored Stella May's simpering, 'Evenin', sir,' and slammed the outer door after himself, so that the little bell screwed to it tinkled angrily.

He stepped into the street. A small, nagging pain throbbed in his chest. The wind was freezingly cold and he struggled hastily into his greatcoat.

He did not know why he was so glad to see Charles in the hallway, when Polly let him in. He had certainly never been fond of him, a boring bookworm, if ever there was one. But today, lurching in from the inclement weather, and being faced with a fairly sturdy young man, wreathed in friendly smiles, had been a relief. A son was a son, after all, especially when you felt old as well as furious.

Now, he washed his trembling hands with carbolic soap and splashed his face with water. Charles had reminded him suddenly of Edward, buried in the African veldt, and the memory hurt him. He went slowly downstairs, to rest in the library until Polly should bang the dinner gong.

After dinner, he sat with Charles by the library fire, a decanter of whisky on a small table between them, and Charles listened patiently to his worries about the poor state of the cotton market; the loss in the Mersey River, the previous month, of a schooner in which Humphrey had had a share; the uncertainty that the Mersey Underground Railway would make money even after electrification; the need to raise capital.

The old man was almost garrulous, thought Charles, and, with a sagacity that his family rarely gave him credit for, he concluded that something had rattled him severely. He was used to his father losing his temper, blowing up like some great Icelandic geyser, but not to his fretting so loquaciously about the ordinary ups and downs of business. Polly's remarks had already made him uneasy. He had always taken his family for granted, assumed that they would be there, in the fine house on Upper Canning Street, ready to greet him whenever it pleased him to come home. Now, he wondered if his mother was more severely ill than Polly had indicated and whether this was upsetting his father.

Humphrey did finally turn to the subject of a post at the University and discussed the pros and cons of it for a few minutes. Then he dismissed the boy on the grounds that he had work to do, and Charles left him hunched over his littered desk, his white hair bunched over his stiff collar and scarlet neck like the feathers of a chilled magpie.

V

In search of Polly, Charles went up to the day nursery. When he opened the door he found a lighted candle on the old candle table by the easy chair and the embers of a fire still lingering in the grate, but no one was there.

He stood uneasily in the doorway and then crossed the room to stroke the nose of the rocking-horse. He looked round the shadowed room. Like everywhere else in the house, it seemed cluttered and neglected. On a table by the window stood a dead maidenhair fern, and on the floor by the chair there was an untidy pile of linen and an open sewing box. The only sound in the room was the steady tick of the clock on the mantelpiece. He smiled at it, almost expecting it to smile back because they knew each other so well. In the bookcase lay the volumes that he and Edward had read as children, and across the top of them had been laid further books. He picked one up. It was a school text on botany and he flicked through it; he was surprised at the careful detail of the notes that Alicia had added on every margin.

He snapped the book shut and rang the bell at the side of the fireplace. If Fanny answered, he would simply ask her to make up the fire.

Polly realized who was probably ringing the nursery bell, and she came hurrying up the stairs. The last flight seemed longer than usual; her knees hurt and she was panting, as she entered the nursery.

Charles was waiting with his back to the warmth of the dying fire.

'Come in, Polly, and sit down. I wanted to ask you quietly a bit more about Mother. She insisted that she was quite well, when I asked her.'

Polly took the chair indicated. She straightened her long, black skirt and her short, afternoon apron, put her feet neatly together, folded her hands in her lap, and looked up at him inquiringly.

'Alicia says mother has been drinking heavily for a long time and that, when she gets the chance, she still does. Why would she do that, Polly?'

Polly responded with prim virtue, 'It int my business to inquire, sir.'

'Come off it, Polly. You're part of the family.'

Polly's eyes twinkled almost girlishly. She relaxed and said, 'Well, sir, I dunno for sure. She's bin goin' slowly downhill ever since I bin here – ever since Miss Alicia were born. Fanny says she used to be really light-hearted and happy when *she* first come. People visitin' her and her goin' to parties and the theatre – and buyin' pretty dresses.'

'Yes, I remember her like that,' Charles answered soberly.

'I can remember when I first come, she were always busy with her charities – and then she had her At Homes. And sometimes they'd give a dinner. Fact is, she were too busy to even take much note of Miss Alicia when she was a baby. But then, after a while, she seemed to lose heart and some days she wouldn't even get up.'

'Has she seen a doctor?'

'Not for years, that I know of. And another thing, sir. She's gettin' so forgetful. At first, I thought it were the drink, but now she's not getting that much. And she *still* forgets. The Master gets awfully cross with her sometimes.'

'Hm. My parents never did see eye to eye.'

'No, sir.'

Servants knew everything, he thought irritably. Feeling rather frustrated, he said, 'Well, thank you, Polly. I didn't want to bother Father.' He did not say that he knew that his father had never taken much interest in his mother, except to make sure she did not overspend.

Polly got up to leave him, and he asked, 'Where's Miss Alicia?'

'In the kitchen, sir. She's bakin' a cake.'

'Cooking? What for?'

'She does quite a lot, sir. Your father – that is to say, the Master – likes a good table – so she helps me a lot.'

'So you're actually the cook now?'

'Yes, sir.'

'And the parlourmaid?'

'Yes, Sir.' As she watched him, she wondered where his eyes had been all these years that he had not noticed how the staff had been cut.

'Who looks after Mother and Miss Alicia?'

'Miss Alicia looks after herself – she runs the house now – and we all do our best for the Mistress.'

'Fanny's still here. I saw her. What does she do?'

'She works real hard, sir. She's got all the cleaning, and the fires to tend and slops to empty and beds and washing – and this is a big house, sir, and real old-fashioned.'

'Poor Fanny,' commented Charles glumly, and then as Polly prepared to leave him, he reverted to the question of Elizabeth. 'I don't think there's anything to worry about over Mother,' he said. 'She's getting on a bit – and I imagine it's natural that she tends to forget things.'

Polly agreed with him, and after she had answered polite inquiries about her own health, she went slowly back down the stairs.

Charles stood staring at the old rocking-horse. He felt suddenly that he could not live in the house; it depressed him. He wondered how Alicia endured it – but then girls were different. If he got a post in the University he would definitely seek lodgings in the town.

VI

The gale finally blew itself out. In the Woodmans' garden the snowdrops flowered late amongst a flood of yellow and purple crocuses. The weeds also flourished and, since there was no one else to do it, Alicia cleaned the intruders out. That evening, she mentioned to her father that they should start a new gardener soon, before the garden ran wild.

Humphrey never used the garden himself. He had paid Mr Bittle to keep it tidy, so that it was in line with those of his neighbours. He said he would think about it, see if he could find a suitable man.

A few weeks later, she reminded him again. In the meantime, she had continued to weed and had given the small lawn its first mowing. 'I can't afford a man,' he had snapped. 'You seem to be doing it quite well yourself – it'll improve your health to spend more time out there.'

Worried that money seemed so short, she had left him and continued to weed and to cut the lawn; in desperation, she left the vegetable patch untouched. She felt she could not face another argument with Humphrey; only two weeks earlier, she had persuaded him that if he wanted to keep his two maids, he must improve their wages, and she had squeezed out of him another shilling a week for each of them. She had concluded that business in the city must currently be in a very bad state, to make her father so mean.

Charles was successful in his application and it was arranged that he should join the University College staff the following October. Meantime, he had to return to Cambridge.

He was thankful to escape from his father's house, and was firm in his intention not to live there; it was so dreary. Even Alicia seemed awfully dull, sitting there with his mother, holding her knitting wool or untangling her embroidery silks and saying little beyond, 'Yes, Mama,' to their mother's fretful utterances. One night he had offered to take both mother and sister to a concert, only to be told coldly by Elizabeth that they did not care to go out at night. When he had opened his mouth to protest that they should do so, Alicia had signalled him frantically to keep quiet. Later, as they were sitting down to dinner, she had whispered an apology to him and explained that, 'If she is crossed, Mama gets nearly as angry as Papa these days.'

'You should go out yourself sometimes,' he had whispered back, as they waited for their parents to come to table.

'I haven't any money,' replied Alicia dejectedly.

'None? No pin money?'

'No.'

'You should ask Father.'

She was quiet for a moment, wondering how to explain her dread of incurring Humphrey's displeasure, the hunch, that over the years had become a conviction, that she was not his daughter and that, if he felt like it, he could throw her out into the street.

In answer to Charles's advice, she said, 'I'm afraid to ask him. He gets absolutely furious if you mention money and it's not good for his heart.'

'I'll ask him for you. He'd never help me at University beyond the bare fees, but he can find a bob or two for you – all daughters get pin money. Have you asked Mother?'

'Yes, several times. But she forgets – and I rather think that Mr Simpkins, her lawyer, is keeping a tighter hold on her income – perhaps Father warned him about her drunkenness.'

'I see.' He began to whistle under his breath; the whistling stopped abruptly, as his father entered the dining-room.

The next time Alicia presented her household accounts to Humphrey, he closed the book with a snap after examining it, and said, 'You may in future take a shilling a week for your own pocket.'

Though Humphrey's lips were clamped together as if he had just swallowed castor oil, surprise and delight shot across Alicia's face. 'Really, Papa? Thank you – thank you very much.' She picked up the housekeeping money that Humphrey had set out on his desk, crept from the room in her usual subdued way, and then ran down to the kitchen to break the good news to Polly.

Polly was grating cheese and she looked up from her work, and said, 'About time, too, luv!' To herself she grumbled, 'The old skinflint!'

VII

During his visit, Charles had gone out to the Vicarage to pay a duty call on Florence and Clarence, and had mentioned idly to Florence that Alicia seemed to have a very dull existence. 'Couldn't you take her with you to a play or a concert or something, occasionally?' he asked uneasily.

Florence had replied defensively that except for visits to her parents and her in-laws, they did not go out much themselves. 'I have Sunday School and Church visitors and the Flower

List and the Women's Embroidery Guild – the Guild is making new hassocks for the church at present and it's a lot of work. I hardly know how to manage myself. Clarence is also very busy – he is writing a book, on top of everything else.'

'God! I don't know how you stick it.'

'Charles!'

'Beg your pardon, Flo.' He chewed his thumb fretfully and decided that Alicia was a lost cause. What boring lives women lived.

Chapter Twenty-One

I

Florence usually visited her mother accompanied by her younger children, but while her boys were home from boarding school at Easter she decided that it was time dear Mama and Papa saw their whole flock of grandchildren. She wrote a note to her mother saying that she and Clarence would bring them for dinner on Easter Saturday, since Clarence would be busy with Easter Services on the Sunday.

Elizabeth was delighted and ordered two dozen eggs to be hard-boiled and then dyed, so that the children could play at egg-rolling in the garden.

'But, Mama,' Alicia protested, 'aren't the children rather old for that? Frank, Tom and Freddie are all young men.'

Elizabeth looked bewildered. 'Are they really?'

'Yes, Mama. I think only Beatrice and Teddy might still enjoy it.'

'Well – er – do what you think fit.' Her mother smiled sweetly at her. Then her smile faded and she looked puzzled.

Alicia told Humphrey of the impending invasion and he grunted acknowledgement. Though he loved Florence and always looked forward to seeing her, he did not enjoy her unruly offspring or the pompous scholar she had married.

Alicia and Polly spent the whole of Good Friday preparing for the visit. To save time, though it cost more, Alicia got the poultryman to bring the roasting chickens already feathered and drawn. She did not dare to buy the Easter Cake, however, and stayed up till midnight in order to bake, ice and decorate one. She had done the same thing at Christmastime, when the whole family had descended on them, and she thought what a relief it would have been if Florence had invited their parents to the Vicarage instead. The older Alicia's male nephews grew the less she liked them. The eldest, Frank, treated her with less respect than a kitchen-maid could normally have expected, and she thought sadly that his pontificating father was not much better. She could not say what it was that bothered her, except that they were patronizing, as if she were her mother's companion-help, instead of her daughter.

The young people did not dare to misbehave when Humphrey was present, so the dinner went off quite well. Afterwards, the three older boys and their father went away to the library to have a glass of port with their grandfather, and five-year-old Teddy and his sisters joined Elizabeth, Florence and Alicia in the morning-room for tea.

The little boy began to whine and be awkward.

Alicia finally suggested that he come with her to the old nursery and have a ride on the rocking-horse.

He accepted with alacrity and was soon restored to good temper. They chose a good jigsaw puzzle for him to take down to the morning-room, and Alicia opened the nursery door to go down again to the family. Lounging outside it was Frank, smoking a cigarette.

He nodded curtly to his little brother, 'Your mother wants you. Hurry up.'

The child clattered obediently down the stairs, while Alicia looked uncertainly at Frank.

He came into the room and shut the door behind him. Suddenly nervous, Alicia edged away from him, so that the centre table was between them. He laughed, and threw his cigarette end into the fireplace.

She said in a light, bantering tone, 'I don't think your father would wish you to smoke, Frank.'

'What Father doesn't know about won't bother him. Come over here and sit on the sofa. We'll have a bit of fun together.'

She was shocked, but she managed to say calmly, 'No, Frank. You know that wouldn't be right – besides, I have to go downstairs to help with the children.'

Her coolness annoyed him. He whipped round the table, caught her by the shoulder and turned her to face him. She tried to pull herself away, but she was pressed against the table and he was a big, heavy youth. He shook her like a dog shakes a rabbit it has caught. 'Come on,' he ordered her roughly. 'Give us a kiss – you Queen of the Midden – if you don't want to get hurt. For a bastard, you're too proud by far.'

He let go of her shoulder, put his arm round her waist and held her chin while he tried to press his mouth against hers. Terrified, she turned her face away, but not before she had seen the savage glint in his eyes.

To stop herself falling backwards on the table, she grasped frantically at the table's edge. Her fingers came in contact with a thin textbook she had left on it. She picked it up, and, as she was pushed backwards, she became for a second sufficiently separated from him to swing it hard against his face.

The swipe was so painful, as the corner of the cardboard cover caught his eye, that he let go of her and staggered back, his hand to his stinging cheek and outraged eye.

In a second, she was round the table and had the door open. 'You bitch,' he shrieked at her, tears running down his face from the injury.

'I'll tell Father,' she snarled back at him, as she ran through the door.

As she closed the door, she heard him him yell derisively, 'Tell Crossing? That'll be funny!'

She feared he would come after her, and she tore down the familiar staircase and across the hall to the green baize door leading to the kitchen stairs. She swung it open, and nearly sent Polly backwards down the staircase. The teacups rattled on the tray and the teapot sent an angry burst of tea from its spout, 'Carefully, duck!' Polly cried. Then she saw her charge's frightened face, and she asked anxiously, 'What's up, luv?'

'It's Frank. He tried to kiss me – it was horrid.'

'Tryin' it on, is he? Run downstairs to Fanny and stay with her. I'll be down in a mo'.'

As the door swung closed behind Alicia, Polly paused for a

moment to rearrange her tray. She heard heavy feet coming quickly down the upper stairs, a door opening and then a bathroom tap running.

'Blast him!' she muttered, and hastened to deliver the tea tray to Elizabeth. 'The dirty warehouse rat!'

When, later, the visitors said their farewells, Frank's sore eye – he had got something in it, he said – drew people's attention. But in the general confusion of departure, no one noticed that Alicia was not present.

II

A shaken Alicia dried the dishes for a loquacious Fanny; she told her nothing about Frank. Then, when the noise of departure had ceased, she went up to escort her mother to her bedroom; she had had to do this recently, because Elizabeth seemed occasionally to lose her sense of the time of day. This evening, however, Elizabeth was already napping in her chair and allowed herself to be helped upstairs to bed without argument.

Though she had defended herself, Alicia had been terribly frightened by Frank's attack on her. What would he do the next time he came? And he might easily visit more often, since he had now finished school and was, in May, to start work with a Liverpool wine merchant. And young Tom and Freddie might be equally aggressive.

Though she did not know the word 'rape' she began to fear some such attack. And what did he mean by 'Tell Crossing?'

It was only when she was drying the dishes that his last words really impinged on her mind. What *did* he mean? Who was Crossing? She wanted to ask Polly if she should tell Humphrey. Would Humphrey laugh at her for refusing to be kissed? Would he say that Frank was her nephew and it was quite natural to kiss his aunt occasionally? But not the way Frank had tried it, she felt sickeningly; he had tried to put his tongue in her mouth.

Trying not to cry with the sense of humiliation that she felt, she ran back downstairs to the kitchen and was relieved to find the two maids, feet on fender before a blazing fire, the earthenware kitchen teapot steaming on the hob.

As she advanced towards them, it seemed that Polly had already told Fanny that Alicia was in some kind of trouble with Frank. Fanny, not usually so demonstrative, put out a tiny, swollen, red hand towards her, and said, 'Come on, luv. Sit down and have a cuppa and tell us all about it.'

Alicia smiled down at her and joined them to tell them exactly what had happened.

'That little twerp!' exclaimed Fanny. ''E aint fit to practise on! But don't you let 'im put you off. There's plenty of nice young men as you'll want to kiss one day.'

'I don't feel like it at the moment, Fanny,' Alicia replied with a shaky chuckle.

'That's better,' Polly said, as she heard the hint of laughter. 'It's somethin' to laugh at! And thank God nothin' worse happened.'

'I'm afraid of next time he comes – because I hurt him – I didn't mean to do more than make him let go, but I think I hurt his eye.'

'Well, luv, whenever he's in the house, you be sure you're with somebody. Stick with your Mam – and with your Pa, if necessary.'

'Shall I tell Father? It's no good telling Mama – she'd forget half the story before I'd finished telling it.'

The maids looked at each other doubtfully. Then Polly cleared her throat and said, 'Mebbe not this time. If he touches you again, you better had.' She thought uneasily that Humphrey might not care if Alicia was mauled a little by the boys; but even he would surely object to rape in his own house. With sudden apprehension, she hoped that he would not make such goings-on an excuse to throw Alicia out. Better he knew nothing, if possible.

They continued to discuss the occurrence, and, also, times when they had themselves been caught in awkward corners by importuning men, until the teapot was empty and the fire had fallen in. Then Fanny went to her little room in the basement. She liked sleeping down there alone; she could occasionally smuggle a man in on a cold winter's night.

Polly and Alicia made their way up to the attic. At the door of her bedroom, Alicia kissed her nanny. Then she said, 'Polly, could I come into your room and talk to you some more?'

She rarely went in to either maid's room, but felt tonight that for some obscure reason Polly's was safer than hers for a secret conversation.

Polly was ready to drop from fatigue, but she unhesitatingly opened the door and let the girl into the chilly room with its black, iron single bed covered with a plain white bedspread. 'What is it, pettie?'

Realizing that something was still bothering the girl, she sat down on the bed and drew Alicia down beside her. 'That Frank didn't do no more'n try to kiss you, did he, luv?'

Alicia replied absently, 'No. I hit him before he could.' She looked down at her hands in her lap, and then raised her eyes to Polly, who was unpinning her cap. 'It was what he said, Polly, that I wanted to ask you. It's something that's been in the back of my mind for years.' She swallowed nervously, 'You see, I said I would tell Father of him, and he laughed in a really nasty way, and shouted, "Tell Crossing?" What did he mean, Polly?'

Polly put her frilled cap carefully on to the bed beside her. She gazed dumbly at the empty wall opposite her and wondered how to answer. Should she deny any knowledge of the reason for Frank's remark and leave the girl guessing?

'Polly?'

She made a great effort to get the story straight and to be cautious. She put her arm round Alicia's waist, and said, 'Well, what I know was told me after I coom here. I haven't never seen Mr Crossing, though Maisie – you won't remember her – she were the parlourmaid when I first come here – she said as he were a very handsome gentleman, your Mam's solicitor, and he visited her often.' She paused and sighed. 'Maisie and

Fanny told me that your Mam fell head over heels in love with him – and when you were born, your Pa – that is, Mr Woodman, said you couldn't possibly be his child – and there was an awful row and Maisie were fired for tattling to the Master about the goings-on.'

Alicia was watching her face with amazement, as all kinds of odd happenings in her young life fell into place.

'For a while it looked as if your Mam would be thrown out the door and you as well – but it would have been a terrible scandal and your Pa's, the Master's, business might well have suffered. It did cause a scandal – a sort of underground one, 'cos Maisie talked up and down the street, and people remarked that, after you was born, Mr Crossing was never at your Mam's dinners – and maybe through the solicitors' clerks it went round that Mr Simpkins had been made her solicitor instead, because of this. Some maids gossip some-thin' awful – and their mistresses find out things from *them*.'

'Poor Mama.'

'Aye. When I first coom here, she were a lovely lady to look at – she were the kind people would gossip about, anyways. Your Pa wouldn't have nothin' much to do with her after that; he put up with her in the house and made her keep house, and I had orders to keep you upstairs out of the way.'

She stopped, and Alicia asked, 'Is Mr Crossing my Papa?'

Polly laughed a little cynically. 'Well, it's a clever child what knows its own father,' she replied. 'But Fanny says as you are the dead spit of 'im, with your nearly white hair and light eyes.'

'And does that make me a bastard, Polly, like that boy said when we went to that New Year's gathering?'

'Not legally, love. Officially the Master is your father, be-cause he never publicly objected to you – and you live in 'is house. But it do leave a kind of shadow on you – it's a kind of excuse for people to feel better'n you, like. And a lot of women was jealous of your Mam's looks, I think, and she were careless of people, sometimes. I've heard her crack jokes about people that were very funny – but kind of cruel to the person they were about. And people don't like that.'

'Yes. She can be quite cutting at times.' Small quivers of fear went through Alicia, as she asked, 'Could Papa throw me out even now?'

Polly smiled. 'I doubt he would. It would cause too much comment – and you're too useful in the house.'

'I wish I could see my real father.'

'Nay, love. Never think on it. He's a married man – that's why he couldn't marry your Mam, even if she could get a divorce. Fanny says his wife were an invalid.'

'I suppose this explains why, when I was small, Papa would shout and rage at me and tell me to get back to the nursery. He still gets very cross with me, if I'm a ha'penny wrong in the housekeeping.'

'Aye,' agreed Polly, her lined face grave.

'And Mama doesn't really care about me, does she? She's never taken me out with her – and I've never had parties like other girls – and the idea of bringing me out just died.' Alicia's tone was bitter, as the resentment of years began to surface.

'I wouldn't say she doesn't care for you, luv. Seems to me it were all too much for her – and you know she hasn't been herself for years now. She sent you to school proper – and I heard her fighting the Master about sending you to Blackburne House.'

'Did she? Mama really does believe in education, I know – she helped Charlie for years. But it wouldn't have hurt her to take me out sometimes, would it?'

'I know, luv, and when I think on it I could spit blood.' Polly tightened her grasp around Alicia's waist. 'But . . .' She paused, and looked at Alicia squarely, 'You know, he's beaten her something cruel more'n a few times and I 'spect she's had as much as she can take.'

'Papa! Beat Mama?'

'For sure. You must've heard her cry out sometimes.'

'I've heard them shouting at each other. I didn't know that men like Papa hit their wives! I thought only working . . .' She stopped, realizing that she might offend Polly.

'That only working men did it?'

'Yes.'

'Ha! Don't you believe it. You just thank God if you get a husband wot don't beat you.'

'I'll never get a husband – I don't go anywhere to meet anybody. And I doubt if Papa would give me a dowry, to help me, if I'm not his daughter.'

Polly agreed cautiously. 'You shouldn't count on it, luv.'

Alicia turned to Polly and put her arms around her. 'You know, Polly, I think you – and Fanny – are the only people who love me. Don't ever leave, Polly,' she implored.

'Nay, luv. I'll never leave you. You're my baby.'

'I wish I was,' replied Alicia, as tears began to run down her face.

'Nay. You take care of your Mama, duck. She needs you. She's had enough.'

'I suppose I must. But, oh, Polly, it's so terrible to feel that there is something the matter with you which is not your fault – it really is.' And she wept.

III

Alicia began to observe Elizabeth and Humphrey with new, informed eyes. Like others with very narrow experience, she had assumed that her family was a typical one, that, despite all the love stories saying otherwise, married couples lived dull, parallel lives, communicating only with spiteful remarks. Now, she wondered if her family were exceptional.

She felt a growing bitterness against her mother for not having made an effort to guard her from the results of her indiscretions, to give her lover's daughter a better chance in life. She thought passionately that if she had had a baby by a man she loved, she would have treasured it as being part of him; instead, she had hardly seen her mother during her childhood; it was Polly who had mothered her.

She realized suddenly that she owed a tremendous debt to Polly and to her godmother, Sarah Webb. Without them, life would have been insupportable.

Why didn't Mama run away? she wondered.

The answer came readily; for the same reason that her daughter could not; the lack of money and the lack of decent occupations in which to earn it.

She might have gone to her sister, Aunt Clara, in West Kirby, ruminated Alicia; she would probably have sheltered her. But Aunt Clara's competence from their father was not very large either, and being so delicate she might not be able to tolerate a baby in the house.

When considering Humphrey, Alicia could believe quite easily that he had beaten her mother; she had suffered many painful clouts from him herself when she was younger and had strayed downstairs.

One Spring evening, when Humphrey had been particularly rude because the dinner was not to his taste, Alicia had flown down to her usual refuge, the kitchen, and said forcibly to Polly, 'The only way out of this is to run away. You heard him, Polly, when you were serving. He's impossible!'

A very concerned Polly spent an hour warning her about the fate of young women who had neither home nor work. 'You could try for a governess's job,' she said, 'but it lays you open to a lot of nasty things – a governess isn't family and she isn't a servant – she don't belong nowhere – and the men of the family can take advantage of her, though you'd be safer if you was a good deal older. And another thing, once you leave here, the Master might not let you return.'

With patience, she talked the angry girl into a better frame of mind, though when she said soothingly, 'One day some nice young man'll want to marry yez and you'll have a home of your own,' Alicia smiled grimly. Her mirror too often showed her a nondescript girl in gold-framed glasses and frumpy clothes – and dowerless.

'I doubt if Papa would even pay for my wedding,' she said sarcastically to her long-suffering nanny.

IV

When Florence arrived with Teddy on one of her periodic visits to her mother, Alicia felt suddenly sickened by her. If Frank knew the secret of her birth, he must have learned it, directly or indirectly, from something his parents had said, and she wondered what her flustered sister really thought of her.

Both sisters' attention was, however, diverted to Teddy. As they entered the morning-room, the little boy ran ahead towards his grandmother's chair. Elizabeth, startled, looked up from the photograph album she was leafing through and asked blankly, 'And who are you?'

At first, Florence thought that her mother was teasing the child, but she was looking earnestly at him, obviously awaiting a reply.

Teddy stopped, put his finger in his mouth and, after regarding her steadily for a moment, said, 'I'm Teddy, 'course.'

His grandmother's face broke into a gentle smile. 'Oh, yes, of course. How are you, Teddy?'

Florence viewed the tiny exchange with alarm. She went forward to kiss her mother and sit down beside her, while Alicia, more used to her mother's mental slips, went to make some coffee for them.

How could Mama forget a grandchild? She was only sixty – too young to be senile. Yet, now Florence considered it, Alicia was constantly reminding her mother of small items, like the impending visit of Miss Bloom, the dressmaker, or that it was time to go for a little walk up and down the road, or even that, perhaps, she should go to the bathroom.

Inwardly, she became quite agitated, as she considered the implications of Elizabeth's memory loss. She flinched at the very thought of ever having to cope with someone senile, in addition to her husband and children. And, sick or well, Clarence was not likely to tolerate Elizabeth in his house very willingly.

Alicia returned bearing cups of coffee and, as Florence looked up at her and took the proffered cup, she felt a sense of relief. There was Alicia, who, with a bit of luck, would always be there to nurse her mother. A plain, dull young woman with a shadow over her origins was not likely to be married. It would not hurt her to have only a mother to look after – single women had such easy lives.

V

Humphrey hardly bothered to address Elizabeth at all; he barely saw her, except at dinnertime. He dealt with Alicia regarding domestic matters; she had the dual advantages that he did not pay her a salary and, unlike the usual run of housekeepers and cooks, she did not steal.

One autumn evening, as he sat in front of his desk in the library, hands clasped across his stomach, he reviewed his household with the same care that he had just gone over his financial affairs. He felt a little surprised to realize that he no longer felt the wild rage of jealousy which the very mention of Alicia used to produce; it had all happened so long ago, and the fat, untidy woman sitting opposite him at dinner bore no resemblance to the woman who had been seduced by Andrew Crossing. He did, however, feel a lingering sense of defeat; he had originally been very proud to marry Elizabeth, a handsome, fashionable woman highly suited to his station in life. He had been so sure of himself that it had not occurred to him at the time that she did not want to marry him and that they would spend their lives sullenly hating each other.

And now he had dismissed Mrs Jakes. She, he thought, had humiliated him beyond pardon and he had been furious; yet there was a certain relief in being free of her.

VI

A few days after Mrs Jakes' request for help for Stella May and the angry spate between them, physical desire had again driven Humphrey along the familiar street to the small tobacconist's shop.

He had been agreeably surprised to be welcomed as usual, though in the ensuing weeks Mrs Jakes continued to make sly mention of Stella May's needs. She said nothing to Humphrey about the root of the problem which was that she wished to remarry. However, her suitor, a retired plumber, disliked Stella May intensely and wanted her out of the house, seeing visions of himself presiding over Mrs Jakes' lucrative little business. The only way out of this predicament, as far as Mrs Jakes could see, was to marry Stella May off.

In spite of the façade of goodwill, Humphrey ceased to enjoy his encounters with her, and the day inevitably came when, curled up in Mrs Jakes' bed, he failed to perform.

Mrs Jakes was not without skill, but she could not ease the dull ache in his chest nor the feeling of breathlessness which activity caused him. In any case, what was once spontaneous was now mechanical. Though unaware of the ministrations of the sturdy plumber, Humphrey sensed shrewdly that she was no longer really thinking about him, and he resented it.

Mrs Jakes complained irritably that she had been left unsatisfied. He flung himself crossly on to his back, his round paunch humping up the bedclothes, and told her that it was *her* duty to satisfy.

She turned on him angrily. She looked slightly ridiculous, as she sat up beside him, tousled hair, grey at the roots, drooping breasts hanging over the sheet she was clutching round the rest of her body. 'Well, if you don't like what yer getting, yer don't have to coom, do you? I can find others, I can tell yer, as'll be glad of me.'

Too late, she realized that any hope of money for Stella May had gone, killed by a few angry words. As he flung back the blankets, heaved himself out of bed and stalked, naked, to the chair where he had laid his clothes, with his bowler hat set neatly on top of his folded-up woollen combinations, she panted with sudden fury. 'Nice story this'll make when it goes the rounds,' she hissed, and then added spitefully, 'Sufferin' Christ! Wot I've put up with from you, you mingy-arsed bastard.'

He did not answer her. He heaved himself into his under-wear and then sat on a corner of the bed to put on his winter socks, while she kept on raving at him. He was shocked at such a tirade. Outraged, he hurried into his suit and shoes.

Without even looking at her, he clapped his bowler hat on his head, took up his walking-stick and overcoat, and opened the bedroom door, to clump steadily down the narrow wooden stair into the living-room. Here, he paused for a moment to get his breath and to look numbly round the tiny room. Three stuffed pheasants sitting on a mantelpiece draped with green velvet stared at him without malice. In that easy chair by the fire, he had sat with this woman on his knee, regarding her as a humble friend. He had shared her fender ale and her bed, and each month had playfully dropped a couple of sovereigns into the blue glass bowl in the centre of the table. And all that had gone in a trice!

He was glad. In future, he would occasionally find himself a whore. All he wanted now was to go home, shut himself in the library, take a large shot of brandy and sit down by the excellent fire he knew Fanny would have made, until his chest felt comfortable again. And he hoped that Polly had made a roast of beef – she did it very well.

Chapter Twenty-Two

I

That evening, Fanny banged the gong in the hall, as usual, to indicate that dinner was ready. As its final vibrations sank away, she stretched her tiny frame and then smoothed down her apron. She was bored and wished she was going out that night with the warehouseman she had met during her last afternoon off, a chance encounter which had delighted her. She had earlier said to Polly that at the advanced age of thirty-one she was on the shelf; the advent of the warehouseman suggested that her time had been extended.

Neither Polly nor Fanny gave much thought to their future. Though poorly paid, they considered themselves well fed and each had a bedroom of her own, a rare luxury when in domestic service. The big Upper Canning Street house was home to both of them.

Though Billy still wrote to her, Polly had given up any thought of his fulfilling his promise to bring her to Canada, and Fanny thought that the very idea of emigration was terrifying, even if one could raise the cost of the passage.

Elizabeth came slowly into the dining-room. For once, her hair was tidy and she had changed into a plain grey silk dress with a high, boned-lace collar; Miss Bloom had made it for her out of a long-abandoned crinoline dress taken from a trunk in the attic. In the light of the gas chandelier over the table, she looked, Fanny thought, a real lady. She pulled out Elizabeth's chair for her.

Alicia came hurrying through the door to the kitchen stairs, tucking wisps of hair into her bun as she entered the dining-room; her plain black dress with a white frill round its high neck made her look older than she was. As she sat down, she smiled at her mother, who smiled brilliantly back at her.

With her hands tidily behind her back, Fanny stood ready to serve the neat row of sardines set out on chopped lettuce.

'Do you think the Master heard the gong, Fanny?'

'He should've done, Miss; he's in the library.'

'Where's Charles?' asked Elizabeth.

'He's in Cambridge, Mama. He doesn't live with us any more,' Alicia answered her patiently.

'Oh, yes.' Again the bright smile. Elizabeth took her table napkin out of its silver ring and spread it across her lap.

'Give the Master a knock, Fanny,' Alicia requested. 'He may have gone to sleep in his chair.'

Alicia heard Fanny knock on the library door and then cautiously turn the door handle.

She shrieked, 'Oh, Allie! Come here!'

Alicia leapt from her chair and flew out of the room and across the black and white tiled hall. Fanny stood in the library doorway, her hand to her mouth. She turned in dismay to Alicia.

Alicia pushed past her.

On the Turkey rug in front of the fireplace, Humphrey lay face down. He looked as if he were asleep. His laboured breath was like a snore.

Alicia swooped towards him and fell on her knees beside him. She shook him gently by the shoulder. 'Papa, are you much hurt?'

He did not respond, so she tried to turn him on to his back, while little Fanny fluttered uncertainly beside her. He was too heavy to move, so she said to the maid, 'Get Polly – quick – and then run for Dr Willis. Tell him Father has had a fall – or it could be a stroke. Run, Fan.'

Fanny edged round Elizabeth who was approaching across the hall. 'What's happened?' she asked, but Fanny skidded past her, muttering, 'Everything'll be all right, Ma'am,' and sped down the kitchen stairs, while Alicia anxiously felt along Humphrey's arms and legs for broken bones. She looked up, as her mystified mother entered, and told her, 'Papa has had a fall, Mama, and I don't know how much hurt he is – there doesn't seem to be anything broken. Could you help me turn him on to his back, so that I can prop him up with cushions; he might be able to breathe more easily. It doesn't seem to be a faint – his face is very red, still.'

Elizabeth obediently lowered herself on to the rug beside Alicia and, showing surprising strength, helped to heave him on to his back. 'There,' said Elizabeth brightly.

They managed to ease some of the sofa cushions under Humphrey's head and shoulders and then tucked a shawl round him, to protect him against the draught along the floor. Alicia sat back on her heels and surveyed the unconscious man, doing her best to stay calm. 'I'll get him a glass of brandy out of his desk,' she said to her mother kneeling on the other side of him.

Polly's calm voice came from behind her. 'Nay, luv, don't give 'im nuthin' till doctor's seen 'im – he could choke on it.' She bent to help Elizabeth to her feet. 'You sit 'ere, on the sofa, Ma'am, while I undo 'is collar.'

Alicia was already trying, with trembling hands, to get Humphrey's stiffly starched collar undone. Polly pushed her gently away and then skilfully pressed the hinge of his gold stud and pulled the collar loose.

As the maid opened up his collar band and undid his fitted waistcoat, Alicia mouthed silently to Polly, 'What is it, Pol?'

'Stroke, almost certain.'

Elizabeth was saying in a haughty voice, reminiscent of her earlier days, that her husband should have a glass of brandy – and she should, too, to calm her nerves.

'It might kill 'im, Ma'am,' Polly replied shortly, and as she listened to Humphrey's stentorian breathing, she thought it would be better that he died than be paralysed. He could live, she thought, a hopeless log of a man for years and years – and it was poor little Allie who would bear the brunt of nursing him – as if her life were not already circumscribed enough.

Alicia got to her feet. 'Hurry, hurry, Dr Willis,' she prayed.

261

Polly looked up at her and advised, 'You take your Mam and go have your dinner. It's all ready in the dumb-waiter.'

'I don't want anything.'

'Look, take your Mam and go.' She jerked her head towards Elizabeth, who had got up from the settee and was trying to open Humphrey's locked desk. 'You'll be up all night, Allie, one way and another. You must eat.' She twisted herself round and said formally to Elizabeth, 'Dinner is served, Ma'am.'

'Oh, yes, of course.' Elizabeth began immediately to move towards the dining-room, completely ignoring her suffering husband. 'Come along, Alicia. You'll be late,' she said over her shoulder to her daughter.

Alicia grimaced ruefully at Polly, and then followed her mother.

As she hurriedly served Elizabeth with lukewarm lamb chops, potatoes and peas, her mother asked fretfully, 'Why doesn't Fanny serve? Where is she?'

Alicia tried to sound cheerful, as she replied, 'She's gone a message for Papa, Mama. She'll be back just now.'

'And where's Humphrey?'

'He asked us to start. He'll be with us soon.' Alicia had long since learned that detailed explanations were lost on Elizabeth.

Elizabeth shrugged and picked up her knife and fork and began to eat.

Alicia quickly served herself and was nearly through her main course when Fanny returned. She came straight to Alicia. 'He's coomin',' she panted.

Facing Elizabeth's uncomprehending stare, she quietly slipped her shawl off her shoulders and held it behind her.

'Who's coming?'

'Dr Willis, Ma'am.'

'To dinner?'

Fanny swallowed, and looked to Alicia for help.

'He's coming to see Father, Mama. You know he does sometimes.'

'I see. You may serve dessert, Fanny.'

Dr Willis was at the front door before Alicia had managed

to swallow her sago pudding and jam. Rising hastily, as she wiped her lips on her linen table napkin, she said to her mother, 'Excuse me, Mama. I have to see when Father wants his dinner.' She wanted to wring her hands at the uselessness of explaining anything to her.

As the doctor divested himself of his coat and jacket, Alicia poured into his ears the news of Humphrey's fall.

In the library, he took one glance at the recumbent man and exclaimed to Alicia, 'My dear young lady, I am glad you called me.' He quickly put his Gladstone bag down beside Humphrey and then knelt to examine him.

Alicia watched him, white-faced, inwardly terrified. She disliked Humphrey to the point of hatred; but she was dependent upon him – and so was Polly.

Polly had risen from the floor at the entry of the doctor and had silently bobbed a curtsey to him. She also caught Alicia's eye and tried to smile reassuringly at the girl.

As he hastily took out his stethoscope, Dr Willis asked, 'Have you any hot water bottles?'

'Yes, a number of them,' Alicia assured him.

'Kindly have them all filled and put into Mr Woodman's bed. And a good fire in his room – we must apply as much warmth as we can.'

Alicia gestured to Polly and the maid hurried out of the room. The doctor went on, 'I thought that this was what had happened, so I brought a stretcher and my errand lad, John. He and my groom can carry Mr Woodman up to his bed – I remembered that last time I was called to him you had no one to lift him.'

'Thank you,' Alicia answered warmly, grateful for his forethought and his presence.

Having alerted Fanny to the need for hot water bottles and a good fire, Polly was returning to the library. She was caught in the hall by an extremely irate Elizabeth demanding to know where her tea tray was. They both appeared in the doorway and Alicia went quickly to her complaining mother and told her that tea would be a little late. Dear Papa was poorly and

Dr Willis had ordered him to bed. Elizabeth calmed down and greeted the doctor graciously; she still ignored poor Humphrey.

Dr Willis stared at her in surprise. Then he asked Polly to tell his groom and errand boy to bring in the stretcher. He would deal with Mrs Woodman afterwards.

With a quick apology to the doctor for leaving him, Alicia persuaded her mother to go into the morning-room and promised that one of them would bring her tea very shortly. She lit the morning-room gas lamps and sat her mother in her easy chair and put a half-finished jigsaw puzzle on a tray close to her. Elizabeth's attention was immediately diverted, and Alicia fled back to Dr Willis. She met the doctor's men coming in with the stretcher, and was surprised how easily they managed to roll Humphrey on to it.

As they led the men up the stairs, Alicia said to Dr Willis, 'I'm sorry about Mama. She simply doesn't remember anything from one minute to the next.'

'Indeed? Poor lady. Perhaps we can talk about her difficulties later on.'

As Polly had foretold, Alicia was up for most of the night. Between a mother who kept inquiring what the matter was, regardless of how often it was explained to her, and a doctor who seemed to need everything in the house, Alicia thought her mind would split.

She was not allowed in Humphrey's room, while the doctor gave him an enema and drew water from him. Noting Polly's wedding ring, the doctor asked if she could help him, and she did.

When, at last, Humphrey was tucked up in bed, still breathing like a half-stranded whale, Alicia took Elizabeth in to see him. Though Elizabeth had kept forgetting what the turmoil in the house was all about, she did observe it and was restless and uneasy. Now, seeing her husband sound asleep, she realized that it was her own bedtime and that the house was quiet, and she allowed Alicia to put her to bed.

Alicia afterwards went to see the doctor. He was seated by

Humphrey's bedside, his fingers on his patient's pulse. He smiled kindly as, after knocking, the young woman came in.

When she looked down at Humphrey's face surrounded by supporting white pillows, she was shocked. His whole face seemed to have fallen to one side and he was drooling from one corner of his mouth.

Dr Willis rose and drew her quietly out of the bedroom. As he rolled down his shirt sleeves, he said that he felt that her dear father would recover, though not perhaps completely. 'You will need a night nurse and a day nurse,' he advised her. 'I can recommend two reliable women.'

Alicia opened her mouth to protest, but the doctor silenced her with a gesture. 'There are many unpleasant duties in connection with a case like this,' he told her, 'and a single young lady like yourself cannot perform them – and Mrs Woodman herself seems too delicate to undertake them. It would probably be better if the day nurse lived in, if you can accommodate her.'

Alicia wanted to burst into tears. Another room to clean, another mouth to feed out of her limited housekeeping, and then the endless running up and down to serve both nurse and invalid. How was it to be done?

She took a big breath. 'Two things, Doctor. Is it really a stroke? And will he be ill for a long time?'

The doctor hesitated. 'It's a stroke,' he said. 'I think he will get better – but he'll never be the man he was.' He paused and then said more optimistically, 'Good nursing and proper exercise will certainly help him.'

'Of course, he must have whatever you say, Doctor . . .' She thought for a moment and then plunged in. 'Could you advise me, Doctor, how I can arrange for money to pay everybody? Will Papa be able to sign cheques and orders – and things?'

'Not for some time, Miss Alicia. Could Mrs Woodman arrange it?'

'Well, Mama has her own small income. But Papa pays everything and gives me money for housekeeping.'

'Ah, I understand. Your brother – I recollect that you have one – or perhaps an uncle – will have to apply for Power-of-Attorney. Meanwhile, perhaps Mrs Woodman can draw on her funds for a short time.'

'I suppose she could,' Alicia replied doubtfully. 'She does sign cheques.' She sighed, and thanked him.

Dr Willis said he felt that he had done all he could and that he would go home. He would come again in the morning, and, meanwhile, someone should sit with Humphrey. Alicia agreed and led him down to the library, where he put on his jacket again. She asked, 'Did you have time to dine, Doctor? Polly could make something for you.'

He smiled at her, and replied, 'No. But Cook will have saved a meal for me.'

'A glass of wine, then? Do sit down for a minute to rest before you leave; you've been on your feet for hours.'

'Thank you.' He seated himself on a straight chair, while Alicia took her housekeeping keys from her pocket and unlocked a cupboard at the side of Humphrey's desk. She took out a bottle of port, a glass and a tin of biscuits. She poured out a glassful of wine and opened the tin, and put both by the weary physician. No time – at half-past one in the morning – to stand on ceremony, Alicia thought, as she sat down herself on the edge of the sofa.

The doctor thankfully took a sip of wine, and then said, 'Mrs Woodman has not consulted me for years and I always assumed that she was in good health. Has she seen a physician lately?'

'No. She is rarely indisposed.'

'But she forgets things?'

'Yes.'

'Has she been like this for long?'

'It's crept upon her gradually over several years. Recently, I've given up explaining much to her, because she doesn't take it in. Can anything be done about it?'

'No, Miss Woodman, there is nothing. She is ageing – it's God's will.'

Alicia gave a little shivering sigh. 'I presume it will get worse, then?'

'It is probable, unfortunately. She may need a companion – someone to be with her all the time – later on.'

It seemed to Alicia that as she heard these words a portcullis slammed in the distance. Who but she would take care of her mother? Certainly not Florence, if she could get out of it, she thought grimly. And it seemed that Papa would end up a semi-invalid and the responsibility for his care would be hers – and yet he was not truly her papa: he was a man who ruled her life like a despot, knowing that she had no real means of escape from him.

The doctor saw her face whiten. 'Take care of yourself, Miss Woodman. Please feel free to call on me for help.' He rose, and mechanically Alicia went to pull the bell, to call Polly to show him out. Polly, asleep before the dead fire in the kitchen, awoke with a jump and ran upstairs.

In the hall, as Polly handed the doctor his coat, Dr Willis turned to Alicia. 'Would you like me to send telegrams to any of your family for you? I would be happy to do so.'

Alicia heaved a sigh of relief. 'I would be so grateful.'

'Give me the addresses, then.'

She ran back into the study and scribbled the addresses of Florence, Charles, and Uncle Harold in Manchester. When the doctor read the list, he said, 'It would be quicker to send my errand boy to Mrs Browning. I'll arrange it.'

As Polly opened the front door, he hesitated, and then said, 'I have presumed that you would not wish Mr Woodman to go into the Royal Infirmary?'

Alicia stared at him, shocked. 'Of course not,' she responded sharply. 'Hospitals are for the poor.'

The doctor smiled. 'Well, not so much nowadays. You might like to consult your family about a nursing home, though.'

As she bowed her flaxen head on to her clasped hands, she muttered, 'Yes.' She listened dumbly to the clip-clop of the horse's hooves, as the groom, who had been patiently walking the animal, saw the light streaming from the front door and brought the carriage back. The little errand boy had been told to run home and get into bed.

'I'll return in a few hours,' Dr Willis promised, as he ran down the steps. *Poor girl*, he thought. *She'll spend most of her life tending invalids.*

Alicia began to cry quietly. Polly quickly closed and locked the front door. 'There, pettie. There, there. We'll manage somehow,' she murmured, as she turned to hold the girl in her arms.

II

Polly made a cup of cocoa for each of them and then insisted that Alicia go to bed. 'I told Fanny to go up, because she has to be up at five to do the fireplaces and make the fires. You go and get rested while you can; tomorrer, this house'll be like Lime Street station, with all the comings and goings. I'll sit with your Pa and see he's warm an' all. I can nap a bit in a chair by 'im, and find an hour to have a sleep sometime tomorrer.'

Alicia saw the wisdom of this, since Polly could not deal with the arrival of the family the next day. She told her about the nurses who would also be arriving.

Over her cocoa cup, Polly made a face. ''Strewth!' she exclaimed. 'Nurses is the end in a house. Constant trouble, they are. Worse'n havin' cockroaches or rats.' She put down her cup and got up to light the bedroom candles and then handed one to Alicia. 'It'll be better for you, though. There's a lot of heavy liftin' and it's a messy job lookin' after somebody paralysed. I seen it before in the court when I were young.'

Alicia went up to bed and lay crying into her pillow for some time. When she finally knelt down to say her prayers, she asked for strength to do her duty – and then for God to lift the duties from her, if he could, which was almost heresy;

women were supposed to bow their heads and accept, she thought hopelessly.

With a cheerful grin, Fanny called her at seven the next morning. 'Brought you a cuppa, to get you goin', like,' she said kindly. 'I've remade your Pa's fire, and Polly's kept puttin' fresh hotties round 'im all night. And she keeps wettin' his tongue and his lips. He's still breathin'.'

Filled with anxiety, her thoughts tumbling between what might happen to them all if Humphrey died and fear of the intolerable load of nursing if he lived, Alicia gulped down the tea gratefully. 'Fanny, dear, could you make up Edward's bedroom for the use of a nurse – there'll be two of them, one night, one day, but only the day nurse will be likely to sleep here.'

'Oh, aye, that's what our Polly was tellin' me,' Fanny replied philosophically, as she prepared to go downstairs again.

Alicia scrambled out of bed. 'To be honest, Fan, I haven't the foggiest notion how we're going to manage. Florence, Charles, Uncle Harold – they're all likely to turn up.'

Fanny laughed, and responded sarcastically, 'Oh, aye. And all expectin' four-course meals, as usual.' Then she added mischievously, 'You could send Miss Florence down to the kitchen to cook.'

This made Alicia giggle, as she poured water from the pitcher on her washstand. 'Fan, you are naughty! She's always been too busy to learn to cook, as you know.'

'Do 'er good to learn,' replied Fanny downrightly, and hurried out, before Alicia could scold her.

A few minutes later, after she had washed, Alicia arrived at Humphrey's bedside, to find Polly dozing. Her cap was askew and her face was grey with fatigue. Though she jumped when Alicia laid her hand gently on her shoulder, she got up from the chair slowly, acutely aware that she was no longer young. The night had seemed endless, as she had conscientiously boiled kettles on the fire and refilled the hot water bottles round her patient and kept his mouth and lips moist by sponging them with a wet flannel.

'How is he?' Alicia asked.

'Well, he hasn't changed much, 'cept I think he can move just a wee bittie – 'is right hand fingers.' Her voice was doubtful. Then she said, 'I couldn't change 'is sheet by meself, so I waited for you to come. He's in a bit of a mess. He needs washin'.' She yawned and stretched.

'Well, we washed him when he had his heart attack. Is the kettle hot? We can use the bowl on the washstand.'

'We'll need a couple of buckets with cold water to put the sheets in – and all the old sheets we've got.'

'I'll get them, Pol. And afterwards, you should go down-stairs and get some breakfast and then go to bed.'

When they had everything assembled, they used the sheet the helpless man was lying on, to pull him over to the unsoaked side of the double bed and then tucked his hot water bottles round him again under the blankets, while they dealt with the soiled side.

They laid an oilcloth tablecloth culled from the kitchen over the damp patch on the mattress and covered it with several layers of old sheets. Their most difficult task, after washing and changing him, was to get him back to the original side of the bed; he was very heavy and they were both panting by the time they had inched him on to the layer of old sheets. Alicia began to realize why nurses, trained in such matters, had been recommended by Dr Willis.

'You'll have to get a real macintosh sheet to protect the bed, Allie,' Polly said.

'The nurses are sure to want all kinds of things. I do hope Uncle Harold comes soon – he'll be able to arrange the funds.' The two women spoke over the head of Humphrey, completely ignoring the fact that he might, to a degree, be able to understand them and be distressed at being left out of the conversation.

They washed him as best they could, and Alicia wiped the distorted face. Then, taking a clean handkerchief, she dabbed cool water round his lips and over the lolling tongue. As she did it, she spoke gently to him, but he made no response.

They had barely finished when Fanny brought a tall, thin woman up to the bedroom. She wore a navy blue uniform and heavy black shoes. A woven basket trunk was carried up for her by a small street urchin, who stared round the bedroom landing with little bright eyes like a cock robin. She dismissed him at the bedroom door with a penny tip and Fanny took him back downstairs. She turned to Polly and Alicia and announced herself as Nurse Trill. As she divested herself of her jacket, she made it clear that she would do no cooking, laundering or tending of fires. She was entitled to three meals a day plus a tea tray and she had not yet had her breakfast.

Polly took one look at her and cast her eyes heavenward, as if asking for Divine help. War, to the last teaspoon, was instantly declared.

Alicia took her quickly away to Edward's bedroom, which she slowly surveyed. It was apparent to Alicia that it did not please her, but neither said anything, and Nurse Trill took off her bonnet and laid it carefully on top of the tallboy. She then opened her straw trunk and took out an elaborately pleated, starched white confection, which she pinned on top of her head and then tied its strings in a huge bow under her chin. She put on an apron so starched that it crackled when she moved, and then turned to Alicia and, with a queenly nod, indicated that they should return to the sickroom. As they crossed the passageway, she said to Alicia, 'See that my breakfast tray is brought up immediately.'

Inwardly quailing, Alicia promised that she would attend to it as soon as nurse had seen the patient.

Nurse Trill looked at Humphrey with jaundiced eyes. She screwed up her mouth in a grimace which clearly said that, in her opinion, he did not stand much chance. Then she said, 'Dr Willis felt he might be able to take a little water or milk this morning. Please let me have these.'

She was surprised to learn that Humphrey had already been washed and changed, and she looked Polly and Alicia up and down. Polly put her nose in the air and said primly, 'I'm a widow, and I done it for 'im before, when he had an 'eart attack.'

Nurse Trill grunted.

Alicia glanced at Humphrey and was astonished to see him watching them with one eye. The lid of the other eye still drooped.

She went to him and spoke softly to him, explaining that Nurse Trill had come to look after him. She was not sure that he understood. He closed his eye again.

That day, it seemed to Alicia that she and the two maids never stopped running up and down stairs. Fanny answered the door, hauled coal and water, and carried trays to the sick room, in between keeping Elizabeth to her usual routine, as far as possible. Alicia helped her mother wash and dress and took her down to the morning-room, where she took up her embroidery quite happily, having obviously forgotten the events of the previous evening.

About eleven o'clock, Polly was preparing lunch for them all and for the expected invasion of anxious relations, when she suddenly swayed and had to sit down. She called out to Alicia, who was in the cellar stirring the dirty bed linen in the copper. Alicia put down her wooden paddle and ran upstairs. Seeing her nanny lying back in old Mrs Tibbs' easy chair, she ran to her.

'Get me some water, luv. I feel faint.'

Alicia got the water for her and upbraided herself angrily. 'I should have sent you to bed long since. Away you go this minute. I'll watch the lunch.'

Polly temporized and then agreed to go up for a nap. Alicia insisted on escorting her up the long flights of stairs.

III

Dr Willis had earlier been to inspect his patient and confer with Nurse Trill. He was very pleased to see definite movement of the right eyelid and some suggestion of movement down the whole of Humphrey's right side. He spent a considerable time massaging Humphrey, to show the nurse how to do it. She told him indignantly that she knew very well what was required.

Afterwards, he went with Alicia to pay his respects to Elizabeth, who had forgotten who he was but received him most graciously. As he left her, he sighed helplessly.

IV

Alerted by a telegram from Dr Willis, Charles arrived from Cambridge, having been able to pick up a fast train for Liverpool at Birmingham. He ate a hearty lunch, sat with his father for ten minutes, spent about the same time with his mother, who was most surprised to see him, and then left again to visit his friends in Liverpool University.

Florence did not come and Alicia began to feel aggrieved; surely she *should* come – her father loved her.

'Send her a telegram,' advised Polly, when she woke up from her nap, about four o'clock in the afternoon.

'It seems that one of us has to go down to the telegraph office. And I must talk to Uncle Harold if he comes – and you *must* do the dinner – and Fanny's nearly crazy answering the nurse's bell all the time.'

'Well, if she don't come by tomorrer mornin' and we're still stuck, you could run next door and ask Colonel Milfort, if his valet could go down to the Telegraph for yez. Proper nice, they are.'

'Father doesn't think they're nice at all. He won't even bow to either the Colonel or his friend who lives with him – nor will Mama.'

Polly grinned knowingly. 'It takes all kinds to make a world, luv. You take my word for it, you'll be safer goin' into that house than any house I know. Remember to give the valet a bit for himself for goin' for yez.'

'Would you go, Polly? I feel shy.'

'Nay. You'll get more respect than me.'

Early the next morning, Colonel Milfort found the faded young daughter from next door sitting nervously on the edge of one of his leather easy chairs in the front room. An ex-hussar with a pronounced limp from an old wound, he still looked to Alicia a very handsome elderly man.

'Good morning, madam,' he addressed her politely, as he limped slowly across the room towards her. 'What can I do for you?'

Alicia blushed and jumped up from her chair. She apologized for troubling him so early and then explained the need to send a telegram to Florence to tell her that her father had been taken seriously ill.

'Of course, I'll send my man immediately,' he promised. Then he inquired how Humphrey was progressing and wished him an early recovery.

As a gentleman, he could not sit down until she did and his leg was aching intolerably, so he pushed a straight chair under her and begged her to be seated. She complied, and he thankfully sank into a chair himself.

From her small clasp purse, she took a slip of paper with the message for Florence scribbled on it, and handed it to him with a half-crown. 'The change will be a little thank you for your man,' she told him shyly.

The Colonel was amused and pressed the silver coin back into her gloved hand. 'It's my pleasure,' he assured her, as he looked at Florence's address. 'In fact, if you will permit me, it would be much quicker to send Francis to your sister's house on his bicycle.'

The tired young face before him lit up. 'Would you?' she asked eagerly. 'I'd be so grateful. You see, Mama is also not herself – and I badly need Flo's help.'

He nodded understandingly and rose from his chair, to indicate dismissal; he was afraid she might stay half the morning, telling him her woes. They shook hands and he himself saw her out of the front door. He watched her until she was safely inside her own house; then he slowly closed the door. It was the first visit he had had from a neighbour since the local widows had realized that neither he nor the quiet friend who lived with him were interested in women. Behind hands and fans, the word had gone round the district that the two army officers in the house with brown curtains were you-know-whats. Not nice at all.

Alicia told Polly that the Colonel had been an absolute dear.

Florence arrived on her own bicycle in just over an hour. In her haste, she had lost half her hairpins en route and had got bicycle oil on the hem of her grey tweed skirt. She burst into the kitchen, raging. 'When I told Clarence about the Colonel's message, he produced a note from Dr Willis which he had been carrying around in his pocket and had forgotten to give me. He had not opened it because it was addressed only to me, the stupid man.' She pulled the hatpins quickly out of her felt hat. 'How is Father?' Without waiting for an answer, she went on, 'The Reverend Browning does not like eating alone, but I told him he simply must manage, at least for lunch.' With an exasperated air, she flung her hat on a chair and followed it with her jacket. 'I'll go up.'

'Yes, Ma'am,' Polly replied, without looking up from the potatoes she was peeling, and when she had heard the green baize door swing softly shut, she muttered disparagingly, 'Listen to her with the gob! A fat lot of help she'll be.'

V

Florence wept for an hour by her father's bed, while Nurse Trill sat unperturbed by the fire, knitting a grey scarf.

Alicia had hoped that Florence would stay for a few days, but she was bent on returning to her overbearing husband as soon as possible. 'Dear Clarence gets so upset,' she confided to Alicia, as she pushed hatpins into her hat. 'And I've the Women's Bible Study group this evening. I'm sorry that I have to go; I'll come again soon.'

Afterwards, Polly comforted Alicia by reminding her that the night nurse would be coming, and if they all got a proper night's rest, they could manage.

The night nurse proved to be an Irish woman in early

middle-age and Polly took to her immediately. In order to save Fanny carrying up a tray, she cheerfully ate her late supper at the kitchen table before going on duty. Then she ran upstairs to relieve Nurse Trill, who was standing in the middle of the bedroom, her knitting neatly bundled up under her arm, waiting, watch in hand, to retire to Edward's bedroom.

Uncle Harold had arrived that same afternoon, very concerned about his acerbic brother's illness. He conferred with Dr Willis, when the doctor made his evening call. Afterwards, he sat down with Elizabeth and Alicia to discuss the situation.

He soon found that Elizabeth could not recall remarks he had made a couple of minutes before, and he was horrified. Humphrey had, during visits to Manchester, complained that his wife was very forgetful, but it was now clear to Harold that the poor woman's mind was fading completely. He looked at Alicia and she gave a tiny shrug, so he said he would like to rest and took his leave of Elizabeth.

Five minutes later, he and Alicia had a heart-warming conversation in the library and his first question was whether she could manage, with the aid of the nurses, to care for his brother. Dr Willis had suggested a nursing home or even the Royal Infirmary, but was certain that Humphrey would be much more likely to get better if he were in his accustomed surroundings. Alicia had drawn her ideas of hospitals from Polly's lurid tales of certain death if you ever found yourself in one, so she agreed, without hesitation, that he should be nursed at home. 'I'd never be able to face my own conscience, if he died in hospital,' she said honestly.

Uncle Harold was very relieved at her decision and he undertook to see Mr Bowring, Humphrey's clerk, on the following day and to discuss a Power-of-Attorney with Humphrey's lawyer. 'Meanwhile, I'll open a small banking account for you from my own funds, so that you can pay the nurses and the staff,' he told her.

In the days that followed, Alicia discovered that Harold Woodman's idea of a small banking account was quite generous, and, when she wrote her first cheque under the careful direction of a rotund, solicitous Bank Manager, she felt a new pride in being trusted with so much money.

Harold had been quite shocked to learn from Mr Bowring that Humphrey's main bank was the Manchester and Liverpool District Bank.

'A radical bank!' he had exclaimed.

'Yes, sir. Very good bank, if I may say so.'

'I always thought my brother was a Tory.'

'Oh, he is, sir, he is. But the Manchester and Liverpool is very forward-looking. Backed many of Mr Humphrey's investments in times past. And, of course, now Mr Humphrey is doing so well, he is a very prized customer.'

Harold was surprised to hear that Humphrey was doing well. Not too long back, his brother had complained that nothing that he touched seemed to be coming to fruition, and Alicia had said that her father was very hard up.

Mr Bowring begged Mr Harold to be discreet and then brought out Humphrey's account books, which confirmed that Humphrey was reaping quite a fortune.

VI

Once it was apparent to him that his father was not likely to die from his stroke, Charles was thankful to leave everything to Uncle Harold and Alicia. He was busy paying his addresses to a Miss Veronica Anderton, the daughter of a Cambridge don. Since his application for a post at Liverpool University had been successful, he felt, now, that it would be wise to marry the lady before she realized that she might be called upon to help to nurse his two invalid parents. As long as Alicia lived, of course, he comforted himself, he did not have to worry. Still, life could be very uncertain, so he took the first possible train back to Cambridge.

VII

Her mind freed of financial worry, Alicia was able to establish a routine and even keep Nurse Trill reasonably satisfied.

Polly and Fanny thankfully took their usual weekly afternoon off, and Polly suggested that Alicia should do the same, even if it were only to attend church on Sunday evening.

'You don't never get round the shops, neither, never mind church,' Polly said. 'You go while you've got the chance, duck.' She was ironing heavy linen sheets as if her life depended upon it and she slammed the iron back on to the fire as if to emphasize her words. 'It worries me no end, the way you bin kept in these last few years.'

Alicia slowly digested the fact that neither of her parents was in a position to be aware of her absence. 'What would Uncle Harold say, if he arrived and I wasn't here?' she asked doubtfully.

'Och, him? He's a real gentleman – remember how he allus brought you bits of chocolates when you was a kid? He'd have a fit, if he knew how you've bin treated since you left school. I don't mind tellin' 'im what a time you've had, if you like.'

Alicia was so used to being confined, her biggest expedition being an occasional visit to the grocer, that it was strange to her that the cage door was suddenly open.

Polly watched her out of the corner of her eye, as she spat on a fresh iron to make sure it was hot enough. She was relieved when Alicia said suddenly, 'I'd love to walk down to see Aunt Sarah Webb – she's too frail now to come over to see us.'

A few days later, she delighted Sarah Webb with a visit, and she poured out her news of Humphrey and Elizabeth to the old lady. Elizabeth's steady decline distressed Sarah greatly. She said sadly, 'I've seen it coming for some years – but we have simply to be patient with her. It happens to all of us, sooner or later.'

After this first plunge, Alicia took her shilling pocket money each Friday and, sometimes, spent most of it on tram fares, happy to sit on a slatted wooden seat and watch the great city go by.

VIII

One Friday afternoon, a letter came for Polly from Billy, and she read it while leaning against the back door jamb to get a little fresh air while she waited for the kettle to boil for Elizabeth's and Nurse Trill's tea trays.

Billy wrote fairly regularly three or four times a year, but no letter had puzzled her as much as this one did, so she showed it to Alicia as soon as the girl returned, glowing, from a brisk walk in Princes Park.

'He's got 'imself a new job,' Polly explained. 'Workin' with 'orses in a stable – he always did love 'orses when he were in the warehouse. Says the pedlar chap's gone 'ome to Montreal – but he does a bit o' peddling 'imself, still, when things is slack at the stables.'

As Alicia began to read the badly printed letters and was amused, as usual, by the total lack of punctuation, Polly went on darkly, 'What's worryin' me is he's all mixed with them Chinamen again – he's forever talkin' about this man, Huang. Says he's gone into partnership with him and put some of his savin's into making Huang's Café look nicer, so as to draw a family trade – and feed weddin's and parties – says he built shelves and tables for him. Throwin' his money down the drain workin' with 'eathens! Needs his head examining,' she fulminated.

Alicia laughed, as she turned over the page and read on. 'Well, you never know. Perhaps there is no nice restaurant there – it could be a good idea. I see that he says his main aim is still to get a farm. He wants to run horses on it. ' She looked up at Polly. 'Horses should be a pretty safe thing – people always need them.'

Polly made a face. 'He's proper daft,' she said, and returned to her ironing. 'I hope he gets enough to eat.'

'I expect he can always get a meal in the café.'

'At the rate he's goin', he should stick with his stable, silly bugger. Savings is savings,' and she thought of her sovereigns still sitting in their pillbox at the back of her dresser drawer. A lump rose in her throat at the sudden memory of Edward.

Alicia smiled impishly at Polly's rank disapproval and took off her hat and coat. Despite the constant worry of two sick people, she had begun to feel much better since being able to go out. She now said cheerfully, 'I'll take mother's tea up, if Fanny is busy.'

As she went upstairs with her mother's tray, she wished she could convince Elizabeth to visit her old friend, Sarah Webb. She had tried on a number of occasions and had once got Elizabeth partly down the road towards Sarah's house, only to have her suddenly baulk and almost panic. No amount of reminding her of her dear friend had persuaded her to go a step further. Alicia had had to bring her home.

Despite her mother's persistent refusals to go out, she had twice been found wandering down the street in her house slippers. Now, the front door was kept locked and the key was removed, for fear she strayed and became lost. Sometimes, she would find her way downstairs to the back garden and would meander amid its increasing wildness. Polly locked the door to the alleyway.

When she entered the morning-room with the tea tray, she found her mother standing by the window, staring pensively out of it.

She turned a bright face to Alicia, and inquired, 'Have you a stamp? I must write to Andrew.'

Alicia put the tray carefully down on to the table beside Elizabeth's favourite chair. 'Andrew, Mama?'

'Yes, dear, Andrew Crossing.' Then seeing the surprise on Alicia's face, she added a trifle impatiently, 'My lawyer. He always makes me save some of my allowance and I want to ask him to let me draw a little more from the Bank – you're not getting enough pocket money and I want to increase it now you're fifteen.'

Alicia swallowed hard, and answered carefully, 'It's very sweet of you to think of me, Mama – but Mr Simpkins is your lawyer. Of course, he hasn't been to see you for ages, so I'm not surprised you've forgotten.'

The smile faded from Elizabeth's face and, to Alicia's distress, tears welled up in her mother's eyes and rolled slowly down the fat cheeks.

'Oh, Mama, don't cry.' Alicia eased herself round the intervening furniture, and went to put her arms round her mother. She took out her handkerchief and wiped away the tears. 'Come and sit down, Mama, and have your tea. You'll feel better, and if you wish we'll send for Mr Simpkins. Who is Andrew Crossing, Mama?'

But the curtain fell once more over Elizabeth's mind and Alicia did not get any pocket money from her mother; the lawyers continued disinterestedly to transfer the same sum each month from the Trust established by her grandfather to her mother's banking account, and it began to be difficult to persuade Elizabeth to write cheques to pay Miss Blossom, the old dressmaker, or for cash for her other small needs.

Chapter Twenty-Three

I

Though it took months, Humphrey did make a partial recovery and managed to get around the house with the aid of a stick. He tried hard to deal with his affairs again and his clerk, Mr Bowring, became such a frequent visitor to the house that Alicia had a table put in the library for him to work at.

Humphrey's temper, never good, became worse. His irascibility sometimes reduced Polly and Alicia to tears; Fanny kept as far away from him as possible. He was frequently unpardonably rude to Elizabeth, but she would simply look at him in a bewildered fashion and it was clear that within a few minutes of his biting attacks, she had forgotten what he had said.

His patient clerk, Mr Bowring, mindful that he was getting to the end of his own working life and that he would in old age be largely dependent upon whatever small sum Humphrey settled on him, kept very quiet and did his best to care for Humphrey's interests and to guide him where necessary.

When Humphrey first saw the housekeeping book, he flew into a temper at Uncle Harold's generosity; but when his brother came from Manchester he finally accepted his explanation that there had been many unexpected expenses in connection with his illness. With some temerity, Harold pointed out to Humphrey that, in addition to the expenses entered in the book so meticulously by Alicia, Alicia herself needed both clothing and pocket money.

'You owe your life to that girl's patience with you,' he said. 'With Elizabeth sick herself, nobody in this world is going to look after you the way she does. She attains her majority this coming year and could very well leave you if she is not happy. My wife pointed out years ago that she hadn't a decent garment to bless herself with and she's dreadfully shabby now.'

Harold was aware of Alicia's likely origins, but had, in an absent-minded way, always treated her as his niece. Now he said, 'I realize why you dislike her so, but you could regard her as a valued employee. If she left, you would have to pay heavily for someone else.'

Humphrey saw the sense of the argument. Mr Bowring was instructed to pay Alicia a wage of eight shillings a week. Mr Bowring opened his mouth like a landed goldfish at the order, and then said quietly, 'Yes, sir.' Poor young lady, he ruminated; he had grown fond of Alicia.

When he paid her, he did not humiliate her by calling the money a wage. He said kindly that her father had instructed him to see that she got some pin money each week, and she flushed with pleasure.

Without asking permission, she continued to take Friday afternoon off and Humphrey found himself facing a frigidly polite Polly whenever he wanted something on that afternoon. Usually, he wanted to be read to, because he could not hold a book or newspaper steady and got too tired when he laid them on his desk to read. He was very angry on the first day he discovered Alicia's absence, but Polly told him coolly, 'I can read to you, sir.'

He was surprised, and asked, 'You went to school, then?'

'No, sir. Mr Charles taught me when I first come here and he were a little boy.'

'Well, I'm damned. Bring in the newspaper.'

So while Fanny kept an eye on Elizabeth, Polly sat primly in the library reading aloud.

Alicia found that there were less expensive ways of dressing oneself than going to George Henry Lee's or to Miss Blossom. She discovered the world of Lewis's, a department store, where for a few shillings she could buy decent blouses, hats, shoes and a thousand oddments; her newfound wealth stretched much further than she had imagined it would. She was very thankful for this, because her father had had a number of visitors during his illness and a few of these gentlemen came regularly to see him. She had had to receive them, since, as she explained, her mother was indisposed. In her shabby skirts and home-made blouses, broken shoes and general air of dishevelment, it was obvious that they had thought her to be some kind of companion-help, and their surprise at finding that she was a daughter of the house had been apparent from their expressions. She had felt hurt.

At first, her father's speech had been so slurred as to be unintelligible to anyone but Alicia, who was with him so much that she was able to follow what he was trying to say. Dr Willis, however, sent a middle-aged lady to see him, and, for what Humphrey regarded as a monstrous fee, she taught him how to improve his articulation. In his frustration, he used to get very angry with her, but she persisted until there was a kind of rueful friendship between them.

On her own initiative, Alicia ordered a carriage one sunny November afternoon to drive him and her mother through the park. While Humphrey was eased into his outside clothes, he shouted at her that it was needless extravagance. Fanny helped Elizabeth into her fur coat and she wandered about the hall saying it was bedtime and too late to go out. Once out, however, they both seemed to enjoy the trip.

Colonel Milfort watched their departure from his drawing-room window. He observed the difficulty with which Alicia managed to persuade her mother into the carriage and then hoist her stiffened father into it. He was also sorry for the girl, whose history he had heard from his batman, who had got it from Fanny.

He limped to his desk and wrote her a note offering the loan of his carriage one afternoon a week, so that her parents might take the air in the park. His batman would be pleased to assist her father in and out of the carriage and to drive it.

Harassed and fatigued, Alicia burst into tears when she read the stiff little letter. She accepted the offer with alacrity, though she expected that her father would raise every objection he could think of, once he knew who had sent it. He had, however, enjoyed the outing that Alicia had arranged; it had given him a sense of assurance that he was indeed recovering his health, so he accepted Colonel Milfort's offer quite gracefully and instructed Mr Bowring to write him a note of thanks. The Colonel was surprised to receive the following Christmas from a grateful Alicia a hand-embroidered desk blotter, which she had worked during long hours of watching her mother.

'Well, damn me!' exclaimed the Colonel, running his fingers over the elaborate workmanship which held the blotting paper in place. He shook it free of its enveloping tissue paper and stumped slowly upstairs to show it to his friend, Major Ferguson, who was lying comfortably on a sofa in the drawing-room window.

The house on the other side of Humphrey's residence was put up for sale on instructions from the heir to the owner; according to Fanny, the heir lived in Jamaica and had no intentions of living in Liverpool. It was bought by a well-to-do carriagemaker, a tradesman called Hunter.

'Proper nice old girl, that Mrs Hunter next door is,' opined Polly, as she heaved a steak and kidney pudding out of a steaming pan of water. 'She'd be good for your Mam.'

'Mama and Papa wouldn't wish to know them, Pol. They're in trade, not commerce.'

''Strewth!' exclaimed Polly in disgust, but said no more.

One day in January, however, when the sun was gleaming softly between the forests of smoking chimney-stacks and when Alicia was about to pass Mrs Hunter's front steps, the lady had just descended from her truly magnificent pale green carriage. Beaming, she left her groom and rolled gently towards the younger woman, to inquire anxiously how her dear father was. They had, she said, seen Dr Willis's brougham regularly at the Woodmans' door.

Alicia was surprised to find that this exuberant lady knew a great deal about her parents and herself, forgetting that Fanny and Polly would indubitably gossip with the maids next door. Made nervous by this sudden revelation, Alicia retreated as gracefully as she could.

Not only did Mrs Hunter wish to ingratiate herself with the ladies in her new neighbourhood, she was also very kind. Armed with a large bunch of grapes for the invalid, she ventured to call on Alicia.

Not sure what to do with her, Polly took her upstairs to the cold, dusty drawing-room, and called Alicia. Alicia explained that her mother was indisposed and unable to receive visitors. She asked Polly to bring tea.

Mrs Hunter stayed half an hour during which time Elizabeth wandered in to join them. Seeing a lady dressed in hat and gloves for visiting, Elizabeth automatically dropped into the role of hostess; it was obvious, however, that she could not keep track of the conversation. Alicia was embarrassed, but Mrs Hunter gave no hint that she realized that all was not well with Elizabeth.

She told her amused husband afterwards, 'I've never seen such a dismal house. Hasn't bin painted in years. And it was that cold – no fire in the drawing-room! Can you believe it? And her poor mother's out of her mind – *non compos mentis*. Between her Ma and her Pa, I don't know how that girl stands it.'

Mr Hunter turned a page of his newspaper. 'So you saw Mrs Woodman? And Woodman?'

'No. According to his daughter, he's up and about, though. I saw him once, driving in the park.'

'Well, I'm glad I was wrong when I said you'd be snubbed,' he responded.

After her visit, Mrs Hunter always stopped to chat when she saw Alicia, and one day asked her to come in for tea. Alicia refused, but explained that it was not because she did not want to; she was simply so busy. She began to enjoy these small encounters with her neighbours, and was quite vivacious with

Colonel Milfort and his friend, Major Ferguson, when they paused in their afternoon perambulations, to inquire after Mr Woodman.

For the first Christmas after Humphrey's stroke, Florence brought her maturing brood for Christmas tea rather than to midday dinner. 'It will save you having to cook so much,' she told Alicia. The visit was, however, quite hectic, and Frank was unsubtly spiteful to Alicia. Clarence spent half an hour with a barely coherent Humphrey, talking about the need for new choir-stalls for his church – woodworm had badly damaged the present ones.

Blithely indifferent to who cooked it or what the menu was, Charles shared a roast capon with Alicia and their mother at midday dinner and stayed on for tea. Alicia cut up some of the meat very small and fed Humphrey in his bedroom. He was propped up in an easy chair beside the bed.

Immediately after tea, Charles left to catch the train for London where he would stay with friends. It was he, however, who suggested that the library was large enough to be adapted as a bedroom for Humphrey, to save running up and down stairs.

Dr Willis saw the convenience of this suggestion and Humphrey liked the idea of being amongst his books and papers again, so a vast amount of furniture-shifting was done by Polly, Fanny and Alicia, including a commode and wash-stand which were concealed behind a folding screen near to the bed.

Being on the ground floor of the house undoubtedly en-couraged Humphrey in his efforts to walk again. Fires in the morning-room and the dining-room, added to the blaze in the library, kept the whole area fairly warm, and he began to set goals for himself, to reach the chair by the door, then the chair in the hall, then to cross the hall. Once or twice, he fell and bruised himself, but after Dr Willis had warned him that he might break a bone, he would ring furiously for Polly or Alicia to help him to move about.

One night, after he had been put to bed, Alicia flopped on

to a kitchen chair and sighed to Polly, 'I'm so tired of it all, Pol.'

'Aye, luv. We all are. But what else can we do?'

And there was no answer.

Sometimes, late at night, Polly would wake up to hear the nursery piano being played and she would lie fretting for Alicia – her baby.

II

In May 1907, on one of his rare visits to his family, Charles confided the news of his courtship to Alicia.

Alicia was thrilled and demanded every detail of Veronica Anderton's looks, likes and dislikes. Charles was so besotted by his prospective wife that he was unable to answer some of Alicia's questions and could not even recall for her, with certainty, whether her eyes were grey or pale blue.

Alicia was inwardly wretched. It was her Twenty-First Birthday, and when her brother came rushing into the house she thought it was to greet her on the day of her majority. Instead, he had come to discuss Veronica with her and had obviously forgotten about the birthday.

The day had also gone unremarked by both Humphrey and Elizabeth; Alicia thought sadly that her mother was becoming increasingly unable to remember anything.

The postman had brought a card and a little silver dish in need of polishing from her godmother, Sarah Webb. Her aunt Clara in West Kirby, immersed in her own invalidism, had also apparently forgotten, and Uncle Harold and his wife, Vera, had never marked her birthdays.

She had been touched by the gift of a violently pink shawl from Polly and Fanny, who must have spent hours late at night to produce it without her knowledge.

Now, as a sudden storm of rain beat against the window-panes, she tried to keep her attention on Charles's problems. And he certainly did have a difficulty, because a prospective daughter-in-law might be reluctant to enter a family where she could have to care for sick parents.

'Not that she'll have to worry while you're here,' Charles was continuing, cheerfully taking it for granted that, while Alicia lived, it was her duty to care for their parents.

Alicia bit her lower lip and reluctantly agreed.

'What shall I do, Allie?'

'You'd better let Father know of your intentions, before you pop the question formally, don't you think?'

Charles sighed. 'Yes, I must.' He stroked his golden brown moustache thoughtfully. 'I wonder how much he'll give me, to start us off?'

Alicia made a face and carefully turned rightside out the sock she had been darning. 'You had better ask him.'

'Can he stand a visit, do you think?'

'He'll have to. He's reading. Mr Bowring's gone home.'

Charles rose and sighed again. He was surprised to hear Alicia chuckle, as she looked up at him and said, 'Don't expect too much!' He realized suddenly that Alicia appeared more self-assured than she used to. In the old days, he thought neither of them would have dared to make even the smallest joke about Humphrey.

At the sight of his son, a bored Humphrey thankfully closed the volume on the sloping book rest in front of his chair; he had difficulty in retaining what he read and even in turning the pages himself.

Charles did his best to smile, despite the smell of urine and excrement pervading the room from the commode behind the screen. What a mess the fine library looked, with a bed set in the middle of it, he thought depressedly.

Humphrey received his son's news with interest and asked some details of Professor Anderton and what dowry Charles expected Veronica to bring. His speech was very slurred and Charles had to concentrate hard to understand him. He seemed, however, to find Charles's replies to his questions acceptable and promised to dictate a letter to his clerk for

Professor Anderton. 'I don't suppose your mother will write,' he added.

'She can't, Father. She simply doesn't remember what I tell her.'

'Hm. Turn down the light for me. My head aches and it's bothering my eyes. And get a whisky out of my cupboard – have one yourself.'

Charles stood up and adjusted the central gas-lights.

'Not that far,' his father told him testily, and Charles hastily turned the four lamps of the chandelier up again. He then got two glasses and a bottle of whisky out of his father's side cupboard and poured out two modest shots. He handed one to his father.

'God's teeth! Can't you even pour a decent sized whisky?'

Charles quickly added more to his father's glass, and then sat down in a chair opposite to him and slowly crossed his own legs. Would the old man come up trumps and provide a decent sum towards his marriage expenses?

Humphrey conveyed his glass to his mouth with some difficulty, while he laboriously meditated on how little he could get away with without losing standing with the Andertons. It always hurt to part with money, and the thought of it raised his blood pressure.

The silence began to depress Charles, and he said, 'Veronica is an only child, as I mentioned. She wants Alicia to be her bridesmaid and Florence her Maid of Honour. Her best friend would be another bridesmaid.'

Humphrey's head began to throb. 'Alicia?' He turned his gaze slowly upon his son. 'Alicia will not attend the wedding.'

'Father! She's my sister. Why not? Veronica's very keen about it.' He uncrossed his legs and leaned towards Humphrey, his face shocked. 'I understand that you and mother may not be able to come – but girls love weddings.'

'Alicia has to attend your mother and me.'

'Oh, surely, Father, Fanny and Polly could do that for one day.'

'They don't do things properly,' Humphrey retorted grumpily.

'But . . . just for a day, Father. It would do Allie a world of good – might introduce her to some decent fellows – it's time she got married.'

'Nonsense! She's not the marrying kind.' His voice rose. 'We should, in any case, not be left to the care of servants.' As he spat out the last words, saliva dribbled down his chin. His face went slowly purple and he trembled visibly.

Charles did his best to control his own anger and bewilderment. He said persuasively, 'I do understand your personal difficulties, Father, but surely it could be managed. Poor Allie will be frightfully disappointed – and so would Veronica – she . . .'

'Stop arguing with me. I will decide . . .' The empty glass fell from his hand and shattered on the brass fender.

For a second, the noise deflected Charles's attention, but then he snarled furiously, 'I won't stop arguing. Allie *must* come.'

'You say *must* to me? How dare you? Get out of this room. When you can be polite, come back again.' It seemed to Charles that his father's face swelled up and that his eyes suddenly protruded like glass marbles.

'Father!'

'Get out!'

Charles jumped angrily to his feet. He strode out of the room, slamming the door behind him, while Humphrey shouted something incomprehensible after him.

He stood quivering in the hall, and then went across it to the morning-room, to find Alicia.

During his absence, Elizabeth had come downstairs and, as he entered, Alicia was holding her arm and was trying to persuade her to go upstairs again. Elizabeth was resisting vigorously.

At the sound of the opening door, Alicia looked round. She said in an embarrassed fashion, 'Could you leave us for just a minute, Charley?'

'Of course.' Charles carefully shut the door again and wondered what womanly business meant that he had to leave them. 'Christ!' he muttered savagely.

The door was quietly opened behind him and he turned quickly. His mother smiled charmingly, 'Charles, dear. How nice.'

'Come along, mother,' Alicia said sharply. 'We have to go upstairs.'

'Why?'

Alicia blushed unaccountably and looked uneasily at her brother. 'Mama, I explained to you.'

'But Charles is here.'

'We'll be down again in a minute. Charles, dear, do go into the morning-room. We shan't be long.'

Mystified, Charles did as he was bidden and stood leaning against the mantelpiece. What the hell was the matter with the family this afternoon? He heard Alicia and his mother arguing, as they ascended the stairs.

It was about five minutes before they returned and, as his mother slowly lowered herself into her chair, Charles raised a querying eyebrow towards Alicia.

'Had to take her to the loo,' mouthed Alicia over her mother's head. Her face went scarlet. 'She wets herself otherwise,' she said baldly.

'O Lord!' muttered Charles.

Oblivious of any embarrassment, Elizabeth began to ask Charles how he was doing at school. He replied absently that he was doing all right – poor Mother seemed to be falling apart. He turned to Alicia and told her that he had had a row with their father over Alicia being a brides-maid.

Alicia was not altogether surprised at the news. As she pulled out a chair and sat down near her mother, she asked, 'Was he *very* cross?'

Charles hesitated before answering and watched his mother trying to find the right colour of embroidery silk in her basket. Then he said, 'He was simply furious.'

'Oh, goodness! He would hate his routine to be upset.' She

rose, and said a little anxiously, 'Perhaps I had better see if he is all right.'

'Why?'

'Well, you know we're not supposed to upset him – it might cause another stroke.' She moved towards the door.

'Oh, come on, Allie. He's all right. Fancy getting all het up about Veronica's bridesmaids!'

She nodded to him. 'Talk to Mother for a bit. I'll just take a peep at him.'

He heard her quick footsteps on the tiles in the hall and the opening of the library door. She was back in a second, her face white.

'Charley, come quick! I think he's dead.'

From Elizabeth came a startled cry. Her comprehension was fleeting. Then her face went vacant again.

Chapter Twenty-Four

I

In his Will Humphrey left Florence ten thousand pounds and Alicia a shilling for candles.

Polly and Fanny were sitting modestly at the back of the big upstairs drawing-room, which had been hastily cleaned for the gathering of the family; they had each been left one hundred pounds and felt they had been meanly dealt with. 'What's a shilling for candles?' Fanny whispered to Polly, as Mr Derby, Humphrey's solicitor, droned on.

'Dunno.'

'Will the Mistress be all right?'

'Aye, I think so. She'll get the use of the ould fella's money and when she dies Master Charles'll get it.' Aunt Vera, Uncle Harold's wife, turned and hushed Polly, and the two maids immediately became models of demure quietness. They watched, however, a sudden stir on the other side of the room, as Alicia got up from her seat beside her mother, the insulting sentence ringing in her ears. Mr Derby paused in his reading and the remainder of the group stared at her as she edged round the room to get to the door.

As the door clicked behind her, Mr Derby cleared his throat and continued, and the family turned back to hear that Humphrey had bequeathed his gold hunter watch, his seals and other personal jewellery to his brother, Harold Woodman.

Alicia had not expected that Humphrey would leave her anything; she was, she told herself, probably not his daughter. She had been shocked, however, to be humiliated before the family, when his Will was read, and, indeed, Mr Derby regretted it; he did not know who Alicia Beatrix Mary Woodman was and had unwisely assumed that she was probably a younger sister of Humphrey's who had displeased the family; he had certainly not expected a quiet, sensitive-faced young woman to be seated in front of him.

Alicia ran down to the kitchen and stood in front of the great, old-fashioned range, her arms clasped across her chest as if she had been wounded. The warmth of the fire was comforting, but, yet again, she felt herself hemmed in by circumstances not of her own making.

'How could Papa be so cruel?' she asked herself. Her nephew, Frank, sitting there with his parents and siblings, must be sniggering. Did they all know about her? She shrank from having to meet them again. And Uncle Harold's tall, dignified sons and their wives, to whose weddings she had not been asked? Did they know? Their mother, Aunt Vera, must know – probably knew more than Alicia herself did.

She heard the green baize door in the hall open and then Florence's voice, calling in a hoarse whisper. Reluctantly, she went to the foot of the stairs, 'What's the matter?' she inquired listlessly.

'Mother's soaked her dress and the chair,' Florence whispered again in great agitation. 'What shall we do?'

'Take everybody into the dining-room for cakes and wine – it's all ready. Send Polly down here to make the tea, and tell Fanny to serve. I'll take care of Mama,' Alicia responded practically. In the background, she could hear Elizabeth inquiring in a piercingly clear voice where Humphrey was.

After she had cleaned up her mother, Alicia did not again mingle with the funeral guests. Florence, as the eldest daughter, could do the honours. When the guests left, nobody thought to come to say goodbye to Alicia.

After Uncle Harold had seen his wife and family off to catch the train to Manchester, he returned, and Polly, as she took his hat and coat from him, was glad to see him. 'Are you staying overnight, sir?'

'Yes, Polly. As the Executor, I have to spend some time with Mr Derby. Where is Miss Alicia?'

Polly directed him to the morning-room, where he found Alicia entertaining her mother by going through an old photograph album of Charles's. He contented himself with taking Alicia's hand and telling her warmly that she was not to worry. 'We'll have a good talk in the morning,' he said, with an uncertain glance at Elizabeth who appeared to be regarding him as an intrusive stranger. He said to her, as he loosed Alicia's hand, 'I'm your brother-in-law, Harold.' He leaned over her chair and kissed her, and she gave him one of her brilliant, almost arch, smiles.

II

Uncle Harold proved to be very helpful. The house now belonged to Charles and he would have liked to live in it after he was married. He felt, however, that he could not turn his mother out and he was determined that his new wife should not be made responsible for his mother's care, which she would be if they moved in – even if Alicia stayed with them and became her mother's personal attendant. It would be better to rent another house for the first years of Veronica's and his marriage.

Thankful not to have to move, Alicia discussed with Uncle Harold her mother's growing incapacity, the doctor's assurance that it would grow worse and the problems of managing such an inconveniently large house.

With Alicia, Uncle Harold toured the place from cellar to attic nurseries, and then he conferred with Charles. Charles told him irritably to arrange any alterations he felt necessary, the cost to come out of his father's Estate.

The old basement kitchens were closed off, and after much trailing in and out by muddy-booted workmen, all grumbling that it could not be done, the butler's pantry on the ground floor was made into a modern kitchenette with a gas-stove.

Gas-fires were installed in all the rooms still in use and the nursery floor simply had its doors closed and was left to gather dust.

'I know it saves steps,' Polly confided to Fanny, 'but when I locked me old bedroom door, I cried. Master Edward and me was so happy in it – and when I put a dust-cover over the rocking-horse in the nursery, it were like losing an old friend – Master Edward loved that horse.'

Fanny nodded glumly. With a fine, new bedroom on the first floor, she would not in future be able to ask a man to spend the night with her, as she had been able to when alone in her basement bedroom. But you can't have everything, she told herself, and never having to carry another hod of coal, never having to face the dust and soot of open fires again, was an overwhelming relief. 'All you has to do is strike a match and the fire's there,' she thought incredulously.

'Will your maids stay with you?' asked Uncle Harold of Alicia.

She looked at him in surprise. How could anyone imagine Polly and Fanny leaving her? 'Of course,' she assured him. Then she asked slowly, 'Do you think we could pay them a bit more? They are shockingly badly paid.'

'I imagine so,' Uncle Harold had replied cautiously. 'I'll ask your Aunt Vera what the usual wage is at present.' They were seated at the dining-room table, a mass of papers between them, and he looked at the pale, earnest face before him, and then went on, 'I can justify a salary for a companion-help for your mother, since she is far from well, and I would like, my dear, if you are not offended, to pay you this salary.'

He saw the startled surprise on Alicia's face, and added, 'It's the only way I can think of to provide for you.'

Alicia flushed, and then nodded sadly, 'A shilling for candles,' she said ruefully.

'Yes. I don't know what made your father cut you out of his Will,' he lied. 'But we have to live with it. So I hope you will accept the salary.'

'Thank you, Uncle Harold. Yes, I will.'

'I think your mother's affairs also need attention, don't they?'

'Yes, they do. She is no longer able to sign cheques for her clothing – and she used to buy books.' Alicia swallowed at the recollection of her mother's pitiful decay, but she sighed with relief when a few weeks later he was able to arrange for her signature to be acceptable on her mother's account, subject to Elizabeth's lawyers overseeing the Bank's Statements. He also opened a Housekeeping account for her and she was astonished at the generosity of the amount he felt she needed. With Charles's and his permission, she had the hall repainted and a new stair carpet laid.

No amount of money would halt the ruthless march of Elizabeth's illness, so it was decided to continue the use of the library as a bedroom and this, too, was redecorated before putting Elizabeth's bedroom furniture into it, so that it looked familiar to her.

As she became more and more irrational, Elizabeth acquired a stubborn fixation which made it almost impossible to persuade her to do something quite normal, like taking a bath. She became terrified of her own reflection in a mirror and, to avoid this happening, some mirrors were removed while the others were draped over.

Dr Willis insisted that, no matter how difficult Elizabeth was, Alicia must continue to go out at least once a week and leave her mother with the maids. 'You must maintain your own health,' he warned her. 'Where would Mrs Woodman be without you?'

Though in earlier days Elizabeth had had a friendly relationship with Polly, she seemed now to tolerate Fanny better, perhaps because the younger maid made less fuss over her and retained the formal status of servant with her, something to which Elizabeth had been accustomed all her life. Fanny never argued with Elizabeth, but simply used the standard phrases of a servant, however inappropriate, to beguile her to the bathroom or to eat.

Supported by Uncle Harold's interest and her spirits raised

by the improvements to the house, Alicia was able to cope better with Elizabeth. The three women took it in turns to watch the benighted invalid, so that no one was herself nearly driven mad by Elizabeth's insane questions and illogical behaviour. And there was always the freedom of Friday afternoon to look forward to.

In the back of Alicia's mind, however, lurked fear of the future. What would happen to Polly and herself when her mother died? The best she could hope for would be that either Charles or Florence and Clarence would give her a home; an extra pair of female hands was always welcome in either kitchen or nursery, particularly when there was no obligation to pay their owner anything. One of them might also give Polly and Fanny jobs, since they were well-trained servants.

As she considered such a gloomy outlook, a slow, burning revolt against her own probable fate grew in her. It would be better to try for a post as governess or lady's companion, where at least she would be paid, and she began quietly to prepare for this and to save all that she could from the salary so kindly contrived for her from Humphrey's Estate. Polly was getting old, she worried, and she hoped that she might be able to help her financially, if necessary.

Late at night, she would sometimes leave her sleeping mother and run upstairs to practise on the grand piano in the huge, unused drawing-room. So that she could teach music, she put together a series of children's pieces and made notes on how she would introduce a child to it. She also spent time during her mother's afternoon naps studying from her old school text-books and putting together short lessons on a variety of subjects. When engaged in replying to Elizabeth's aimless and persistently repeated questions, she did some pieces of fine needlework to show a prospective employer or did pencil sketches, which she could show at the same time, to indicate that she could teach these ladies' accomplishments.

One Friday afternoon, she went to the Windsor Street library and borrowed two travel books and one on the care of pets, with an eye to having background knowledge for a post as Companion. Later on, she read a number of books on etiquette, for the same purpose. She became known to the librarians and began to regard them as her friends.

Christmas brought several letters. Charles wrote that, because of his family's being in mourning, he and Veronica had decided to be married quietly in Cambridge during the Christmas holidays. He realized, he said, that Alicia must look after Mama and would not be able to attend. Alicia presumed that Florence or Clarence had explained to him why she had been cut out of his father's Will and she smiled sardonically. Veronica's parents did not send her a formal invitation, so she blinked back her tears of disappointment and threw his letter into the fire.

There was a joyful letter from Billy to say that he had taken up a quarter-section of land in Alberta, a whole one hundred and sixty acres, he exulted, and he was clearing it while he worked part-time at the stable; he did not mention the excruciating, back-breaking work this entailed, but instead said that the land was the beginning of a real hope that he could bring Polly to Canada and have a place for her to live. It might take a few years yet, but he would do it.

Such a pang went through Alicia as she read this that she felt it difficult to say, with conviction, to Polly that it would be wonderful for her to go. How could she endure being separated from Polly? She would be totally alone.

As Polly read the letter again, she pursed her lips and said, 'Why don't he get married?' The idea that Billy might actually fulfil his long-ago promise made her suddenly nervous; she was not sure she wanted to meet a collection of Chinese, Red Indians and Frenchies.

'Perhaps he isn't the marrying kind,' Alicia responded lightly, as she remembered the short, inarticulate boy who had helped to weed the now totally neglected garden.

'He wrote once as there was more men than women in Alberta – maybe that's why,' Polly suggested, on consideration.

Alicia agreed. The talk of marriage reminded her of the other ceremonies in her Book of Common Prayer, and she asked idly, 'Was I ever christened, Polly?' She looked up from the tray of rice she had been cleaning, while her mother napped. They were in the new kitchenette and Polly had put down her letter, while she got out her new cookery book, *How to Cook with Gas*, to check the heat setting for a rice pudding. At Alicia's question, she turned round and smiled. 'Of course, you was, duck. The Reverend Clarence done it. Your Mam and Miss Webb stood for you – god-mothers, like. Now what put that idea into your head, all of a sudden?'

Alicia shrugged. 'Well, I wonder why I was never confirmed?'

'Confirmed?'

'Yes. You know – made a full member of the Church.'

Polly was gingerly lighting the gas oven and her reply was a little muffled, as she leaned into it. 'Probably nobody remembered to have you done.' She got up from her squatting position and closed the oven door. 'Now, Master Charles, he were done at school – I remember because your Mam gave me a parcel with a present to post to him.'

Alicia shook the cleaned rice into a basin in order to wash it. As the last grains plopped in, she said slowly, 'You know, Polly, it seems to me that nobody ever thought about me, except you.'

Polly smiled. 'Well, you always was my baby, luv.' Then, as she shook sugar for a rice pudding on to the small, brass scales in front of her, she added, 'Master Edward loved you like anything – remember?'

'Yes, he did – and I loved him so much. How I wish he'd lived, Polly. Both our lives might've been different.'

'Aye, they might've bin,' Polly sighed. Then she reminded Alicia, 'Your Mam cared enough to see you went to school, though. I remember she had a real set-to with the Master over it.'

'Surely school is every girl's right?'

Polly sniffed. 'Nobody never sent me to a proper school, except to Dame School to learn me letters. Even so, if Master Charles hadn't taught me, I wouldn't be able to read nor write now.'

'Nowadays, you'd have been sent to the Board School.' Alicia ran water from the tap over the rice and drained it. Polly concentrated on her recipe and did not reply to Alicia's comment.

'Polly, do you remember long ago, when we went out on New Year's Eve to the top of Upper Parliament Street, and that horrible Ralph Fielding from down the road called me a bastard?'

Polly glanced warily at her out of the corner of her eye, as she turned to get flour and lard out of the small pantry behind her. 'Yes?'

'When I finally found out what the word meant, it made me feel sick, Polly, and lots of things I'd never understood fell into place. I knew why the girls at school weren't allowed to be friends with me. It seemed so terribly unfair, Polly, because it wasn't my fault,' she said dejectedly, as mechanically she assembled the rice pudding. 'And then when I understood the absolute repudiation that *a shilling for candles* meant, I felt totally publicly humiliated. It confirmed my worst fears about Papa's feelings for me.'

'Well, I told you before, love, that he were your Papa as far as the law were concerned.'

'But not as far as his feelings were concerned. He often made my life a misery; he was quite different with Florence. Do you suppose that Charles's in-laws or his Veronica know the story about me?'

'Seeing as you wasn't asked to their wedding and Miss Florence and the Reverend was, not to speak of Mr Harold and all his kids, they must've got wind of it – people would talk about the Will and ask questions – and a proper nice piece of gossip it would be. I'm sorry, pettie.'

Alicia half-closed her eyes. She felt despised and rejected, and she wondered if the feeling would be with her all her life.

Aloud, she said to Polly, 'I've tried so hard, Pol, to be a good daughter.'

Polly smiled wryly at her. 'You've bin more than good, chook.'

III

In the Spring of 1908, Charles and Veronica rented a newly-built house not far from Seacombe Ferry, on the other side of the River Mersey from Liverpool, from which Charles could commute easily to the University every day. Upper Canning Street, also, was not very far from the University and Charles dropped in occasionally to see his mother, though Veronica declared that was too far for her to visit. Charles's visits were short because Elizabeth no longer knew him with any certainty and he did not seem to have much to say to Alicia. Her absence from his wedding was never mentioned.

Florence also called from time to time. In an absent-minded way, she was gushily polite to Alicia but, as with her brother, any sense of ease there had been between them was gone. She, also, did not stay long.

'I bet Clarence has told her to have as little to do with me as possible,' Alicia thought shrewdly, well aware of her brother-in-law's ambitions. Her manner towards Florence became stiff and cold.

Viewing her small savings nestling in an old tea caddy, there were days when Alicia felt like taking flight; the money would last her for a little while. Yet, now she knew about Andrew Crossing, she felt an enormous pity for her mother who had, in some way, become locked into a marriage which did not suit her. Pity, a sense of duty and a fear of censure, if she left, kept her by her mother's bedside. She could almost hear the acidulous voices if she deserted a sick parent, 'You can expect wicked, outrageous behaviour from a bastard – nothing good in them.'

It became impossible to leave Elizabeth alone for a second,

even if she were sleeping – she might wake up. She would wander all over the house, absently turning on all the gas lights without lighting them or aimlessly tearing up books and papers when she came across them. She occasionally smashed crockery by throwing it on to the floor and there was always the fear that she would fall downstairs or, as she once did, get into the bath and turn the taps on until she was soaked and the bath flooded. She was still physically quite strong and it was easier to follow her round the house than to try to persuade her back into her room.

'She's like a clock without a pendulum,' Polly once remarked in despair, as she sorted a pile of stinking bedding and clothing, the result of Elizabeth's incontinence. 'And yet she looks that well you'd never believe it.'

IV

Next door, Colonel Milfort quietly died of cancer and his heart-broken friend sold the house to a well-to-do grocer with a large family, who referred to Elizabeth as *that madwoman next door*. He forbade his wife to have anything to do with a family with the stigma of lunacy about them. This did not stop his children, when they met Alicia in the street, pointing at her and sniggering and, sometimes, calling 'Loony, loony,' after her. She passed them each time with slow, grave dignity and finally they gave up.

'District's goin' to pot,' said Fanny, in disgust, when she heard the racket the children made in the next-door garden.

The irrepressible Mrs Hunter, the Woodmans' other neighbour, continued to be extremely kind to Alicia and the young woman often had tea with her in her opulent, overstuffed drawing-room. Alicia found it comforting to be told that she was doing a wonderful job in caring so well for her poor Mam and to be presented with vases of flowers or bunches of grapes for the invalid. She became very fond of the stout lady.

Quite frequently, on her day off, Alicia would go down to tree-lined Rosebery Street to see her godmother, Sarah Webb, who was housebound by acute arthritis. 'It's just old age, my dear,' she would tell Alicia, as the girl put into her tortured hands bunches of roses or daffodils culled from the Woodmans' wild garden.

Alicia wept bitterly when, in January 1911, the old lady caught influenza and slipped out of life, a wise, erudite woman who had taught Alicia far more than the girl realized.

Alicia felt that her own life was slipping away without any of the normal consolations that made human existence worthwhile. Sarah Webb had done her best to contribute a lot of small happinesses to her goddaughter's lot and, without her, Alicia felt a terrible mental loneliness which even Polly could not fill.

Uncle Harold came periodically to check her accounts and discuss house repairs and any other small needs. It was he who first suggested a professional nurse to help Alicia with her mother. Remembering Nurse Trill, Alicia felt that such a person might only drive her mother to even greater perversity and stubbornness, so she replied uneasily that she did not think that the time had yet come for such help. 'Fanny is better with her than any nurse would be,' she added. 'Between the three of us we are managing – and Dr Willis is very helpful.'

V

Not too long after Sarah Webb died, when Spring bulbs were beginning to flower in the Woodmans' garden, Alicia helped Polly to peg out newly-washed sheets on the clothes-line. Both women were suddenly petrified by a great roar just above their heads. As Polly told Fanny, 'We dropped a sheet on the lawn and ran like 'ell into the house. There were an aeroplane right over our heads – could've nearly touched it. We'd never seen anything like it before – scared stiff we was.'

Upstairs, a terrified Fanny had held a panic-stricken

Elizabeth firmly in her chair. 'Thought it were an earthquake,' she responded to Polly.

'Bloody madman! Ought to be put in Bedlam,' fumed Fanny, when, the next day they saw pictures of the plane in the newspaper. 'Ought to make a law about them.'

'Really, Fanny dear. There's no need for bad language. Aeroplanes are a fad – young men are always trying dangerous things,' Alicia rebuked her.

As if to belie her words about a passing fad, the selfsame young man, Mr Henry G. Melly, flew his plane safely to Manchester and back, the following day.

'He'll fall out one of these days,' prophesied Fanny, shaking out dried towels as if she were shaking the young man for his foolhardiness.

In a port, the loss of men and ships at sea was common news, but, as Alicia said, 'Nobody has to risk his neck in a noisy thing like a plane while we've ships and trains.'

'Nor drive them motor cars,' interjected Fanny huffily. 'Going around as if they owned the street. I were nearly run over the other day – and the horses is frightened to death by them – rear up, they do, as soon as they hear one comin'.'

'Upper Canning Street is getting quite busy, and I'm always afraid of Mama, somehow, wandering out and being killed,' Alicia replied, giving voice to an anxiety which had been with her for some time.

'Na, I bin keepin' the door locked – and I always keep the key in me apron pocket – never put it down anywhere; so I can answer the door quick enough and yet make sure your Mam can't pick it up,' Fanny assured her briskly.

VI

It was Fanny who returned from her afternoon off, one August day, looking like a sparrow that had been mauled by a cat.

Her best black straw hat was a tattered wreck and her greying hair hung like rat-tails down her back. She sobbed to

Polly that she had been caught up in a fracas outside the *Legs o' Man* public house in Lime Street. Some railwaymen hanging round the station had begun to bait the constables on duty there. The police were nervous because there had been riots in the city as a result of a railway strike.

'Them buggers waded in with their truncheons and I got it. Me back hurts like hell, it does.' Polly had never seen her friend so upset. Fanny's face was drawn with pain, as she went on aggrievedly, 'And I were only talkin' to ever such a nice fella as was down there to see what was happening.'

'Come on up to your bedroom,' Polly suggested, 'and take your frock off so I can have a look.' But when, upstairs, she quickly commenced to unhook Fanny's print summer dress, the woman cried out in pain.

Polly stopped immediately. 'Maybe you should go to the Dispensary,' she suggested uneasily.

'Not me! They might send me to the 'ospital.'

'Well, look. You sit down here and I'll go and tell Allie. She's with her Mam. I think you've broken somethin'.'

Very concerned about her old friend, Alicia sent Polly for Dr Willis. She dared not leave her mother unattended, so Fanny sat alone in her bedroom, weeping with pain.

Dr Willis was annoyed at being asked to come to a servant at nine o'clock at night and sent his young partner, Dr Bell.

Though glad to see him, Fanny was horrified when he calmly took out a pair of scissors and cut her out of her best summer frock. She gaped at him and yelped, 'Wot you done?'

'You're more important than the dress, Miss Barnett,' he comforted her, as he peeled the dress back to expose purple bruises on Fanny's back.

As his delicate fingers probed round the wounds, Fanny sniffed back her tears. Nobody had ever called her Miss Barnett before.

He turned to Polly. 'I don't think anything is broken. Have you any arnica in the house?'

'Aye. Miss Alicia's bound to have some.'

307

'Bathe Miss Barnett's back with it, and I will give you a little laudanum to help her sleep tonight and tomorrow night.' He took a tiny bottle from his bag and dripped a little liquid into it from a bigger bottle. He corked it down firmly and handed it to Fanny.

'Thank you, sir.'

'Take care of yourself, Miss Barnett, and don't get caught in any more riots. You'll feel discomfort for some days, but the bruises and cuts will heal.'

Fanny looked up at him with wonderment, her pain forgotten. What a lovely man! *Miss Barnett!*

The encounter sparked a devotion which was to last her into old age. Many, many years later, she was to become his housekeeper.

On his way out, the young doctor met Alicia standing anxiously at the door of her mother's bedroom. Polly introduced them and Alicia shook his hand.

He looked at her with little interest, as the full glare of the evening sun struck her through the landing window. It showed him a very tidy, slim woman of almost no colouring, a firm mouth clamped too tightly, as if she, too, might be in pain. After he had answered her anxious inquiries about Fanny, he mentioned that Dr Willis had asked him to find out how her mother was, since he had not seen her for several weeks.

Alicia sighed. 'She is, as usual, totally forgetful. We never leave her alone, except when she has had her usual dose to make her sleep at night.'

She watched him descend the stairs with Polly and then went back to pick up her mother's sewing, books and jigsaw puzzles with which she had tried to amuse her.

Her mother's coordination was becoming worse, she thought sadly. She would put a few stitches into a petticoat that had lain in the sewing basket for months, and then drop it irritably because she could not place the stitches as she wanted. She could still occasionally manage a simple jigsaw puzzle, when someone sat by her and encouraged her to try, but her only true enjoyment, as far as Alicia could see, was to listen to her playing light classical pieces on the drawing-room piano. So every afternoon, of late, she had seated Elizabeth in an easy chair while she herself played. Somewhere in the recesses of her mother's damaged brain there seemed to linger a memory, not much more than an instinct, that the piano represented much happier times, when Elizabeth had played at parties she had given. Perhaps, thought Alicia, Andrew Crossing had stood by her to turn the pages for her. Nothing, however, would persuade Elizabeth to try to play once more, and as the music swirled around her, tears would run slowly down her mottled cheeks.

Alicia allowed her mind to stray from her tidying up and her sleeping mother, while she considered Dr Bell. She could not remember ever speaking to such a young professional man and she wondered if he were married. Then she told herself savagely not to be such a fool. She was not free to marry while her mother lived. Furthermore, she was now twenty-five years old, too old for marriage.

Chapter Twenty-Five

I

One February morning in 1913, Alicia received a registered letter from a West Kirby lawyer, informing her of the death of her Aunt Clara. He enclosed a freshwater pearl necklace left to her by her Aunt. She had died, he wrote, from a severe bout of influenza and he regretted having to send her such bad tidings. As the Executor of her Will, he needed to know the names and addresses of any other relations who should be informed.

Alicia berated herself for not going to see her Aunt on her afternoons off; but she had flinched at spending her precious few hours of freedom sitting beside yet another invalid, and she had kept deferring a visit. Now it was too late. She had, however, written to her at Christmas and Easter, ever since she had been a small girl, which was how the lawyer must have found her address. The fact that he needed the addresses of other members of the family indicated that Aunt Clara had not received letters from either Florence or Charles.

With tears in her eyes, she wrote to the lawyer and gave the addresses of Florence, Charles, Uncle Harold and, finally, of Uncle Henry in Ceylon, who she believed was the final inheritor of her maternal grandfather's estate. Uncle Henry, she remembered with wry amusement, had never been known to write to anybody and she had no recollection of his visiting her mother – he must have come home at one point or another, she ruminated, but she could not remember his doing so. She wondered if he had managed to live until now – long enough to collect a part of the Reversionary Interest from his father's Estate now available to him.

Alicia also wrote immediately to Charles, who went to West Kirby to check that his aunt had received proper burial and a suitable monument. The lawyer had seen to both matters, as instructed by Aunt Clara in her Will. 'Do this, so that I am no trouble to my young relations,' she had told the lawyer.

On his return, Charles came straight to see his mother and Alicia.

'Have you told Mother?' he asked Alicia.

'No. I didn't think I could make her understand.'

In some dim way, Elizabeth always seemed to recognize her son, and, when he told her gently about her sister, Clara's, death, she seemed to understand, because she exclaimed quite clearly, 'Oh, no!' She did not cry, however, and was soon talking in a fuddled way to herself.

'What about Florence?' Charles inquired.

'I thought I'd let the lawyer do it. I felt I could not stand Florence gushing all over Mother, who might be frightened and yet not understand what had happened. Flo always flounders so – perhaps because she's so tired.'

'She's not really tired,' he replied with a grin. 'She used to be worn out with the children. But since they left home, she is become pretty spry. She still runs all the church's women's groups. She just takes to her couch when Clarence is at home.'

'What on earth for?' Alicia was startled by this peculiar behaviour.

'Well, you *know*. Our Clarence always wants to leap into bed, even at his age. And Flo isn't the type.'

'Charles, I think you are being very vulgar.'

'No, I'm not. It's a reality of life – and it's great fun, if you haven't had absurd, old-fashioned ideas put into your head by a lot of school ma'ams – and so many women have.'

'Charles, you're talking to a single woman who knows nothing about the secrets of marriage.'

'Sorry.' He grinned down at her, and she felt suddenly left out, deprived of the knowledge of what fun was.

What was fun? Though Polly had explained matters of sex

quite baldly to her, she had not suggested that there was particular *fun* in it. What was she missing?

She looked back on the dragging years of her adult life, spent trying to care for her parents. Now she had given up even trying to entertain her mother, which, at one time, when she had got a response from Elizabeth, had been an entertainment for herself. Now life was a steady, deadening routine, enlivened only by her afternoon off.

To try to keep Alicia from going out of her mind herself, Polly increasingly encouraged her to do all the shopping and go for walks in the park. When Mrs Hunter invited her to tea next door, she would say firmly, 'Don't worry about your Mam. Fanny's very good with her. You go for an hour.' Polly herself rarely went out, except to visit her sister, Mary, on her day off or perhaps to go with her to a music hall.

With the same upright carriage as her mother, Alicia would walk through Princes Park, even onwards to Sefton Park, a nondescript, middle-aged-looking woman, plainly dressed in a long grey skirt and a matching three-quarter length coat nipped in at the waist. Her fair hair was covered by out-of-date hats, trimmed and retrimmed with bits of satin culled from the boundless odds and ends of her mother's old clothes stacked in trunks in the attic. Two large hatpins anchored the hats to her head and were regarded by her, as by most women, as a useful weapon if attacked. But none of the young bucks who strolled through the park at the weekends would make a pass at such a prim-looking lady, and, anyway, the park keepers were always in evidence to keep order in their domain.

Other residents of Upper Canning Street had become accustomed to seeing her in the street and nearby shops. They would bow politely and pass on, though many of them had never heard the scandal of her origins. They had, however, heard of her mad mother. As one sharp-tongued inhabitant put it, 'It's a most peculiar household, I hear. A crazy old woman and a couple of servants who don't know their place and live as if they were part of the family; the craziness must run *in* the family. And then Colonel Milfort used to live next door to them – and we *all* know about him. Now there are the Bottomleys there – a very loud, vulgar family – not nice at all; I don't allow my children to mix with theirs. The whole of that end of the street seems to have gone down dreadfully.'

So nobody spoke to Alicia.

Fanny visited the other maids up and down the street and often talked to the Bottomleys' skivvy, as they both scoured their respective front steps. Fanny called the neighbours a lot of jangling old biddies, and she would throw her scrubbing brush into the bucket of dirty water at the bottom of the steps, and say viciously sometimes, 'I'd like to scupper 'em. Our Missus and Miss Alicia is the very salt.'

In the hope of getting some help and, perhaps, a little social life for Alicia, Uncle Harold went out to visit Florence, without result.

'They are simply too busy to take on anything else,' Alicia told him gently, when he mentioned his visit and his reason for it.

'They're simply too selfish,' he replied downrightly. He had tried without success to persuade his wife to invite Alicia for a little visit, to give her a holiday. His wife had loftily refused, saying, 'She is not a member of the family. Why should I be bothered with such a bore?'

For the sake of peace in his household, he had not pressed the point. He had said soberly to Alicia, 'You're carrying a very heavy load for the family. And anything I can do to lighten it, I will do.'

She had kissed the old man impulsively, and he had gone red in the face with embarrassment.

II

One evening, as her mother continued her eternal pacing up and down the room and Alicia watched her as she sewed herself a blouse, her mother began to mumble and tears to course down her face.

It was not the first time in her slow decline that Alicia had seen her weep, but it grieved her, and she jumped quickly from her chair and ran to Elizabeth to put her arms around her.

Elizabeth recoiled as if she had been attacked and pushed Alicia away. Then she backed away from her daughter, like a frightened cat. Shocked at her obvious alarm, Alicia stood staring uncertainly at her.

After a few seconds, Elizabeth resumed her unsteady pacing, and coming back across the room, she finally faced Alicia head on. Not knowing what to do, Alicia tensely held her ground.

Elizabeth, seeing her full face, said brokenly, through her tears, 'Alicia, dear.'

'Mama,' Alicia responded tentatively, and moved slowly towards her mother. They embraced warmly. Alicia was crying. Her mother had never held her like this before.

'I must have scared her when I ran to her,' she chided herself.

'When is Andrew coming?' Elizabeth asked, as she slowly loosed her hold on Alicia. She spoke much more clearly than she had done for a long time.

Perplexed, Alicia answered her, 'I don't know, Mama.' She slowly took out her handkerchief and wiped her mother's wet cheeks.

Andrew? Andrew Crossing, of course.

Deadly curious, she asked, 'Do you miss him, Mama?'

But Elizabeth's tattered brain had closed off. She smiled her usual charming smile and turned to walk some more.

Thereafter, Alicia always moved very carefully in her mother's presence and instructed Fanny and Polly to do the same.

It was, however, the last time that Elizabeth recognized her daughter, and, as Alicia steadied her mother when she walked, fed her, washed her, dressed her and dealt with her total incontinence, she would weep herself and cry, 'How long, O Lord, how long?'

III

Alicia and Polly were great newspaper readers; the arrival of the morning paper was often the only interesting event of their day. Fanny, however, had never learned to read and she got *her* news from the seamen and dockers she picked up around the Pier Head on her days off. The seamen sailed in rusty freighters to Hamburg and Trieste, to Istanbul, Odessa and Murmansk, to Madras and Vladivostock, and every port in between. Though they did not see a great deal of the places in which they docked, they picked up gossip in the bars and streets. When they returned home and had exhausted their complaints about women, and the food in the ships of their various great companies, they enlarged upon what they had seen and heard abroad. So it was Fanny who first said that the constant quarrels between the Balkan States would lead to a very big war. Alicia and Polly pooh-poohed the idea; the only place to be afraid of was Germany, and the Kaiser would never actually make war on his English royal relations.

On June 28th, 1914, Francis Ferdinand, heir to the throne of Austria–Hungary, and his wife, Sophia, were assassinated by Bosnian students while on a visit to Sarajevo, a lovely, almost oriental town, which few people in Britain had ever heard of.

Absorbed in their daily struggle to cope with Elizabeth, Polly, Fanny and Alicia were unaware that the death of this dogmatic prince would turn their lives upside down. They spent the last fragile days of the world they knew encouraging and half-carrying Elizabeth downstairs to the garden, to get the sun. The weather was perfect, the half-wild roses ran riot up the brick walls of the garden and Alicia wished, as always, that she had time to keep the garden tidy.

After they had set Elizabeth down in a chair on the over-grown path, she seemed to enjoy the warmth and colour and forgot her earlier intransigence. She leaned back and watched small, fat clouds drift across the sky. Alicia cut a rose, removed its thorns and gave it to her to hold.

Polly sat down on the back steps and began to turn the pages of the evening newspaper, and as she perused the headlines, she said uneasily, 'Aye, I'm that glad our Billy's away in Canada. I wouldn't want 'im in a war – though he's no kitten by this time. Same age as you, add a year – too old to fight.'

Since her mother seemed at peace, Alicia knelt down and began to weed round a clump of delphiniums. 'Billy seems to have done awfully well in Alberta, doesn't he?'

'Aye, he's a bright lad is our Billy, and he always did love horses. Now he's got land to breed them on, he'll not look back.'

Alicia smiled. 'He'll be sending for you at last, Pol.'

'Not he. He's forgotten wot he promised; and anyways I wouldn't leave you, luv.'

IV

It was in January 1915, that Fanny dropped a bombshell.

After Elizabeth had been put to bed, the three of them were seated round the gas-fire in the morning-room. Between the two maids, on the floor, sat a jug of ale which Fanny had fetched from the nearest public house; it was a custom which Alicia had never queried because the maids had nearly always enjoyed an evening pint together.

Fanny cleared her throat and, without preamble, announced, 'I'm goin' into munitions next week.'

Alicia's heart missed a beat and the little colour in her cheeks fled. Polly put down her glass and asked belligerently, 'Wot you mean?'

'I'm goin' to fill shells with – well, with whatever they fill shells with.'

'You're going to *leave* us, Fan?' Alicia was incredulous.

Fanny shuffled her feet uneasily and her ale slopped into

the hearth. She cursed under her breath. Then she replied steadily, though averting her eyes from Alicia, 'Yes, Miss Allie. They pay like a ship's crew on leave – you wouldn't believe how much. And I haven't got nothing saved for me old age, except what your Pa left me.'

'You're crazy,' Polly told her sourly. She took a sip from her glass, and then said, 'It'll cost you more 'n you earn to live.'

'No, it won't. I bin talking it over with some of the other maids what has left – they've got good clothes and all from it.'

Alicia was suddenly terrified. Suppose Polly left as well! What would she do? She glanced nervously at the older woman and, as if she had read her mind, Polly turned to her. 'Don't take on, luv. Your old Polly's got more sense.'

Though her lips were trembling, Alicia smiled at her. But Fanny, also, was a most important part of her life and she was very fond of her. She gave a quivering sigh and said, 'I'm really sad, Fan. I know we don't pay you an awful lot. But you can be sure of it every week – and you've got a good bed and food – and uniform.'

Fanny shifted uneasily in her chair and put out a hand to touch Alicia's knee, as she replied, 'I know, Miss, and don't think I'm not grateful. But this is a chance for me to put something by – and I don't never want to see the inside of a workhouse again – I seen enough when I were a kid.'

Alicia tried to still the frightened beat of her heart and could not. The war was suddenly in her own home, and she did not know what to do.

'Think it over, Fan, before you make up your mind,' she urged through dry lips.

'I thunk about it, Miss. I thunk about it a long time. Mebbe Mr Harold can get you some help.' She took a sip of ale, and then went on a little defiantly, 'And somebody's got to fill shells.'

Reluctantly, Alicia agreed.

This idea of helping in the war had already begun to

percolate into kitchens and drawing-rooms. Women rolled bandages and knitted balaclavas and gloves for soldiers. A few brave women had volunteered to drive ambulances in France; and the newspapers had reported that women, dragging their long skirts behind them in the mud, had helped with the winter ploughing, because so many farm labourers had simply left the fields to volunteer.

Alicia got up from her easy chair and began to pace up and down the room. 'I'll miss you terribly, Fan,' she said suddenly, and burst into tears. Fanny whipped out of her chair and put her arms round her, and they cried together, while Polly stared into her ale glass. She was so tired already. How would they manage?

'I'll come to see you both,' Fanny was promising.

A fat lot of help that would be, Polly thought sourly.

Chapter Twenty-Six

I

With Fanny gone, the dining-room was left to gather dust. Cooking was reduced to the simplest recipes.

In fact, shopping for food began to take up more time than the cooking of it. The shops were short of many items, and of staff, too, as more men and women went into factories; people were not yet reduced to queuing, but they had to wait longer to be served and often had to carry their parcels home, because errand boys tended to serve behind the counter, instead of doing deliveries.

Elizabeth's physical health deteriorated, but she could still heave herself out of bed and walk, and had, therefore, to be watched all day. Time off for both Alicia and Polly became a distant memory. Nevertheless, Alicia decided that to improve their diet, she would try to dig a part of the garden and put in some lettuces and tomatoes. One day in early March 1915, she put on a pair of boots and her shortest skirt and began to clear an old flower bed, while Polly ironed linen sheets in the library, now her mistress's bedroom, so that she could keep an eye on the stricken woman and get some work done at the same time.

Alicia had just driven a spade into the heavy earth, when a shocked, male voice with a strong Liverpool accent stopped her. 'Miss! You shouldn't be doin' that!'

Frightened, she turned. A soldier in an infantry private's uniform stood behind her, cap in hand. She pushed back the old straw hat she was wearing and surveyed him coldly. 'Who are you and what are you doing in my garden?' she snapped as strongly as she could.

The man's face, already reddened by exposure, turned an even richer colour. 'Sorry, Ma'am. I come through the garden door. I come to see Polly. I'm her brother.'

'Billy!' She let the spade drop, rubbed her dirty hands together and then held out one to be shaken. 'How nice to see you. Polly will be thrilled. We both look forward to your letters so much. What are you doing here?'

'I come over to join the Army, Miss. Didn't write 'cos I reckoned I'd be here almost as soon as a letter.' He shook her hand shyly.

'Polly's ironing in Mama's room,' she told him. 'We have to watch Mama all the time, so we take work into her bedroom and do it there.' She smiled at him. 'Come in.'

She led him into the house, stepping calmly out of her muddy boots and putting on her slippers, as she entered, something no lady would do in front of a gentleman. Billy carefully wiped his boots on the tattered doormat. As she took him through the old kitchen, which smelled of damp and mould, and up the back stairs, she asked him, 'Have you joined the British Army – or are you with a Canadian contingent?'

'I come over with some horses for the British Army, Miss, about six months ago, and joined the South Lancs. What a voyage, Miss! Never again – lost 'alf the horses, with broken legs.'

She stopped in the hall, and told him almost coquettishly, 'Billy! You fibbed. It doesn't take six months for a letter to come from Alberta. You should have let us know you were here.'

'Well, Miss, I thought Polly'd be all upset if she knew I were in the Army – thought it better to show meself when I were settled in, like. She's goin' to be as cross as two sticks, anyway,' he said sheepishly.

'I doubt it.' The frank, light eyes surveyed him and his clumsy uniform. 'I think she's going to be very proud.' She opened the door of the library, and said to Polly, 'Come out a moment, Polly. I've a surprise for you.'

Polly glanced at Elizabeth, for the moment sitting quietly

in a chair by the window. She put down her iron and came to the door. Billy could barely restrain his sense of shock when he saw the pale, gaunt, grey-haired woman. Polly?

But it *was* Polly and she had clasped him in her arms and was weeping on his shoulder. 'Billy, luv. Billy.'

'Take him into the morning-room, Polly. Make some tea,' Alicia urged her, as she took off the sackcloth apron she had been wearing. 'I'll stay with Mama.' She felt suddenly left out and wished that she cared for Charles like that.

With his arm round Polly's waist, Billy turned to her and said, 'If you'll excuse me for sayin' so, Miss, don't you do no more diggin'. I'll come over tomorrer in civvies, and I'll do it for you in a trice. I got three days' leave and me sister, Mary, isn't goin' to want me round the house all the time.'

'That's very kind of you,' she responded warmly, with the same grace her mother had had.

'Yes, you let 'im do it, Allie. Keep 'im out of mischief.'

Billy's dark eyebrows went up in surprised query. No *Miss Alicia*? Just Allie?

Alicia smiled, and went quietly into her mother's room and shut the door. Elizabeth, disturbed, turned and burst into angry incoherent speech.

In the shabby morning-room, Billy put his peaked cap down on to the sideboard. 'Is the Missus still ill?' he asked.

'Sit down, luv. You don't know the half of it.' Polly gestured to an easy chair. His question opened a dam, and Polly poured out the story of Elizabeth and of Alicia's bleak life looking after her and after Humphrey. Though she did not complain about her own harsh life, it was half an hour before she remembered to get up and make some tea.

Early the following morning, while Alicia was quickly putting Elizabeth's breakfast tray together, before the invalid woke up from her drugged sleep, she pushed back the lace curtain and peeped through the kitchenette window. Outside, there was a light mist which made the garden look soft and vague. Through it, however, she could see Billy digging with an even, methodical rhythm which she envied. She smiled.

'Will he have had breakfast?' she asked Polly, who was stirring a pan of porridge on the gas-stove.

'I doubt it,' replied Polly glumly. 'Our Mary don't have that much, what with the rent of her new Corpy house and her hubby drunk half the time.'

'Well, ask him in to breakfast – there's lots of porridge – and make some toast.'

Later on, when Alicia came back to the kitchenette, to eat her breakfast at its little table while Polly watched Elizabeth, he was still sitting, elbows on the table, lingering over a cup of tea. As Alicia entered, he hastily stood up.

'Sit down. Be comfortable, Billy,' she told him, an unusual cheerfulness in her voice, as she helped herself to porridge from the pan on the stove. It was exciting to have a visitor, other than Dr Bell or Uncle Harold.

As she sat down at the table, she glanced at him. This morning, he wore a pair of breeches with boots and leather gaiters. Knotted round his neck was a red and white cotton handkerchief. His eyes were brown, she noted, narrowed like a sailor's, as if used to seeing great distances in a bright light. The mouth was wide, quirked up at the corners to suggest much laughter. The sleeves of his union shirt were rolled up to reveal hairy forearms tanned by strong sunlight. As she began to eat, he hastily rolled down his shirt sleeves and reached for a heavy, plaid jacket with leather patches on the elbows. When he moved, a collar stud flashed below a strong, red neck. On a drain-board by the sink lay his dark, flat cap. He smelled palpably of the stable, and she remembered that he had come across the Atlantic with a herd of horses.

Feeling suddenly a little shy in such silent male company, she urged him to have another cup of tea. She filled his cup and poured one for herself.

Except that she had filled out and become a woman, she was very like the child he remembered, he thought as he considered her out of the corner of his eye. Her hands were red from work, but the rest of her skin was still incredibly white; there was none of the leathery look of Prairie women. There were a few lines on her face; yet her mouth, pink as a white kitten's nose, was as innocent-looking as that of the child he recalled so vividly.

He suddenly became aware that she was staring at him over the rim of her cup, alert grey eyes making him feel uneasy and tongue-tied. She had overcome her nervousness and was thanking him earnestly for digging the garden. She did not offer to pay him and he was grateful for her not doing so; it confirmed to him in a subtle way his status as an up-and-coming young man.

Her next words, innocently spoken, put him back in his slums, and he was secretly angry. She said, 'Do you remember when you used to come here as a boy and Polly squeezed some breakfast out of Mrs Tibbs for you?'

'Yes, Ma'am,' he replied stiffly. She passed the sugar bowl to him and he took some and then stirred his tea quickly. And I've come a long way since then, Queen, he told himself crossly. And no matter what she may be thinking, I'm sitting here with her as if I were an old friend. And she int much different from Edmonton women I know – she's not the usual stiff madam as lives round here. I remember her like I remember nobody else except me Mam, jumping down from a tree and showing the longest legs and the prettiest little ass I ever saw in a pair of divided pantaloons.

'Are you still working at the stables – I mean when you're not in the army?'

He looked surprised and, with a spoon halfway to her mouth, she chuckled. 'You must forgive me, but I always saw your letters – in fact, I often wrote part of the replies, until Polly got good at writing.'

'Did you really, Miss?'

'Yes. It was like having a pen-friend.'

He was nonplussed at this revelation and was not sure how to reply. Finally, he said carefully, 'Well, I hope we are friends, Miss.'

Alicia smiled at him, as if amused at his embarrassment. 'Of course we're friends. You're Polly's brother and Polly's been like a mother to me.'

He slowly put down his cup, proffered a hand scarred from old blisters and she took it and they solemnly shook hands.

They grinned at each other like two small boys making a blood oath. 'Now we're really friends,' said Alicia, and then she reminded him of her question about the stable.

'Yes, Miss. Me job's there for when I go home. It's not a great job, but it brings in ready cash for setting up on the quarter-section, and it's kept me, meanwhile. I got a hay crop last year and some grain. And if you'll forgive me mentioning such a thing, I can't keep me mares in foal fast enough to meet the demand.'

'Do you live there?'

'No. I live over the stable. I got a Metis family livin' in a one-room cabin out there, lookin' after it while I'm away, and Ernie, me friend wot owns the stable, has promised to go out and check on 'im, an' all.'

A little later, he went away to spend some time with his other sister, Mary, while her husband was at work. He returned in the evening, however, and screwed some cup hooks into a shelf for Polly, while she prepared dinner; without asking Alicia, she made enough for four.

'What happened to that Chink you lent money to?' she asked idly.

'Huang? I didn't lend him the money 'cos he wasn't sure he could pay back. I bought a half share in 'is café when he were fairly on the rocks – it were only a little hole in the wall, but not a few bachelors used to eat there. So I took a chance on him. You should see it now – quite respectable, it is – fourteen tables and a coffee bar – built 'em all meself. 'Is wife and son and daughter help 'im, and sometimes of a Saturday night I give 'im a hand in the kitchen. Full, most nights, he is. Pays me me share every three months on the dot. We don't make a lot – but, you see, one day we will.'

'Strewth! Why on earth did you enlist – you got more'n plenty to do?'

'Well, you can get a white feather handed to you in Edmonton, same as you can in Liverpool, if you look young enough and aren't in uniform – and I didn't want no bloody feathers. So I talked it over with Ernie and with Huang and then, when there was a herd of horses goin' on the train to Winnipeg, I come over for nothin' for takin' care of 'em. I wanted to be in a Liverpool Regiment – and they was recruitin' for the South Lancs when I got here – and I thought that'd do.'

'Blow the feathers! You was plain stupid, our Billy. You should've stayed out of it and sold them horses and made money out of 'em. You could get yourself killed.'

'Well, this little lot's not going to last long. Finished by Christmas, they reckon. Then I'll take you back with me. You'll like it there. You'd be married quick as a wink, if you want to – lots of fellas there, not so many girls.'

'Don't be daft. Anyways, how can I leave our Allie before her Mam dies? The old girl could live a few years yet and Allie can't manage by herself.' She lifted the lid from a pan of potatoes and tested their readiness with a fork. Then she went on, 'It's so unfair on Allie, 'cos her Mam never really cared a damn about her – it were me that brought her up.'

He was silent for a moment, as he watched her drain the potatoes over the sink. Then he said slowly, 'I'd like to take Miss Allie as well, if she'd have me.'

'What?' Polly whirled round to look at him, steaming pan in hand. 'Now I know you're daft, lad. You don't know 'er – and she's a lady.'

'Not too much of a lady,' replied Billy shrewdly. 'She's got more'n a bit of you in 'er. And things is different in Alberta. The way I'm goin', I could use a wife what can hold her head up amongst the best. And it int true I don't know her; we used to work in the garden together with that ould gardener fella. I thought she were a princess – and I still do.'

Dumbfounded, Polly stared at him, her steaming potatoes forgotten. 'You serious?'

''Course, I am. I always wanted to do it. Only I thought she'd sure enough be married before I could give 'er the kind

of home I want to give 'er. Even now, I can't give her anythin'
grand – but I'm gettin' there, and I'm still not so old.'

'Well, she int married.' Polly plunked the saucepan she was
holding on to the draining board and picked up a fork to mash
the potatoes. 'She's never had a dog's chance of gettin' married;
her parents saw to that – she's been too useful to 'em.'
Then she said carefully, 'You'd better wait till you've finished
winning the war, before you ask 'er.'

He stretched himself, and said, 'Oh, aye. I don't want to
leave 'er a widow.'

Polly shook her fork at him. 'Now, remember, I don't know
what she'll say – because she'll think first of her Mam – she
knows where her duty lies. So don't take it too personal, like,
if she says No.'

II

Billy's sister, Mary, prevailed upon him to stay with her on
the last day of his leave, so he did not come again to see Polly
and Alicia. A couple of days later, however, they received a
letter from him saying that he was to be trained as a sniper,
'Seeing as I'm used to handling a hunting rifle.'

'I thought only rich people went huntin',' Polly remarked,
as she put the letter down on the kitchen table.

'Well, he told me when he was here that he and his old
pedlar often fed themselves by hunting or trapping.' Alicia
picked up Elizabeth's breakfast tray to carry it into her room.

'Hm, Canada must be a proper queer place. Don't they have
no butchers nor fishmongers?'

Billy never went for his training. With a number of other
ill-trained men, he was rushed across the Channel and found
himself with Haig's 1st Army, ready to attack a place called
Neuve Chapelle. At first it seemed that the proposed break-
through across the German lines would succeed; and a
sickened, terrified Billy was thankful to a long-forgotten God
for his survival. But his little unit ran out of ammunition, and

the curtain of artillery fire which, on the third day, was supposed to soften up the enemy line, faltered for the same reason. Pinned down in a shell hole by the weight of German fire, Billy lay beside a weeping wounded man. With his field dressing, he did his best to staunch the blood from a ghastly rip in the man's back, to no purpose. He died, and Billy lay by him while machine-gun bullets rattled overhead. He himself screamed, when a swordlike piece of flack smashed into his left shoulder.

Desperate for help, he managed to inch himself out of the hole and then fainted. After dark, he was found by a Canadian medical orderly crawling round, looking for the wounded amongst the dead.

He languished for some months in a London military hospital, while they tried to save his arm. As his next of kin, Mary received a postcard saying where he was. Whey-faced, she hurried over to see Polly. Because her husband tended to beat her if she left home, she rarely visited Polly and the very presence of her, hammering on the back door, indicated disaster.

Once he was able to move about, Billy wandered round the overcrowded ward and helped the nurses to dish out food to their patients. From other outraged wounded, he learned that the shortage of ammunition had been caused by strikes and slowdowns ordered by trade unions seeking to oust unskilled people, like Fanny, from the factories.

'Ought to put the bloody skunks in the Front Line and see how they like it with no ammo,' he raged as his useless left arm reminded him of a life full of special problems to a man with only one working arm. He was suddenly glad that he would be going back to Canada. 'Who needs mates who'd betray yez like that?' he asked himself bitterly.

A worried Polly asked Alicia if she could possibly manage Elizabeth alone for one whole day while she went to London to see Billy. She had decided that this was a time when one of her long-hoarded sovereigns had to be spent.

Alicia agreed immediately, and Polly set out with a little

basket of precious butter and sugar and some apples from the garden, to augment Billy's spartan hospital diet.

III

It was an extremely difficult day for Alicia. The moment she left the invalid to prepare a meal or go to the bathroom, Elizabeth would begin an unsteady perambulation through the house. The weather was cold and if Alicia turned off the gas-fires, Elizabeth became chilled; if she left them on, she feared that her mother might brush against them and set her skirts aflame; Elizabeth was, in any case, capable of turning them on and leaving them unlit.

At one point, Alicia guided her mother into the kitchenette and sat her down on a chair, so that she could prepare dinner and watch the older woman at the same time. Elizabeth objected violently to the strange, little room and the unaccustomed chair, and she had to be taken back to her library-bedroom. In despair, Alicia tied her into a small easy chair, with the aid of a couple of long scarves, and left her there; she shrieked steadily until Alicia returned with a tray of hastily assembled cold food.

She gave her protesting mother her bedtime sedative a little early and thought frantically that, if anything ever happened to Polly, she would have to find a nurse to help her. 'But where would I get a nurse in wartime?' she wondered hopelessly. 'They'll all be nursing the wounded.'

It was nearly midnight before she heard a key in the front lock. She ran to the door, to meet an equally exhausted Polly.

She helped Polly off with her coat and hat and took her into the morning-room. Then she brought her a tray of tea and sandwiches, which she had made ready as soon as Elizabeth had gone to sleep.

As Polly thankfully drank her tea, she described a white wraith of a man, still recovering from losing a great deal of blood and still in bandages. Her eyes filled with tears. 'They'll discharge 'im in Liverpool 'cos he volunteered here. He's finished for the Army.'

Alicia had picked up the sock she was knitting for one of Mrs Hunter's many warwork projects, but now she laid it in her lap. 'Poor man!' she exclaimed. It hurt her to think of the sturdy, self-confident digger of her garden being crippled. 'Life is too hard,' she meditated wretchedly. 'Even without a war.' Then, trying to be practical, she asked, 'Just how badly wounded is he?'

'It don't look as if 'is left arm is going to be much use to 'im. The doctor were talkin' of takin' it off, at first. But he wasn't havin' none of that. He hurts somethin' crool.'

'Will they send him to a Convalescent Home?'

'They might. Otherwise, he could go to Mary's while they fix up 'is pension. He says he's got to find his own way to Canada 'cos he enlisted here.' Polly leaned back in her chair to rest her tired head and a tear trickled down her cheek. 'I'm afraid of Mary's hubbie, Mike, kickin' up a fine to-do, if he stays long with them. It were bad enough when he spent his leave there. Mike's got a filthy temper.'

Alicia leaned over to clasp Polly's hand, 'Now, don't take on so, Polly dear. We'll think of something.'

While the older woman sniffed back her tears and poured herself another cup of tea, Alicia looked out of the window at the darkened garden and remembered contented afternoons helping Billy and Mr Bittle do the weeding. She turned back to Polly, and asked slowly, 'I wonder if Billy would like to stay with us while he's convalescing?'

Polly's head jerked upwards in surprise, and Alicia went on, 'We've got oceans of room, Pol. I imagine he wouldn't need much actual nursing. Do you think his wound would need dressing?'

'I doubt they'll let him out of 'ospital till it's fairly healed.' Polly paused while she considered the suggestion. 'He'd need to be helped, washin' and dressin', till he learned to manage himself, poor kid. But Mr Harold would have a fit, wouldn't he?'

'I think he'd agree if we wanted it very badly; he's tremendously kind and he's never refused any reasonable request I've made. It's Charles who might try throwing his weight about – not that he can really say much; neither he nor Veronica has ever given us an iota of help. Of course, this is really Charles's house – but I think Uncle Harold could deal with him.'

'And Miss Florence and the Reverend?'

'To hell with both of them,' replied Alicia trenchantly. 'Poor Billy's worth ten of them.'

'Now, our Allie,' reproved Polly. 'She's your sister.'

'Fat lot she cares about me. It's you who've borne with me all these years. Without you, my life would have been impossible. And it's *your* brother who needs help now – and probably very little, at that. Rest and quiet and good food – and we can provide that. We're stuck in this house, anyway, with Mama.'

There was quiet, except for the popping of the gas-fire. Then Polly smiled and said, 'Aye, Allie, I'd be so grateful – and I'm sure our Billy will be, too.'

'Well, ask him if he'd like to come,' Alicia replied, with quiet determination; for once in her life, she thought savagely, she was going to do what she wanted to do.

To forestall any snubbing of Billy, Alicia wrote to Charles, telling him of Billy's wounding and discharge and saying that he would stay in the house with them until he could get a passage to Canada. She said firmly that it was the least they could do for a man who had come six thousand miles to help them win the war.

Charles was, at first, shocked that a servant's brother should stay in his house, but when he read Alicia's letter to a very stout and petulant Veronica, he was surprised that she replied calmly, 'Polly's brother? Well, I expect he'll behave like a servant and not step out of line or steal anything. And what can you say? A wounded man?' So Charles made no objection.

Drained, and haunted by the horror of what he had seen in France, a sad and disillusioned Billy came thankfully to them.

At first, he was very quiet and spent a good deal of his time either propped up with cushions in an easy chair in the dining-room window, where he was not disturbed by the rest of the household, or sitting in the little kitchen, talking to whichever woman happened to be there.

He accepted humbly Polly's aid to wash and dress and managed to make a joke with Alicia over her having to cut up his meat for him. With every other task, he struggled with his one good hand. When he first arrived, he was too shaky to walk far, but one dry winter day he went carefully down the front steps and walked along beside the railings of the houses until he had encircled the block. Several men spoke to him and a number of women smiled at him gently, paying their respects, in effect, to his hospital-blue uniform. Their kindness cheered him up, and the next morning Alicia found him clumsily pulling up the empty stalks of her Brussels sprout crop, his bad hand tucked into his jacket pocket.

On two occasions, Polly walked with him to the Royal Infirmary, for examination, and the doctors there encouraged him to try to use both arm and hand, without much success. He went before several military Boards for consideration for a pension. The officers on the Boards tended to bully, regarding him as a possible malcontent who would malinger in an effort to get a pension.

Finally, he stood up and told them to stuff their goddamned pension – he could manage without it. As soon as the doctors felt they had done all they could, he wanted his discharge, so that he could go back to a decent country. Leaving the Board unified in rage, he stalked out.

He had written to Ernie, who owned the Edmonton stable, and asked him to send him his fare back to Canada from the monies he was managing for him. Alicia slit the envelope of Ernie's reply for him, and he read the letter with obvious satisfaction. 'Says business is roaring along and to hurry home,' he told Alicia with a grin. 'Soon as I cash this Draft, I can pay something for me board,' he said.

'What rubbish,' Alicia responded roundly. 'Father's Estate is quite large, according to Uncle Harold; it can certainly feed a wounded soldier for a while. I am sure Uncle Harold would be most upset if I took a penny from you.'

They argued for a few minutes, but she could not be shifted, so he went out and, after cashing the Draft, bought her a huge bunch of flowers.

She looked at them in wonderment, when he handed them shyly to her. No one had ever bought her flowers before. 'Why, Billy! Thank you.' Impulsively, she leaned over the bouquet and kissed him on the cheek, and went away to find a vase, leaving him a little pink, and surprised that so little could make a woman happy.

He had found it hard to come to terms with the fact of having only one good arm, but, as his general health improved, he began to think constructively again and his natural optimism asserted itself. Polly was thankful to hear him whistling one morning after he had, for the first time, managed to shave himself, no easy task with a cut-throat razor.

Alicia noticed his effort, offered some iodine for one or two cuts and congratulated him on being able to do it. Now that he had the money for his return home, she meditated sadly, it was only a matter of time before he found a passage, and she realized she was going to miss him intensely. Never before had she enjoyed the company of someone her own age; she had always silently endured her noisy nephews and nieces. But Billy was fun, always ready to make a joke at his own predicament or to help her where he could, even to sitting with her rambling mother so that both Polly and she could enjoy one of Fanny's visits together.

Fanny was far from well. Her skin had turned an unhealthy yellow. 'It's the stuff we put in the shells,' she explained. 'But the money's good,' she added defensively.

'You look dreadfully tired,' Alicia told her, surprised that someone used to working very hard indeed could actually appear exhausted.

'I'm all right,' she replied heavily, and got up from her chair. 'I'll go in to see your Mama for a minute.'

IV

Another day, while Alicia fled to the grocer's and the butcher's, Billy asked if he could sit with Polly in Elizabeth's room.

'Oh, aye,' said Polly. 'She don't know anythin' and she's all washed and tidied. Come and 'ave a bit of a jangle.'

So Billy sat with her and watched her trim Brussels sprouts. He felt restless, anxious to go home and pick up his life again. But he was not yet legally discharged from the army, and he was having difficulty in booking a passage home; both problems would not be solved for some weeks.

'I heard Miss Allie playin' the pianner in the big front room upstairs,' he said idly.

'Oh, aye. She loves 'er pianner and 'er weeds; takes 'er mind off things.'

'Weeds?'

'Aye, she tries to study a bit after her Mam goes to bed 'cos when her Mam dies she'll have to earn her living as a governess, she says. She's determined she's not goin' to live with Mr Charles or Miss Florence – unpaid servant she'd be for the rest of her natural.' She carefully divested a sprout of its collar of yellow leaves, and then asked, 'Unless you want to take her to Canada, like you said?'

Billy did not answer, at first. Finally, he muttered reluctantly, 'I love her, Pol, and I want her, but I'm a proper nobody compared to her. And now, well, who'd want me?' Then he said, more cheerfully, 'But you should come back with me, Pol. You owe it to yourself to enjoy life a bit.'

'I couldn't leave the girl to look after this alone,' Polly responded, gesturing towards Elizabeth babbling in her chair by the window.

Billy did not reply. As his strength returned, he had begun to desire Alicia in a very active way. Yet, when he examined the cobbled scars all over his shoulder in the dressing-table mirror, and when he massaged his practically useless hand, he flinched at the idea of showing such a horrid sight to any woman, never mind a gentlewoman. And thinking of his small ranch, he wondered how he would ever manage horses with one arm.

Polly was fretting, 'I don't know what'll become of her once her Mam dies. Being a governess is worse'n bein' a maid, sometimes.'

'She could emigrate to Canada herself – and teach school,' Billy said suddenly. He gestured towards the woman in the window. 'You're always sayin' her Mam never did a thing for her and now she don't even know her. Any decent woman could look after Mrs Woodman; the girl's daft to stay with her, give her whole life to her – let her sister have a go for a change.' He leaned forward and tapped Polly's arm, 'Believe me, we're that short of women in some parts of Alberta, she could come out and teach school for a term – and I promise you she'll be nicely married before the next term begins. And you must come, too; there's many a settler as would be glad of a woman as smart as you.'

Polly laughed, 'Go on with with yez!'

'I'm tellin' you God's truth. And neither of you'd be lonely, 'cos there's lots of men as have wives wot play the pianner and know how to behave like her. You could live like a lady yourself, given a bit of luck.'

'You're kiddin'?'

'No, I'm not. The minute her Mam's laid to rest, you both emigrate. I'll help both of yez get settled.' Though he sounded light-hearted, he wanted to yell at the unfairness of life; the thought of watching Alicia walk up the aisle of McDougall Church with some smug lawyer or doctor made him burn with jealousy – but it was better than thinking of her being a governess in England. He got up from his chair and began to walk up and down, clasping his useless arm across his waist with his good arm.

V

Late that evening, as they prepared Elizabeth for her bath, Polly told her of Billy's suggestion. They were all together in the huge bathroom, and Elizabeth was protesting strongly, as Polly undressed her, while Alicia tested the heat of the bathwater by dipping her elbow in it. Though Elizabeth had grown very thin because they could not persuade her to eat very much, she was still surprisingly strong, and it took their combined efforts to lift her into the bath without dropping her. Polly's remark had, however, sent Alicia's spirits soaring and she wondered why she had not herself thought of emigration.

Once in the soothing water, Elizabeth settled down and, panting, Alicia handed her a sponge to hold. Polly said, 'I'll wash her. You go out in the passage for a minute and get your breath back.'

Alicia thankfully accepted Polly's offer and went out of the bathroom, closing the door behind her. The passage was dark, except for the faint penetration of the hall lights downstairs. She leaned thankfully against the wall and closed her eyes. Canada? Where no one would care about her illegitimacy, even if they found out, or would know about her poor, mad mother; a place where she could begin again.

'God damn it! Jaysus help me!' The door of the old guest room opened, and an enraged Billy shot out, a shirt clutched over his naked chest. He spun round to the head of the staircase, and, not noticing Alicia, he leaned over the hall banister, and called, 'Polly! Pol! Could you come up for a sec?'

There was no response and, fulminating to himself, he came slowly back towards his room.

He was embarrassed to see Alicia in the passageway. 'Can I help you?' she asked. 'Polly's bathing Mama.'

He modestly whipped his shirt in front of his chest. 'I'm sorry, Miss Allie. I didn't see you. Could you ask Polly to come in, when she's done with your Mam? I damped me vest when I were washing me face, and I can't get into a clean one. I tore the old one when I were getting it off of me,' he finished with a rueful laugh.

She moved towards him instinctively, used to helping invalids day in and day out. She said, 'I can do it for you, if you'll let me. I dressed Papa often enough.'

He looked at her warily, and swallowed.

'Where is your vest?'

'On the bed, Miss.'

'Come on, then. I'll get it on in a second for you.'

He wondered if she realized what she was about. He was not her Papa – and at that moment, seeing her slender form in the half light, he did not feel the least like a father.

He said carefully, 'Thank you, Miss,' and led her into his room.

The winter sunshine streamed through the lace curtains and showed the botched-up shoulder in painful detail. It also showed an otherwise well-knit man garbed only in hospital-blue trousers.

Alicia was jolted by the sight of him; she lowered her eyelids and picked up the recalcitrant vest, stretched it and then threaded the helpless arm carefully through one sleeve. She came close to him while he bent his head so that she could get the neck of the vest over it. She felt a tumultuous madness in her, but she gritted her teeth as he lined up his right arm and wriggled himself into the garment. Her hands touched his bare flesh, as she pulled the garment straight down over him.

Billy took one look at the wide, imploring eyes suddenly looking into his own brown ones. 'Oh, God!' he muttered, and pulled her to him with his good arm. As he kissed her, he felt her slender body nestle to him. She put her arms round his neck and held him tightly. Blood racing, he turned her so that her back was against the door, which clicked shut behind her. Then he kissed her properly, his tongue exploring her mouth.

She hardly knew what she was doing or where it would lead

to, but she realized, at last, as Billy caressed her, what had driven her mother into the arms of her father, Andrew Crossing.

'Allie, luv! I'm ready to get her out!' called Polly from the bathroom.

He let her go immediately and she stood leaning against the door looking at him bewilderedly, but behind the confusion there was a hint of laughter in her face. She bit her lip and then smile at him beguilingly. He leaned against her again and said, 'I love you, our Allie.'

The smile was wiped off her face. 'I love you,' she replied thickly. 'But I can't marry anyone because of Mama – you know that.'

He kissed her neck above the stiff, white frill of her dress and felt her tremble. Then he told himself desperately that he must keep his head. He moved away from her slowly, to pick up his shirt. 'You'd better go to Polly,' he said dully.

She let out a long, sobbing sigh and turned and opened the door.

Chapter Twenty-Seven

I

'Billy, you dumb street mutt! What did you do to her? She were lit up like a street lamp last night.' This from Polly the following morning, as she dumped Billy's breakfast porridge in front of him.

'I kissed her,' replied Billy, a little sulkily.

'Holy Mother! Is that all? I'd like to see what she'd be like when you really got goin'.'

Billy slapped his good hand down on the table. 'Happy she'd be, that's what. I'd see to that.'

Polly sniffed, and peered out of the window at the blackness of a winter morning, eased only by the faint glow of a gaslight in the street and the flood of light from her own kitchen. She turned back to her brother.

'Well, you'd better marry her, then. You can't play around with her like she was some kid from back of Boundary Street. Not with folks like she's got. And if you marry her, you'd better watch your step, boy, or you could end up quarrelling like a pair o' cats – just 'cos you mayn't understand wot's the custom with folk like her.'

'I want to marry her and I think she'd marry me, even though I'm stuck with a useless arm,' Billy replied irritably. 'If Ernie at the stable can make a full-blooded Cree, complete with feathers, happy, I can do the same for her. And *you* brought 'er up, not her Mam. You must've taught her plenty. It's her Mam wot's the problem – she's ripe for the loony bin, she is.'

'Now, our Billy! Would you've let our Mam go into Bedlam?"

'Na, 'course not.'

'Well, she's the same about her Mam.' Polly sighed, and then said, 'If Mr Harold could get me some help, I could stay with her Mam and you take *her* to Canada.'

'Oh, no,' Billy replied firmly, 'I'm goin' to get you off this bloody treadmill an' all.' He picked up his spoon and began slowly to eat his porridge. 'I'll think of somethin'.'

'Maybe we should talk to Dr Bell and ask him. And then get hold of Mr Harold, her uncle. He's proper kind.' Desperate with sudden desire to be free herself, she said, 'Truth is, we've both gone on from day to day, and neither of us – nor her brother – ever really sat down and thought about what to do. Allie were here, so everythin' was all right and they left her to it.'

She picked up her porridge bowl and quickly put it in the sink, and warned him, 'Now, Allie'll be down in a minute to get her breakfast. You be careful what you do.'

'I'm not goin' to rape her,' he replied crossly. 'Anyways, I'll be most of the day up at the Royal Infirmary while they try to make me arm work.'

A few minutes later, when Alicia entered the kitchen, she was bitterly disappointed that he was not there. Polly, about to go to Elizabeth, explained that he had gone to get ready to walk over to the hospital.

The glow had gone out of Alicia. 'It's too far for him to walk,' she said. 'I feel angry every time he has to do it.'

'Let 'im try, luv. He's got to get strong again.'

With a leap of pure passion, Alicia remembered the strong embrace of the previous evening. She swallowed, and agreed. She had not kissed him out of pity or to comfort him; the kiss had been a spontaneous outpouring of a terrible longing which had grown in the months of his quiet stay with them. He was a lively, intelligent man, and the very thought of his return to Canada had been crushing.

She had agonized through the weeks of being with him; she was sure that to give any inkling of the love she felt would have encouraged a man when she could not marry; that he might have responded by simply becoming her lover never occurred to her. Though her mother had had a lover, she knew that nice girls got married and were faithful; Polly said so.

Reluctantly at first, though increasingly as the day progressed, she began to think, like Billy, of how her mother could be cared for by someone else. Not by Polly, she was determined on that; Polly had done enough.

By late afternoon, she was telling herself to stop worrying; she was basing her desires on one kiss. It was ridiculous.

Could Billy, perhaps, stay in England? In this house?

She was combing her mother's long, white tresses, as the idea occurred to her. She paused, comb poised, and considered what the situation would be.

There would not be much work for him in England, other than labouring, she thought sadly. These days, an uneducated man was fixed firmly at the bottom of the ladder. Would Charles or the Reverend Clarence help him to get started in some small business?

'Don't be funny,' she told herself, as she gently combed. 'They don't even help *you*.' And she shuddered, when she considered how her brother and her brother-in-law would treat Billy if they met him, no matter how well-dressed he was or how good his manners were. To them, class was class.

She did not see Billy when he came home and ate his warmed-up dinner in the kitchen with Polly. He was tired, depressed and in pain, so Polly got him a hot water-bottle and sent him up to bed.

II

Late that evening, Fanny rang the front door bell, and Polly answered the door.

'Didn't want to come up the back track,' Fanny excused herself, as she slipped inside. 'It's that dark.'

Polly replied, with a friendly grin, 'Och, nobody cares which

340

door you coom through; there's only us here. How's yerself?'

Fanny sighed, as she took off her coat and hat and laid them carefully on a hall chair, smoothing the hat's tremendous satin bow. 'Well, I'm not too clever,' she said. 'I bin off sick a while. Goin' back tomorrer. We don't none of us keep too well in that place.'

'Well, coom in. It's nice to see yez.' She ushered the little woman into the old morning-room, and while she took a box of matches and knelt to light the gas-fire, she urged her to sit down. After she had slowly got up off her knees and had lit the gaslight, she glanced at Fanny's face and exclaimed, 'Holy Mary! You look like a Chink!'

Fanny promptly put a finger to each eye, to pull them into a slant. 'Chinky, Chinky Chinaman, chop, chop, chop,' she said with a wry laugh. 'Foreman says its the TNT wot does it.' She looked around the shabby room. 'Where's our Allie?'

'She's in with her Mam, changing her napkins.'

'Aye, poor soul! And her such a fussy lady,' Fanny exclaimed. 'She always took such good care of her looks – till the Master broke her spirit. God, he were a son of a bitch.'

'He were. He int much missed,' responded Polly drily. 'She's proper daft now. Don't know nobody nor nothin' much.' She went towards the door. 'I'll get a bevvie. Be back in a min!'

Over a glass of light ale, Fanny began to describe the various men from the factory that she had been out with and their sexual abilities. Then she triumphantly listed the hats and dresses she had been able to buy. At the end of the inventory, her voice trailed off and an uneasy silence fell between them until Fanny picked up the conversation again. 'It's proper scary, workin' there – you never know the minute when you'll be blown to glory.'

Polly got up from her chair. 'I'd not take the risk,' she said with a grimace. 'What about coming into the other room to see our Allie and the Missus? Allie'll be glad to see you.'

Elizabeth was sitting up in bed, her delicate, lined face almost saintly in its new-found thinness, giving no hint of the violent behaviour of which she was capable. Alicia was struggling to heave open the big sash-window to get rid of the odour in the room. Fanny went across to her, pushed her out of the way and lifted the window easily. She grinned at Alicia, and said, 'It's a knack. How are you, duck?' She ignored the woman in the bed.

Alicia put her arms round her and kissed her, while she exclaimed at her sickly complexion. Elizabeth gave a frightened murmur, a quavery questioning.

Fanny turned to her without hesitation, curtsied and said, 'I'm Fanny, Ma'am. Come to make the fire up.'

As if she understood, Elizabeth smiled slightly, and Fanny winked at Alicia. The maid moved towards the gas-fire and inquired, regardless of the lateness of the hour, 'And how are yer, this morning, Ma'am?'

Alicia watched fascinated. Though her mother did not reply, she inclined her head as if acknowledging the inquiry.

Fanny muttered to Alicia out of the corner of her mouth, 'Take her right back far enough and she often understands. Never had much difficulty with her, even when she got real uppity and lashed out at me. I could always settle her.' She turned to the bed and made a little curtsey to Elizabeth again. 'Has she had her evening cocoa yet?' she inquired of Alicia.

'Not yet. It's an awful job getting it down her.'

'Let me try giving it her.'

Polly, anxious to see what would happen, broke in and urged Alicia to let Fanny try.

Ten minutes later, Elizabeth was sipping cocoa quite contentedly from her invalid cup. Fanny held it for her and gossiped to her about small happenings of years back. It took longer to persuade her to swallow her sleeping draught, but Fanny did finally succeed.

Still playing her part as a young maid, Fanny put the cup back on its little tray, curtsied and quietly left the room. Polly followed her.

Outside the door, they looked at each other and giggled helplessly. 'Really, Fan, you are a one!' Polly exclaimed admiringly. 'And, you know, Dr Bell always says to get out photo albums of when she was a girl. And it's true – she'll often sit quiet and let you show her old pictures, as if she remembers.'

After Fanny had gone, Polly made some more cocoa and gave Alicia a cup to take up to bed. 'You go and get a good night's sleep, duck.' She leaned towards the girl and kissed her. 'And you don't worry about nuttin'.'

'Little do you realize,' thought Alicia miserably.

III

Polly took another cup of cocoa and slowly climbed the stairs to Billy's room. The candle she was carrying dripped grease on to the stair carpet. She paused and looked down at the offending spot for a second, and then continued up. Who cared about the carpet? It was Allie she was bothered about.

The flicker of candlelight on his face roused Billy from sleep. He turned and groaned, as the movement pained his shoulder.

'I brought you some cocoa and a bickie, chooks. How you feelin'?'

'I'd hate to tell yer.' Billy heaved himself up clumsily, and she quickly put the cup down on a side table, and pushed a couple of pillows behind him. Then she handed the cup to him carefully, so that he could grasp the handle.

While he drank the scalding brew, she pulled up a straight chair and sat down by the bed. She folded her hands in her lap and watched him quietly. Then she asked, without preamble, 'You sure you want to marry our Allie?'

'Don't talk daft. You know I do.'

'Well, does she want to marry you?'

The answer was slower in coming. 'I dunno for sure, now I'm a one-armed Jack,' he said. 'And there's her Mam holdin' her back in every way. I can't solve that one either; if she don't want a disabled man, she could use her Mam as a polite excuse, come to that.'

He looked down at the muddy contents of his cup, his face

so filled with despair that Polly wanted to hold him to her as if he were a small boy.

'I'm afraid to ask her – formal like, in case she turns me down. A kiss is one thing; marrying is another.' He looked up at his sister, and added, 'I couldn't bear to be turned down. I've had enough. All me life I've dreamed and worked for her, in a manner of speaking. And here I am, stuck with this bloody arm.'

Polly wanted to cry; in the world she had come from a man with the use of only one arm was a dead loss – how could he labour?

'That's no way to think,' she told him sternly, and she asked, 'Could you earn enough to keep her, do yer think?'

'Oh, aye. I bin lyin' here thinkin' for hours. There's timber on my quarter-section – I already built a cabin wot Simon Yellowknee, the Metis who's carin' for me horses, lives in. With him to help, and maybe one or two of me neighbours, I reckon I could put up a better cabin for her. And I always intended to run more horses.' He sighed heavily, while Polly waited for him to continue. 'I'm always goin' to have to pay help, 'cos I doubt if I can plough or carry sacks, but it can be done. And there's steady money coming in from the café – not a lot, but the way things are going, it'll grow; it were a lucky strike that I bought into that and didn't just lend 'im the money – it could end up being the best thing I ever did. A real friend, Huang is.'

'What about the stable?'

'I'll have to talk that one over with Ernie. When I think of it, by the time I left, I weren't actually handling horses that much – we'd a couple of stable lads, and it could be that I can manage more'n I think . . .' His voice trailed off. 'It could be I'll have enough without workin' for him.'

'Well, it don't look as if either of you would starve.' Her voice was forcedly brisk and cheerful. 'And you haven't allowed as she might help you a lot – she's a smart young woman when she's given half a chance. I bet she could learn how to breed horses and care for 'em.'

'A lady?' exclaimed Billy, scandalized.

'Aye, some great ladies with titles is very knowledgeable about 'orses.' She got up and took his cup from him, and then began to rearrange his pillows. 'Now, you listen to me. Tomorrer, you ask her proper – and you tell her what the odds are – don't hold nothin' back. And see what she says.'

'And what about her Mam?' He sounded bitter.

'Well, chook, you're not the only one as has bin thinkin' – and I might be able to solve that one.' She made a wry face at him and then laughed at his surprise. 'I got to get help from a lot of people – and Christ only knows if I can swing it – but first you got to ask her.'

IV

When Alicia entered the little kitchen the next morning, after giving her mother her breakfast, she blushed scarlet and muttered, 'Good morning, Billy.' She did not look at him, as she scraped the saucepan clean of porridge and dumped the sticky mass into a dish.

Billy emerged from the protection of the morning newspaper, and said, 'Hi.' He carefully folded up the paper as best he could with one hand and put it down beside his teacup.

She sat down opposite him and sprinkled sugar thinly on to her porridge. I behaved like a street woman, she chided herself silently. What will he think of me?

She nearly choked on a mouthful of her breakfast, when he asked suddenly, 'Allie, will you marry me?'

She put her spoon down slowly, and swallowed, while she picked up her table napkin to wipe her mouth. Tears welled up, and she exclaimed, 'Billy, darling, you know I can't.'

He licked his lips. 'Why not?'

'Well, you know I can't leave Mama.' In her distress, she sounded irritable.

'Is that the only reason?'

'Well, of course, it is. Why else should I say No?' Tears were running down her face. 'I love you, I love you.' The words burst from her.

In an instant, he was on his feet and by her chair, his good arm round her shoulders. 'Don't cry, luvvie. I can't bear it.' He held her against him. 'Come on, chook, cheer up. I didn't know ladies cried when men popped the question!'

She picked up her table napkin and wiped her eyes and giggled suddenly. But then she said, snuggling her face into him, 'I don't know what to do.' He felt her heave a great shuddering sigh. 'Oh, Billy, dear. You're the sweetest thing that ever happened to me.'

'And you don't mind the mess I'm in?'

'Your shoulder? For goodness' sake, Billy! I'd still love you if you were in a bathchair!'

Billy stroked her back, and said slowly, 'That's the best thing that anyone ever said to me.' He bent and kissed her upturned face.

Her porridge went cold while the kiss lasted, and then he drew back reluctantly, and told her, 'Our Polly says as she thinks she knows how to get your Mam cared for – proper,' he added the last word quickly, as mixed doubt and fear showed on her face. 'Not in a madhouse.'

'How?'

'She wouldn't tell me, but she's goin' to talk to you today.'

'She's not taking on the job herself?'

'No – that is, I don't think so. I think she wants to emigrate.'

Alicia made a wry face, and sighed. 'What a lovely dream, Billy.'

'Well, supposin' for a minute she can do it?'

'Yes?'

He hesitated. 'I don't have any fancy manners,' he said a little shyly. 'And, honest, I don't know how you'll put up with me at times. But there's some nice women around Edmonton who like to play pianners and speak nice – you'd have friends. Would you really come to Canada with me – serious?'

'With you, Bill? Of course. I'd go anywhere with you.' She clasped him more tightly.

'Well, Polly says I'm to tell you as best I can what we'll do there. And I can't promise you the earth, mind, and it'll be hard work.' He loosened her arms gently from round his hips, and turned to sit down again on his chair. 'Now, you come here and sit on me knee and I'll tell yez.'

'Billy, I couldn't sit on your knee!'

'Yes, you can, you silly judy. Come here.'

Chapter Twenty-Eight

A little later on, Alicia carried to her mother's room a bundle of brooms, dusters and tins of polish, in order to clean it. She moved mechanically, as if in a trance. She wanted to drop her brooms and run back to the kitchen and cuddle again with Billy. How on earth could she let him go back to Alberta without her? The idea was unbearable.

As she opened the old library door, Polly glanced up from easing Elizabeth into a clean, white blouse. 'So he asked you?' she inquired knowingly.

Alicia leaned the brooms against a wall, and smiled dreamily back. 'Yes.' She pushed a few wisps of hair back into her bun, and then said, 'But I don't know what to do – he said you had some ideas.'

Polly quickly buttoned Elizabeth into her blouse and led her slowly to a couch in the window. Then she went over to Alicia and hugged her. 'I don't want to raise your hopes too much, luv, 'cos we got to get a lot of people to help. But the most important one is Fanny.'

'Fanny?' Alicia came out of her dreamy state immediately.

'Yes. You know she's gettin' sicker and sicker in them munitions. If it weren't for the money, she'd give it up, I'm sure. And for all she's a proper little man chaser, she don't like bein' 'arassed by men as she is being.'

'In the factory?'

'Oh, aye, she is.'

'How horrid!'

'Oh, aye, it is. So my line of thinkin' is, let's ask her to come to look after your Mam. Offer her a real housekeeper's job with a good housekeeper's wages.'

'Polly! It's a marvellous idea – but she couldn't manage alone – she's so small, for one thing. And to get nurses would be impossible – they're all going to the army.'

'Your Mam don't need professional nurses – only very kind and patient women. Now, at present there's many a soldier's wife with kids who can't make ends meet and yet can't leave the children for long; I bet that in the smaller streets round here, we could find half a dozen as would take turn and turn about for a few hours a day and be thankful for it. Mr Harold would have to pay 'em well, but Fanny could teach them and keep them in line – she knows what's to be done; and she's methodical, too.' She paused for breath, and then went on earnestly, 'Doctor did suggest a nursing home a while back. But you couldn't get her into one now, even if you wanted to, with all the wounded crowding in.'

Alicia agreed to her last remark. Then she said slowly, 'With your idea, she would be in her own home. Do you think such women would mind the washing and the cleaning up? It's a disgusting job, sometimes.'

'Women as has had three kids close together is used to such things. And a lot of them will've nursed, or seen nursed, old folks in their own homes – they'll know.'

Alicia nodded agreement. She slowly put down the brooms and dusters she had been carrying. As Polly watched her, she went over to the *chaise longue* in the window where Elizabeth reclined, fretfully kicking off the shawl over her feet. She looked thoughtfully down at her. Though at the moment her mother seemed comparatively quiet, Alicia knew she could get up at any moment, to rant and tear off her clothes and defecate on the polished, oak floor.

Elizabeth ignored her daughter's approach and Alicia slowly raised her eyes to stare out at the busy street. What Polly offered meant a new life to her, perhaps a hard life, but one with a person beside her who loved her. It was made possible, she thought, only because Elizabeth now recognized nobody. She felt a sense of desolation at the emptiness of her mother's life and at the terrible price she, her daughter, had had to pay for it. She had given her youth, as she did her duty in nursing Mama – and Papa, who had, so unwillingly, given her a home. She had paid a frightful toll, and it had been taken for granted by most of those around her, she thought bitterly.

She glanced down again at Elizabeth. She found it difficult to believe that this benighted woman was her mother who had once loved a tall, blond man with the same passion that Alicia felt for Billy – and the result had been an unwanted, neglected child who had become a servant – and only Uncle Harold had really tried to make the servitude bearable.

'If Mama had cared at all for me, she could have had my devoted love – instead of pity and duty,' she ruminated and felt again her childhood sense of being shut out by Elizabeth.

She turned slowly back to Polly, and said acidly, 'Dear Florence and dear Charles are going to have a fit.'

'Do them good. No reason why Mr Charles and his Missus shouldn't live in this house, if they're worried about your Mam; then they could supervise Fanny.'

'You're right.' Alicia's voice was suddenly brisk. 'I think we'd better start by talking to Dr Bell.'

Dr Bell felt that Polly's suggestion was workable. 'I remember Miss Barnett well,' he said with a smile. 'And, of course, she's been with Mrs Woodman nearly all her life.'

While Billy fretted impatiently, Alicia wrote to Charles and to Florence. They both arrived with their spouses the following day, Charles and Veronica first.

'Get married?' exclaimed Charles disparagingly. 'Who to?'

'A rancher from Canada called William Tyson.' Alicia sat calmly in front of him in the morning-room, her chin set defiantly in the air.

'What an incredible idea,' Veronica exclaimed, fear clutching at her heart. She sat down suddenly in Elizabeth's old chair by the window.

The surname of Alicia's proposed husband sounded vaguely familiar to Charles but he could not place him.

'Where did you meet Mr Tyson?' he inquired, watching his apprehensive wife out of the corner of his eye.

'I wrote to you about him nearly twelve months ago. He's Polly's brother.'

'What?' This from Charles.

'You couldn't marry a servant!' expostulated Veronica.

'I resent your remark!' Alicia flared. 'He can keep me and he's a very decent man. I see no reason why I can't marry him.'

According to them, there were a thousand reasons, and also according to the Reverend Clarence and Florence, who panted in about half an hour later, the most compelling one being the unspoken one that none of them wanted to care for Elizabeth.

The family row, through which Alicia fought her way stoically, was vicious. Apart from anything else, they said Alicia was betraying her class.

White with rage at the insult to Billy, Alicia announced that she would make arrangements for the care of Elizabeth with Uncle Harold, since he was their father's executor.

'But I'm her son,' shouted Charles indignantly.

'Then you look after her,' Alicia snapped back. 'Behave like a son.'

She swept from the room, beside herself with anger which she had never expressed before.

Chapter Twenty-Nine

I

Alicia fled to the morning-room and shut herself in. She was trembling from the aftermath of the quarrel and sat down on her mother's old chair by the window, her hands clenched in her lap. The winter afternoon had closed in and it was almost dark. The gasfire was unlit and the room was cold. She put her head down on her knees and began to cry with great, hard sobs.

She barely heard Charles slam the front door after him when the family left. She was terrified that they would find some way to *make* her stay with her mother, make her break her engagement. Clarence had, after all, the awesome authority of the Church behind him and Charles was a brilliant scholar. She felt that beside them she was a nobody, simply a woman who should obey.

Would kind Uncle Harold feel that Billy was beneath her? Or that she should not leave her mother to a servant, however good?

Polly had been sitting mending in Elizabeth's room, while she watched her mistress. She heard in the distance the sound of angry voices and made a wry face, but she dared not leave Elizabeth who was restless and fretful. Poor little Allie. She wished that Billy was at home, but he had gone to visit his sister, Mary and his nephews and nieces.

A few minutes after the family's stormy exit, he came running up the front steps, whistling cheerfully. He let himself in and, after struggling out of his blue overcoat, went in search of Alicia. He found her still in the darkened morning-room, quiet now, except for an occasional dry sob.

He was beside her in a flash, his good hand on her bent shoulder. 'Luvvie! What's to do? What's up?'

She raised her head and turned to look up at him. Then she wailed, 'They all came and shouted at me. They said I was deserting Mama. All kinds of dreadful things.' She put her arms round him and laid her face against his rough, serge trousers, and began to cry again. 'Four of them, all going at me at once.'

'Aye, luv,' he soothed. 'They're not worth givin' away with a pound o' tea. Don't you fret. I'm goin' to marry you, come hell or high water. Then they'll have to do somethin' about your Mam.'

'But I can't simply leave her!'

'Na, of course not. You get a hold of your Uncle Harold. You always said as you got along with him, and he's the man what looks after your Papa's money, isn't he? He can fix to pay Fanny good wages and maybe talk some sense into your brother and sister.'

Alicia took out her handkerchief and wiped her eyes. 'I hoped a little bit that they might be pleased I was going to be married – and one of them might volunteer to look after Mama,' she said unhappily.

He pulled her up from her chair and held her to him. 'What does it matter whether they're pleased or not? We're goin' to be six thousand miles away, and I can tell you that there's people there as'll like you and be your friends. They'll be more like family to you than your brother and sister ever will.'

That night, Alicia wrote to Uncle Harold. He arrived at his late brother's house the following afternoon, perturbed and tired after an argument with his wife, Vera, about the suitability of Alicia's proposed marriage.

To Alicia, he looked very frail and she realized, for the first time, what an old man he was. She offered him a glass of brandy from the last bottle in Humphrey's cellar. He accepted it gratefully and leaned against the back of the settee on which he was sitting. Polly had brought up the brandy and, at a gesture from Alicia, she stayed in the room, hovering in the background while Alicia explained to him the details of the plan suggested by her.

He listened quietly, nodding his head from time to time, until she had finished. Then he cleared his throat, and said, 'I think I should meet Mr Tyson, first, if he's at home.'

Agreeably surprised, Polly went to find Billy, helped him into his hospital blue jacket and watched while he hastily combed his hair.

With some trepidation, he marched into the morning-room and stood respectfully in front of the old man, his left hand tucked into his buttoned-up jacket.

Uncle Harold looked the young man up and down and then held out his hand to him. 'Sit down, Tyson.' Billy shook hands and then perched on the edge of a straight chair.

Harold Woodman asked which Regiment he had served in and how he had been wounded, to which Billy replied briefly. Then he asked what Billy proposed to do when he was discharged, and, with some enthusiasm, Billy told him about his quarter-section and how he hoped to continue to raise horses. Hesitantly, he spoke of his share in Huang's cafe and how they were building it up; he was not sure what Uncle Harold would think of such a business venture. Uncle Harold, being a very shrewd businessman himself, thought it could be a remarkably good investment, and he said so. Then he held out his hand to Billy, and said, 'I've neglected to congratulate you; you're a lucky man.'

'I know it, Sir.'

'When is the wedding to be?'

Billy glanced at Alicia, who smiled at him. 'Soon as we can fix up Mrs Woodman,' he said firmly.

'And then you'll take Miss Alicia to Canada?'

'Yes, Sir. And me sister, Polly, here, so Miss Alicia won't feel lonely, Sir.'

'Can you pay the fares?'

Alicia interrupted here, to say, 'Between the three of us, we can, Uncle. I've saved from the salary you've been paying me and Polly has some savings, too.'

Polly thought it wise to bob a curtsey, and add, 'Yes, Sir. Between the three of us we've plenty enough.'

Alicia could do far worse with an Englishman returning wounded from the War, Harold Woodman ruminated, as he weighed up Billy. Unlike Charles, he remembered his own father's humble beginnings and how he had laid the foundations for the prosperity of his sons, Humphrey and Harold.

He chatted amiably for a few minutes with both Polly and Billy and then said that he was rather tired and would be glad to rest for a little while, so they left him with Alicia. Billy felt he had found an ally.

Alone with Alicia, Harold Woodman relaxed. 'Nice fellow, you've got there,' he remarked, as he took a sip from his glass.

Alicia was delighted by his approbation. She smiled.

'Mind you, my girl, you have to realize that he has been brought up differently from you. Are you prepared for that?'

'Do you mean that he's a working man?' Alicia bristled slightly. 'He's made his own way since he was twelve – and that's good enough for me.'

Uncle Harold laughed. '*My* father began life as a shoemaker,' he told her. 'But you have been fairly protected in your life.'

'To all intents and purposes, I was brought up by two maidservants, one from the workhouse and one from the slums,' she responded sharply.

He was hurt by the bitterness of her tone but he knew she was right.

II

That afternoon, Billy took a note from Alicia to Fanny's lodgings asking her to come over in the evening.

While Polly patiently sat with Elizabeth, a mystified and slightly flurried Fanny was installed in the morning-room with

Billy and Alicia, a large glass of Humphrey's port in front of her.

'What's up?' she asked suspiciously.

When they told her of their engagement, she jumped up and embraced them both in turn, with whoops of pleasure that would have done credit to an Indian on the warpath. 'I knowed it!' she shouted. 'I seen 'im lookin' at yez.'

Laughing, Alicia disentangled herself from her and restored her to her chair. She then went carefully through Polly's plan with her. She finished up by saying, 'I hope you can come, Fan. I hope you can.'

Fanny had listened soberly and was thrilled. She was careful, however, not to express too much enthusiasm. She would be employed by Old Fishface's family and if they were anything like him where money was concerned, she felt she should play hard to get.

She drank her port, while they waited. She saw herself as companion-help to an invalid lady, a person of dignity, garbed in good black bombazine with a jet necklace and earrings – and a black silk apron to indicate her status. And best of all, savings locked up in a proper tin cash box in her bedroom.

'I wouldn't consider it for less'n the wages I'm gettin' now,' she told them. 'And I would need help 'cos I got to have me days off. And somebody'd have to help me lift her.'

Though Billy understood Fanny's ploy, Alicia did not and her face fell at Fanny's lack of enthusiasm.

Fanny saw her disappointment and felt that she had been too hard on her. She relented a little and said smilingly, 'I always loved your Mam, and I'm sure I could manage her as well as you could. I bin with her nearly all me life – and coming back would be like comin' home. Only I'm determined to improve meself.' She folded her hands primly in her lap to indicate her firmness about this.

Uncle Harold will never agree to wages equivalent to those of a munition worker, though Alicia despairingly. Aloud, she promised to talk to him.

III

That afternoon, after taking a short nap, Harold Woodman spent a few minutes lying contemplating the ceiling of his late brother's bedroom while he considered the best way of coercing either Charles or Florence into caring for their mother.

Then as a strategy occurred to him, his wrinkled face broke into a smile. He knew all the combatants fairly well and he earnestly wished for his sister-in-law to have the best possible care. He told Alicia that he would take the electric tram out to see the Reverend Clarence Browning and that he would probably be late in returning.

He accepted a quick lunch and left to get his tram without further explanation, leaving a very doubtful Alicia. Billy kissed her and told her, 'Cheer up, luv. I'm goin' to put the pressure on by booking passages to Canada – and we'll get the banns read.'

'How can you, Billy, without first settling about Mama?'

'We can and we will,' he replied grimly.

Equally grimly, Uncle Harold sought the help of the Reverend Browning.

After pleasantries had been exchanged and it was explained that Florence was giving a bible class in the church hall, Uncle Harold expressed the opinion that she was not strong enough to take over the care of her mother, if Alicia got married.

The Reverend Browning was very surprised at this; he had rather expected to be pressed into taking in his mother-in-law, after seeing how adamant Alicia was about going to Canada. His relief that this was not likely to be so was very great and he willingly undertook to go with Uncle Harold to see Charles.

Pleased that he had succeeded in his first manoeuvre, Uncle Harold surveyed the enemy over a cup of tea brought in by Clarence's elderly maid. Florence was, in his opinion, a disorganized fool. It would be far better to pin the responsibility on to Charles and his wife. Charles could move into what was, after all, his own house, close to the University. And Charles' wife, he knew, ran her home and children in an orderly manner. Cutting out Florence on grounds of ill-health would stop the brother and sister trying to push the burden on to each other. And getting the Reverend Browning on his side would, thought Harold, bring the weight of church opinion onto a reluctant Veronica.

After writing a quick note of explanation to be given to Florence on her return from her class, they set out by tram and ferry to Seacombe.

The family delegation was received by Charles and Veronica with little enthusiasm. They were expecting guests for dinner and were about to go upstairs to change into their dinner clothes.

'How sweet of you to call,' gushed Veronica, half her mind on her dinner party, despite apprehension about the reason for the unexpected visit.

The Reverend Browning beamed on her, his clerical collar shining in the gaslight, while Charles shook hands and offered them a drink.

Uncle Harold sat down in the most comfortable chair and took a glass of Madeira as if he expected to be there for some time. Charles's heart sank, as he handed the smiling Clarence a glass of port.

Harold Woodman wasted no time. He went straight to the point, outlining Alicia's plan to marry and the need for Elizabeth to have suitable care. 'You are legally responsible for her,' he told his nephew, and the Reverend Browning nodded agreement in a most annoying way. 'She's actually living in a house that you own close to the University. It would be easy to move your family into it.'

Veronica looked at him, appalled. Charles was about to reply, but before he could, Harold outlined the plan to employ Fanny to nurse Elizabeth. 'I am the administrator of your father's Estate and she can be paid out of it, as can any extra help she may need.' He handed his glass back to Charles to be refilled.

'What about Flo?' Veronica managed to interject. 'She's her daughter.'

Clarence broke in smartly. 'She's far from well, almost prostrate after the row she had with Alicia the other day. I fear for her mental stability if she had more responsibility laid upon her.'

Charles raised an eyebrow. 'She seemed all right when we saw her.'

Clarence gave him a look reserved for those who failed to pay their tithes to the Church, and Charles quailed.

'How can we move?' Veronica wailed. 'The children would have to change schools and that house needs renovating from top to bottom, I've no doubt.'

'Good schools in Liverpool,' Uncle Harold replied inflexibly. 'Renovate the house when you're in it.' After two Madeiras, he was beginning to feel that nothing could stop him. 'You'd move quickly enough if poor Elizabeth were dead.'

'Uncle!'

'Well you would, and you know it. Move now.'

'Could we put mother in a nursing home?'

'Find me one not full of wounded.'

'Your dear mother, alas, may be called to her Eternal Rest in the not too distant future,' suggested Clarence. 'In my experience, such cases, once bedridden like your mother is, do not last very long.'

Charles longed to choke the man, and the argument continued until a very young maid knocked at the door and, on being told to enter, announced that the first dinner guests had arrived and that she had put them in the upstairs drawing-room.

Veronica looked at her in despair. 'Tell them I'll be with them in a few minutes. Serve them sherry.'

The maid withdrew and Charles said to Harold Woodman,

'Veronica and I will have to discuss this. Our entire life will be upset, if we move.'

'You'll enjoy it,' his uncle assured him. 'It's a fine house – only needs painting and some new rugs. Might do Elizabeth good to see you and get to know her grandsons – seems to me they've never been near her.'

Regardless of the fact that his own children had not visited Elizabeth for years, the Reverend Clarence turned a shocked face upon Veronica. 'Really?' he inquired in a tone which suggested that immediate damnation awaited her.

The accusation was true. If it were known to their acquaintances, she would be shamed. She bit her lips and bent her head in the face of clerical disapproval. Then she rose and said flatly, 'We have dinner guests. I must go to them.' She did not ask the visitors to eat with them.

Charles was standing uneasily with his back to the fire. His uncle again reminded him flintily of his legal obligations. 'You haven't much time,' he warned him. 'And Veronica should see Fanny Barnett – I'm sure she'll find her very capable.'

Foreseeing a long and bitter fight with his wife, which he knew he must win, Charles nodded, and then saw both gentlemen to the door.

Uncle Harold took the Reverend Browning to the Adelphi for dinner.

IV

Despite her uncle's assurances that all would be well, Alicia doubted it and wept when she went with Billy to arrange to have their Banns read in All Saints Church. She was surprised to hear that Billy also ranked as being of the Church's parish, since he had stayed so long in Humphrey's old house.

She cheered up considerably, however, when a stony-faced Veronica and Charles arrived a couple of days later. They looked over the house and decided which furniture should be discarded and where they would put their own belongings. Then they went in to see the invalid.

Charles hardly recognized the shrunken, restless figure in the bed and Veronica, who was not totally unkind, felt some pity for the mother-in-law she had never seen before. Alicia agreed stiffly to arrange for Fanny to go to Seacombe for an interview. Uncle Harold had already arranged a suitable salary with her, Alicia told Veronica. She should get into touch with him in Manchester about any more help she required.

Billy kept out of the way and concerned himself with hunting down a passage to Canada. Polly began to sort and pack her belongings and encouraged Alicia to do likewise.

Mr and Mrs Hunter, next door, heard from their servants that Alicia was engaged, and they offered the use of their carriage to the bride and groom on their wedding day. The good lady, when she found there was no one else to do it, also insisted that she and her daughters would have a little reception for them after the ceremony. Then she took Alicia shopping to buy a suitable dress. 'We have to bear in mind that almost everyone is in mourning, dear,' she said sadly, as they window-shopped. Alicia agreed and they settled on a pretty grey material and a matching hat. Miss Bloom's successor made the dress.

Alicia and Billy would have sworn that they had few friends in Liverpool, but it was surprising how many people Mrs Hunter suggested should be invited. There was Mary and Mike and Billy's nephews and nieces, Uncle Harold and his wife, his sons and their wives, and, of course, Florence and Charles and their spouses and children. Alicia rather dreaded the attendance of her nephews and nieces, particularly Frank, but since Mrs Hunter was the hostess she trusted that the party would go off well, despite them.

Fanny simply did not turn up for the shift at the munitions factory which followed her interview with Veronica. She moved into the house and began to take over the care of Elizabeth. Veronica had been agreeably surprised to be faced with an obviously well-trained servant at a time when they were at a premium; Fanny had looked her new mistress over shrewdly and decided she was manageable. A deal was struck.

Alicia was happy to have her friend back and the whole tenor of the household began to be more cheerful. With Fanny helping, Billy and Alicia took long walks in the park together like the lovers whom Alicia had so envied years before.

Billy received his formal discharge from the army and bought himself a civilian suit. Seeing him so neatly dressed seemed to Alicia to symbolise a break from the past for him as well as for herself. She thought, 'I don't care who comes or who does not come to the wedding. I've got Billy and Polly and a new start – and I'll have children in a new country, legitimate ones. I couldn't ask for anything better.'

She smiled at Billy, shy in his new apparel, and said, 'You can walk me down to the dressmaker. I'm going to try on my wedding dress.'